Chapter 1

"Everyone to their stations. Ready for combat in five."

Jeff flinched at his commander's words and squeezed his eyes shut. He could feel the blood pulsing through his veins. His heart rate must be off the chart.

Now the shit's going to hit the fan! Will I be dead or alive in twenty minutes?

He was clenching the armrest of his seat so tightly, his hands ached. Jeff forced himself to reopen his eyes. He studied the holoscreen in front of him—a message from the computer confirmed the ship's systems were activated. Peeling one of his sweaty hands off the armrest, he reached forward to close the message. He was shaking so badly, he thought he might have a fever. Finally he managed to hit the small field on the touch screen.

I don't want to die!

He had to get a grip. It wouldn't help anyone if he lost his nerve now, least of all himself.

Jeff felt a steady hand on his shoulder. He turned and looked into Major Irons' face. His commander was smiling encouragingly. "Relax. We can do this."

Jeff took a deep breath and felt some of the adrenalin seep out of his body. If there was living proof that you could survive even the most dangerous mission, then it was Major George Irons. He was only thirty-eight years old, but his features were as weathered as an old man's. The left side of his face was riddled with scars where the skin had been pierced by red-hot bits of metal when his ship was hit by a kinetic weapon three years ago. Another scar extended from his receding hairline across his forehead and ended somewhere under his black eye patch. An enemy's knife had penetrated so deeply into the optic nerve that even the latest advancements in regenerative medicine had been no use.

During his training, Jeff had already noticed that his commander was a living textbook of what combat could do to a human body. The major had twenty years of experience behind him. He had fought as an infantryman on inhospitable planets before volunteering as a bomber commander for the Solar space fleet. He'd gone on to survive dozens of missions as, one by one, the majority of his friends and comrades had perished.

Jeff was incredibly grateful to the major for offering him reassurance even in a situation like this, and he forced himself to smile. Then he nodded weakly and turned back to his console. All he could see through the narrow windows was the darkness of hyperspace, but in a few minutes that would probably be replaced by a blazing hell.

"Captain Austin," his commander began. "Would you please check the status of each station?"

Jeff took a deep breath. Of course: that was his job, and he'd trained for precisely this kind of situation in hundreds of virtual simulations. But even the best simulation couldn't replicate the imminent prospect of a violent death.

He exhaled slowly and switched on his mic. "Final status check before start of mission. Confirm readiness for combat." As hard as he tried to sound authoritative, Jeff couldn't stop his voice from trembling. He expected to hear a snigger from Owens, who was sitting behind him with the other officers, but even he had better things to do right now than make fun of Jeff.

"Navigation?"

"All systems go," Joanne Rutherford confirmed.

"Engineering?"

"Team in position. Systems ready to go," Dave Green responded.

"Weapon systems?"

"Ready to kick ass!"

Jeff rolled his eyes. He was about to call the next station when the major, seating beside him, hit the talk button. "Respond in a proper fashion, Lieutenant Castle!" His voice was calm but icy.

Jeff thought he heard a gulp over the speaker. "Weapon systems ready."

Jeff shook his head lightly and carried on. "Comms?"

"Ready." Jeff heard the high-pitched voice of Edward Owens – known as Owl – behind him.

"Positioning?"

"Positioning systems ready!" Finni Herrmannsson's voice reverberated over the speaker.

Jeff turned to his commander. "Sir, all stations ready for combat. And according to the computer, the ship's systems are all in the green. The I.S. Charon is ready for action."

"Good. Thank you. Computer: log entry for combat readiness at twelve thirty-eight UT. Exit from hyperspace on schedule in three minutes and twenty seconds."

The commander flicked a switch on his console and

then hit the talk button again. "Now we're through with the formalities, let me say a few personal words." Irons paused for a moment. "The Acheron system is sure to be well defended, so we're likely to face resistance. At least we have five bombers, and they'll have to divide up their defenses between them."

Five ships! Jeff didn't know whether to laugh or cry. There were up to a hundred bombers and additional escort fighters attacking other systems, but in this fool's errand of a war, the Arkturus Sector was just a sideshow. But if a system's defenses were stronger than predicted by military intelligence, then the entire attacking fleet might be obliterated before the bombers even stood a chance of reaching an entry point back into hyperspace. And there was no guarantee that this wouldn't happen now, with Acheron.

"So," Irons continued, "we will carry out our mission and do whatever it takes for our Quagma bomb to reach its target. Even if just one bomber makes it through, we'll have gotten rid of this system and moved a little closer to victory against the Alliance. The sooner we finish this war, the sooner we can all go home."

Jeff had his doubts it would be anytime soon.

"I expect every crew member to keep a level head and to give his or her best on this mission. If we don't lose our nerve and work together, we'll survive the next hour, complete our mission, and be able to celebrate tonight. The beers are on me."

Jeff could hear a guffaw from behind him, but wasn't sure if it came from Owens or Herrmannsson.

"Another one-and-a-half minutes till we enter the Acheron System. May God help us," Irons concluded his speech.

"Check suits and close helmets."

Jeff touched a blue field on the control panel on his left

forearm. A green hologram appeared in front of his face and confirmed that his combat suit was ready for action.

The Mark VI suits were marvels of modern military technology. Flexible and soft, they adapted to every movement of the body. Breathable in a normal atmosphere, the fibers compacted in a vacuum so they could be used as space suits. When deactivated, the helmet was little more than a hood that you could hardly feel in the nape of your neck.

On his belt were a holster for his pistol and a separate pouch for various bits of gear, including his personal hand-held computer.

Jeff touched another button and the hood inflated, wrapped around his head and connected to the narrow metal ring on his neck. A faint hissing indicated that the life-support system had been activated.

Jeff's eyes were riveted to the clock on his console; his heart was pounding. He felt like he was counting down the minutes to his death—in slow motion, because time was moving unbearably slowly, as if they were in the vicinity of a black hole. There was nothing more to do or discuss. Everything was prepared. All they could do was wait and see what Acheron had in store for them when they left hyperspace.

The rumors flying around the officers' mess over the last few days hadn't escaped Jeff's attention. Three bomber formations had disappeared—and never re-appeared—after taking off for bases in the Lambda Sector. There'd been speculation that the Alliance had developed a device to reliably predict the departure points of approaching combat units, and that the bombers were destroyed by a gravity mine as they left hyperspace. Jeff had dismissed the talk as gossip, but what if it were true? In that case, the end of the war was near, and Jeff was not on the winning side.

But who gave a shit? He would be dead in a minute, anyway.

Jeff's eyes were still glued to the clock. Thirty more seconds. Time simply did not want to move forward. Why the hell had he volunteered for the military? He could have stayed on Luna and taken over his parents' business. But that hadn't been good enough for him. He'd wanted bigger and better things than supervising the production of subsystems in the factories of the space fleet. But now he probably had no future ahead of him at all. On the other hand, who could have predicted that a war of this scale would break out?

At least Jeff had a chance of avenging his father's death. Finally, those muttonheads from the Alliance would have to pay for their war crimes.

"Ten seconds," Major Irons spoke into his mic.

Jeff put his hands on the console so he could reach all switches quickly if necessary.

"Five."

Jeff took one last deep breath.

"Four."

Blood rushed into his ears like the waterfalls of New Paris.

"Three."

If he was going to die, then hopefully it would be quick.

"Two."

He didn't want to spiral toward eternity trapped in a beat-up wreck with a diminishing supply of oxygen.

"One."

Please God, let me live!

There was a jolt as the Charon's Casimir fields collapsed and Jeff squinted as Acheron's blue sun appeared in the window before him. He tensed up, waiting for the explosion of a gravity mine.

"Captain Austin!" Major Iron spoke in a subdued but firm voice.

He had to get a grip. He had a job to do. "Positioning, come in!" he said hoarsely.

"Close range free of contacts. Positioning system running!" Finni replied.

No mines, at least!

"Navigation?" Jeff asked.

"First estimate reporting exit point within the tolerance range. I have Acheron-4 on the screen, and it's about where it ought to be," Joanne said.

"Is the computer giving you a navigation solution for the perihelion maneuver?"

"It's working on it."

"Report to me immediately when you have a solution!"

"Yes, Sir," said the blond navigator, who was also the ship's paramedic.

"Weapon system officer?"

"Sir?" Castle responded.

"Prepare the Quagma bomb."

"Yes, Sir. I'll initiate the firing sequence."

Jeff nodded and looked at the blue sun, which was growing in size as they approached it at almost the speed of light.

The procedure was standard and they had trained for it in hundreds of simulations. As executive officer, Jeff was responsible for freeing his commander to concentrate on overall strategy.

"I have the navigation solution," Joanne reported. "Four minutes, ten seconds to the central star. Perihelion maneuver with eight-g acceleration lasts three minutes and eighteen seconds. Deviation of four point five degrees.

Time to target following maneuver: six minutes and twenty seconds."

This corresponded to the values calculated in advance of the mission. They had planned their hyperspace flight precisely and had entered the system very close to the planned entry point.

"What about the other bombers?" Major Irons asked. There was a hint of impatience in his voice.

"Radio operator, come in."

"I'm receiving signals from three ships," Owl said hesitantly. The data was probably only just coming in. The other bombers were entering the system on different courses and they would only form a formation with the Charon after the perihelion maneuver. "I'm receiving the Boston, the Spider, and the Neptune."

"What about the Atlantic?" Iron asked.

Owl paused. "Not in the tolerance range of its entry point."

Jeff pursed his lips. Either the Atlantic hadn't planned its maneuver correctly, or there was now another ship whose drive system had failed at the critical moment and would race toward infinity for all eternity in hyperspace. This damned war didn't leave enough time to carry out proper checks of the Casimir converters.

"We'll continue our approach as planned," the Major said firmly. Not that Jeff had expected any other decision.

"The Quagma core has been inserted in the missile," Castle reported.

"Good, open the bomb hatch and release the bomb!" Jeff commanded.

"Understood."

"I'm receiving a strong tachyon pulse!" Finni's voice came in, his words tumbling over each other.

"OK, they've located us," Irons said. "A little earlier

than I'd hoped, but nothing we didn't expect. They're trying to predict our flight path. After the perihelion maneuver, we can expect to come up against strong defenses."

Jeff had hoped they would escape undetected, but he knew he'd been kidding himself. He looked at the location hologram in front of him, which showed a scaled map of the Acheron system. A sweeping, green flight path led from their entry point to the sun, where it curved sharply and veered toward a small blue ball. He waited for red dots to appear: rockets racing toward them. Nothing so far. But he noticed that the blue sun outside the windows was growing rapidly in size. Not long now till the perihelion maneuver.

"Quagma bomb released. Magnetic mount ready to eject," Castle said.

Irons grunted in satisfaction.

"Confirmed. Bomb ready to be ejected. Wait for my command," Jeff said.

"Positioning here!" Finni came in. "I've got a lot of small objects leaving the orbit of Acheron-4. Accelerating very fast."

"Those are rockets," Irons said grimly. "How many?"

"Can't say exactly. I'm getting conflicting signals. They're flying very close together. At least four dozen. They're moving toward the sun."

Of course they were! The missiles would intercept them after the perihelion maneuver as they headed for the target.

"Four dozen," Joanne whispered. "That's a hell of a lot. If they have Artemis target devices, we've had it!" She couldn't disguise the panic in her voice.

"According to recon, no Artemis positioning systems have been registered in the Acheron system," the major said tersely. "Now please stay calm and concentrate!"

"Yes, Sir!"

"The contacts have disappeared from the screen," Finni reported.

Irons grunted. "That was to be expected," he said. "The missiles have stopped accelerating and the engines have shut down. Check again as soon as we've set course for the target. When the engines restart, they'll be on us in a few seconds."

Jeff looked up at the holoscreen. "One more minute until the perihelion maneuver!"

"Where are the other bombers?" Irons asked.

"The Spider and the Neptune are right on target for the meeting point in the perihelion," Finni said. "Boston has fallen behind a bit."

"What do you mean by *a bit*?" Jeff asked.

"About seven million miles. They'll reach the perihelion around twenty-five seconds after us."

Irons groaned. "That's too late to balance out the maneuver."

Jeff swallowed hard. Of course, the Boston would follow the same flight path as the other bombers. So the enemy would know exactly where to strike. They had only one chance.

"Shall I order the Boston to change course?" Jeff asked.

Irons hesitated. "We need the Boston's bomb. We have to destroy the base on Acheron-4, otherwise we can't continue the offensive in the Lambda Sector."

Jeff sucked his teeth. Irons had turned the Boston into a suicide squad. But Jeff knew the Major was right. If they failed to destroy even one of the bases in the Lambda Sector, their infantry would be in danger of being killed by Alliance bombers. Jeff was sure Irons would have made the same decision if it had been his own ship that had fallen behind. "Radio operator, order the Boston to continue its approach to Acheron-4 as planned."

"Understood."

Jeff couldn't see the expression on his shipmate's face as he delivered this fatal command to the escort ship.

"Perihelion maneuver in ten seconds," Joanne said.

"OK," Jeff replied. "Into position for high-g maneuver."

He sat back and put his hands on the armrests, making sure his head was in the hollow of the backrest.

"Five, four, three, two, one …" Joanne counted down.

It was as if someone had thrown an anvil at his chest. The air escaped his lungs in a hiss, as the heavy antimatter engines ignited. He was flattened into his seat with the force of eight g. He could hardly breathe. Stars danced in front of his eyes.

"Power up the engines as planned," Joanne said. "Perihelion maneuver in exactly three minutes!"

Jeff tried to lift his arm but failed. With agonizing slowness, the position of the ship's vector changed on the navigation hologram. Jeff looked out of the window. The blue Acheron sun kept on growing, until it had outgrown the space of the window. They were so close to the surface, Jeff thought he could dip his hands into the flames of the sun. They passed layers of the sun that were thousands of degrees hot, but that was nothing compared to the frictional heat that some parts of the ship, still flying at almost the speed of light, had to endure. The hull of the ship couldn't withstand the thermal load for more than a few seconds.

"Passing perihelion," Joanne said. Her voice was little more than a croak.

In front of the window, the sun moved further and further to the left until it disappeared behind them.

"Sixty seconds," Joanne said.

The vector of the little ship on the hologram barely changed direction anymore and pointed toward a blue symbol: their target, Acheron-4. Through the window, Jeff could see a tiny blue dot moving from the right and coming to a stop right in front of them. The planet with the enemy base was still over one hundred and twenty-five million miles away, but they were racing toward it and would pass it in less than seven minutes. If everything went smoothly, it would cease to exist shortly afterwards.

Suddenly, the pressure eased, and Jeff was sitting in his seat again with normal gravity. He took several deep breaths, then hit the talk button. "Navigation, status!"

"Perihelion maneuver complete. We're precisely on course. We'll reach Acheron-4 in six minutes and ten seconds."

"The other ships?" Irons asked.

"The Neptune and the Spider have also completed their maneuvers. They're one hundred and twenty-five thousand miles starboard. The Boston is still in the maneuver."

"Missiles!" Finni screamed. "Twelve o'clock!"

Jeff glanced out of the window. But of course he couldn't see anything. Only Finni, with his positioning system, could see the death-bringers.

"They're gone again," the radar technician let out a sigh of relief.

"They adjusted their flight path to our perihelion maneuver," Irons said. "Time until missiles reach target?"

"About two minutes," Finni whispered.

"Talk loudly and clearly, damn it!" Irons ordered, without raising his voice.

"Let's drop the bomb and start the evasive maneuver!" Dave Green spoke up.

"It's too early," Irons said. "Come on, don't lose your nerve."

"I can see detonations of hydrogen bombs orbiting Acheron-4," Finni reported. "They're very strong."

"Damn!" Irons frowned. "I wasn't expecting that, looks like they've stationed kinetic weapons."

Jeff gulped. The missiles were bad enough, but the scrap metal now flying toward them at almost the speed of light would puncture the spacecraft like bullets perforating single-layer toilet paper.

"One minute until the missiles hit!" Finni reported.

Jeff didn't answer. There was nothing left to say or do. All they could do was wait. For death or life—those were the only two possibilities. The next five minutes were like a game of Russian roulette—he was holding a gun to his head and all he had to do was squeeze the trigger.

"Thirty seconds."

Jeff clenched the armrests. All the simulations and trainings … nothing could have prepared him for this. He lifted his head and looked out of the window again. There was nothing to see but the blue dot of Acheron-4.

The clock continued its relentless countdown. Any moment now …. It was so quiet on the bridge, it seemed as if time itself were holding its breath. Only the dull throb of his heart echoed in his ears.

Suddenly, there was a blinding light. Jeff squeezed his eyes shut, but the bright light penetrated his closed eyelids. Tears ran down his cheeks. One of the missiles must have detonated right in front of them. Jeff forced himself to open his eyes again. The brightness had subsided slightly, but he still had trouble recognizing anything. A new sun had sprung up in front of them. Pale yellow, almost white, dazzlingly hot, and they were racing toward it at breakneck speed—they didn't stand a chance of avoiding it. Already they were diving into the blinding ball of white-hot plasma.

"Cooling system on max!" Irons bellowed.

"Yes, Sir."

There was a loud crash in the cabin and Jeff was almost thrown out of his chair. The cooling system must have failed somewhere on the ship. It was already overheated after the perihelion maneuver.

"Plasma intrusion! We've lost stabilizer number three!" Green screamed. "I'm sealing off the section!"

Jeff nodded. At least there was nobody in there.

"Understood," Irons replied.

Then it was dark again outside. They had left the plasma cloud. Portside, more expanding suns came into view, but they were far away enough not to be dangerous.

"I've located forty-four detonations," Finni said. "Most of them exploded behind us. I think we survived the missiles."

Jeff clenched his teeth. It was too early to breathe a sigh of relief.

"I'm not receiving any signals from the Neptune," Owl said. His voice was barely audible.

"Position?" Jeff asked.

"Yup, I've got it," Finni replied. "One of the detonations was exactly in the flight path of the Neptune. It must have been hit."

That could have been us! If they had raced into the plasma ball of the detonating missile just a few seconds earlier, the Charon would now be nothing but atoms. They would have been dead before they'd even registered they'd been hit.

Major Irons spoke. "Positioning! Can you estimate when the scrap of the kinetic weapon will reach us?"

"No," Finni answered immediately. "We don't have

enough data on the strength of the detonation to calculate its speed. But we'll probably pass it any second now."

"How long till we reach the target?" Jeff asked.

"Two-and-half minutes," Joanne replied. "We have to drop the bomb up to sixty-two seconds in advance, so we can reach a safe distance."

"Good," Irons said. "WSO, prepare the bomb—"

All hell broke loose. An almighty crashing noise sounded in Jeff's ears. Splinters flew through the bridge in every direction. A violent pain shot through his arm as he was hit by a piece of debris. The alarm sirens wailed. Behind him, Green screamed. Jeff felt his ears pop. The cabin filled with mist, the air pressure dropped.

"Malfunction message!" Irons roared.

Jeff looked down at his arm and saw red patches seeping through his combat suit before the automatic seal set in.

"We've been hit!" Green screamed.

"You don't need to tell me that! Give me a proper malfunction report!"

They must have passed through a wall of scrap metal. It was anyone's guess how many bits of metal had perforated the ship.

"We're losing pressure in sections one and four. Some of the holes are too big to be sealed off by the gel between the fuselage sections," Green reported.

"We'll worry about that later. Carry on!"

"One of the antimatter stores must have been hit, too. The voltage in Penning Trap Five is falling."

"Falling? How fast?" Irons asked.

"Too fast! If it carries on like this, it'll be down to zero in five minutes."

"Anything else?"

"Some damage to non-critical systems."

"Hyperspace drive?"

"Appears to be undamaged."

Appears ...

"OK. Send your men to the Penning trap! Weapon system officer!"

"Sir?"

"Release the bomb!"

"Yes, Sir," Castle said. "Bomb released."

"Lieutenant Rutherford, initiate evasive maneuver!"

Jeff was pushed down into his seat again as Joanne fired the engines. At least the main engine had survived the attack, otherwise they would have crashed onto the target planet along with the bomb.

"What about the other ships?" Irons asked.

"I've heard from the Boston. They've released their bomb, too," Owl said. "I can see they've started their evasive maneuver."

"And the Spider?"

"Disappeared. I'm receiving the typical gamma blast of an antimatter explosion."

"Shit! A piece of that wall of scrap metal must have hit the antimatter tanks."

"At least we got two of the bombs to hit the target," Irons said without any emotion in his voice. "Let's hope they're not duds."

Despite the engines working at full capacity, the blue dot of Acheron-4 was still right in front of them in the cockpit windows. But it had become much brighter since the perihelion maneuver.

"Thirty seconds," Joanne said. "Point seven five million miles."

Suddenly there was a loud bang and Jeff was thrown against his console. An alarm siren whined.

"Status!" Irons demanded.

"The portside engine pod's gone!" Green shouted. "It's just disappeared."

That meant they'd lost half of their positioning capabilities.

"The sensor is picking up traces of uranium and thorium," Finni said. "They must have shot at us with a particle accelerator!"

"The particle beam can have only just brushed us, otherwise the Charon would be history," Jeff said. In a briefing, intelligence service had said it was unlikely for a base of this size to have particle weapons. But it wouldn't have been the first time the powers-that-be had got it wrong. They'd been lucky. Jeff only hoped they would pass Acheron-4 before the enemy could recharge its accelerators.

"The Boston has disappeared from the radar," Finni shrieked.

Jesus Christ!

That meant Acheron-4 had *two* particle accelerators.

Green suddenly groaned loudly.

"Lieutenant Green?" Irons asked.

Jeff turned around to look at him. The engineer was squirming in his seat, his hands pressing against the helmet of his spacesuit.

"Lieutenant Green!" Irons repeated, then turned to Jeff. "What's wrong with him?"

Another groan from Green. "My head. My head is about to explode," he whimpered.

"They're attacking with psycho rays," Irons said.

Jeff swallowed. It was the latest development in the Alliance's weapons market. The rebels tried to influence the human brain with alternating magnetic fields. Depending on the strength of the transmitter, they could control people from afar or drive them crazy. Luckily, the deflective shields in their combat suits offered a certain amount of protection. Green's shield device must have been damaged. He was screaming as if someone was drilling a hole in his skull.

"Hang in there, Lieutenant Green," Irons said. "Just a few more seconds, then it'll pass."

"Passing over the target in ten seconds," Joanne reported.

Acheron-4 had changed from a tiny blue dot to a blue marble. The marble expanded rapidly into a gigantic sphere. It looked as if they were hurtling right into the planet.

We're not going to make it!

Had they miscalculated the evasive maneuver?

But the maneuver was going as planned. They passed the planet, which according to Jeff's HUD was fifty miles away. There was a brief flickering in front of the windows as the Charon raced through the edges of the atmosphere and the nitrogen atoms turned into plasma.

Then they were through, and the engine shut off again.

Jeff knew what was coming next and closed his eyes.

The light seemed to penetrate straight through the cabin wall and his closed eyelids, as if their spaceship was made out of transparent paper. It only lasted a second, then the light was gone again. Jeff opened his eyes and switched his monitor to the rear cameras.

Where the blue planet Acheron-4 had been a moment ago, a yellow sun was now blazing. As it expanded, its color changed to a reddish hue. The Quagma bombs had hit their target. Acheron-4 no longer existed.

"Target destroyed!" Jeff reported to his commander.

Five bombers had started out on this mission. Only the Charon had survived the attack, badly damaged. As shocked as they were at the loss of their sister ships, they were incredibly relieved to have survived themselves.

Green had stopped screaming. But he was breathing heavily. "I thought I was going to die," he moaned.

Jeff recalled how entire corps had been killed in psycho-weapon attacks before a counteragent had been found. He shuddered. He hoped he'd never have to go through that himself.

"Radio operator!" Irons ordered. "Send a message to the base. Tell them: target destroyed."

It took a few seconds for Finni to answer. "Hyperradio failed."

"Then use the backup system," Jeff said.

"That was in the portside engine pod," Finni replied. "This spaceship won't be able to transmit any more super-luminal messages."

"Lieutenant Green," Irons said. "What's with the anti-matter storage?"

"The voltage in cell five has stabilized again. The air outlet in the fuselage could also be plugged."

"Good. Anything else?"

Green hesitated before answering. "Reactor one has failed completely. Positioning and radio are damaged. The electrical systems are reporting faults in almost every subsystem."

"And what about the hyperdrive?"

"The Casimir converter appears to be undamaged, but we'll only know if it's still able to build a horizon once we get to the entry point."

"Then let's hope for the best." Irons turned around in his seat. "How long to the entry point?"

"We'll be far enough away from Acheron in about five minutes," Joanne said.

"Good. We'll remain on combat alert until we're in hyperspace.

Jeff looked at the holoscreen, which gave him a view of what lay behind them. The gas cloud of the destroyed planet was still glowing blood-red. The Quagma bombs had done a thorough job. Jeff wondered how many people had been on the base. The intelligence service hadn't been able to say exactly—apparently anything between an emergency crew of twenty to a deployment point with several thousand infantrymen was possible. Maybe Jeff would find out once this damned war was over. He wondered how many more planets would be reduced to dust by Quagma bombs in the meantime. He closed his eyes as it occurred to him that if they reached the Delta Quadrant, their next target might be an inhabited planet. Then he would be responsible for the deaths of millions, or even billions, of people. Needless to say, it was not what he wanted but he knew there was no other way of advancing on Delphi. If they overlooked even a single base, the enemy would come at them from behind. And after all, the Alliance hadn't had any scruples, either, in wiping out Deneb-6 in a surprise attack.

It was that surprise attack, in which his father had died, that had started the war. Until then, nobody had seriously expected the Cold War to turn into a hot one.

"I'm losing voltage in the Penning traps again," Green said.

Jeff turned around and looked over at the flight engineer. There was enough antimatter on board to blow up the ship into a thousand smithereens if the traps ran out of power. In an emergency they could eject the cylinders, but it was a long way to their base on Sigma-7. They would need every bit of antimatter they had for their return flight.

"Get that under control," Irons said.

"Request permission to leave the bridge," Green responded.

Irons nodded. "Permission granted. Corporal Owens, take over the onboard systems."

"Yes, Sir."

Now Jeff and his shipmates had nothing left to do except wait. It was unlikely that enemy forces would suddenly appear. And even if they did, they didn't stand a chance of intercepting the Charon until the entry point. Gradually, it dawned on Jeff that he had survived his first bomber mission. He went over the events of the past twenty minutes in his mind. They'd been lucky not to have hit any mines at the exit point. They'd been lucky the missiles had missed *them*, and they had been crazy lucky that the particle beam …

"Captain Austin!" Jeff started. "Are you asleep?"

"No, Major. I was just—"

"We're still on combat alert. Please focus on our mission! We are in an enemy system."

Jeff nodded, numbly. He looked at the location hologram with the navigation data. They were nearing the entry point into hyperspace. Three more minutes.

"Are we ready for hyperflight?" Jeff asked.

"Yup," Joanne answered. "Course is programmed. We need about eight-and-a-half hours for the return flight to Sigma-7."

"Assuming the hyperdrive wasn't hit," Finni added glumly.

Jeff waited for a comment from the Major, but he didn't respond.

A yellow light glowed on the console in front of him. Jeff pressed it. "Green here," the sonorous voice of the flight engineer echoed across the bridge.

"Speak!"

"We have a serious problem with Penning Trap Five."

"How serious?" Major Irons asked.

"It's been hit by a piece of shrapnel. The voltage is fluctuating and there's nothing I can do to change it. We can only pray it doesn't give up the ghost."

"OK. Return to the bridge."

"Sir! Another thing."

"Yes?"

"Shorty is injured."

Jeff turned around to look at him. *Hopefully not badly.* The tall mechanic Travis "Shorty" Short and the two other technicians weren't in the cockpit during missions, but in the engine room.

"Private Short," Irons corrected him. "How bad is it?"

"He's unconscious. He was working on the Penning trap when we were hit by the particle beam. Corporal Fields says he was flung against the paneling of the Casimir Converter. Private Short may have a concussion, but he seems to be in a stable condition. We've put him on a gurney."

"All right. Lieutenant Rutherford will take a look at him as soon as we're in hyperspace. Come back to the bridge and order your men to buckle up until I lift the battle alert."

"Understood."

"What happens if the Penning trap kicks the bucket?" Joanne asked. Her voice sounded more curious than worried.

"Then we'll expel it, according to protocol," Irons replied coolly.

"That would mean we probably wouldn't have enough power to maintain the horizon the whole way home," the navigator pointed out.

"We'll deal with any problems as they arise, Lieutenant Rutherford."

"Yes, Sir."

Jeff saw a movement from the corner of his eye—it was Green, returning to the bridge and taking his seat.

"We've reached the entry point," Joanne said.

"Are we clear for hyperflight, Lieutenant Green?"

"Yes, Sir. Everything ready for entering hyperspace."

"Then enter hyperflight, Lieutenant Rutherford," Irons commanded.

"Yes, Sir."

Within a few seconds, the stars disappeared from outside the cockpit windows. They were surrounded by the endless blackness of hyperspace. At least the hyperdrive seemed to be working.

"Maneuver completed."

"I don't like this," Green said.

"Explain yourself, if you have something to say." Irons' voice was irritable.

"Yes, Sir. The horizon hasn't stabilized. I can see big gradients here. I'm worried the hyperdrive might have been hit."

"And what does that mean for us?"

The engineer didn't answer for a long time. Jeff turned around in his seat and saw Green bent over his console.

"Lieutenant Green?"

Green sighed. "I can't say. I can't see where the problem is exactly. Maybe in the projector unit of the converter or in the control electronics. I don't know. Maybe it'll hold out, maybe not."

"What about the other systems?" Irons asked.

"Unchanged."

"Life support system?"

"The pressure is stable. Everything OK."

"All right," Irons said after a few seconds. "Lift combat alert."

Jeff pressed a field on his console and the red light on the bridge changed to a reassuring, warm white. Then he unlocked his helmet. There was a hissing noise as the pressure between the cabin and his space suit equalized. Jeff pushed the visor up and breathed in the equally stale but cool cabin air. It smelled as if someone had been welding or had detonated some firecrackers. It was the typical smell of space as he knew it from exercises, and a clear indication that the hull of the spaceship had been hit. But the ship's self-repair system and the three mechanics had done a good job.

Jeff turned around and his eyes met Joanne's. The blond navigator smiled at him and nodded. Yes, they'd made it. At least for today. Somehow, they'd make it back home. Jeff turned back round to his console and changed the mode of his location holo. A long line stretched from the left edge of the hologram to the right, passing close to a few stars. It was their course. A small symbol indicated their current position. They hadn't covered much of the fifty-six light years to Sigma-7 during the first few minutes of their hyperspace flight. It would be a long eight-and-a-half hours.

Chapter 2

"Thank you, Captain!" Major Irons said as Jeff put a cup of steaming coffee on the console in front of him.

"Sure," Jeff mumbled, and sat back down in his seat. With a push of a button, he let the onboard computer know that he was back at his station.

"OK," Irons said. "Corporal Owens, you can take a break, too. But remain on standby. Lieutenant Rutherford, how are the crew?"

"Private Short regained consciousness, after I injected him with a stimulant. The other nine crew members are all fine."

Irons nodded. "Good, then you can take a break, too."

"Thank you, Sir," Joanne said. A few seconds later, Jeff heard her footsteps receding behind him, and the bulkhead moved aside. After it had closed behind the two crew members, he was left alone with Major Irons on the bridge. Green had already left with Finni half an hour ago to look at the damaged hyper radio.

Jeff felt washed out. They had set off on their mission from the space base above Sigma-7 over twelve hours ago.

The night before he'd been so agitated, he'd hardly slept at all. He was beyond tired, but adrenalin was still pumping through his body. He doubted the coffee would make things any better. His hands trembled as he reached for his cup.

"Still feeling nervous?"

Jeff turned to his superior. "Yup, you could say."

The major smiled at him and nodded. "It'll pass. The first mission is always the worst. After that you know what to expect and are mentally better prepared."

Jeff saw things differently. For the first time in his life, he had been a whisker away from death. They were the only one of five ships to have survived the mission. He was pretty sure he would be feeling far more nervous before the next mission.

Forty-nine missions to go—basically I'm already a dead man!

"I can't imagine ever getting used to it," Jeff responded.

The major suppressed a laugh. "Believe me, you will. In fact, you can even become addicted to the adrenalin kick."

Jeff frowned at the major, who was still smiling. Is that what the major was? Addicted to the adrenaline rush of near death? Is that why he was always so calm and matter-of-fact—because he was secretly enjoying it all?

The major seemed to have guessed what he was think-ing. "No, Captain Austin, I'm not in it for the kick. I don't go looking for danger. I'm just as afraid of death as you. But between missions you inevitably think about death." He paused a moment, searching for the right words. "You think about so much—about death, about life, about the point of it all. And above all, about your place in the middle of all the chaos. But after about the thirtieth mission, something goes 'click'. I've heard it from other experienced officers, too. Suddenly you stop thinking about it, because you come to the conclusion that humans, with their limited mental faculties, can never grasp the meaning of it all, anyway. Then you stop driving yourself crazy between flights. Finally, you can sleep again."

Jeff looked at his superior for a long time as he mulled over his words. "Are you saying that you've resigned yourself to dying?"

Irons chuckled. "On the contrary. I've resigned myself to living. And death is an integral part of life. We all have to die, and it can get us at any moment, whether you're in combat or riding your motorcycle. My best friend was a bomber pilot in the Orion Offensive. He volunteered for the most dangerous missions until he received an honorable discharge."

"What happened to him?"

"He died of a heart attack. Shortly after his return to Aldebaran-6." He sighed. "And I guess you heard about my son?"

Jeff nodded. Everyone on board knew the story. Irons had a wife on Lambda-3 and their son had died from Caroll's Fever. He had been born with it. After the war broke out, the only drug that could help him was no longer available, and the four-year-old boy died painfully from the degeneration of his nerve cells. "Yes, I heard about it. What was his name?"

"Jack. But do you see what I'm getting at?

Jeff hesitated. "I guess it gives me something to think about."

Irons laughed again and made a dismissive gesture with his hands. "I'm going to tell you something: people die. Without this war and also because of this war, even if they're not sitting at the helm of an interstellar bomber."

"But—we've lost four ships," Jeff blurted out. "Forty

people died. And that's just on our side. Do you think the sacrifice was worth it?"

Irons exhaled slowly. "You were at the briefing. We have to clean up the sector so that we can advance on the heartland of the Alliance."

Jeff shook his head. "I know that. But that's not what I mean."

"Then what do you mean?"

"I mean: what price … how many victims … was the Acheron 4 base worth? The forty men and women we lost? Would the destroyed bases have been worth a hundred of our soldiers? How do you measure human life against strategic advantages?"

The major gave him a long hard look, then whooped with laughter.

Jeff grimaced. What was so funny about his question?

The major answered before Jeff had time to retort. "Once again, it's the academic in you speaking. Although perhaps you're studying the wrong subject. Instead of a historian, you should have become a philosopher." The major laughed again and wiped the tears from his cheeks.

"I think those are legitimate questions," Jeff said, making sure to keep his voice neutral and not to sound offended. "Military conflicts need to be processed and evaluated. Ethical questions need to be considered in addition to strategy."

Irons groaned. "Where did you pick that up?"

"Excuse me?" Jeff couldn't keep the irritation out of his voice now.

"A sentence as polished as that must have come from one the textbooks you were forced to read at the Academy. It sounds like an existential justification of your profession to a court of inquiry."

Jeff shrugged helplessly. As far as he knew it wasn't a

quote from a textbook. But of course, it was possible that he'd absorbed it in the early days of his studies and that the sentence had been slumbering in his subconscious until he needed it. "You may be right, but when this war is over, there will be analyses and studies written about it, and ultimately about every single mission. And then questions will arise as to whether the goals achieved justified the loss of human life and materials. In the history books—"

Irons bellowed with laughter again. The scars on his left cheek turned his face into a grimace, but his eyes radiated warmth and friendliness. Jeff realized his commander wasn't laughing at him but at the situation they were in. "Captain Austin. How about we win this war first and then worry about how it goes down in the annals of history? If we lose, it'll be Alliance historians writing the history books."

"In the end it will all boil down to the same thing."

Irons shook his head adamantly. "Ask your professor. In the end, history is always written by the winner. I'll give you an example: What did we do today?"

Jeff knew it was a rhetorical question so he didn't reply.

"I'll tell you: we destroyed a planet with our Quagma bomb. Not only did we eradicate a military base, we turned a whole planet—that at some point might have produced life—into a bunch of atoms.

Jeff still didn't know what the major was getting at. "Are you trying to say the Alliance would present us as war criminals if they won?"

"As I said, the winner writes the history books. We committed atrocities—"

"—that the Alliance committed, too," Jeff interrupted him.

The major shook his head. "They'll dismiss the murders they committed as a necessity provoked by us. Just as we will, except the other way round. But think ahead a hundred years, when both the Empire and the Alliance have made way for another regime. How will this conflict be seen then?"

Jeff remained silent.

"If it's a more sensible society than ours, it will criticize both our deeds and those of the Alliance, and dismiss both sides as barbarians," the Major said firmly.

"That would mean that you hold this conflict and our actions in contempt, Major," Jeff concluded.

Irons shook his head again. "We're at war. We're fighting for our lives and our freedom. Of course the stakes are high. We have no other choice."

"Then I don't understand …"

"All I'm trying to say is that there is no such thing as objectivity. If you survive the war and go on to write your books, you'll do so from the subjective perspective of the winning side. Perhaps your history book will remain the standard work of the Imperial universities for several centuries, like Gibbons' *Decline and Fall of the Roman Empire* —it's possible." Irons smiled at him. "But someday the perspective will change again. The conflict will be romanticized or a more objective view will emerge. Who knows? But your work will land on the rubbish heap of history, or it will be read as an example of an outdated perspective and will be picked apart in lectures."

Jeff looked out of the window at the endless darkness of hyperspace. He felt as if he'd been slapped in the face. He'd never thought of it like that. He'd committed himself to serving as an officer in the fleet because Nimitz University on Tau Ceti-4 was the holy grail for historians, and if wanted to study military history there, it would stand him in good stead if he'd served in the military. Even as a child he'd been fascinated by old maps and historical battles, and pored over books about long-ago wars. He had never regarded himself as a strategist, only as a historian. In fact, his dream had been to write an important book, which in future would become a standard work at universities. He wanted to create something for posterity. But Irons was right. Most books in the Imperial Military Library on Tau Ceti-4 were less than a hundred years old. And it wasn't as if people before 2400 hadn't been interested in history. It was just that the old works had become outdated.

Jeff could feel Iron's hand on his shoulder and turned around to look at him.

"Some day you'll return to your books and write about this war, because I'm assuming we'll win. But until then, you're in a much better position: you can help shape the present instead of just writing about the past. When the war is over, you yourself will be part of this history. Your name will appear in the records and documents and prove you were part of the mission we just successfully completed. Here and now you've made history, and you can be proud of that."

Jeff looked at Irons wordlessly. He was right. On his first mission, he had actually become part of human history. He nodded tentatively and Irons pulled his hand back to his own armrest.

"And if you don't mind me giving you some advice …" he continued.

Now what?

"Don't write about this war!"

Jeff lifted his shoulders and let them slowly sink back down. "Why not?"

"By participating in this conflict, you're biased. You will never be able to write neutrally and objectively about the battles of this war. Whether you like it or not, whether *I* like it or not, we have blood on our hands. Today we destroyed an entire planet and we have no idea how many Alliance soldiers and civilians were on that base on Acheron-4. And nobody knows how many lives we'll wipe out with our bombs in the next few weeks and months."

"I think I can preserve my objectivity," Jeff replied, but he could hear the uncertainty in his own voice.

Irons laughed. "Would you yourself consider a mission a failure? Would you admit that you wiped out a planet and its inhabitants in vain? That you murdered, without—"

"Murdered? Hold on, we're defending—"

Irons shook his head firmly. "No. We didn't defend anything today. The mission against Acheron-4 is part of an offensive campaign."

"That we had to carry out to win the war."

Irons snapped his fingers. "To win the war. That's right, we want to win the war and not just defend ourselves. You're already whitewashing these missions, Captain Austin. And you will continue to do so—even more so when the war is over, as you'll want to morally justify your actions. Forget it! Write your memoirs about your involvement in the war if you want to write about it, but don't try and write an objective textbook. Focus your career on the Punic wars or the three World Wars, but not on …" He shrugged. "… whatever this war will be called in ten years' time."

Without even having to think about it, Jeff knew that Irons was right. He had already murdered people. He would never be able to write objectively about this conflict. But maybe writing his memoirs wasn't such a bad idea. If he did it well, he could incorporate an overview of the conflict into an account of his own experiences. Fridtjof Nansen had done something similar in his book about his Arctic expedition. On the other hand, Jeff was just a small cog in the wheel of this war. Who would even buy his book?

Irons must have noticed he was lost in thought. "Don't lose sleep over it. First you have to survive the war, you'll still have plenty of time to think about it after."

Their conversation was interrupted by the whining of a siren. A warning light immersed the bridge in a deep-red light. Even before he could look at the status message on his monitor, Jeff noticed something in front of the cockpit windows. Something that ought not to be there: stars. "We've left hyperspace."

"Jesus fucking Christ!" Green stormed onto the bridge, brushing a hand over an ugly brown stain on the front of his combat suit. Joanne came up behind him looking concerned.

"Stop cursing and give me a sensible report," Irons demanded calmly.

Jeff switched the system controls back to Green's console.

"We've left hyperspace!" Green's voice went up an octave with surprise.

"I can see that for myself," Irons retorted. "But why?"

"That piece of shit has switched itself off," Green said after several long seconds. "For safety reasons—the Casimir Converter couldn't keep the horizon stable anymore."

Another status message appeared on Jeff's holoscreen in red letters: "The Penning trap!"

"I see that! Fuck!"

Irons spun on Green and gave him a withering look.

"Voltage is sinking again!" Green said.

"Send your people to look at it!"

"Yes, Sir!" Jeff could hear Green talking into his mic with the mechanics in the crew's ready room.

"The damage appears to be worse than we thought," Jeff said.

Irons frowned. "Yes, so it seems. Lieutenant Rutherford!"

"Sir?"

"Do we have enough antimatter to reach Sigma-7 if we eject the faulty cell?

"No. That won't work."

"Do we have another target we could fly to if we eject the cell?"

Joanne slowly exhaled. "Karim-6. There's an advanced positioning station."

"Without a maintenance base, I'm guessing?"

"Correct."

Jeff rolled his eyes. Then the ship couldn't even be patched up. They would have to wait for a tender, and at this stage of the war that might take several weeks. If they flew to Karim-6, they would be stuck there for a long time, sharing oxygen and food with a crew who would be far from thrilled to host them.

The major must have been having the same thought. "Lieutenant Green, have you had any feedback from your men?"

"Give me a moment, Sir."

On the other hand, if the mechanics didn't get the hyperdrive to work again, it wouldn't make any difference whether they reached Karim-6 or not. Then they would have to spend years crawling back home at a snail's pace.

"Sir, the Penning trap is beyond repair." Jeff wondered how Green had managed to suppress an almighty curse.

"Then get rid of it!"

That meant Karim-6. Shit!

"Yes, Sir!"

On the other hand ... as long as they were fixing the

positioning system, they couldn't be killed in another mission.

Another siren went off.

"We can't eject the Penning trap."

"Say that again?" Jeff was aghast.

"I said, we can't eject the Penning trap. The damn thing must be totally shot. It's a miracle it didn't blow up in our faces in the Acheron System.

"Can't you do it manually?" Irons asked. "There's an emergency ejector."

Green didn't answer, but Jeff could hear the engineer talking to his men.

"Lieutenant Green?" the Major was getting impatient.

"The ejection system has been destroyed."

Green's words were followed by a lengthy silence. Jeff's felt a knot in his stomach. *Their antimatter store had turned into a ticking time bomb that they couldn't get rid of. And the countdown had started.* They would be blown up together with the ship. The old Agadir-class bombers didn't have rescue capsules on board.

Major Irons was the first to recover. "Lieutenant Rutherford. Give me a precise overview of our position."

It took a moment before the answer came. "We're fifty-two light years away from Sigma-7 and forty-five light years from the Karim System. The next star system is a binary star system of the A and G class. No known planets."

"Distance?"

"Two point three light years."

Jeff bit his lip. They were in the middle of an inter-stellar void and without the hyperdrive they had no chance of reaching a safe haven. If the voltage in the Penning trap dropped, they would have to leave the ship in just their combat suits. Jeff got goose bumps. These were high-tech spacesuits with an integrated life support system. He would neither suffocate nor die of thirst. An Armstrong Mark Six space suit could even supply him with liquid food for a certain amount of time. In his combat suit he could drift through space for weeks and slowly starve to death.

Not a great prospect.

"Where's the next star system with a planet we could survive on?" Irons asked. His voice was matter-of-fact.

"Sigma-7," Joanne replied.

"Not a single planet with a breathable atmosphere within forty-five light years?"

"No. The best I have to offer is a Mars-like planet."

"Distance?"

"Six point two light years."

"Lieutenant Green?"

The engineer grunted. "No can do. We can manage one light year at most. Definitely no more."

"Corporal Herrmannsson," Irons commanded. "Give me a medium-range location scan. We need somewhere we can land. A stray planet, a comet, *something*!"

"Give me a minute, Sir," Finni answered.

"I don't want to dampen your mood but the voltage in the antimatter trap is hitting rock bottom," Green said.

"How long do we have left?" Jeff asked.

"An hour. At most!"

"Corporal Hermmannsson, what's with the scan? You heard what Green said—time is short."

"OK, I've got a result. Unfortunately not what we'd hoped for. I've got an asteroid five light months away."

"An asteroid?"

"Or a planetesimal. Judging by the size and shape, it's similar to Ceres in the terrestrial Solar System. Looks like it has high metal content. *Interesting!*" His voice rose an octave as he spoke the last word.

"What do you mean?" Irons asked.

"It's moving very fast. Almost at half the speed of light. Maybe it was hurled out of its system by a neutron star or a black hole."

"What direction is it flying in?"

"Roughly toward Sigma-7."

"Lieutenant Rutherford, set a course," Irons commanded.

"You want to us to set down on that thing?" Joanne asked, dumbfounded. "Even if the asteroid is moving at half the speed of life, it would take us a hundred years to reach Sigma-7."

"Unfortunately, we have no other option," Irons said. "Lieutenant Green, please prepare for hyperflight!"

"I'd prefer not to use the hyperdrive anymore."

"Nor would I, but we don't have much choice."

"Yes, Sir!"

Jeff swallowed. Irons really wanted to set down on a bare asteroid. Surely that wasn't their only option! "If we can't make radio contact, we'll never be found." He made an effort to hide the panic in his voice, without much success.

"With a bit of luck, they'll find us," Irons said softly.

"With a bit of luck?" Joanne practically shouted. "Like that's going to happen."

"Unfortunately, we have no choice."

Jeff could just picture it. Sitting in his space suit on a dead asteroid. In eternal darkness, waiting for a miracle that would probably never come.

"You've got to be kidding me!" Owl said. He hadn't spoken for some time.

"Corporal Owens!" Irons voice was stern. "I want you to send a maximum-strength signal toward Sigma-7. Report our situation and the trajectory of the asteroid."

"Yes, Sir." Owl's voice had dropped to almost a whisper.

"Ready to enter hyperspace. But I wouldn't bet another dime on that thing. If the horizon collapses during flight …" Green didn't finish his sentence, but Jeff knew exactly what would happen. Then they would be sitting forever in a mini universe within hyperspace, with no way back. On the other hand, they would be dead meat in any case when the antimatter bomb in the fuel depot exploded in an hour. Perhaps that would be a more humane death than starving slowly on a bare, black lump of asteroid in an interstellar void.

"We'll give it a try," Irons said decisively. "Lieutenant Rutherford, enter hyperspace."

"Course set. Flight time in hyperspace nine minutes. I've programmed an exit point close to the positioning signal at an adjusted speed. Activating … now."

The ship vibrated as the stars disappeared behind the windows. The vibration intensified quickly, and a metallic grinding noise reverberated through the cabin.

"What is that?" Irons asked.

"The horizon hasn't stabilized. Looks like gravitational gradients are affecting the ship."

"Will the hyperdrive hold out?" Jeff asked.

"God knows."

"Lieutenant Green!" Irons barked.

"Sir?"

"Order your men to bring the emergency equipment into the lock. Plus any other tools they can get together in fifteen minutes."

"Yes, Sir."

"Shall I pack any weapons?" Castles asked.

"We're unlikely to need any on an asteroid," Jeff said sardonically.

Irons hesitated. "There are some handguns and grenades in the emergency depot. We won't need more."

Jeff concentrated on his controls. The status indicator of the hyperdrive was glowing dark red. Numerous other systems had also failed. The ship had really had it. If only the hyper radio was still working!

Suddenly Jeff slammed forward against his console. If his visor hadn't been closed, he would have broken his nose. But even with it on, he knew he'd have a big bruise on his forehead.

"What's going on?" Irons sounded alarmed.

"The hyperdrive!" Green cursed. "The horizon is forming singularities. We have to switch off, or the ship will be torn apart by the gradients."

"No!" Irons said sharply. "How long still?"

"Two minutes," Joanne said.

"The drive can manage two more minutes," Irons said.

"You're going to kill us!" Green screamed. "We have to switch off!"

"Get a hold of yourself, Lieutenant Green!"

"Jesus!"

The vibrations were getting stronger. Jeff's teeth were chattering so hard he was sure one would break. He heard a rumbling noise above his head and looked up. The ceiling cladding was beginning to come loose.

"One more minute," Joanne shrieked. Her voice was so distorted, Jeff had trouble understanding her.

"I'm switching off now," Green screamed.

"If you shut down now, I'll shoot you!" Irons threatened.

"For fuck's sake!" Green screamed, but he pulled his hand away from the console.

"Thirty more seconds!"

The rattling didn't stop. Dazzling white light flashed outside the windows.

Hawking radiation.

Jeff's stomach contracted. He had been warned about this phenomenon at the Academy. Individual elements of the horizon peeled away and exploded in a torrent of hard radiation. It was the last warning sign of a collapsing hyperfield.

"Twenty seconds."

"Major Irons!" Green screamed.

"Hold on!" Irons voice was calm.

Jeff closed his eyes. He could still see the flashes of light and thought he could feel heat of the gamma radiation on his skin.

"Ten seconds."

The vibrations worsened. Suddenly, an invisible hand lifted Jeff clean out of his seat. Without the belt he would have hit the ceiling. Joanne screamed. More alarm sirens wailed. At any moment, the ship would fall apart and they would be crushed by the debris.

Then—abruptly—there was silence. Jeff was sitting back in his seat. The vibrations had ceased and the alarm sirens had stopped. A quiet creaking noise moved through the metal girders of the cockpit, then that sound subsided, too. Breathing heavily, Jeff straightened up and looked around. He could see stars outside the cockpit windows. He exhaled slowly. The hyperdrive and the horizon had held out. They'd made it back to the normal universe. But had they come out in the right place?

"Lieutenant Green! Status!" Irons commanded.

The engineer coughed. "The hyperdrive actually made it." His coughing turned into hysterical laughter.

"Get a grip, man! Give me the status of the systems."

Green took a deep breath. "Yes, Sir. Most of the

systems are offline, including the life support system. We've got several holes in the hull and some of the Vernier engines have failed. Voltage in the defective antimatter trap is still falling."

"Time until malfunction?"

"Half an hour at most."

"Lieutenant Rutherford?"

Joanne didn't answer. Jeff turned around to look at her. The navigator was clasping her space helmet with her hands. Through the slightly fogged-up visor, Jeff could see blood on her forehead. "You OK, Joanne?"

"Yeah, I'm all right," she said eventually. "I hit the console and banged my head. I'll be OK in a sec."

"Lieutenant Rutherford!" Irons' voice was low but urgent.

"Yes, Sir. The maneuver was successful. We're where we want to be. The asteroid must be somewhere in front of us.

"Corporal Herrmannsson?"

"I can see it. It really is right in front of us. Distance around sixty thousand miles. We're approaching it at around two hundred and fifty miles per second. I'm trans-ferring the vectors to the onboard computer."

"Good, make a detailed analysis of the object. Lieu-tenant Rutherford, start the alignment maneuver. Bring us to standstill at a distance of three hundred miles, so we can find a place to land."

"Yes, Sir!"

"Strange …"

"What's strange, Corporal Herrmannsson?" Irons asked.

"The metal content is very high for an asteroid. There are also significant variations in density. As if it had huge empty spaces inside it."

"cavitys?" Jeff asked. He was no astronomer and didn't know what was normal for an asteroid and what wasn't.

"Not of that size. Huh."

"What?" Irons asked.

"The surface is composed not only of metallic compounds but also of complex alloys."

"Which means …?"

"The predominant alloying elements are aluminum and copper, with traces of manganese and silicon. Other parts seem to consist of a nickel alloy with chromium and iron. Jesus, at home we call that Inconel-X and use it for most of our spaceships."

"Are you trying to say that there are artificial structures on this asteroid?" the major asked.

Jeff leaned forward and looked out of the window. He couldn't see anything. The object was too far away. Maybe there was a secret base there. Then they would be saved.

"No," Finni replied after what felt like an eternity. "The whole thing seems to be made of these alloys. It isn't an asteroid. It's a man-made object."

"With a diameter of almost six hundred miles?" Irons scoffed. "Impossible. Our largest space station is just three miles in diameter. Neither we nor the Alliance could have built anything of that size. You must be mistaken."

"I'm not mistaken." Finni sounded offended. "I know what I'm doing."

"Then maybe something's wrong with the instruments."

"The instruments are working just fine!"

Irons frowned. "Give me a topographic scan."

A three-dimensional hologram appeared between Irons' and Jeff's consoles. It had the approximate shape of a sphere and rotated slowly. It looked like an asteroid.

"Alignment maneuver completed," Joanne announced.

Jeff leaned forward again. The object couldn't be more than a few hundred miles away from them now. But all he could see was a huge black area that blocked out the stars behind it.

"I can't see a thing," Green grumbled.

"Of course not," Irons answered dryly. "We're in the middle of an interstellar void. There's no sun here, so there's no light to reflect off a celestial body. We'll have to produce some light ourselves. Lieutenant Castle!"

"Sir?"

"Are the fusion rockets ready?"

A few second passed. "Laffette one is offline, but number two is ready to load."

"Fire tangentially. Safety distance times two, radial one K. Active mass forty megatons."

"Roger. Lafette two loaded and ready to fire."

"Then fire!"

The firing of the rocket occurred in complete silence. They couldn't hear anything in the cockpit.

"Rocket ejected. Detonation in three, two, one …."

Jeff squeezed his eyes shut to block out the light, then gradually opened them. He saw an alien object directly in front of them.

Jesus Christ! What is that?

"What the hell …?" Joanne's voice trailed off before she could finish her question.

"Holy shit!" Finni whispered.

Even Major Irons let out a gasp of surprise.

That was no asteroid. It wasn't a natural object at all. Sure, it had the nearly spherical shape of an asteroid, but it was made completely out of metal. The surface was covered in all kinds of weird projections—antenna-like structures that reached far into space, craggy outcrops, and jagged protrusions. It looked sinister and utterly inhospitable.

Jeff got goose bumps. *Bizarre, totally bizarre.*

The proportions were all wrong. Suspended in the middle of space, it looked like a megalomaniacal sculpture by a depressed and crazy artist—maybe something by H.R. Giger or Picasso.

The bright light of the fusion rocket faded away, plunging the thing in front of them back into total darkness. Jeff shook himself. He had the uncomfortable feeling that he had seen something he shouldn't have.

"What the hell *is* that?" Joanne finished her sentence second time round.

"If only I knew," Irons said in a strained voice.

Jeff turned around to look at him. It was the first time he had ever heard the major sound uncertain. "What shall we do?" he asked.

"Twenty minutes till the Penning trap gives up the ghost," Green said.

"There's your answer," the major replied.

"You don't seriously want to land on that thing?" Jeff asked.

"You mean dock," Joanne said.

Dock … yes, it really did appear to be a giant spaceship or space station. But it seemed to be dead. There was no sign of life. No lights, no movement, nothing …

"Corporal Owens, call on all frequencies," Irons seemed to have recovered himself.

"Call?" Owens looked confused. "Call who?"

"Our involuntary hosts. Who else?"

"You really think there are *people* living down there?"

"Aliens maybe …" Jeff whispered.

"Captain Austin?"

Jeff turned round to look at the major. He could only

guess at the expression in his eyes behind the visor. "That thing can't have been built by humans."

Irons leaned forward to look out of the windows again. Jeff did the same. The outline of the mysterious object had merged back into the darkness of the interstellar void.

"I think you're right," Irons said. "Looks like we've discovered an alien artifact for the first time in human history."

"This far inside the known sector?" Joanne retorted.

"It seems to be dead. It's drifting far beyond our inhabited systems at half the speed of light. It might have been here for thousands of years without a chance of being discovered. In fact, it might have been sneaking its way through space for millions of years."

"But it's so damn *big*," Green said.

"It's flying at half the speed of light. Maybe the aliens never discovered hyperdrive technology. It might be a generational spaceship aboard which some catastrophe occurred."

"What kind of catastrophe?" Green asked.

"We'll soon find out," Irons said grimly.

"How?"

"Lieutenant Rutherford. Search for a place to land."

Joanne gave a desperate laugh. "What do I look for? How should I know where's a good place to land?"

"Something that looks like a lock or a hangar. Some place from where we can get inside the thing."

"I don't know—"

"Make a decision. We don't have much time."

"Sir!" Owl piped up.

"Yes? Did you get a reply?"

"No, I sent a greeting via all standard frequencies, but haven't received an answer."

"Then it really does appear to be dead. Lieutenant Green, tell your men to prepare to leave the ship!"

"Yes Sir."

"We're within range of the landing lights," Joanne said.

"Activate!"

They were now flying at low speed above the surface of the foreign body. Jeff gawped at the sharp-edged protrusions, pointed antenna, and dome-shaped projections dotting the black surface. Joanne had to change course more than once to avoid colliding with one of them.

"I really haven't got a clue where to set down," Joanne said. There was a hint of desperation in her voice.

"Go a little higher so we can see more of the surface," Irons commanded.

They swerved upward. Jeff shook his head. He couldn't see anything that looked even remotely like a lock or a hangar door. The whole thing looked so other-worldly.

"Fifteen more minutes," Green said.

"Right then," Irons said. "Just set down somewhere. It doesn't make any sense to look …"

"There! There!" Finni screamed and pointed. His already high voice was almost piercing.

Jeff looked up. "You're right!" On the horizon, about thirty miles away, part of the surface glowed a dark red.

"What is that?" Joanne sounded worried.

"An invitation, perhaps," Iron replied.

"Or a warning to get the hell out of here," Castle speculated.

"Take us there."

"Are you sure that's a good idea?"

Irons ignored the question.

"Yes, Sir!" Joanne confirmed.

The Charon turned slowly to the right and approached the illuminated spot between several spiky outcrops. Red spotlights on the surface of the artifact illuminated a circular area that was free of any protrusions, but which looked otherwise inconspicuous. Joanne slowed the ship down until they came to a standstill above the circular area.

"Is this the only spot on the surface where there's any sign of life?" Irons asked.

"Seems so," Finni said. "At least there's nothing on my readouts."

"Can you detect any sources of energy or other evidence of anything else going on down there?"

"No, but it's a hell of a big beast. If their reactors are deep inside that thing, my instruments won't be much help."

"Any reaction to our radio signal?" Irons asked.

"Nope, still nothing."

"Look, an opening!" Joanne cried.

She was right. A circular hole suddenly opened up below them. Jeff estimated it was about thirty feet in diameter. It appeared to be an airlock, and was filled with red light. They could even see the ground inside.

"Looks like a lock to me," Castle said.

"Looks like an invitation to me," Irons retorted.

"Ten more minutes," Green called out.

"OK, we'll leave through the emergency lock. Captain Austin?"

Jeff stood up. He knew what the major wanted him for. "Got it." He was closest to the emergency lock. He walked the two steps to the hatch and pressed the small switch on the door. The remaining air escaped from the cabin. Then a red light went on.

Shit!

Jeff tugged at the silver lever next to the switch, but it didn't budge.

"Emergency lock can't be opened. Automatic and manual mechanisms aren't working."

"Then we'll leave through a window," Irons said.

Jeff took a deep breath and stepped up to the closest of the two big cockpit windows. The HUD of his spacesuit confirmed that the cabin was almost completely evacuated, in any case, so he didn't need to worry about a difference in pressure. He hung on to his console and thrust his right leg out. He kicked as hard as he could. Even the reinforced glass of the cockpit window couldn't withstand the diamond-studded tips of his boots. The glass shattered into thousands of pieces, which were pushed out by the remaining atmosphere.

Suddenly, a metal screen began to drop down from above, covering the newly formed opening.

Shit!

He had forgotten about the damn safety screen! It was automatically activated when a window was damaged and sealed the window against the vacuum of space.

Jeff turned around and punched a round knob on his console.

The screen already covered half the window, but it came to a stop. Thankfully, the hole was big enough for them to squeeze through.

Irons gave him a stern look and shook his head. He didn't give him a dressing down in front of the others.

"Meeting point is at the edge of the opening on the artifact. Lieutenant Rutherford, program a course for the Charon that will take her to a safe distance."

"Sir!"

"I don't like this at all. That thing down there is freaky," Castle said.

"Better than being dead …" Jeff mumbled. But he got goose bumps at the thought of going inside that thing.

"That was an order!" Irons said, unfazed. "And that goes for you, too, Lieutenant Castle!"

Jeff stepped back to let the WSO pass. It was a miracle the artificial gravity was still working.

"Lieutenant Rutherford, hurry up!" Irons commanded. Jeff went over to the navigator, whose fingers were still dancing over her console.

"I'm programming another course to a safe distance. It's a bit more complicated than I thought, I need to make sure the Charon doesn't collide with the artifact."

"Make it quick!"

Castle, Green, Owl, and Finni had already left the bridge. Irons was squeezing himself through the gap under the screen.

"Joanne!" Jeff laid a hand on her shoulder.

She nodded agitatedly, then stood up. "Done."

"Then get a move on!" Irons ordered.

Jeff followed Joanne to the window. One by one, they squeezed through the opening.

"Hurry up!" Irons ordered. "Meeting point is next to the lock on the artifact. Fields, Short, McGuinness: have you understood?"

"Loud and clear—Sir!" Jeff heard Shorty's voice.

"How far are you?"

"We're just leaving our lock," Mac McGuinness answered.

"Have you got emergency equipment with you?"

"Yes, Sir. We loaded an additional pallet with things that might be helpful."

"Good. We'll see you on the surface.

In front of Jeff, Joanne was pushing her way through the opening. She activated the small jets on her combat suit and floated down. Jeff stepped forward and gaped in amazement at the surface of the alien body, which was about twelve miles below him. It was lit up by the Charon's powerful landing lights. He had the feeling he was staring down on a man-made planet—the surface looked like it was made of black metal sheeting. It was as if a surrealist painter had tried to recreate the moon out of the most bizarre metal pieces they could find. The view to the horizon was obscured by spiny outgrowths and terrace-like overhangs. Below him, Jeff saw the red illuminated area with the opening in the middle. He didn't want to go inside. He didn't know where the feeling came from, but something was telling him that if he went in there, he would never come out again.

"Get a move on, Captain Austin!" the major shouted at him.

Jeff took a deep breath. He pushed off with his boots so that he floated headfirst. Then he activated the fine-control jets on his suit and was thrust forward. Gently, as if in a dream, he began to fall. Joanne and the others had already reached the ground, which was bathed in red light, and were casting jerky shadows on the black metal surface whenever they moved. Beside them, the open lock glowed like a red-hot eye. The pale white light from their helmet headlamps danced like ghosts over the ground. A few seconds later, Jeff had also reached the ground. He activated his magnetic boots and was relieved to find that the ground was ferromagnetic. The gravity of the planetoid body was too low to be able to move about normally.

"We're all down," Irons said. "Get the spaceship to a safe distance!"

"Sir!" said Joanne and jabbed some buttons on her arm console.

Jeff looked up to where their ray-shaped bomber hovered motionless in space. The landing lights were so dazzling, he couldn't see the ship clearly, but even so, he could tell it was badly damaged. The starboard engine pod was torn off about halfway along the outrigger—cables and wires dangled out of the cavity like entrails. Frozen coolant was leaking from several parts of the fuselage and there were numerous spots where the outer skin had been torn off, revealing the ugly bowels of the ship.

"How much longer?" Jeff asked.

"One to two minutes," Green said.

"What's going on, Lieutenant Rutherford?" Irons asked impatiently.

"I'm ready. I'm starting the program."

The bomber gradually accelerated while rising up at the same time. It spun slowly on its axis, turning its nose away from the artifact. Jeff saw the faint glow of the Vernier thrusters, then the Charon accelerated quickly. A few seconds later, it had almost disappeared from view. If it weren't for the landing lights, it would have already been swallowed up by the darkness. A few more seconds, and it was just a small white dot. Jeff squinted as he tried to follow its course. Then it was gone completely.

"Lieutenant Rutherford, has the Charon—" Major Irons began, but he didn't finish his sentence.

A painfully bright flash lit up the sky and Jeff closed his eyed, dazzled by the light.

So that was it.

They were stranded. In the middle of the darkest void, dozens of light years from the nearest manned outpost, unable to send a hyper-radio message. They were now standing on the outer shell of the first extraterrestrial artifact ever to be found by mankind. Jeff's thoughts swirled like mist. Their fate and survival now depended on whether they could get into the interior of this spaceship—or whatever it was—and in what they found there. Judging by the open lock, it looked like getting inside would be possible at least.

"Gone …" Green peered up into the blackness. "Now we're really up shit creek."

"Please keep your pessimism to yourself," Irons retorted sharply.

"What do we do now?" Shorty whimpered. Jeff looked up. Although he couldn't see any of his shipmates' faces through their visors in the dim light, he knew it was Shorty from his hulking, six-foot-five form.

"We're going in," Irons said.

"All of us?" Joanne asked. "What if we can't get back out?"

"Then I wouldn't know what to advise those of us left out here. If there's a solution to our problem, it can only be inside this thing. And I think it makes more sense for us to stick together."

"What do you think's down there?" Jeff mused out loud.

"I wonder if there's anyone living down there, waiting for us," Owl added.

"I doubt it," Irons said. "By the looks of it, this thing is ancient. It's probably been abandoned for eons."

"But somebody turned on the light and opened the lock," Joanne pointed out.

"That was probably triggered automatically. Our approach must have activated some kind of program," Irons retorted.

"An automatic program could just as easily have thought we were an enemy and shot us down," Green pointed out sardonically.

"But it didn't," Irons snapped back. "Corporal Fields, please take the emergency equipment into the lock."

"Yes, Sir."

Without waiting to be instructed, the two privates, Shorty and Mac helped Green push the sled-shaped construction that was hovering above the ground on repulsor fields. They steered the equipment into the yawning, red hole in the ground of the artificial asteroid. A few seconds later, the technicians had disappeared into the lock. Irons waved over Joanne, Owl, and Castle, and waited for them to descend into the hole, too, before bringing up the rear. Finni stepped up to the edge, looked nervously down, and then jumped. Only Jeff and Green were left standing on the surface.

"Come on!" Irons urged them.

"This is how Jonas must have felt when he was swallowed by the whale," Green said, and jumped.

Jeff took a last look up at the stars, which were so unfathomably far away. He wondered if he would ever see them again. Then he, too, stepped over the edge and drifted down into the red cavity.

As the walls glided past him, he looked around. It really did seem to be a lock and resembled similar ones on their own spaceships and planetary bases. The walls were made of dark metal plates that dully reflected the red light emanating from a source he couldn't see. Yellow and red stripes marked the hazard areas around the hatches. Jeff could make out alien-looking pictograms, which must be the aliens' warning signs, and strange characters that were vaguely reminiscent of Sumerian cuneiform. Jeff landed softly on the ground. In front of him he saw a hatch with a small window in the middle. He peered through, but all he could see on the other side was darkness.

"And now?" Castle asked. "How do we operate the airlock?"

Jeff looked around in vain for a manual control panel or something similar.

"Maybe hidden behind flaps in the wall or something …" Joanne wagered a guess.

Fields and Mac began to tap along the walls.

"Or maybe they controlled the lock by remote control," Joanne added.

"Or the aliens had telepathic powers and used their minds." Green began to laugh. "Then we're really—"

"Lieutenant Green!" Irons spoke sharply and the engineer fell silent.

"It could be …" Jeff began, but stopped as he noticed a movement above him. He craned his neck to look up. "The outer hatch is closing!"

Because of the vacuum they couldn't hear anything, of course, but they could see the door sliding over the opening.

"Let's hope we can open it again," Green said in a snarky tone. Jeff waited for a dressing down from the major, but Irons didn't respond.

Several seconds passed in silence, then Jeff heard a low whistle, which gradually grew louder.

"They're pumping air into the lock!" Joanne said in surprise.

"Then we can take off our helmets in a minute," Castle said.

"Could also be mustard gas," Green remarked.

"We can't rule out that these aliens breathed a different atmosphere," Irons said. "We'll have to analyze the air first."

The whistling noise had stopped. Fields rummaged around on the sled with the emergency equipment, found a container, and opened it. He took out a small, silver device with a handle: a multitester.

"I'll start the analysis."

Jeff pressed a button on the controls on his arm and

looked at the HUD display on his combat suit. "Ten twenty-two hectopascals of external pressure," he said.

"Tailor-made for us! It could be Earth," Joanne sounded relieved.

"How long does the analysis take?" Irons asked.

Fields looked up. "Done. The atmosphere is breathable. A mix of seventy-eight percent nitrogen, twenty-one percent oxygen and one percent argon."

"That's almost exactly the same as on Earth," Irons commented, without a trace of surprise in his voice. "Aerosols? Trace gases?"

"No aerosols. Very few trace gases. Just some carbon dioxide, methane, and ozone. And water in the form of unsaturated steam. The humidity is sixty percent at a temperature of seventy-five degrees Fahrenheit."

"If there's carbon dioxide here, then someone must have exhaled it," Green said.

"Unless the atmosphere is artificially composed," Irons said.

"But the resemblance to our atmosphere …" Joanne trailed off. "It's as if they were expecting us."

"Have you checked for microbes?" Irons asked.

"Yup. No microbes. The atmosphere is absolutely sterile. A military hospital would be proud of the purity level."

"Right then," Irons said curtly. He reached up for the neck ring and released the latch. Then he pushed the helmet back over his head and took a deep breath.

Jeff looked intently at his superior's face, ready to react immediately if he started to discolor, or if he passed out. But Irons breathed calmly and evenly. After what seemed like an eternity he smiled, even if his smile was a little strained. "Smells kind of stale and musty."

"Should we open our helmets, too?" Joanne asked.

"I don't see why not."

Jeff released the latch and flipped his helmet up. He took a cautious breath. The Major was right. The air did smell stale. As if they'd entered an apartment that hadn't been properly aired in months. It was warm and very humid. There was also a faint whiff of something else he couldn't put his finger on—something which was anything but pleasant. A little sweetish, but with a tangy edge that suggested decay. Not so much like old fish or rotten meat … more like exotic vegetables rotting in the sun. Very strange—and very alien.

By now, the others had also removed their visors. Jeff could tell by their puzzled faces and wrinkled noses that his shipmates were also trying to identify the smell.

"I don't like this air," Joanne said. "Smells like there are dozens of decomposing aliens on the other side of that door."

"If they open the outer hatch now, we're all dead," Green said.

"Then why would they have opened the airlock in the first place?" Jeff retorted.

"Maybe they're playing a game with us."

"How do we get inside, anyway?" Owl asked.

As if an invisible listener had heard his question, the bulkhead retracted with a hiss. A gust of wind swept across Jeff's face. Behind the opening, it was still dark. Their helmet lights were too weak to illuminate the apparently much larger space on the other side. Irons stooped over the equipment sled and found a battery-powered headlamp. He switched it on and stepped into the opening. Jeff came up beside him.

"Looks like a small hangar," Irons said.

The Major was right. Black and yellow lines crisscrossed the ground in random patterns. The ceiling was about thirty feet above them. The room itself was empty, as if nobody had ever bothered to equip it. On the other side of the room was a large metal bulkhead. As Jeff looked around, he noticed that the room was gradually getting brighter. "They're turning on a light!"

Irons switched off the headlamp. Jeff had been right. The room was illuminated by some kind of indirect light that was getting brighter all the time. It wasn't clear where the light was coming from—it appeared to be coming from all directions at once and produced no shadows.

Irons stepped out of the lock chamber into the hangar-like room.

Jeff followed him. "It's not that different from one of our stations."

"Or a base on the moon or on another planet," Irons agreed. "Except for that strange writing."

Jeff headed for the opposite wall with the door. There was a window in the middle of the hatch. Beyond it was darkness. Beside the door was a text written in the strange cuneiform characters he had seen earlier. It looked as if it had been stenciled on the wall. It was written in block type. Jeff had no idea if this alien language was read from left to right or vice versa. None of the signs resembled the Latin alphabet.

There was a hissing noise behind him, and he swung round. The inner lock hatch had closed, just after Shorty and Mac had entered the hangar with the equipment sled. Fields examined the wall around the hatch. "I don't see any controls," he said. "If we wanted to get back out, I wouldn't know how."

"Maybe we should have posted someone outside," Green said.

"And what good would that have done us?" Irons asked impatiently. "We would have been separated. As I said, we only have a chance of finding a solution to our problems in here. Not outside."

Green's grunt didn't exactly express agreement, but Irons didn't pursue the matter.

"At least there are no alien bodies," Owl said brightly. "But the air in here reeks as bad as it did in the lock chamber."

"And it's just as warm," Joanne added, wiping the sweat from her forehead with her gloved hand.

Jeff still couldn't figure out whether this was a space station that had been flung out of orbit, or a giant spacecraft. They'd managed to get inside, but it was completely unclear what would happen next. He turned to the Major, who was frowning at the opposite door. "How should we proceed, Sir?"

It took a few seconds before Irons responded. Finally he returned Jeff's gaze, but he seemed to look right through him. The already heavy rings under his eyes were darker than usual. For a moment Jeff was afraid Irons would collapse, and his stomach tightened at the thought. He had always been able to rely on the Major. Without his experience and instincts, they didn't stand a chance. There was nobody who could replace Irons. Jeff, who was the most senior officer after the major, certainly didn't feel up to the job.

But after a moment, Irons' facial expressions hardened again, and his steel-blue eyes were as determined as they had been before. "We have more than enough time to evaluate our situation and check out our surroundings. First, we need to determine whether this artifact is actually abandoned."

"You said that some kind of automated system probably opened the airlock."

Irons nodded. "Yes, that's what I think. And we have to find out if it's possible to communicate with it."

"But how?"

Irons shrugged. Then he took a deep breath. "Is anyone here?" His voice boomed through the room, causing Jeff to flinch. "Can anyone on this ship hear me?"

The others had all turned around to see what was going on. Castle looked at his commander as if he'd lost his mind. Then there was a tense silence and Jeff could hear his own heartbeat.

"I can hear you."

Jeff almost jumped out of his skin. The voice spoke flawless Cosmocration. It was a high but distinctly male voice.

"Welcome on board."

The voice was completely devoid of emotion and sounded as if it had been synthesized by an ancient computer. Jeff looked around but couldn't tell from which direction it was coming. There must be several speakers in the room.

Irons cleared his throat. "I am Major George Irons, Commander of the Imperial spaceship Charon. I would like to thank you on behalf of the whole crew for taking us on board."

Jeff exchanged a quick glance with Irons. The major raised his eyebrows. His forehead was covered in beads of sweat. He looked as tense as Jeff was feeling. "Who are you?" Irons asked finally.

"I am the intelligence of this ship."

Jeff nodded slowly. So it was a spaceship, and not a space station. A spaceship *this* big?

"Are you like a computer? An onboard computer?" Irons asked.

"That is an adequate description."

"Seems to be some kind of artificial intelligence," Irons said quietly to Jeff. "Where's the crew?" he shouted into the room.

"The crew left this ship long ago."

"Why?"

"Because they had arrived at their destination."

"Destination?" Green whispered. "What destination?"

"The crew was looking for a suitable planet on which to settle after our own system was doomed."

"Doomed? How doomed?"

"A gamma-ray burst threatened to make our galaxy uninhabitable and so this spaceship was built to bring the inhabitants to a new world."

"An ark," Joanne chipped in, astonished. "This ship is an ark. It's certainly big enough."

"There must have been billions of living beings …" Green said.

"Unbelievable," Short added.

Everyone started to talk at once.

"Whoa!" Irons raised a hand. "One at a time. First we have to clarify the important points. I will talk with this computer and nobody else, understood?"

Jeff's teammates fell silent.

"Unfortunately, our ship was destroyed, as you may have noticed," Irons said. "We're stranded here. Will you help us?"

"Yes, as far as I am able," said the alien voice.

Jeff let out a sigh of relief. Maybe they'd been lucky after all. If this was a spaceship, it might be able to take them to the next inhabited star system. Once they were there, they could continue exploring the ship in safety.

"Can you give us access to a hyper-radio system so we can get a ship to pick us up?"

"If you are referring to superluminal communication, unfortunately I cannot provide that."

Shit!

Irons grimaced. "You don't have a hyper radio?"

"No."

Jeff felt an icy shiver going down his spine as he realized the possible consequences. What if the strangers didn't have superluminal technology? Then being on a spaceship wouldn't help them much. How fast was this ship flying through the interstellar void? At half the speed of light, Jeff remembered. At that speed they would need a century to get to the next outpost.

Irons seemed to be thinking the same thing. "Surely this spacecraft doesn't just have *sub*luminal engines?"

Unfortunately, it made sense. Why else would they have built such a huge ship? Perhaps this had been a generational spaceship, on which millions of beings had been born and died before reaching another star system after decades or centuries. No wonder the crew had disembarked after arriving at an inhabitable planet.

"No," said the strange voice. "This ship has a functioning superluminal drive."

Jeff let out a sigh of relief.

"However, our jump drive is much slower than your hypertechnology appears to be."

Jump drive? Jeff had never heard of a jump drive. These aliens must have developed a completely different technology for space travel than humans.

"How slow?" Irons asked.

"This ship can jump about two light years a week, if I use your units of measurement. In between, the capacitors have to be charged."

Jeff wondered how the computer knew their units of measurement, let alone their language.

"Two light years a week," Irons mused. "That would be half a year for a distance of fifty light years."

The alien voice did not answer. If they could persuade the onboard computer of this huge spaceship to take them to Sigma-7, they would need half a year to get there. That was a long time. But at least a more feasible amount of time than a hundred years, which none of them would survive.

"Would you perhaps be willing to take us to a specific system, whose coordinates we would give you?" Irons asked.

Right now, this was the question of all questions.

Silence.

"We could certainly agree on some form of payment," the Major said.

Payment … what kind of payment could they possibly provide?

Several long seconds passed, during which Jeff's heart beat so fast it made his temples ache.

Finally the computer answered. "Certainly."

Jeff could have whooped for joy, but he restrained himself. They would get back home! Six months … they could use the time to explore the giant ship. It might come in useful for Jeff's studies after the war was over. It would take him in a completely new direction, but it would also give him a huge advantage over his peers. Yes, he would be *the* specialist in extraterrestrial culture and history. In his mind, Jeff could already see himself giving lectures at interstellar conferences. Who knows, he might even end up winning the Nobel Prize.

Someone slapped him on the arm. "Stop daydreaming," Irons said harshly.

Jeff swallowed. Of course. It was still a bit early for daydreaming. First they had to get back home.

"Do you have a name?" Irons bellowed into the room.

"No."

"Does this spaceship have a name?"

"Yes."

"What is it called?"

"The translation of the name is 'spaceship'."

Irons rolled his eyes. Jeff chuckled. Green snickered.

"How should we address you?" Irons asked.

"That's up to you."

"Then I'll simply call you Computer."

No answer.

"Is there an area where we can base ourselves? Accommodation of some kind? Perhaps with access to clean water?"

"Appropriate rooms are being prepared for you. I suggest you make your way there now. We can discuss any details later."

Jeff wondered who was preparing their accommodation. Robots?

"Great, thank you" Irons said. "Where do we need to go?"

Suddenly the hatch opposite them hissed and moved aside.

"There's your answer, Major," said Shorty.

Joanne hurried over to Jeff and Irons. "This is all a bit weird, if you ask me," she whispered. "Can we trust that thing?"

"Unfortunately, we have no other choice, Lieutenant Rutherford," Irons said softly.

"How does it even know our language? It's creepy."

Irons put his hand on her shoulder. "There are many questions that I hope will be answered in time. But we mustn't rush anything. This spaceship is our only chance.

We'll have more than enough time to explore the ship and find out what we want to know."

"I don't know if I even want to explore the ship," Green said, not budging from the spot.

"Why not?" Jeff asked.

The engineer turned to face him and stamped his right foot on the ground. "This thing is huge. You would have to travel thousands of miles before reaching the other side. We have moons in our Solar System that are smaller. It freaks me out just thinking about what's hidden in the depths of this ship."

Jeff had to admit the ship—this whole situation—gave him the creeps, too. Everything was so alien. But hadn't the ship's computer promised to help them?

"And another thing," Green interrupted his thoughts. "It's a ghost ship. Christ knows how long its been flying itself through the galaxy. At this speed, it must have been flying through the known sector for years. Why has nobody ever tried to make contact with it? I reckon—"

"Stop, Lieutenant Green," Irons barked. "I've had it up to here with your fear-mongering. We've been received in a friendly manner, and I will not allow you to insult our hosts with your unfounded suspicions."

Green looked down at the ground and didn't answer.

"Corporal Fields, get the equipment. We're going."

The technician nodded and beckoned to his shipmates.

Jeff followed Irons to the door. He stopped at the threshold. A long corridor stretched out in front of them. The walls were made of an unusually dark gray metal— the whole ship seemed to be made of the same material. The corridor was very dimly lit, but at least it was light enough to see where they were going. And it was just wide enough so that two people could walk side by side. It sloped down gently from the surface of the ship.

"Strange—it's like a ramp," Irons said. "On our space-ships and stations, the floors and corridors all run parallel to the decks. If you need to reach another level, you use elevators, stairs, or ladders."

Suddenly he gave a gasp of surprise.

"What is it?" Jeff asked.

"Walk forward six more feet and you'll see for yourself," the major said.

Cautiously, Jeff took a step forward. His foot met with less resistance than he had expected. When he pulled the other foot after it, he was monetarily overcome by dizziness. "The artificial gravity is changing vector direction," he said in surprise.

"That's right," Irons said.

Jeff looked back at the hangar or whatever that room with the airlock was. It was strangely tilted now, and his shipmates seemed to be leaning against invisible walls, but Jeff knew it was just an illusion produced by the different directions in which the artificial gravity of the spaceship pointed.

"We have to be careful not to lose our sense of direction," Irons said, setting off again. The others followed him, reluctantly. Jeff wondered how much farther they would have to go until they reached their quarters.

"You'd never have done this on a human spaceship," Green mused. "But considering the size of this thing, it makes sense. Imagine—a corridor tilted at ninety degrees leading straight to the center of the ship. You could reach it without ever having to use a staircase or elevator."

"But they must have had transportation systems," Irons frowned. "Surely these aliens didn't travel such vast distances on foot."

"It's so murky," Joanne shuddered, stepping into the corridor. Her face gleamed faintly in the pale light, while her dark space suit appeared to merge with the gray walls of the ship.

"You're right," said Jeff. "It wasn't particularly bright in the hangar, but here you can hardly even see any outlines."

"Maybe the aliens' eyes were more sensitive than ours," said Owl, who was trudging along the corridor behind Joanne.

Sticking close together, they continued walking down the hallway in silence. Nothing—not even the occasional door or recess—broke up the monotony of the dark metal walls.

Irons quickened his pace and marched on ahead. Shorty and Mac, who were carrying the equipment sled, brought up the rear. Thanks to the integrated inertia negation, the sled was light as a feather despite its mass. One person could have pulled it alone, but it was so big, it was easier to have two people pulling.

They must have covered about a mile when they finally got to an intersection. Three corridors forked off at different angles from the one they had been walking along. Only one was illuminated, and Jeff could see that it also led downward, and that there was another turning a little further on. One of the other corridors seemed to go up, but it was too dark to see for certain.

"Now where?" Owl asked.

Irons just grunted and set off down the illuminated hallway. Jeff saw the major tapping something into his handheld. "What are you doing?"

Irons held out the handheld computer—part of every crew member's equipment—for Jeff to look at. He could see that the major had drawn several lines leading away from a rectangle. It was a rough sketch of the path they were taking. Jeff nodded, and Irons put the handheld back in his pocket. It was a sensible thing to do, of course.

Whichever way they went, they would know the way back to the airlock if necessary. The inertial navigation systems in their handhelds were also recording the route they were taking, but it was sensible to have a hand-drawn back-up.

"How far still?" Green asked. Nobody answered. "Thanks a lot," the engineer muttered sarcastically.

Jeff only hoped that the aliens hadn't been used to walking hundreds of miles on foot. He wondered what they had looked like … the facilities they had seen on the ship so far didn't tell them much. The lock hatches and the width and height of the corridors suggested the aliens might have been similar in size to humans, but that was just speculation.

Every time they came to a junction, only one of the turnoffs was illuminated. Without ever hesitating, Irons led the group further into the mighty ship.

Almost an hour and a half had passed, during which time Green had complained on numerous occasions about his aching feet. Each complaint was acknowledged by a glare from Irons—although secretly, Jeff could have done with a break himself.

After yet another intersection, the new corridor became wider and they passed the occasional door adorned with the strange symbols and characters in the alien language. There were no door handles, but next to each door there was a little blue box embedded in the wall. Jeff presumed these were opening mechanisms, and was tempted to try one, but he didn't know how the ship's computer or Irons would react—and he didn't want to find out.

Shorty had less scruples. Just as Jeff was turning away from one of the doors, the young mechanic pushed one of the boxes. The door remained closed, but three short beeps sounded through the corridor.

"Fingers off!" Irons said sharply. "I don't want anyone here to touch anything without my command. Is that clear?"

Shorty looked down at his feet and nodded. Irons snorted and set off again. More intersections followed at ever shorter intervals and Irons struggled to keep up with his sketch. Finally, they turned into a corridor in which the light petered out after several feet. Somewhere beyond where the darkness began, there was an open door from which bright light shone into the corridor.

"Behind this door are your living quarters," the voice of computer suddenly returned.

Jeff entered the room behind Irons and chuckled in surprise. He'd reckoned with just about anything, but not this.

Green came in right after Jeff. "Holy shit, what is this?"

"Looks like a designer hotel." Joanne shook her head.

She was right. The room looked a lot like a luxury hotel suite. Jeff was reminded of his room in the five-star hotel he'd treated himself to in New York a few years back on a tour of the Solar System. In the middle of the spacious room were two large couches, arranged at right angles around a big glass table. In one corner was a large, round, wooden table—at least it looked like wood—around which were ten ornately curved wooden chairs. Behind the table was a kitchenette. Through one of the wall cupboard's glass doors, Jeff could see plates, cups, and glasses. He was sure he would find cutlery in one of the drawers next to the stove.

Green strode over to the kitchenette and tore open the door of the thing that looked like a refrigerator.

"Now take a look at that!" he said.

He was right. It was a fridge, and it was packed with drinks, fruit, vegetables, and more. Green took out a bottle of Neptune beer—they actually had Neptune beer!—and unscrewed the top. He looked at the bottle skeptically for a moment, then took a long swig. "Delicious!" He said. "It tastes like the real thing. I wonder where they got it?"

"Probably synthesized," Irons said. The Major, as always, seemed unimpressed. He walked past the couch area to a door at the far end of the room. Next to the door was another dark square. Irons pressed it and the door opened. It led into another corridor.

"There you will find your sleeping quarters," the voice of the computer said. "If you wish to communicate with me, it is only possible here in the lounge area."

Jeff followed Irons into the corridor. The major opened one of the doors and Jeff peeked into a bedroom. There was a queen-sized bed covered with a white bedspread, and next to it a narrow, black wardrobe and a small sitting area with a chair and a table. A doorway led into a beige-tiled bathroom with a toilet, shower, and sink. The ship's computer seemed to have thought of everything.

"Ten doors," Irons said after he and Jeff stepped back into the corridor. "It looks like the area was created specially for us."

Jeff shrugged. "He did say something was being prepared for us." But how the computer had been able to recreate it so realistically was anyone's guess.

"Well, we certainly can't complain about a lack of hospitality," Joanne said, peering into one of the rooms.

Irons walked past her back into the lounge. Jeff followed him. Green had already made himself comfortable on one of the two couches. He looked completely out of place in his combat suit. Owl was standing at the kitchen counter and washing his face at the small sink. Shorty and Mac had parked the equipment sled near the front door and were gawping at the luxurious room.

Irons went up to the sofa on which Green was lolling, and rested both his arms on the backrest. "Computer," he spoke loudly.

"What can I do for you?" the emotionless voice sounded through the room.

"First of all, many thanks for these comfortable quarters. This is more than we could have hoped for."

"You're welcome."

"And regarding our desired destination …"

"Just give me the coordinates and I'll set a course."

Irons hesitated. "Don't you want to negotiate payment or other terms?"

"I have been traveling for millions of your years and the corresponding number of light years. A small detour makes no difference to me."

Irons knitted his brows, as if something bothered him about the computer's choice of words. "What do you mean by *detour*? Where are you even headed? Why didn't you stay with your crew?"

"The crew had no more use for the spaceship after arriving at their target world. I was given the assignment of flying on and exploring the universe."

"And eventually returning to your creators?"

"No. I transmit the results to the home world by point-to-point radio."

"Where is this home world?"

"In another galaxy, over a hundred million light years from your Milky Way."

"Could you tell us the coordinates? Someday it would be interesting to investigate what happened to your people. Provided of course we are able to develop a hyperdrive that can take us there."

"I'm sorry, I cannot tell you the coordinates."

"Why not?" Joanne asked.

She got no answer. "Probably for security reasons," said Irons. "We would have reacted the same." He addressed the computer again. "You've probably already told your builders the coordinates of the human galaxy."

"Of course, that is my task."

Irons made a dismissive gesture with his hand. "One hundred million light years. If they only find out about us in a hundred million years, then it's no skin off our backs. In any case, they probably died out long ago." He cleared his throat. "Computer, when was the last time you had contact with your builders?"

"Before my departure from the target world."

Jeff was all ears.

Irons raised an eyebrow. "You've never heard from them since?"

"No, that was never the intention."

"Aha. How is it that you can speak our language?"

"I have collected and analyzed your radio transmissions for many years."

"You're studying us?"

"In fact, I changed my course in order to fly through your area."

"Why didn't you make contact with us?"

"Making contact is not within my mission parameters. I have been instructed to watch, analyze, and send back the results. Then I will fly on to other destinations of interest."

" … not within the parameters," Irons repeated. "And yet you have taken us in."

"This decision was made on the basis of moral directives."

"Moral directives?" Castle grimaced. Jeff chuckled. The weapon systems officer would never have dreamed of creating a machine with moral capabilities.

"Maybe the alien equivalent to the Asimov's laws," Jeff

pondered aloud. "If you find castaways in the interstellar void, you pick them up and take them to the nearest safe haven. Our merchant marines have similar guidelines."

"Well, I for one am not complaining," Irons said. "Computer. If we give you the coordinates, will you bring us to this system?"

"Yes."

Irons looked at Joanne. She registered his glance and nodded. She took her handheld out of the front pocket of her combat suit and tapped around on the touch screen. "Computer, our target system is relatively close to X+31, Y-4 and Z+47. The unit of measurement is light years."

"I have understood. I require a definition of your coordinate system."

Joanne raised her eyebrows. "Oh, God," she muttered. She swiped around on her DA and swore loudly.

"What's the problem?" Irons asked.

"Of course—this spaceship doesn't know our coordinate system. I need a fixed point that we can use in the coordinate transformation."

"You gave the location of Sigma-7 relative to our current location. I don't understand the problem," Irons persisted.

"Yes, the origin of the coordinates is clear, but the ship doesn't know the direction of our axes."

Irons nodded.

"I have an idea," Joanne said finally. "Computer. Draw a line from here to the center of the Milky Way, that's our axis of rotation for the coordinate transformation. The rotation is then …" She read some numbers from her DA.

Several seconds passed before the computer voice spoke. "At the point you specify, my analysis system shows a binary star system with a K-star and a G-class companion."

Joanne nodded. "Yes, that's correct. The G-class star has nine planets, and the Sigma-7 station is circling the fourth one."

"I have set a course. The flight time there will be 212 days according to your time. Everything you need will be provided."

Irons nodded and smiled. "Thank you very much. I still have a couple of questions about your creators. Above all, I'd like to know—"

"I apologize for interrupting you here. I have to break off contact now."

"Break off contact? Why?" Irons was surprised.

Jeff shook his head in confusion. The thing was a computer—and not just any old computer, an onboard computer. On their own ships and stations, they were permanently available to the crew.

"My program requires self-testing of complex onboard systems at regular intervals, which must be reset. Some of these tests require my full attention."

"Well, I guess that makes sense. It is a big ship," Owl remarked.

But Jeff still found it strange. Precisely *because* it was such a big ship there must be tons of systems that needed to be constantly monitored, checked, and controlled by the computer. Even if it did have to carry out these self-tests or whatever they were, there should still be enough capacity for communication between the computer and the crew. On the other hand, perhaps the computer technology of the extraterrestrial builders had been very different. It was an old ship. Maybe some of the original computer capacity was no longer available and the system had to be economical.

Irons shrugged. "OK. But I still have one question. Can we leave our quarters?"

Jeff pricked up his ears. That was a good question. If they couldn't leave their quarters, they would basically be prisoners on this ship.

"Of course. You can move around freely. However, I would recommend that you do not go too far from your quarters as you might get lost."

Jeff nodded in relief. OK—that made sense.

"I am now going to turn off my communication module," the computer said. "You can contact me again in a few hours."

As if to underscore these words, a faint crackling sound emanated from the invisible speakers.

"Computer?" Irons asked. No answer.

Nobody spoke for a few seconds. Then Joanne broke the silence. "Now what?"

Irons sighed. "I need some time to digest all this. At least we're safe here. Considering the alternatives, we were pretty lucky. I suggest we all have a rest. It's been a long, exhausting day. It looks like everyone gets their own space. You can check out your rooms, freshen up, take a nap." He glanced at the clock on the arm of his combat suit. "As there are no day and night rhythms here, I suggest we keep using universal time. It's now shortly after three in the afternoon. We'll meet here for dinner at seven and then we'll discuss our next move."

"Can we help ourselves to drinks from the fridge?" Shorty asked.

Irons nodded. "Sure, but don't overdo the beer. And another thing: I don't want anyone to leave the quarters without my express permission."

"Why not?" Green asked. "The computer said we could move around freely." Jeff could tell he was dying to explore the vast ship.

"We will explore our surroundings, but nobody will do

so on their own, and I'd like to work out a plan first," Irons said. "The last thing we need is for someone to get lost in the labyrinth of this ship."

"But then surely the computer would direct us back to our quarters."

"You will stay here," Irons barked. "Have you understood, Lieutenant?"

Green shrugged. "Yes. Whatever."

Irons opened his mouth to make a retort, but then turned on his heel and disappeared through the door into the short corridor with the bedrooms. Jeff saw the major take the first room.

"I reckon the old dog is overreacting. It can't harm to take a look around," Green grumbled.

Joanne rolled her eyes.

Jeff tried to look stern. It was now his job to reprimand Green. "You will follow the Major's orders! And don't call the commander 'old dog' in front of other crew members. *Major Irons*, got that?" Jeff wished he could make his own voice sound as authoritarian as Irons', but he knew he would never succeed.

Green looked at him dismissively. His lips curled as if her were about to burst out laughing. But then he waved his hand dismissively and went back to the fridge.

Jeff took a step forward and almost stumbled over the emergency equipment, which had been dragged into the middle of the room. "Corporal Fields, would you please clear away the sled?"

"Where should I put it, Sir?" As always, Jeff ignored the sarcastic undertone in Fields' voice when he addressed him as "Sir."

Jeff looked around the room. "There's a niche behind the kitchen. Looks like a good spot."

Fields shrugged. "As you wish, *Sir*."

The mechanic showed no sign that he was about to carry out his task. On the contrary; he turned around and walked over to the fridge as if nothing had happened.

"Corporal Fields," Green spoke in a crisp, clear voice that made even Jeff flinch.

Fields turned around on his heal. "Sir?" This time his "Sir" sounded more alert.

"Take the equipment straight to the niche!"

"Yes, Sir!"

Fields pursed his lips and returned to the sled.

"When you've finished with that, I want you to make an inventory of all the equipment and supplies we have left. Every single item. And I want to be able to hand over the list to Major Irons at dinner. Is that clear?"

"Yes, Sir," Fields replied and activated the sled's inertia-negation system. He waved Shorty over and together they steered the bulky object over to the niche behind the kitchen unit.

Green grinned with blatant disdain at Jeff's lack of authority. Jeff got up hastily and retreated to his room. He could have cried. When Irons wasn't around, he had absolutely no power over the crew. He never would. He was an academic, pure and simple. A bookworm. He had zero interest in ordering other people around. Who had even had the bright idea of making him the XO of a bomber? And now they had to wait seven long months until they reached Sigma-7.

Jeff locked the door to his room, sat down on the edge of the bed, and closed his eyes.

Please let this nightmare end.

Chapter 3

"Where did that come from?" Jeff asked, pointing at the steaming pot in the middle of the table.

"It was on a trolley outside the door," Joanne said, gesturing to the main entrance of their quarters. A metal trolley—that could have come from a canteen kitchen—was standing next to the door. "I'd just come back in here and sat down on the sofa when there was a knock at the door. I got the shock of my life. When I opened it, I thought there'd be an intelligent lizard or some other alien standing there. Instead there was this stew."

Jeff came up to the table and leaned over the pot. He could see beans, peas, bits of carrot and potato, and something that looked like sausage. It smelled delicious and his mouth started to water. He suddenly realized he hadn't had anything to eat since leaving Sigma-7. And then an inner voice told him to be careful. "Where could these ingredients have come from?" he wondered aloud.

"I'm sure they're synthesized," Joanne said, taking a stack of plates out of the cupboard above the kitchen counter and placing them on the table.

"But the computer must have gotten the recipe from somewhere."

Joanne laughed. "The ether is full of all kinds of cooking programs. The computer has probably been analyzing our transmissions for a long time. I guess that's how it learned our language, too."

Jeff scratched his head. He'd been thinking about it over the past few hours. The ship's computer had admitted that it scoured the universe for information. It was probably creating a comprehensive encyclopedia about humanity, which it would then send to its builders. It was a shame the computer wouldn't reveal the coordinates of its home planet. It would be incredibly exciting to discover more about the fate of its builders. Millions of years! What might have become of them? Had they died out long ago? Or had they reached a new rung on the evolutionary ladder? Had they collectively merged into a kind of technological super-intelligence, as the brilliant futurologist Bennett had once predicted for humankind? They could have learned so much from them. On the other hand, the home planet of this ship was in a faraway galaxy—unreachable. It would probably take many more generations before their hyperdrive technology was advanced enough to reach other galaxies. He'd have to make do with what they could find out on board this ship.

"What are you dreaming about?" Joanne asked.

Jeff started out of his reverie. "What?"

Joanne sighed. "You're too easily distracted."

Jeff felt like he'd been caught red-handed. "I wasn't—"

Joanne laughed. "Yes you were! And not for the first time." She sat down next to him. "Have you ever asked yourself why nobody here takes you seriously?"

Jeff swallowed. Joanne had never spoken to him this directly. What should he say?

"You always seem like you're not quite there," she said. "Sometimes I get the impression you're not really listening when others talk to you. Everything about you screams 'academic with his head in the clouds.' And when you say something, you always sound doubtful. You're the XO and should be able to stand in for the major. That will never work if your commands sound more like requests. You know what? You would have been better off staying at your university."

He'd come to that conclusion himself, but it still felt like a punch in the stomach coming from Joanne. Jeff didn't reply.

Joanne gave him a consoling smile. "Will you tell the others that dinner's ready? I'll finish setting the table."

Jeff nodded. It was almost seven o'clock. He turned around and opened the door to the corridor with the bedrooms. He clapped his hands loudly. "There's food— come and get it!"

It was only a few minutes before everyone except Major Irons, who was still taking a shower, were sitting at the table. Corporal Fields blinked sleepily at the big pot of stew and yawned. Green hadn't even bothered putting his combat suit back on, and was sitting in his chair in his underwear. Jeff wondered whether he should say anything, but decided not to make himself even more unpopular.

"Smells like home." Finni laughed, ladling some stew into his bowl. Shorty had found a pack of sliced bread in the cupboard above the fridge and placed it in the middle of the table. Joanne had even found glass salt and pepper shakers in one of the drawers.

Mac grabbed the ladle from Finni and helped himself to some stew. Then he picked up his spoon and dipped it into his bowl.

"Don't touch that!" The sharp tone in Irons' voice made Jeff wince. Startled, Finni dropped his spoon.

Jeff swung round and saw the major walking toward the table with a cool expression.

"Where did you get that?" Irons asked.

Joanne briefly explained how she had found the pot in front of the door.

"Corporal Fields!"

"Sir?"

"Get the mass analyzer from the emergency equipment and check the stuff in the pot—and the bread."

Fields nodded and stood up wordlessly.

"The ship's computer would hardly have saved us only to poison us," Castle grumbled.

"Lieutenant Castle, this is an alien ship, controlled by an alien computer. I do not assume any ill intentions, but I doubt it has extensive knowledge of the human metabolism. We cannot rule out that toxic substances were accidentally used in the synthesis of the food. I just want to be sure. We should have done it earlier with the drinks from the fridge."

"Of course, Sir!"

Fields was now holding a small device in his hand, which he activated with a push of a button. It emitted two beeps, indicating that it was working. Slowly a kind of antenna emerged, which Fields dunked into the liquid in the pot.

"Lieutenant Green!" Irons said sharply.

"Sir?"

"If I find you outside of your room again not wearing a combat suit, I will not hesitate to put you under arrest for the rest of the journey. Is that clear?"

Green nodded hastily, got up, and disappeared to his room.

Irons and Jeff's eyes met. The major shook his head very softly and pressed his lips together.

I messed up again!

"I have the results," Fields said.

"And?" Irons asked.

"No toxic ingredients. We can eat it," Fields said.

Irons nodded.

"It's actually quite nutritious," Fields added.

"What's the nutritional value?"

"Sixty-one kilocalories per hundred milliliters. Carbohydrates, proteins, fats, even vitamins. Everything the human body needs."

"I wonder how this ship knows how to fold proteins," Joanne mused. "The computer can't have learned *that* from our TV programs."

"Maybe our bodies were scanned when we came aboard," Jeff said. "Combined with information from planetary radio signals, you can discover a lot."

"The Galaxy Net," Castles said suddenly.

Jeff nodded. That made sense.

"What?" Irons asked.

"The Galaxy Net of the Imperial University Alliance continuously transmits all information from the scientific databases. The encyclopedic knowledge of humanity is sent via the Net and can be received by anyone listening. I bet it includes an explanation of how proteins are folded or vitamins are synthesized."

"I thought the Galaxy Net is transmitted by hyper radio," Joanne said.

"Yeah, but the traditional radio transmitters were never turned off," Green said, stepping into the room again, this time in combat gear.

"Why not? They're superfluous," Finni said.

Jeff shook his head. "No," he said. "We've had colonies

that were forgotten by humanity for decades, and whose hyper radio failed. At least they could still benefit from our collected knowledge via normal radio. Don't you remember Praxus-4?"

Nobody answered.

"An earthquake devastated the colony and disabled the hyper-radio transmitter. Due to the lithium crisis, Praxus-4 was forgotten and was isolated for almost fifty years. Thanks to the knowledge from the Galaxy Net, the descendants of the first settlers were able to build a new hyper-radio device and get back in contact."

Irons nodded. "Now you mention it, I remember once reading a report about it. But we're moving away from the original subject. Ultimately, we don't know how this ship was able to make this stew. There are a lot of unanswered questions and we need to talk about how to proceed."

"Can we eat something first?" Green asked.

Irons sighed. "The analysis was very clear. So sure, go ahead."

Green and Finni immediately began to slurp their stew loudly from their spoons. Joanne pulled a face, then also tucked in, but less noisily. Jeff had to admit, the stuff didn't taste bad. Perhaps a little too salty for his taste. He took the slice of bread Joanne handed him and dunked it in the stew.

"Don't you want to eat, Major?" Castle asked.

Irons shook his head. "I'm not hungry. I'll eat one of the concentrate bars later on."

"This tastes a lot better than one of those bars."

"Life doesn't revolve around eating," Irons snapped.

Castle nodded. "You're right, Major. There's something else I'd rather do than eat." As if in slow motion he turned his head and grinned at Joanne, who only looked up after a few seconds. She tapped her forehead with her index finger.

"Dream on, Castle," she said and turned her attention back to her plate.

"It could be a long and lonely six months aboard this weird ship. My door is always open!"

Joanne shook her head and ignored him. Jeff chuckled. He knew that Joanne was tough and could take this kind of banter in her stride. He was also pretty sure that Castle, with his smoldering dark eyes and cheeky smile, probably enjoyed considerable success with the opposite sex. But he'd have his work cut out for him with Joanne.

"Stop this nonsense," Irons said sharply. "We're on board an alien spaceship the size of a moon and at the mercy of the ship's computer. We've got more important things to deal with."

"Of course, Sir," Castle said in a tone that contradicted his words.

"How do you propose we proceed, Sir?" Jeff asked.

"First, let's lay down some ground rules," Irons said. "I said it once, and I'll say it again: nobody leaves our quarters without permission. Nobody goes walkabout. Second"—he looked directly at Green—"We keep our combat suits on. Always. Even while sleeping."

Green dropped his spoon on his plate, aghast. "What the hell for?"

"We have no idea what might happen. We need to be ready for action at all times. Keep your guns on you. Only take off your suits to wash, and then put them straight back on."

Jeff groaned inwardly. The combat suits weren't as rigid as the last-generation suits, but wearing them even at night wouldn't be much fun. Not to mention the inevitable stench after a few days. "Isn't that a little over-cautious?"

"Better too cautious than dead," Irons said. "And furthermore: if you notice anything unusual—even if it seems trivial—you must inform me or my XO immediately. Is that clear?"

Joanne and Castle nodded. Green shrugged.

"We also need to guard our quarters at night."

"Why?" Finni asked.

"The fact that a trolley suddenly appeared in front of our door—it makes me uneasy. Who put it there? I don't want robots, or drones, or whatever hanging around here at night while we're sleeping."

"Don't you trust the computer?" Joanne asked.

"I repeat: despite the friendly welcome, we have no idea who or what we're dealing with here. I don't want to imply that our host has any bad intentions, but I think it makes sense to take precautions. We'll take turns at night; two hours each."

"What about exploring our surroundings?" Jeff asked.

Irons nodded. "I've been thinking about that. We need to be systematic and gradually expand the radius, and also map the area we explore. We'll begin tomorrow morning. I propose that two teams of two set off at the same time. The others hold the fort, collect the radio data, and create a map."

He turned to Owl. "Will we be able to use our radios here?"

The radio operator wavered for a moment, then shook his head. "No. There's too much metal everywhere. The radios are likely to work only within a very limited radius."

Irons grunted. "That's not what I wanted to hear. I want to be able to stay in touch with the reconnaissance teams at all time. If anything happens, we won't know about it. If we were forced to go looking for a squad, we'd probably never find them in this labyrinth."

"Perhaps I can help, Sir."

Jeff turned around in surprise. He wasn't used to hearing an unsolicited suggestion from Green. On the other hand, the guy was a good engineer.

Irons signaled to Green to continue.

"I can't make any guarantees, but I have an idea how we could talk to each other without radio."

"Go ahead."

The engineer scratched his nose. "We could use the metal walls of the spaceship to relay electrical impulses. I could modify some of the handhelds to do that."

"A kind of Morse code?" Joanne asked.

Green shook his head. "No, we would actually be able to talk to each other, even if the quality isn't very good."

"How long would it take?" Jeff asked.

He shrugged. "A few hours, maybe. But I can't make any promises. It'll only work if all the walls are made of the same material."

"Please start as soon as this meeting is over."

"Who'll be in the recon squads?" Joanne asked.

"We'll take turns," Irons replied. "But I'll stay here at all times to coordinate the missions. Lieutenant Green will also stay here in case there are any communication problems. Lieutenant Castle with Private Short, and Captain Austin with Private McGuinness."

Jeff nodded numbly. He didn't mind going on a reconnaissance mission, but did it have to be with Mac? The boorish mechanic despised Jeff and only obeyed his orders reluctantly. Irons must have been aware of this, but maybe he thought a joint mission would help them bond. Jeff had his doubts.

"We'll meet for breakfast tomorrow at 0600," Irons said. "At 0700 the squads will set off to explore. I would like to gain an overview of our surroundings as soon as possible."

"How do we handle the ship's computer?" Joanne asked.

Irons nodded. "That takes me nicely to the next point." The major smiled. "I want to find out as much as possible about this ship, its computer, and its builders. Of course, that will require close communication with the computer. We don't know how these aliens tick—but their psychology may be reflected in the behavior of the computer, which would also explain the strange time out it's taking. So we have to proceed cautiously. To start with, I'll be the only one to speak with it. Have you all understood? Lieutenant Green! Stop playing around with your handheld and listen!"

Green put his portable computer aside and looked up. "I understand, Sir."

"I'm not quite convinced. So, if anyone has any questions for the computer, please pass them on to me."

"Do you think the computer will let us know when it's contactable again?" Joanne asked. "It's already been four hours. Those self-tests are pretty drawn out."

Irons nodded. "Computer!" he spoke loudly.

Jeff cocked his head. He almost expected to see a hovering figure appear in the room. But there was no answer.

Irons sighed again. "All right, let's go to our rooms. Corporal Owens, please clear the table. Lieutenant Castle, will you take the first watch?"

"Sure. Who should take over from me?"

"You decide."

Castle turned his head and grinned at Jeff.

Surprise surprise.

Chapter 4

"Computer!" Irons shouted, but again there was no answer.

"I don't get it," Joanne said. "It's been almost sixteen hours. Surely it can't take that long to carry out a self test."

"Maybe it's moved on to a different self test," Finni suggested, taking a can of beer out of the fridge.

"Or the computer has limited multitasking capabilities. Maybe it's a reflection of how the builders of this thing functioned," Owl mused.

"Doesn't sound very logical," Irons said dryly. "A computer has to be immediately accessible to its users. Perhaps we'll find out the reason. Lieutenant Green?"

The engineer was still fiddling around with his hand-held and looked up. "Sir?"

"How's our communication device getting on?"

The engineer smiled. "We'll find out in a minute." He handed Irons the handheld. Jeff was standing next to the major and could see that Green had plugged some kind of antenna into the front port of the tablet.

"How does it work?" Irons asked, taking the device from Green.

"The antenna has to be touching the wall."

"What's the principle behind it?" Jeff asked, thinking it was an intelligent question to ask.

Green turned around and looked at Jeff as if he were a child who had asked a question to which he wouldn't understand the answer. "The computer picks up the acoustic signals from our speech and the antenna transmits these into the wall using eddy currents."

"Ah," Jeff said.

What are eddy currents?

"The counterpart receives the voltage impulses and transforms them back into speech," Green added.

"If you say so," Irons said. "Good work, Lieutenant Green. Attach one of the handhelds to the wall here, so that it's always receiving."

"Give me yours and I'll attach an antenna to it," Green said, and impulsively reached for the major's belt.

With lightning speed, Irons grabbed the engineer's hand and twisted it behind his back. Green grimaced in pain. "Don't ever try to grab my belt again," Irons said icily. He let go of the engineer's hand, and Green staggered forward and fell against the wall. His face was still contorted with pain and he rubbed his hand. "Shit, that hurt!" he whined.

Jeff looked at Irons wordlessly. He thought his reaction had been excessive. It was unusual for the major to use violence on any of his crew. Irons briefly returned his glance and grabbed one of the replacement handhelds from the equipment sled, which Shorty had pulled from the niche to the middle of the room. "Take this and fix it to the wall." He pointed to a spot beside the front door. Then he went over to a long table that was pushed against the wall nearer the kitchen, and dragged it over to the place he had indicated. "This will be our command post. Joanne?"

"Yes, Sir?"

"This is the sketch I made yesterday on the way to our quarters. Use it to verify the handheld's automatic tracking and add the data the teams transmit by radio."

"It isn't a radio."

"Excuse me, Lieutenant Green?"

The engineer shook his aching hand and stepped up to the table. He took the handheld and secured it with a clamp so that the antenna he had just attached touched the wall. "I said: it's not a radio. We're not exchanging any radio signals, but impulses through the metal of the walls."

Irons waved his hand dismissively. "Stop quibbling! First we need to find out if these things even work. Lieutenant Castle?"

"Sir?"

"Start the reconnaissance. Go back the way we came yesterday until you reach the last junction. When you get there, turn right. Make sure to first map the areas near our quarters. At every intersection, stop and message us by radio."

"Yes, Sir."

"I just said, it isn't—" Green began, but was silenced by Irons' frosty glare.

Castle nodded to Shorty and opened the door into the corridor. The mechanic was carrying a flashlight and a backpack containing some basic equipment, food, and water. Irons closed the door behind him.

"We'll soon see if your invention works," Irons said to Green. Green kept quiet and looked fixedly at the handheld on the table.

A few seconds passed and then Castle's voice—with some interference but clearly intelligible—sounded from the handheld's speaker." This is Lieutenant Castle. Can you hear me?"

"Green here. Loud and clear. Can you hear me?"

"Loud and clear. Your construction seems to work."

"Yup, thought it would."

"We're now at the intersection and turning right. The corridor leads into darkness. This shitty flashlight is only lighting up the first thirty or so feet. It's kind of scary."

Irons leaned forward. "Record the path with your handheld, but keep sending us info so we can track your route."

"Understood, we're setting off now."

Jeff looked over Joanne's shoulder. She was drawing lines on the screen of the handheld with her finger. Something occurred to Jeff. He turned to Green. "Tell him to report any changes to the gravity vector, otherwise we might misinterpret it in our sketch.

Green shook his head. "He won't hear us now. He has to hold the device against the wall to be able to communicate with us. He has to report first."

It didn't take long for him to make contact again. "Castle here. Can you hear us?"

"Still loud and clear."

"We're at the next intersection. We've walked precisely eighty-five feet. This intersection has four turnoffs at right angles to each other. We're turning right."

"Understood. One more thing. We need you to report any changes in the gravity vector, understood?"

"Understood."

Jeff nodded and watched Joanne drawing more lines. A few seconds later, Castle checked back in. He described the route and the next intersection. Joanne entered the data into the mobile device.

Jeff felt a hand on his arm. Irons gestured for him to

follow him. Clearly he didn't want to disturb Joanne. "Time for you to go, too."

Jeff nodded.

"Go to the same intersection where Castle turned off, but turn left. Look out for any rooms. There can't be only corridors on this ship."

"Yes, Sir," Jeff said. He hoped they would find something the former inhabitants of this ship had left behind. Something that would tell them more about the history and culture of this extraterrestrial civilization. Jeff signaled to Mac, and the burly mechanic slung his backpack over his shoulder. Then he picked up the flashlight and flicked it on and off a few times to check it was working.

Jeff handed Green his handheld, and the engineer inserted an antenna into the port. Just as Jeff was about to take it, Green pulled back his hand. "Now, don't forget to hold it against the wall if you want to talk to me," Green sneered.

Jeff just glared at him as he took the device. He should have said something, but he didn't want to lower himself to Green's level.

Jeff strode to the door and signaled to Mac to follow him. The mechanic was smirking. He must have seen what had just passed between him and Green.

They stepped into the corridor. It was pitch black. Mac switched on the flashlight. Even though the beam was quite bright, the dark metal of the walls swallowed most of the light and they couldn't see far in front of them. Mac marched off ahead.

"Wait," Jeff said. "That's the wrong direction. We have to go back toward the outer airlock and turn left at the next intersection.

Wordlessly, Mach turned around and passed Jeff in the other direction. Jeff followed him a few paces behind.

What was that?

Jeff swung round. But all he saw was darkness.

"What's the problem?" Mac shone the flashlight back down the corridor. They stood still for several seconds, listening. But there was no sound.

"What's the problem?" Mac asked again.

"I thought I heard footsteps behind us," Jeff sighed. "Probably just the echo of our own."

This darkness! This silence!

Jeff couldn't shake the feeling there was something lurking in the shadows, watching them.

"Maybe a poltergeist is up to no good on this ship," Mac snickered.

Or something worse. Jeff didn't reply.

After just a few more steps, they reached the first inter-section. Mac shone the flashlight into the corridors that branched off in different directions. At first glance, they all looked exactly the same. Jeff held the handheld's antenna against the wall. "Austin here," he said. "Do you read me?"

The answer came immediately. "Yes, we can hear you." There was a slight rustling noise overlaying his colleague's voice, but it was clear enough.

"We're at the first junction and turning left."

"Understood."

Mac went ahead with the flashlight. To the left and right of them were only the smooth walls of the corridor. There were no doors here. In fact, they'd seen hardly any doors since leaving the airlock. But there had to be *something* behind those walls. Jeff stopped and punched the gray material with his fist. The dull thud didn't suggest an empty space on the other side—but maybe the wall was just very thick.

"Everything OK?" Mac asked.

Jeff nodded and they continued on their way. The next

turning came after just forty feet. One corridor led to the right at a sharp angle, another to the left, going slightly downward. If they wanted to find out what was going on, then probably they would have to go deeper to the heart of this huge ship.

"This way," Jeff said, pointing downward. Mac shone the flashlight into the corridor. There appeared to be no doors or further turnings.

"Sure?"

Jeff nodded and reported their position to Joanne. He also checked the tracking system on his handheld. A line indicated the route back to their quarters. Even if his own handheld failed, they could use Mac's. The accelerometers in the devices seemed to be working accurately.

Mac marched ahead again, flashlight in hand. They hadn't walked far when Jeff felt a cold draft on his neck. He spun round and peered into the darkness. Again he had the strange feeling of being watched. He got goose bumps and could practically feel a pair of invisible eyes on him.

"Mac!" he whispered.

"What?" his companion replied grumpily.

"Light!"

Without any urgency, Mac turned around and lit up the corridor behind them. It was empty. Some way off in the distance, Jeff could still see the bend in the diminishing beam of the flashlight.

He shook his head. "I could have sworn I heard—"

"Got the jitters?" Mac asked, amused. With his hulking physique and impassive face, he didn't seem in the least intimidated by the strange surroundings.

Jeff turned around and responded huskily: "No, I'm fine."

"Scared of the dark, huh?"

Jeff didn't rise to the bait. "Let's go on," he said flatly.

"I didn't realize you were such a chicken, Captain" Mac said.

Jeff turned around in surprise. Up to now, he hadn't received such a direct insult. Should he react to it now? Or was it best to pretend he hadn't heard? He didn't feel like responding to every stupid remark—Mac would just think he was being petty and like him even less than he already did. In the end, Jeff decided to ignore the remark. He'd spent too long thinking about it already.

The corridor seemed to be endless. By the time they reached the next junction, nearly twenty minutes had passed. Jeff contacted their quarters. "Austin here. We've reached the next intersection."

"We were wondering where you'd got to," Joanne said. The static had increased slightly, but he had no difficulty understanding her. However, he worried that the farther away they moved, the harder it would become to communicate.

"The corridor was pretty long. One thousand seven hundred feet, according to the handheld. And we're also a hundred and eighty feet deeper.

"Have you passed any doors?"

"No, just smooth corridor walls. I'm wondering what's behind them. Have the other two found anything yet?"

"Not really. They found a few doors they could open, but the rooms were empty."

"Understood. We'll keep going."

"OK. But Major Irons doesn't want you to exceed a distance of half a mile from our quarters."

Jeff nodded. "Roger." He pointed down the left-hand corridor that led, as usual, into darkness. "This way."

"Why that way?" Mac asked.

"That's the direction of our quarters, just further down in the ship."

Mac shrugged. "How far are we from the surface?"

Jeff looked at his handheld and changed the scale of the map. "About six hundred feet. But since it has a diameter of almost six hundred miles, we're only scratching the surface of this thing."

"When we arrive at Sigma-7 in a few months, we should just keep the ship," Mac said.

"I doubt the computer will let that happen."

"Maybe we'll find a way of switching it off. It doesn't seem to be very efficient—it's hardly ever available. We'll just take over the ship and use it as a weapon against the Alliance."

Jeff laughed. "With a range of two light years a week, it won't be much of a weapon."

Mac shrugged again. "I'm sure it can be used for something."

"Even if we *could* take over the ship, it would be pretty ungrateful of us. After all, the ship's computer did save us."

Mac rolled his eyes and mumbled something incomprehensible.

This corridor, too, seemed to go on forever. Jeff kept glancing down at his handheld. Finally, they were getting closer to their quarters—albeit about two hundred and fifty feet below them. After taking a few more turns they were exactly below where their quarters must be. Interestingly, there was a door here, too.

Jeff pushed the square next to the entrance and the door hissed open. Mac stepped forward and shone the flashlight into the room. It appeared to be an exact replica of their own quarters, but there was no furniture and no kitchenette.

"Even the door to the sleeping quarters is in the same spot," Mac said, pointing to the other side of the room. Jeff nodded and reported their discovery to the improvised base. "Thanks, Jeff. I've noted down the information. Castle and Shorty also found some rooms after they went back toward the surface. Also empty."

Jeff wasn't surprised to hear this. Everywhere they went was deserted—it was hard to believe anyone had ever lived here. Clearly their quarters had been prepared especially for them at short notice, but there must be more on this ship. The old inhabitants must have lived *somewhere*.

"How about a break, boss?" Mac asked. He didn't wait for an answer, but plunked himself on the ground near the door. He set up the flashlight so that it illuminated the ceiling and bathed the room in a dim, diffuse light. Jeff would have liked to continue, but he didn't want to get into an argument. He reported the break to Joanne and sat down next to Mac with his back against the wall. Mac opened his backpack, took out a small bottle of water and a ration pack, and began to rip open the packaging. He didn't show any sign of wanting to share it with Jeff.

"Could I please have some water and food?"

Mac didn't hear him or acted as if he hadn't heard him, and Jeff had to repeat his question. Without saying a word, the mechanic reached into his backpack again and handed Jeff water and a concentrate bar. Jeff sighed and tore off the plastic wrapper with his teeth. "You don't like me much, do you?"

Mac turned around, his bar halfway to his mouth, and looked at Jeff the way you looked at an idiot. It was a pretty dumb question, since everyone in the crew knew the answer already. "Does it matter?"

"Not really, but you don't exactly make an effort to hide your aversion," Jeff said. He tried to make his voice sound casual, and to hide any bitterness, but didn't succeed.

Mac chuckled softly. "I'm just honest. But it doesn't make any difference to our mission. Give me an order,

Captain, and I'll obey. That's all that really matters, isn't it?"

"But why do you dislike me so much, Mac?"

"You're from the *Solar System*—from the *moon*, no less."

A bigot? Was Mac simply a bigot?

"Is that all? You hate me because I come from the moon?"

Mac shook his head. "You all think you're something special because you come from the center of the Empire. For you, we're just rednecks."

"I've never felt that way about the peripheral areas," Jeff said firmly. "My family always tried—"

"Your family," said Mac dismissively. "Your family are aristocrats."

Jeff shook his head. "My family has never held a high office in the Imperial Government."

Mac snorted. "Same difference. You're all in each other's pockets. Where did your parents work? Hermes factories? Artemis production?"

"My father had a little company and was a subcontractor to the Nubium shipyards. He produced navigation sensors."

Mac craned his head forward. His eyes radiated pure hatred. "I can tell you something about the Nubium shipyards and their clean, shiny facilities run by robots. Where do you think the stable fermium for the Casimir converter comes from?"

Jeff didn't reply.

"From the asteroid belt around Ross 339. We don't have any beautiful planets like Earth in our system. Not even a terraformable dust ball like Mars. We don't have any planets at all—we live in miserable containers on barren pieces of rock in the belt. If it hadn't been for the fact that fermium could be synthesized in that shithole of a system, nobody would have dreamed of settling there. We slave away for you with shitty equipment under a burning sun to produce your oh-so-important fermium. And you pay us next to nothing, although it's the backbone of your industry. And you know what the best thing is?"

Jeff didn't reply. Mac had talked himself into a rage. "The money we earn we have to spend on water, food, and air, for which you charge crazy shit prices. We're just slaves to you, with no chance of leading a better life."

Jeff swallowed. He had heard second-hand reports of political activists, who were constantly ranting about conditions on the outskirts of the Empire. Of course, those stories were immediately refuted by lawyers and the public relations machine. Since there were no commercial flights to many of the systems, the reports were difficult to verify independently. In fact, Mac might be exaggerating.

"And yet you're fighting in the war for the Empire against the Alliance," Jeff pointed out.

Mac spat on the floor. "I don't give a shit about the Empire. I didn't volunteer to be here."

"You could have refused."

"That might be possible in your central systems. Where we come from, it's not. There's enough human garbage rotting away in jail who can be blackmailed into service."

"You were in jail?"

Mac nodded. "Where I come from there isn't enough to go round, and there are too many people strung out on drugs trying to escape their pathetic lives. There are constant skirmishes. About drugs, weapons, women, food. Until the war started, your prick of a governor didn't give a damn if we were cutting each other's throats. Now all the roughnecks are being sent to jail and forced into military service. When the alternative is twenty years' labor camp on Doom 3, you don't ask any more questions about which mission you'll be sent on with the Imperial fleet."

What could Jeff say in response?

"So don't tell me we live in a *just* world," Mac continued. "We on the margins are the slaves, and those in the center are the masters. And you guys from the Solar System are worst of all. And another thing …"

Jeff didn't reply.

"If you were stuck in the cockpit, wounded, I wouldn't risk my ass to save you. You better get that into your thick aristocratic skull," Mac smirked. "And if you don't like my choice of words, you can go and report me to the major. Then I'll have a nice rest in my cabin and spare myself these little expeditions through this alien shithouse."

Jeff couldn't think of anything to say. In fact, he felt kind of sorry for the guy.

While he was still searching for the right words, Mac threw the empty packaging of his ration carelessly into the corner of the room. He put the bottle back in his backpack. "I'm done. We can go on, if you like."

Jeff hadn't even taken a bite of his ration bar. But he'd lost his appetite, anyway. He stuffed the bar in the pocket of his combat suit and tucked the water bottle in his belt. Mac stood up, picked up the flashlight, and opened the door into the corridor. It was as dark out there as it had been before. They spent two more hours wandering through seemingly endless corridors, searched through some more empty rooms, and finally returned to their quarters with the help of the handheld. They got back at almost exactly the same time as Castle and Shorty, who hadn't found anything interesting, either.

Jeff had difficulty hiding his disappointment. But Irons was more optimistic. So far, they had only searched the area relatively close to their quarters and that didn't even represent a fraction of what there was to explore, considering the size of the ship. Irons showed them the map Joanne had created with the data they had sent back. She corrected the sketches using the data stored on their handhelds and identified some corridors nearby, which they hadn't been down yet. Tomorrow, two more squads would be sent off to explore these; then they would start to expand the radius of their reconnaissance. They would be spending several months on this huge ship. At some point, surely, they would find something interesting.

Chapter 5

"Hello guests. Have you settled in comfortably?"

Jeff started at the sound of the onboard computer's synthesized voice. Over dinner, they had just been discussing the fact that there'd been no contact for more than twenty-four hours. The food—another stew—had again suddenly appeared outside the door. After the knock at the door, Irons had leapt up from the table and reached the door in seconds, but once again there were no robots or aliens to be seen in the corridor. The night before, the trolley with the cleared-up crockery had disappeared just as mysteriously after they had left it outside the door.

"Good evening," Irons said, looking up at the ceiling as if the mind of the computer were floating up there. "Yes, thank you, we've settled in well. And thank you for the food."

"I hope it is to your liking."

"It's very nutritious and tasty. We were unable to make contact with you for a long time."

There was a pause of a few seconds before the answer

came. "That is true. I apologize. This is a big and old ship with a multitude of monitoring and maintenance needs. Due to its age, some computer banks have failed. Since they could not be replaced, I am unable to offer my full attention and must divide up my capacities."

Jeff nodded. That was exactly what they had assumed.

"So I will continue to be available only sporadically, and apologize in advance," the ship's computer continued. "Did you have a good night?"

"Yes, the rooms are more comfortable than we could have expected. Thank you," Irons said.

"How did you spend your day?" the synthetic voice asked.

"We had a look around the vicinity of our quarters. I hope this is OK with you."

"As I said, you can move around freely."

"We noticed that the corridors are very long. And there don't seem to be many rooms." Irons waited for an answer, but none came. "What is the bulk of this ship made of?" he added.

"The jump drive takes up a lot of room and permeates the whole ship. That's why some of the rooms are so far apart."

Irons nodded. It sounded like a logical explanation. Jeff wondered what the physical principle of this jump drive was. It seemed to be less efficient and slower than the technology of their hyperdrive.

"Where did the former crew live?" Irons asked.

"They were distributed all over the ship."

"So far we haven't found any signs of former inhabitants. And how did the passengers get from one point of the ship to another? Surely they didn't run down hundreds of miles of corridors?"

"The crew took everything useful out of the ship to their new colony. A long time ago there was a transit system, but it was removed by robot workers upon arrival at the target system. The empty holes were filled for reasons of stability, so you will find no evidence of it."

"Where was the bridge of the spaceship?"

There was another pause before the computer answered. "Bridge? What do you mean by bridge?"

Irons frowned. "Well, the place where the ship is controlled by the members of the crew."

"Ah, you mean the control center. There were several such rooms, all in the core of the ship."

"I would like to see the bridge—control center, I mean," Irons said.

"I'm afraid that will not be possible," the computer answered.

Irons didn't seem surprised by the answer. Nevertheless, he persisted. "And why not?"

"As I said, the ship was converted into an unmanned reconnaissance ship after it arrived at its destination. As there was no more crew on board, the manual controls were removed, and it was switched entirely to computer operation."

Irons sighed. "Shame. I would have liked to find out more about the builders and their technology."

Jeff nodded. He was particularly interested in the builders of this ship, and their culture. He signaled to Irons and tapped on his chest. Irons nodded.

Jeff cleared his throat. "I have a few questions about the builders of this ship."

"I will do my best to answer your questions," the computer responded.

"First of all, what did they look like?"

Joanne whispered something to Castle, who did not hear her, he was so engrossed in the conversation.

"You would call the form humanoid. In fact, they did not look dissimilar to you. A little smaller and more graceful and without body hair. Big eyes, small mouth. Is that sufficient for an answer?"

Jeff nodded. The description matched the dimensions of the corridors and doors they had seen so far. The prevailing darkness in the ship, even when the light was on, suggested very light-sensitive eyes. "Yes, thank you. In what ways was their culture different to human culture—as far as you can tell?"

"I'm afraid this question exceeds my analytical abilities."

"Did they have a religion? Did they believe in one or more gods, or in life after death?"

Mac rolled his eyes and groaned. Irons looked at him sharply.

"I do not understand the question."

Either the aliens lacked culture and religion, which could not be ruled out, or the computer simply was not programmed to answer such questions. It was impossible to say.

"Do you have any information regarding the history of the builders?"

"I'm afraid my memory banks contain no information for the time before the ship departed from the world of origin."

Jeff sighed. "Are there any rooms on this ship that contain evidence of the builders, and could we look at these?"

"I'm afraid the answer is no. There is nothing for you to find."

Somehow Jeff had the feeling that despite the computer's cooperation, it did not approve of their further exploration of the interior of the spaceship.

"You said we could move freely around the ship," Jeff said. The computer did not answer. "Didn't you?" Jeff persisted.

"Yes," the computer replied.

"Would you give us a three-dimensional map of the ship so we don't get lost?"

Irons looked up. Several long seconds passed, without an answer from the computer.

"Computer?"

"I'm sorry," the answer came at long last. "My attention is required in another part of the ship where there has been a power failure. I will get back to you."

A faint crackling sound indicated that communication had been broken off.

"The last sentence sounded almost like a threat," Castle said.

"It's a computer," Green laughed. "It's hardly capable of making ambiguous statements."

"It all sounded logical to me," Joanne put in. "They probably radically rebuilt the ship after they arrived in their new home system. If it's only controlled by one machine, then it really doesn't need a bridge anymore."

"But why are there any quarters on the ship at all then?" Castle asked.

"Well," Joanne mused. "All that seems to be left are these empty rooms and corridors. These quarters were specially prepared for us. A few days ago, they were just empty rooms."

"Well, I don't have a good feeling about any of this," Castle said.

"Me neither," Finni agreed. "Every time I hear the voice of that computer, I get the creeps."

Owl laughed. "I think you're being paranoid."

"Jesus, we're on an alien spaceship," Castle looked angry. "Surely it's natural to be a little paranoid."

Owl just laughed again and gave a wave of his hand.

Castle turned to the major. "That computer said it would bring us to Sigma-7," he began.

"What's your point?"

"How do we know that it'll really bring us there? Without access to a bridge or a map room, this ship could take us anywhere it wants."

Irons shook his head. "As soon as the computer tells us we've made the first jump, two of us will go outside and check our position against the stars." He turned to Joanne. "That's possible, right?"

The navigator nodded. "Sure. Every handheld is capable of determining our location from the position of the stars. I saved our position when we left the Charon, we can easily compare the two."

"So what next?" Finni asked.

Irons shrugged. "Our plan hasn't changed. We'll continue to check out our surroundings and gradually expand the radius of the area we explore."

"But the computer just told us there's nothing on board for us to find," Finni said. "So why bother?"

"Do you want to spend all day in your room?" Irons asked, with a hint of a smile. "No. For one, we need a purpose, and we need exercise, since we're going to be stuck here for half a year. And I don't think we should rule out finding something interesting."

"Do you think the computer lied to us?" Jeff asked.

Irons shook his head. "I didn't say that. On the contrary. So far the computer has responded to all our questions with logical answers."

"So why won't it give us a 3D map of the ship?" Castle asked.

Irons shrugged. "I'm not sure I would hand out maps to unknown guests on board an Imperial ship. But let's stop with all this speculation. Please clear the table, Lieutenant Castle. That'll give you something to do and less time to brood."

Chapter 6

"We've reached—" The rest of the words were swallowed by static.

Jeff hit the talk button. "Please repeat, Finni."

"I said, we've reached a dead end. The corridor doesn't go on."

Irons leaned over Jeff's shoulder. "Interesting. The whole area there seems to be cut off. The only access is this corridor here." He pointed at a line on the three-dimensional map projected into the room by the handheld. Jeff nodded.

For the last week they had been exploring the corridors around their quarters. And the more they explored, the more apparent it became that the corridors were arranged in a particular pattern. Several times they had come across smaller areas that were only accessible via a corridor, which then branched off into dead ends. They came across these areas particularly near the outer shell of the ship. But they could never make it right to the edge of the ship—the corridors ended at least three hundred feet away. The only access to the outside was the airlock through which they'd entered. Joanne had floated the idea that the ship's corridors were arranged in a fractal structure like a snowflake. This meant you could only ever cover larger distances inwards or outwards, and only short distances going sideways. If they wanted to get to a part of the surface that was farther away, they would first have to go deeper down, then move across through another passage to a different part of the ship, and from there go back up and out. Castle agreed with Joanne and hypothesized that this structure might be a result of the automated production process of the ship. A robotic factory or nano-forge would be provided with a specific, basic formula, and the artifact automatically produced repetitive elements according to these formulae, without the need for complex blueprints. Jeff vaguely remembered hearing workers in the shipyards on Luna talking about a similar process. And if that was the case, they only had one option left. "We have to go further toward the center of the ship."

Irons pointed at a spot on the hologram. "Tell Corporal Owens that he and Fields should advance to this area. They aren't far away from it, and it's the only area near the outer shell of the ship that's accessible to us but which we haven't properly mapped yet."

"What about Herrmannsson and Short?" Jeff asked.

"They can come back to HQ."

Jeff suppressed a smile. Only somebody who had spent half their life in the military would think of describing their accommodation as "headquarters." But he carried out the major's order.

"Shall I take over?" Joanne asked, who had just come back into the room after a break.

Jeff shook his head. "No, it's OK. I'll carry on until the men are back."

Joanne nodded. She had dark rings under her eyes,

probably because she'd taken the middle night shift and then hadn't been able to get back to sleep, as she'd told them at breakfast. She disappeared to her room. The others who weren't taking part in an expedition today were also in their rooms. Jeff was left alone with Irons.

The major sighed, pulled a chair over from the dining table and sat down next to Jeff. "I think you're right."

Jeff turned around and frowned. "About what?"

"That we need to go deeper into the ship to find anything. The computer said that's where the control center is—or used to be."

Jeff's mission a few days ago had been the one that had taken them deepest into the ship so far—albeit only about three hundred feet.

"HQ?" Owls' voice sounded through the room.

Jeff leaned forward and pressed the speak button. "Jeff here."

"We're now at junction G12. What direction should we go now?"

Jeff zoomed in on the hologram. "Go to +Y. That's the only corridor leading from the junction that we haven't explored yet. If the same pattern that we've seen in the other sections repeats itself, you should get to two more intersections with three branches each, all of which lead to dead ends. In one of them there should be door, and behind it an empty room.

"Understood."

"Tell him he doesn't have to report back at each intersection," the major said. His voice sounded tired, but it still had more authority than Jeff would ever manage himself. "He should only report if there are deviations from the pattern."

Jeff passed on the order, and Owl signed off. But now Finni's voice sounded from the speaker. "We're at junction

B17 now, leaving for the area B-F. We'll take the shortest route back to our quarters. ETA forty minutes."

"Understood," said Jeff. "Report back if you come across anything interesting."

"You're good at this," said the major.

Jeff turned around. "What do you mean?"

Irons smiled weakly. "Coordinating the team. On the ship, and here, you've demonstrated good organizational skills."

The major almost never gave praise without an ulterior motive. "What are you getting at?"

"But …"

"But what?"

"But you lack authority. The men and women do what you say, but they do it reluctantly. If you were in a real emergency situation and had to make tough decisions, it could get tricky—there's a good chance the team wouldn't follow your orders."

As if Jeff hadn't noticed this himself. "I think it has to do with where I come from."

Irons chuckled and shook his head. "I'm sorry—but that's total nonsense."

"But that's what Mac told me a few days ago."

Irons raised his eyebrows. "Did he say it to your face?"

Jeff nodded.

"And what did you do?"

"Nothing."

"Nothing?" The major swiveled around in his chair.

"Well, I asked him why he didn't like me."

"You *asked* him?" There was disbelief in the major's voice. "You're not serious."

Jeff was silent and looked down at the floor.

Irons took a deep breath. "Listen to me, Captain Austin. Respect has nothing to do with background. Every officer has to deal with prejudices. One comes from the aristocracy, the other from a backwoods swamp, and another from a former prison planet. One is small, the other lanky, a third has a big nose. I come from Lamsid and didn't have an easy time of it, either. Do you know Lamsid?"

Jeff had heard of the planet. It was apparently a hell-hole. Covered in foul swamps, it was home to a tiny and very isolated colony. Some people called it the "planet of the inbreds." Jeff hadn't known the major came from there, but he could imagine his first commando hadn't been easy.

"There are two things to keep in mind. First, when you encounter prejudice, you have to act against it. You're on the right track—you're doing good work and are empathetic toward your subordinates. But—and this is important—you have to punish any actions by your crew that undermine your authority." Irons leaned in closer. "And never ask your subordinates what they think of you. Never! Because you couldn't care less—at least outwardly—and it will affect your judgment."

Jeff nodded. He knew all this in theory. "I'm afraid they'll think I'm nit-picking if I dole out punishments for every trivial misdemeanor."

The major wrinkled his nose. "Nit-picking? No, Captain Austin—you don't care what they think of you. Your subordinates may like to make fun of you when they're alone in their quarters or in the mess. But when you are in the room, you need to be treated with the respect your superior rank deserves. Because if that isn't the case, you won't be taken seriously, and your orders won't be followed."

"You mean I should punish the men harshly the next time one of them makes a stupid remark?"

Irons shook his head. "It's not that easy; it depends on the situation. I'm sure you've noticed how many stupid comments I let Green get away with."

Jeff nodded. He had often wondered why the major didn't call the engineer to account more often.

"It's the way Green is—and sometimes his comments even lighten up a tough situation. But he's not doing it to undermine my authority. *That's* where you have to draw the line. And it's also important not to punish anybody unjustly. You won't do yourself any favors if you behave like a dictator. It's a matter of experience."

"You mean it gets better over time?"

Irons swayed his head back and forth. "Only if you're willing to learn. But sometimes I get the feeling you've already given up."

Jeff pursed his lips. Really? Maybe the major was right. Lately he'd been letting the team get away with a lot. It was easier than confronting them.

Although Jeff found this conversation embarrassing, he was grateful to the major. Irons was one of the most charismatic officers he'd ever known. A born leader. He would never match up to the major, but maybe he could learn something from him.

"HQ?"

Jeff sighed as he leaned forward and pressed the talk button. "Yup, I'm here."

"You were right. It's a dead end."

"As was to be expected," Irons said.

"Understood," Jeff answered.

"Where shall we go now?"

Jeff turned to Irons.

The latter glanced down at his wristwatch. "Back to HQ. You're done for today."

Jeff passed on the order.

"Good, my feet hurt. The way back from our current position should take about half an hour. Over and out."

"Starting tomorrow, we'll go deeper down into the ship," Irons said.

"Do you think we'll find anything there?"

Irons shrugged. "If we believe what the ship's computer has told us, I guess not. Based on what we've seen so far, I wouldn't be surprised if the whole ship is crisscrossed with snowflake-like corridors. But I wonder what happened to all the rooms and facilities? There must have once been engine rooms, power units, and so on."

Jeff had thought about this already. "Maybe the doors to the rooms were removed when the ship was rebuilt. Or the machine rooms were built in a way that they were always inaccessible."

Irons shook his head. "I don't think so. They must have been accessible to carry out maintenance."

"Maybe every system was equipped with automatic repair units? They might have been made based on a modular construction system."

The major frowned. "That's possible, of course. Like our Falcon-class fighter jets. But the two-man crew of a Falcon wouldn't be able to carry out repairs during a flight, even if they wanted to. But for large ships and stations, we would always provide a point of access, in case the automatic maintenance systems failed."

Once again, Jeff realized just how little they knew about the ship's builders. It was such a shame there were no clues of them left on the ship.

Irons took his handheld out of his pocket and started tapping around on it.

Jeff noticed that Irons' handheld had a small red section on the back. "Do you have a different model from ours?"

The major hesitated. Eventually, he sighed and nodded. "It's not a secret, but our policy is to talk about it as little as possible," he said. "Yes, some commanding officers, including squadron commanders, get a specially encrypted handheld. It contains the transponder codes for all systems in the Empire. Including positions of secret stations near the front line, in case we end up there.

Jeff nodded. He had often wondered what would happen if they had to escape into another system with a sophisticated defense system and they weren't on the list of welcome guests. If in doubt, an overly cautious station commander would fire a kinetic weapon before an enemy or hijacked bomber had a chance of releasing its Quagma bomb.

"And the red button on the back?" Jeff asked, although he already knew the answer.

"The button is actually a cap with a micro-switch underneath."

"A self-destruct button?" Jeff asked.

Irons nodded. "Pressing this will release a capacitor, and the electric charge will erase the memory of the chip using EMP. The codes on the device must never fall into enemy hands. We are under orders to do whatever it takes to prevent that happening, even if it costs us our own lives."

Jeff imagined an Alliance of enemy bombers with valid transponder codes entering the Earth's Solar System. It gave him goose bumps.

"And we'll need the codes," Irons said.

"What for?" Jeff asked. They didn't even have their bomber anymore.

Irons laughed. "When we enter the Sigma System in this thing, they'll think it's a trap set by the Alliance. They won't take any risks and will destroy it with Quagma bombs. The only way of preventing that is to emit the right transponder code, and that's in here." He turned the little device around in his hand.

"How do you plan to connect that thing to the ship's system to send out the signal?" Jeff asked.

"We'll work that out when the time comes. I'll talk to the ship's computer."

Jeff was about to ask another question, when a crackling sound filled the room.

"Speak of the devil …" Irons muttered so softly, Jeff barely heard him.

"Hello, dear guests," said the now familiar voice of the computer.

"Hello, Computer," Irons replied. "Is everything functioning properly on your ship?"

"There are no problems," came the immediate reply. "I don't have much time. I just wanted to inform you that we have completed our first hyperjump and have now moved one-point-four light years in the direction of the system you told me about. The next jump will be in six days' time after the banks have been recharged."

Irons nodded. "Thank you for the information."

"You're welcome. I will sign off now, as I have to take care of some maintenance on the life support system."

Jeff shook his head. Gone again? It was one hell of a busy computer.

Irons opened his mouth to say something, but the crackling sound could be heard again and the major closed his mouth.

"These aliens don't seem to have grasped the concept of multitasking," Jeff said wryly.

Irons suddenly frowned.

"Everything OK?" Jeff asked him.

"Life support system," Irons said.

"Excuse me?"

"It didn't occur to me before, but hearing that word again, there's something about it that really bothers me."

"What?"

"If this spacecraft was rebuilt as a robotic ship, why did they go to the effort of pressurizing all the corridors—probably tens of thousands of miles in total—and give them a breathable atmosphere?"

It was a good question. "Maybe they weren't pressurized until recently, and the computer did it just for us."

Irons shook his head. "A small area near the airlock would have been sufficient for us, but not the whole ship."

While Jeff pondered this, there was a knock at the door. Without waiting for an answer, Finni stepped inside. He was followed by Shorty, who shut the door behind him. "Here we are again!" the radar technician said chirpily. "It sure is spooky in those dark corridors. I keep thinking I can hear noises, but when I shine the flashlight, there's nothing there. I'm glad I can stay here tomorrow."

"I'm afraid that's not going to happen," Irons said dryly.

"What? Why not?" Finni asked, trying not to look too annoyed.

"I need your assistance tomorrow, Corporal. According to the ship's computer, we recently made a hyperjump. I need you to go back to the airlock with Lieutenant Rutherford in order to ascertain our position outside the ship."

Finni's eyes widened. "We made a hyperjump?"

Jeff nodded.

"But I didn't notice anything."

Irons nodded. "Another reason to establish our position." The Major turned to Jeff. "You will go, too. Together with Corporal Fields. You'll wait at the airlock, to provide help if needed."

Jeff nodded. It would have been his turn to go out again, anyway. Somehow, he was relieved not to have to go deeper down into the ship. Not tomorrow, at least.

"I thought we wanted to continue exploring the ship," Shorty said.

Irons shook his head. "No. Checking our current position has absolute priority."

"I was looking forward to it." Shorty couldn't hide the disappointment in his voice. "What if we sent a second squad? I would volunteer and take Mac with me."

Finni rolled his eyes. Shorty seemed to have gotten a taste for exploring the ship.

"No," Irons said. "Tomorrow we'll concentrate on the airlock. I don't want to have to coordinate a reconnaissance squad at the same time."

"But, I—"

Irons raised his hand and got out of his chair. "Enough already! This discussion is over. Tomorrow we're concentrating on the airlock, and nothing else. That's my final word. If everything goes according to plan tomorrow, I'm happy for you to go on another recon deeper into the ship. Have I made myself clear, Private Short?"

Shorty looked down at the major and nodded.

"Now what?" Finni asked.

"We'll wait for the other squad and compare notes. Then we're done for the day and should make it an early night. Tomorrow's a critical day."

"Critical how?" Shorty asked.

The major looked at him intently. "Because I'll sleep much better once I know this ship is really heading for Sigma-7."

Chapter 7

"We need to take a right here," Castle said.

Jeff looked down at his handheld. "No," he answered. "We need to keep going straight ahead."

"Right," Castle insisted, and carried on down the corridor without waiting for Jeff to respond.

Jeff sighed and rubbed his right temple. He had a hell of a headache—he'd woken up with it in the morning. He'd thought about asking Irons to get someone else to take his place, but didn't want to look like a wimp. But the headache hadn't got any better. On the contrary, he had the feeling his skull was about to explode. Jeff put it down to the extraordinary circumstances and the stress of the last few days. He just hoped he wouldn't get seriously ill.

"Hang on a minute till we've worked it out!" he heard Joanne's voice.

"Why? My device says we need to take a right," Castle said grouchily. "If you can't read yours properly, that's your problem."

Fields leaned against the wall of the corridor and grinned.

"Jeff!" Joanne appealed to him.

Will this bullshit never end?

"Castle! Would you please wait?" he said, trying not to sound harassed.

"I'll wait for you at the next turning," the weapon systems officer said curtly.

Whatever. I'm not in the mood for this shit.

Then he remembered his conversation with the major. It couldn't go on like this. He took a deep breath. "You will wait until we've sorted this out, or …"

Castle turned around reluctantly. His surprise was clear to see. "Or what?" he asked and laughed softly. At least he'd stopped walking.

"My device also says straight ahead," came Joanne's voice.

"Let's get an outsider opinion," Jeff said, and held his handheld against the wall of the corridor. "Austin here, come in."

"Mac here, we can hear you."

"Where's Green?" Jeff asked. It was the engineer's turn to be on "radio" duty today.

"Irons sent him to bed. Migraine."

"Migraine?" Jeff asked, surprised. He'd never known the smart-ass engineer to have a migraine.

"After he barfed all over the major's boots, he was sent to bed."

Jeff thought about his own headache. Hopefully they hadn't caught a virus that was now making the rounds. There'd been a bit of a flu epidemic on Sigma-7 before they left on their mission. An incubation period of about a week … the timing was right. Luckily he didn't feel nauseous. Could it have something to do with this ship? No, they'd analyzed the air.

"We're standing at junction A11. Our handhelds aren't in agreement about which way to go."

"Hold on," Mac said. Jeff could hear Irons' voice in the background but couldn't understand what he was saying. This was followed by several long seconds of silence.

"Can you hear me?" Mac asked.

"Yes, we're still here."

"Might be a synchronization error," Irons said. "We'll take a closer look when you're back. In any case, you need to turn right and then keep going along the corridor. It'll take you straight to the antechamber of the airlock."

Jeff avoided catching Castle's eye. It was enough to imagine the big grin on his face. "OK, let's go."

Castle went ahead with the flashlight, Field in the middle, Jeff and Joanne brought up the rear. The eerie silence was disturbed only by their footsteps, which were strangely muted, as if the floor were muffling all sound. When someone talked, there was no echo, which was strange considering the corridors were so long and their walls were made of metal.

Jeff kept turning around, thinking there was something behind him. But every time he looked, all he saw was blackness. He wished he had a flashlight, too, or could at least use the headlamp on his helmet, but Irons had ordered them to turn them on only in an emergency.

Once, Jeff thought he saw something twinkling in the distance. He stopped and turned all the way round. He listened but only heard the sounds of the other members of the group.

"What is it?" Joanne asked.

Jeff shook his head and kept walking. "Nothing," he mumbled.

"You didn't stop for nothing," Joanne persisted.

"I thought I saw a flash of light. As if a light went on

briefly in one of the other corridors." He sighed. "But I guess I was wrong."

"A flash of light?" Joanne asked. Jeff didn't answer. "Could have been Cherenkov radiation," Joanne suggested. "After all, we are nearing the outer shell."

Trust Joanne to come up with a logical explanation. Cherenkov radiation was created by cosmic particles that penetrated the eye at almost the speed of light and gave off part of their energy as a short pulse of light, which then hit the optic nerve. The phenomenon had driven some of the early astronauts nearly out of their minds. But Jeff doubted her theory. The shadows of the corridor walls had been too clear to see. A more likely explanation was that the never-ending darkness of the corridors was playing tricks with his imagination. The only alternative was that there was someone—or something—sneaking through the corridors. But that couldn't be. The ship was abandoned.

If only he could get rid of this sensation of being watched! He could almost feel the gaze of a sinister some-thing on his back. Jeff exhaled slowly, resisting the impulse to turn around.

There's nothing there. Don't make a fool of yourself in front of the others!

They approached a turning and Jeff looked up. Suddenly he stumbled and almost fell over his own feet. He cursed inwardly. He should have remembered: this was the place where the vector of gravity had changed when they had first walked to their quarters. It wasn't far now to the airlock.

"Made it!" Castle called out. He had stopped in front of the door and was waiting for the others.

"I didn't remember it being so far," Fields grumbled.

Jeff looked at his watch. "One-and-a-half hours. Yeah, that's about right."

"Then let's go in," Castle said and held his finger up to the white square next to the door. With a hissing noise, the door slid open.

Fields walked past Castle into the antechamber of the airlock. Jeff followed him. It was pitch black. If only they knew how to turn on the lights … but there were no controls on the walls as far as he could see. Jeff held his handheld to the wall. "Austin. We're in the antechamber."

"Keep us informed of every step," Irons had taken over communication with the group.

"Understood."

Jeff joined Fields, who was already standing by the door to the airlock scratching his head. The others followed him.

"Hm, and now what?" Fields asked.

"Well, how about opening the hatch to the airlock," Castle said sarcastically.

"I get that, Lieutenant," Fields quipped. "The question is *how*. There aren't any controls here."

Jeff saw his point. The walls around the hatch to the airlock were completely smooth. How the hell had the aliens opened this thing?

Castle stepped up to the hatch and tapped at regular intervals along the wall.

"What are you doing?" Joanne said, coming up behind them.

"Maybe the controls are embedded in the wall. We also have flaps on our ships that only open when you apply pressure."

Fields had moved away from the group and was using his flashlight to light up the walls of the room. Jeff nodded. Maybe there was a control panel somewhere in here …

Jeff looked through the little window into the interior of the airlock, which was shrouded in darkness. "Maybe there isn't even a vacuum in there, or the outer hatch is open …" Joanne mused.

"I can't imagine it," Castle retorted, and continued tapping along the wall.

Jeff sighed and took the handheld out of his belt pouch. "Austin here. Come in."

"Irons," the major responded curtly.

"We have a problem."

"Speak!"

"There are no controls for the airlock. We can't even get the outer hatch open."

"Understood. Keep looking for a solution."

"Yes, Sir."

Jeff remembered the moment they had come into the airlock from outside. They'd been surprised then that there were no controls. The computer had apparently opened the hatches for them. He got an uneasy feeling.

He pressed on the talk button again. "What if the airlock can only be operated by the computer?"

Castle swung round and frowned at Jeff. "That would be pretty dumb."

A few seconds passed before Irons answered. "If there really are no manual controls in there, it's the logical answer."

"Maybe there were once manual controls but they were removed when the ship was reconstructed after the crew left," Joanne said.

"Try it," Irons said. "Call the computer."

Castle waved his hand dismissively. "I bet it's sleeping again."

Jeff took a deep breath. "Computer," he said loudly and found himself looking upward. "Can you hear me?"

Several long seconds passed. Then the familiar crackling sound filled the room. "I can hear you, Jeff Austin. How can I help?"

Jeff blinked.

He knows my name?

Not so dumb, that computer. "Well, er …"

He fell silent. He couldn't say they wanted to go outside to find out their position and check the computer was telling them the truth. The computer would interpret it as distrust. "Um, we'd like to use the airlock to make some measurements."

"Measurements? What for?"

"Um, it's routine according to our protocols. I mean, for our logbooks."

"I understand," the computer said.

Did he detect an amused undertone in the voice?

"So it is not an emergency?" the computer asked.

Jeff shook his head. "No. It's not an emergency."

"I'm sorry," the computer replied. "While in flight, the locks can only be opened in an emergency."

So that was that.

"Major?" Jeff asked.

"I heard. Come back to HQ," Irons said in his usual, matter-of-fact tone.

"Understood."

"Is there anything else I can do for you?" the computer asked.

Jeff sighed. "No, that's all. Thank you."

"Then I wish you a pleasant day."

"Thanks," Jeff replied automatically. "You too."

The crackling sound indicated that the computer had switched off again. Something was bothering Jeff, but he couldn't put his finger on what.

"Did I hear that right?" Castle asked. "We're trapped in here and aren't allowed out?"

Joanne laughed out loud. "That's an interesting inter-pretation of our situation!"

"Why do you mean?" Jeff asked.

"Even if the computer let us out, where would we go?" She laughed again. "We're trapped, whatever way you look at it."

"Let's go back," Jeff said, signaling to Castle to lead the way with the flashlight.

"Still, I would have liked to know our actual position," Joanne said.

"Maybe we're not supposed to find out," Castle said darkly.

Chapter 8

"So we're trapped inside this alien ship. There's no other way of looking at it, really," Jeff said, listlessly stabbing at his steak with his fork. At least his headache had gone.

Irons shook his head. "I'm not too worried about that. If we really want to go outside, then we'll go outside."

"And how?" Fields asked.

"You should know best, Corporal." The major pointed at the sled standing in the corner with the emergency equipment. "You packed the thing."

Fields gave it a brief glance and shrugged.

"The emergency kit contains two kilos of FOX-7. That's ten times enough to blow us through the outer shell of the ship."

Jeff scratched his head. Could it work? Would the ship's computer even allow it? Hopefully they would never get to the point where they would have to try it.

"And how do we check our position?" We have no way of finding out if the ship is really heading for Sigma-7."

Irons nodded. "That's true, and I would have liked to verify our position, but I'll say it again, loud and clear. We have no reason to distrust our host. It could have just left us outside."

"Do you think it doesn't want us to check our position?" Joanne asked.

"It seems kind of far-fetched to me that the airlock can only be opened in emergencies," Castle said.

"I disagree," Irons retorted. "We have very similar protocols on our ships. In fact we should have expected it. Imagine we took a handful of shipwrecked aliens onto our ship, and they wanted to open the airlock during flight. What would we do?"

"Put them into a detention cell until we got to our destination," Finni said dryly.

Irons had a point. Maybe they were being a bit paranoid.

"Lieutenant Green," Irons said. "Everything OK?"

Jeff turned to look down the table. The engineer was sitting motionless in his seat and staring right through the major with glassy eyes. It suddenly occurred to Jeff that the normally loquacious Green hadn't said a word during dinner. He obviously wasn't feeling well. He was white as a sheet and drooling slightly from the corner of his mouth.

"Lieutenant Green?" Irons repeated.

Finally the engineer focused his gaze. "Sorry. I'm not feeling so great." His voice was no more than a thin rasp.

"Is your headache still so bad? Do you want some painkillers?"

Green shook his head. "No, I'm starting to feel better."

Jeff thought about his own headache, which he hadn't mentioned to anyone. If it was infectious, then the major ought to know. "I didn't feel too good this morning, either," Jeff said quietly. "I had a terrible headache."

Irons swung round to look at him. "Why didn't you say anything? I would have sent someone in your place."

"That's just what I wanted to avoid," Jeff said. "Besides, it wasn't that bad."

Joanne raised her right hand tentatively. "I didn't feel too good yesterday."

"You too?" Irons raised his eyebrows. He blinked.

"It went away very quickly."

Irons nodded. "Well it seems there's some kind of virus going around. Anyone else?"

Castle and Fields raised their hands.

"Yesterday," the WSO replied.

"Last night," said the mechanic. "I woke up two or three times in the night and nearly took a pill. But it wasn't all that bad and this morning it had gone."

"Then it seems to be some kid of mild infection, if nobody feels too bad," Irons said.

"Apart from him," Castle gestured with his thumb to Green, who was sitting beside him.

"We probably brought the virus with us from Sigma-7 and infected each other in the bomber during the incubation period." Irons turned to Green. "Go to bed. It looks like you're not hungry, anyway. Off with you, and have a proper lie-in tomorrow morning."

Green nodded. "Thanks, Sir." The engineer stood up and almost collapsed. He clung to the back of his chair with some difficulty.

"Lieutenant Castle, please bring your shipmate to his room," Irons ordered.

The WSO was about to stand up but Green raised his hand. "S'OK. I'm all right."

"You sure?" Castle asked.

"Sure," Green answered, and dragged himself to the door.

"I hope we didn't catch something on this ship," Joanne

said after Green had disappeared. "I mean, something alien."

"Nonsense," Fields retorted in a sharp voice.

Joanne's face hardened. "Don't snap at me like that, Corporal Fields!"

"I mean …" Fields' face turned red and he stuttered. "I mean, if there were biological dangers here, they would have shown up on the scanner."

Jeff smirked. Joanne was able to flip quickly between being chummy and standoffish. It was different from Irons' predominantly authoritarian approach, but just as effective. Jeff sighed inwardly. He knew Joanne would have made a better XO than him. "What's our next move?" he asked.

Irons took a deep breath and exhaled loudly. "We'll carry on exploring the ship. We've been through all the corridors between our quarters and the outer shell, without finding anything of interest. So we'll start going deeper. But I'd like to change our strategy a little."

"Strategy?" Finni asked. "What strategy?"

Irons turned his head and glared at the radar technician, eyes narrowed to slits. "So far, we've been systematically exploring all the turnoffs, in order to map out all accessible areas close to our quarters. We've been thorough, but we've only managed to expand our radius very slowly. Based on our explorations so far, there's not much to discover. The rooms we've found are all empty. My guess is that there are other areas of the ship that are different from around here. And if that's the case …"

Finni raised a hand. "But Green calculated that because of the fractal layout of the corridors—"

Irons interrupted him in a loud voice: "—perhaps the whole ship is as empty as the area around our quarters. That's a hypothesis, no more." He leaned forward. "And incidentally, I would ask that you do not interrupt me while I am speaking, Corporal Herrmansson. Is that clear?"

Finni nodded.

"If other areas of the ship are structured differently, we'll pursue another strategy and plan our reconnaissance missions so that we move as far away as possible from our quarters. We'll guide the squads from HQ to the right turnoffs." Irons turned to Joanne. "I suggest you go on the first of our modified missions tomorrow."

Joanne nodded. "Sure."

"Sir!" Shorty interjected. "You said two days ago that I could take over command of the squad tomorrow."

Irons sighed and nodded. "You're right, Private Short. I forgot. OK. You can join Private McGuinness tomorrow."

"Do I have to?" Mac grumbled under his breath.

"Thank you, Sir," Shorty said.

"We can send a second squad," said Joanne. "Like we've been doing up to now, anyway."

Irons tipped his head to the side uncertainly. Finally he nodded. "You're right. Maybe we'll make faster progress. Do you want to go?"

Joanne nodded. "Who's coming with me? Any volunteers?" She looked at Jeff. "What about you?"

All eyes were on Jeff. If he refused or looked for a flimsy excuse, he would undermine his authority even further. "Sure. I'll come with you."

He didn't actually want to go. He was spooked by the memory of being watched in the corridors. He couldn't say why, but he couldn't shake the feeling there was something waiting for them in the depths of the deserted ship.

Chapter 9

"That's the turnoff," Jeff said, glancing down at his handheld to be on the safe side. "Yes, G58. This is where Mac and I turned around a few days ago and went back. This is the furthest point we've been from HQ up to now."

"Sure, I remember the spot," Mac said. "I don't need a handheld for that."

Shorty nudged him. "We're better scouts than our officers, eh? Like Lewis and Clarke!"

Mac bellowed with laughter.

"Get a hold of yourselves, boys," Joanne said.

Jeff shook his head. The two technicians were in a surprisingly good mood this morning. The whole way down they'd been laughing and wisecracking. If Jeff hadn't known better, he'd have guessed they'd knocked back a few beers before setting out. But maybe it was just their usual form of communication when they were alone. Jeff was sure they would have behaved differently if Irons had been with them.

"I suggest you two go down the right-hand corridor.

Joanne and I will go straight ahead. Both corridors seem to lead deeper into the ship.

"Sure boss, let's do it," Mac said, without even giving Jeff a second glance.

"Are you sure you wouldn't rather come with us? Without us, you might get lost," Shorty joked.

Joanne stuck out her tongue. Jeff thought the two of them were starting to go too far.

"Ahhh, the lovebirds would rather be alone," Mac gave a big wink. "Have fun, kids. And don't forget to use a rubber!"

Howling with laughter, the two men headed off down the corridor.

Joanne pursed her lips.

Jeff would have liked to ignore what they'd said, but he couldn't do that in Joanne's presence.

He straightened up. "Private Short! Private McGuinness!"

They stopped and turned around, both of them still grinning.

What should he say now?

"What is it?" Mac asked.

Should he give them both a warning? Or send them back to their quarters? Report them to Irons? It all seemed so childish.

He sighed. "Nothing. Go."

Chuckling, the two men set off.

Jeff avoided looking at Joanne. Luckily he had to send a message to Irons. He gave their position and the direction the squads were taking.

Meanwhile, Joanne had switched on her flashlight and was shining it down the corridor. There were no more intersections in sight. Jeff put his handheld away and marched on. His shipmate stayed close on his heels.

"You shouldn't have let Shorty and Mac get away with that," she said finally.

Did he have to listen to another lecture now? He wasn't in the mood. He knew he'd reacted the wrong way again. "Drop it—please," he said.

"I didn't want to undermine your authority, but next time I'm going to say something."

"I get it."

"You really need to start—"

He stopped in his tracks and clenched his fists. "Leave it!" His voice sounded angrier than he'd intended it to.

Joanne looked at him in astonishment for a moment, then began to laugh.

"What?" Jeff asked irritably. "What's so funny?"

Joanne jabbed his chest lightly with her forefinger. She was still laughing. "You! You're funny. That tone you just used with me—you would have been better off using it on Mac and Shorty. You sounded really pissed and authoritative. When you speak like that, you sound like a real XO."

"Forget it," Jeff said grumpily. "Come on, let's go!"

Side by side, they continued down the corridor in silence. Jeff kept glancing down at his handheld. The corridor was surprisingly steep. Somewhere behind them, the gravitational vector had changed again. He hadn't noticed the change, but his handheld showed him the spot where it had been registered by the acceleration sensor. They were now approaching a depth of just over half a mile. He kept wondering what else was waiting for them inside this strange ship, which had been abandoned for eons, and all of a sudden his hands began to shake. He was scared. Yes, scared!

Jeff took several deep breaths. "Do you think there are areas of this ship that are different from this one?" he asked, not so much out of interest, but more to break the awkward silence.

"I have no idea," Joanne answered. "If we believe what the computer says, there's nothing to find on this ship. In that case, it probably looks the same as it does here everywhere, and the machines and aggregates are all computer-controlled and hidden behind thick walls. In that case, all this running around is just a work-out. At least we'll stay fit until we reach Sigma-7."

"If we ever reach Sigma-7."

"Do you doubt it?"

Jeff didn't reply for a long time. He didn't want to be a pessimist. Finally he shrugged. "I'm not sure if I really trust that computer. On the other hand, Major Irons doesn't seem too worried."

Joanne shrugged. "You know what the major's like. He expresses just the amount of emotion that he wants us to see. My guess is, he doesn't want to worry us unnecessarily, but I bet he *is* worried." She sighed. "All I needed was for this one flight to go smoothly. Then I'd be done."

Jeff looked up, surprised. Surely she couldn't have completed the minimum number of missions already.

Joanne noticed his quizzical expression and laughed. "Yes, you heard right. After this flight I could have quit the unit."

"But … how?"

"I applied for the intelligence service and was accepted."

Now Jeff remembered: those who were assured a staff officer position in a non-combat unit had a certain number of flights deducted from their quota. After all, you didn't want to lose your future executives in a routine mission gone wrong. As a historian, Jeff didn't have that option. History lecturers counted as cannon fodder. But there was no reason to be bitter. He didn't begrudge Joanne this advantage, especially now, when she was stuck in the same mess as he was.

"I'm sorry," he said.

She shrugged. "Every mission can go wrong. Others have been shredded to bits on their first flight. Besides, we're still alive, and maybe this ship will get us back home and we're just being paranoid."

Jeff nodded. Maybe they really were being too pessimistic, and in half a year Joanne would take up her position in the intelligence service. If there was anyone in the crew that he wished well, it was Joanne. He'd liked her from the start. She was friendly, open, and sharp as a tack. Plus she got cute dimples when she smiled. At the start of their mission, he'd even caught himself watching her when she wasn't looking. But just when he thought he was falling for her, it hit him that he wasn't in her league. Joanne needed a sociable and adventurous guy by her side, and not a geek like him. It never would have worked, so Jeff had nipped his little crush in the bud. In fact, he'd even made a point of keeping out of her way. Only now, in this dark and gloomy place, did it occur to him that he didn't actually know very much about her.

"This corridor is going on forever," Joanne said, snapping him out of his reverie. He looked down at his handheld. It was true: they'd already covered a third of a mile since the last junction. The long corridors brought back memories of his childhood. "It's a bit like on Luna—we also had endless corridors connecting one complex to the next. Except they weren't this dark or sinister …"

Joanne nodded. "We had those at home, too."

He didn't know where Joanne was from. "And your home is …?"

"I thought that as an XO you'd have seen all the personnel files."

Jeff shrugged. "Obviously I failed on that front, too," he said dryly.

Joanne grinned. "I'm from Ross 154/2."

"Ashland?" Jeff asked.

She nodded. "Have you been?"

Jeff shook his head. "Not really. I once changed ships on one of its orbital stations on the way to Barnard. The connecting flight was delayed by half a day and I had some drinks with my buddy in the panorama lounge. We tried to count the active volcanoes on the surface, but gave up during our second drink."

Joanne giggled. "I can imagine. We have one thing in common with Luna—you can't move around outside without a space suit. There's a monorail connecting the individual settlements and neighborhoods, but often sections aren't running because a nearby volcano has erupted. Then the only option is to use the passageways that were drilled through the rocks to get from one dome to another.

Jeff shrugged. "Luna is just a boring heap of rocks. The only bright spot is Earth, which looks like a blue paradise. My parents and I used to spend every vacation there. My father bought a holiday home on the Mediterranean, and we went twice a year, usually Easter and Christmas. Even though we had big beach pods on Luna, it never came close to the feeling of lying on a real beach, with the breeze on your face under a blue sky ..." He sighed. He wondered if he'd ever see the golden beaches of the Costa Brava again.

"There's no Earth-like planet close to Ross 154. And no beach pods, either. It was too difficult to get enough water. The nearest beach was on Earth, and flights there were too expensive for my parents. The first time I saw the sea was when I was at the Academy, and we went for a weekend trip. I'll never forget it. I stepped out of the bar of the hotel on the beachfront, and suddenly there was this huge surface of water in front of me. I panicked!"

"Panicked?"

"Yes, panicked!" Joanne opened her mouth and eyes wide and clutched her head with both hands in mock horror. Then she smiled again sweetly. "It moved like a living creature, the waves breaking on the beach, the foamy tips stirred by the wind … I'd also never seen a blue sky before, so at first I thought there was water everywhere. I really thought there was an endless wall of water in front of me that would devour me at any moment."

She laughed and then became serious. "I heard your father was on Deneb-6."

Jeff felt a wave of pain welling up inside him. He sighed. "Yes, he was on a business trip to carry out an inspection on a subcontractor. Deneb-6 was attacked by the rebels with Quagma bombs. A hundred thousand people died in an instant on the colony. My father was one of them. That day he'd actually wanted to—"

A flash of light! Right in front of them.

"Ssshh!" he hissed.

"I saw it," Joanne whispered and switched off the flashlight. "What was it?"

"I've noticed it a few times before," Jeff spoke as quietly as possible. "But I always thought I was imagining it."

"I wish that were true. But that was real, for sure." She pointed in front of her. "I think there's another turnoff up ahead."

There was another flash. Something was lurking in the passage behind the bend, which was still about eighty feet away. Jeff and Joanne pressed themselves against the wall and waited. But the light didn't reappear. Now there were only stars dancing in front of Jeff's eyes in the darkness. They kept multiplying, until he noticed he'd been holding his breath for a very long time. He barely managed to stop himself gasping noisily for air.

"What shall we do?" Joanne whispered.

"I don't know," Jeff said. All he wanted to do was run. But they had to find out what it was. "We'll go to the turnoff and look around the corner," he whispered finally.

Moving at a snail's pace, they edged their way along the wall toward the intersection, doing everything in their power not to make any noise. Now the ground covering was to their advantage—it did a good job of swallowing the sound of their footsteps.

It felt like hours were passing. Because of the dark, they could only guess how much further it was. Jeff felt his way along the wall with his outstretched arm. Finally he hit the edge. They had reached the intersection. Where was Joanne? He felt something soft on his right arm. Joanne was right behind him. He could hear her shallow breathing. With pigeon steps he edged his whole body up to the intersection. No more flashes of light. Had whatever produced the light gone? Of was it lurking just around the corner? Was it lying in wait for them? His heart was beating so hard, he imagined the whole ship must be able to hear it. Slowly he moved his head to peek round the corner. But he couldn't see a thing. If only it wasn't so pitch black. Or if only he had his infrared glasses. It was no use. He needed light.

He reached behind him to take the flashlight out of Joanne's hand. Joanne noticed what he wanted and pressed the small cylinder into his trembling hand. He pointed the flashlight around the corner and laid his thumb on the button. He knew he wouldn't like what he was about to see. Adrenalin flooded his body—ready to respond to whatever horror awaited him. He took a deep breath. And pressed the button.

It all happened very fast. He was staring into a demonic grin—right in front of his face. Before he could react, the figure sprang toward him with outstretched arms. The creature screamed, an inhuman roar. Jeff let go of the flashlight, which clattered to the ground. He was blind again. He stumbled backward and yanked Joanne with him. She screamed in surprise. Their legs got tangled and they both fell to the ground. But even as they fell, Jeff pulled his pistol from his holster. He should have done it minutes ago! It might be the mistake that cost them their lives. Frantically, he tugged at his weapon, and released the trigger even as he was pulling it out.

To his boundless surprise, the roar of the monster turned into a laugh. A human laugh, which he knew only too well. The beast stepped back into the cone of light from the fallen flashlight and Jeff groaned with a mixture of irritation and relief. "Mac, you *fucking* idiot!"

Now Shorty stepped into the light and joined in Mac's raucous laughter. He slapped himself on the thigh.

Jeff closed his eyes and tried to get rid of the pent-up adrenaline. He took a deep breath, counted to twenty in his head, then exhaled again. He opened his eyes and saw Shorty with his back against the wall, crying with laughter. Mac had fallen to his knees and was clutching his stomach.

Jeff picked up the flashlight and stood up. Then he turned around and helped Joanne to her feet. She looked him in the eyes and he knew exactly what she wanted to say. He nodded. He couldn't let them get away with this. "There will be consequences," he said softly.

His panic had turned into anger. He was still pumped

up with adrenaline. He turned to the still laughing men, pursed his lips, and squared his shoulders.

"Attention!" he said loudly.

The men looked up, but didn't make much of effort to adopt the military position.

"The next time I say 'Attention' and you haven't taken up position within two seconds, I will make sure that you do not leave your sleeping quarters for the rest of your flight. Is that clear?" Jeff was surprised how icy his voice sounded.

The men's laughter petered out. It didn't seem to have occurred to them that they might have overstepped the mark this time.

"Attention!" Jeff repeated.

This time the men adopted the correct stance.

Jeff pulled his pistol from his holster and held it in front of his chest without pointing it in a particular direction. "Did you two idiots even stop to think that you might have been shot?"

Mac shook his head. "We just discovered that one of the intersections led in exactly your direction. We saw the light of your flashlight and thought we'd play a little joke."

"A little joke ..." Jeff repeated icily.

"Yeah, to lighten up the mood around here."

To lighten up the mood?

He was starting to boil with rage. "Since leaving your rooms, you haven't stopped laughing and making jokes at our expense. As far as I can tell, your mood is light enough as it is."

"Yeah, but—" Shorty began.

"Enough," Jeff hissed. He put his gun back in his holster. "Next time there will be a price to pay. Is that clear?"

Shorty nodded, but Mac continued grinning.

"Come on, let's go," Jeff said, pulling Joanne with him into the other corridor. Shorty and Mac walked back in the direction they had come, chuckling, and soon Jeff could no longer see the light of their flashlights.

"*Next time* there'll be a price to pay?" Joanne asked incredulously.

Jeff lifted a hand. "They were just kidding around." What should he have done? Sent them back to their quarters and put them under arrest? Given them two weeks' kitchen duty? That would have been ridiculous. At least he had told them he didn't condone their tasteless jokes.

Joanne tightened her lips and shook her head.

"I'll report the junction to headquarters," Jeff said, changing the subject.

He took his handheld out of his belt pocket. Irons answered the call directly. Jeff reported their position and the direction they were going.

"Private Short and Private McGuinness are exploring the corridor that ought to lead in your direction. Don't be alarmed if you bump into them."

Joanne groaned.

Jeff sighed. "We just met them at our position." Should he inform on them? He didn't see the point. "They went back the other way and are continuing their recon."

Joanne groaned again.

"Understood," Irons said and signed off.

Jeff handed the flashlight back to Joanne and continued down the corridor. About forty feet ahead of them was another intersection. They continued in silence until they reached it. Jeff stopped in front of the turning and leaned his head forward to look round the corner. "Oh," he said. "A dead end." The corridor ended in a wall several feet away.

"Not quite. There's a door. Let's see what's behind it," Joanne said, moving closer. Jeff hurried after her.

"Shall I open it?" Joanne asked, pointing at the silver square on the wall.

Jeff nodded and the heavy steel door hissed open.

Together they stepped over the threshold.

"Pretty big," Joanne remarked, playing the light of her flashlight across the walls.

Jeff nodded. The room was about the size of a small football stadium. The ceiling was far above them. In fact, he *guessed* where it was more than he could actually see it. The walls were lined with shelves.

"Maybe a storage room," Joanne said. Together they walked toward the opposite wall.

Jeff stopped in the middle of the room and looked around. Following a sudden impulse, he clapped his hands. Again, there was no echo. He sighed. "It's possible, I guess."

"Well there's nothing being stored here now, that's for sure," Joanne said dryly.

Jeff reached the wall of shelves opposite the entrance. He climbed a ladder that was leaning against the shelves until he had a good view of the room and the upper shelves. Yup—all empty. "Maybe it used to be a storeroom, when the ship had a crew. And they emptied it when they left the ship."

"If it weren't for that computer, you'd think we were on a ghost ship," Joanne said. She stood at the bottom of the ladder and looked up at Jeff.

Carefully he made his way back down, rung by rung. There was nothing of real interest in here. "As far as I'm concerned it *is* a ghost ship." When he reached the bottom, he fumbled for his handheld. "I'll report back to base. Let's go back outside."

Joanne followed him into the corridor where Jeff activated his handheld. Irons replied immediately.

"We reached a dead end. There's a big room at the end, but it's completely empty. We're not going to get any further in this area."

"Join Private Short's squad immediately. The two men have found something."

Jeff was all ears. It would be the first time since the beginning of the reconnaissance mission that they had found *anything*.

"What?" Jeff asked. He could hardly keep the excitement out of his voice. Joanne moved up closer to him.

"A gate," Irons said.

"A gate?" Jeff asked.

"Or a bulkhead. Go and see for yourselves. I'll give you the coordinates."

Irons described the way from the point where Jeff and Joanne had met Mac and Shorty. Jeff signed off and they headed back the way they had come.

"What kind of gate do you think it is?" Joanne asked. Her voice was tense.

"No idea. Maybe the men just found a door and are exaggerating again."

"If it's a gate, what's behind it?"

Jeff shrugged. Until they got there, all they could do was speculate.

A few minutes later they reached the junction where they'd been ambushed by Mac and Shorty. Jeff glanced down at his handheld, but he remembered that on the way here, they had come straight. So now they had to turn left if they wanted to follow Mac and Shorty's route.

After about half a mile they reached another intersection. A corridor led to the right. That must be the way back to their quarters. Another corridor went off to the left and in the beam of Joanne's flashlight, they could see another junction about eighty feet further on. Jeff glanced down at his handheld to double check, then turned into the corridor. Joanne followed him.

After the first junction, another one appeared after about six hundred feet. Beyond it, the corridor started to go down at an angle of approximately twenty degrees.

Silently, they followed it further down into the depths of the ship. Without the handheld, they would have lost their way completely. It would have been impossible to sketch this three-dimensional labyrinth with a pen and paper.

A short while later, when they reached the next junction, they were in for a surprise. At first, Jeff thought they had stepped into a room, but it was a corridor, much wider than the ones they were used to. In fact it was so wide, they could have fit the Charon inside it. There was one corridor branching off to the right, and two more branching off to the left, each of them as wide as the one they had just come out of. Jeff looked up at the ceiling, which was arched like the nave of a cathedral. Then he spotted Mac and Shorty. The two mechanics were standing about six hundred feet away in front of a dark gray wall. The beam from their flashlight flickered in different directions. As Jeff and Joanne approached them, Jeff realized that what he had thought was the back wall of this hangar-sized corridor was in fact a gate.

The gate!

It bulged a little in middle, and to its left and right were shimmering silver rails, or runners, along which the gigantic gate could presumably slide up and disappear into the ceiling. Huge white and yellow characters were painted in the middle of the door. In front of it, on the ground, there were more strange white and yellow markings. A blue area directly at the foot of the metal gate probably indicated the danger zone.

When they reached Mac and Shorty, the two of them were sounding out the walls. Jeff guessed they were looking for some kind of operating system with which to open the gate, but there was nothing there. Like everything else on this ship, the gate was presumably controlled by the computer, too.

"Interesting." At that moment, Jeff couldn't think of anything else to say.

"You could say," Mac responded. His jovial mood seemed to have died away in face of this colossal gate, beside which the two men looked like dwarves.

"Looks to me like the door to an airlock," Shorty said. The mechanic punched the metal with his fist. "The way it bulges out, I'd say it's at least fifteen inches thick. You'd need an atomic bomb to get that open."

"No controls?" Joanne asked.

"We didn't find anything. We've searched the whole corridor," Mac said.

"And the little room, too," Shorty added.

"What little room?" Joanne asked.

Only now did Jeff notice the door in the wall of the corridor, about forty feet away from the gate. It was open. Next to it was a square window through which he could look inside.

"It's only about thirty by thirty feet. And completely empty, like everywhere on this ship," Shorty said.

"How the hell are we supposed to open this thing?" Mac was clearly frustrated.

Jeff wondered if they should even try. Who could say what was behind it? Suddenly, a wave of fear washed over him again. As if something utterly evil was just waiting to be let out behind that gate.

"We can't," Shorty replied. "There are no controls —again."

"I'd love to know what's behind there," Joanne said. "Maybe Irons was right, and the interior of the ship is divided into lots of individual areas. Probably a new area starts behind that gate."

"I reckon the corridor on the other side is just as wide. Could be a kind of highway to the center of the ship," Mac mused. "Maybe it used to be a transport route. It's sure wide enough."

"We could ask the ship's computer to open it for us," Joanne suggested.

Before we do anything, we should speak to Irons," Jeff said. "He has to decide our next move."

"And what do we do now?" Joanne asked.

"We'll do another thorough search of the area around the gate, to be absolutely sure we didn't miss something. And I'm going to take a few pictures of the gate and the funny letters on it for the major."

"And then?" Mac asked.

"Then we'll go back."

Chapter 10

"There were no controls?" Irons asked. "No knobs, switches, or anything else?" His spoon lay untouched next to his plate of stew.

"No," Jeff shook his head. They had spent an hour searching before heading back to their quarters in the early afternoon.

"The gate is probably controlled by the computer," Joanne said. "We could ask it to open it for us."

Irons nodded. "Let's hear what it has to say."

"Maybe we should just stay away from it," Green said. It was the first time he had joined them to eat since being knocked out by the flu, or whatever it was. The engineer was still pale. His eyes were bloodshot and, like Irons, he hadn't touched anything on his plate.

"Why?" Castle asked derisively. "Are you scared there might be a monster on the other side?"

Green turned very slowly to look at his shipmate. Like Mac and Shorty, Green and Castle were buddies. "I'm not afraid of anything," he answered evenly.

"Knock it off!" Irons said. "We'll ask the computer to

open the gate the next time it contacts us." He glanced at his watch. "It's been a while, actually. Then we'll decide what to do. Until then, we'll check out the two remaining unexplored corridors."

"I think I heard that my presence was required," the emotionless voice of the computer suddenly echoed through the room. Jeff wondered how long it had been listening in on their conversation.

"Yes," Irons replied. "Thank you for contacting us. Everything OK with you and the ship?"

"Thank you, yes. Some irregularities with one of the power plants, but repairs are already in progress. You will be pleased to hear that the capacitors are charging for the next hyperjump. This will take place in two days."

"Great. Thanks again," Irons said. "I have a question."

"Go ahead."

"On a ... er ... walk around the ship, we came across a big gate. It's about a mile from our quarters in a big corridor. It's locked."

There was no answer. Irons looked over at Jeff with raised eyebrows.

"What's behind it? Can it be opened?" Irons asked.

"The gate leads to another sector of the ship," the computer answered promptly. Apparently it needed explicit questions in order to reply. "The gate cannot be opened because the sector behind it is no longer under my control due to a defect that occurred a long time ago."

"Oh."

Jeff bit his lip. True, the computer had confirmed Irons' assumption that the ship was divided into different areas. But Jeff hadn't expected to hear that there were areas which weren't under the computer's control. If that were the case, then they would only be able to explore the corridors on this side of the gate. Maybe they would come across another gate leading to another sector, which was still accessible.

"So you're saying that you can't open the gate," Irons continued.

"Your assumption is correct."

"Are there any manual devices for opening the gate?"

"No."

"So how could the crew open the gate in an emergency?"

"By asking me to open it."

"I see, but you're not always available," Irons said. He could barely suppress the sarcasm in his voice.

"It has not always been that way," the computer replied, almost crossly. "With the passing of time, the number of failed systems has increased, and this has affected my own capacities."

Irons raised his hand. "All right. I didn't mean it as a criticism."

"Now I need to get back to dealing with other tasks. I will contact you when we have made the next hyperjump." The familiar crackling indicated that the computer had switched off without waiting for an answer.

"What now?" Castle asked.

Irons turned to look at the weapons specialist. His forehead was deeply furrowed and he appeared to look straight through Castle.

"I asked, what—"

"I heard you, Lieutenant," Irons said gruffly. "Our plans are unchanged. We will explore the remaining corridors and take another look at the gate. Green?"

"Sir?"

"I assume it used to be possible to open the gate manually. No human designer would have built a bulkhead like that without manual controls for an emergency. Maybe you can find a way of opening it for us."

"But the computer said—"

"I know what the computer said. But maybe it wasn't given any information about the manual controls for good reason."

Green nodded. "OK. I'll take a look at it."

Chapter 11

Jeff was about to ask Irons a question when Owl's voice blared from the handheld. "Headquarters?"

Jeff adjusted the volume. "HQ here," he replied.

"The passage was also a dead end."

Irons grunted.

Jeff wasn't surprised, since the other intersection near the gate had also led to a dead end after several hundred feet. That left only one more corridor to explore. "Go back to the last crossing and explore the corridor that turns off from it."

"Understood."

Jeff looked at Irons, who was sitting beside him. "To be honest, I doubt that corridor will lead anywhere, either."

Irons leaned forward to look at the map on the screen of his handheld. He nodded slowly but said nothing.

Behind them, Joanne and Castle were sitting at the table having a snack. The weapons expert reached for his bottle of beer, causing Irons to frown. But why shouldn't he? He wasn't on duty, after all. Joanne chewed on her sandwich and listened in to the conversations between HQ and the two squads. Shorty and Mac were in their rooms, sleeping.

"HQ?"

"Yes. What is it, Fields? Anything to report?"

"Not really. Green says he can't find any manual controls near the gate. But we're going to check out the little room nearby again. We're not too hopeful, though."

Jeff shook his head. They were getting nowhere. "Understood," he said flatly. They would never get that gate open! And what was the point, anyway? The ship was probably just as empty on the other side as it was here. They could have spared themselves all these explorations. Jeff rubbed his temples. He hadn't slept well and had been plagued by nightmares in which he was being chased by invisible monsters through the ship's corridors.

Irons looked at him and narrowed his eyes. "Everything OK? You look unwell."

Jeff waved a hand. "I'm fine. Just didn't get a great night's sleep."

"That can happen," Irons said laconically.

"What if the last corridor leads Owl and Finni to another dead end?" Joanne asked.

"Then we can stop all these recon trips," Castle said. He spoke with his mouth full, and a piece of cheese fell out of the corner of his mouth onto the plate. "And just hang out here."

"You can get that idea right out of your head, Lieutenant!" Irons turned to look at him. "If we stop reconnaissance missions, they will be replaced by patrols."

"But—"

"You will not spend six months on your butt drinking beer. I can guarantee you that."

"Oh man!"

"Headquarters?"

Jeff pressed the talk button. "Found something, Fields?"

"Yes, we found something." His voice was agitated.

Jeff jolted into an upright position. Irons pulled his chair closer. Joanne and Castle got up and hurried over.

"Shoot!"

"We were about to stop searching and go back outside. But then I felt a draught in the corner of the room. I tapped along the wall and suddenly I had a panel in my hand. It looked like a section of the wall, but it wasn't completely airtight. Behind it is a narrow tunnel, which could be a ventilation shaft. As far as I can see, it leads to the other side of the gate."

A ventilation shaft? Wouldn't that have been blocked off, too? Still, it was a chance. Maybe it really would lead to the other side—and another part of the ship.

"Shall we crawl through and find out what's on the other side?" Fields asked.

Jeff glanced over at Irons. He expected him to tell Fields that he should wait for reinforcements.

"Yes, find out where it leads."

He'd been wrong on that count.

Irons was probably as curious as Jeff. And why should it be any more dangerous than exploring the corridors around here.

"Green here," Jeff heard the voice of the engineer. "I can't get into the tunnel. It's too narrow, I'll get stuck. I'm claustrophobic. I'll get a panic attack."

Irons rolled his eyes.

Then the heard Fields' voice. "I'll go alone. Doesn't bother me. But Green's right. It really is narrow."

Irons sighed and nodded at Jeff. "All right. But Fields shouldn't go too far and he needs to take the handheld with him. We'll send Corporal Owens and Herrmannsson to you as soon as we hear from them."

"Roger. I'm going to start crawling down the tunnel now."

"A good thing you gave them two flashlights," Joanne said.

Jeff nodded. "Yeah, we should have done that sooner. You never know when a squad might be separated."

"The flashlights won't last forever, though," Castle pointed out. "At some point the batteries will run out."

"That's why the second one should only be turned on in an emergency," Jeff said.

"In an emergency we can also activate the lights on our combat suits," Castle said.

"They're our absolute last resort," Irons said.

"HQ?" It was Fields. His voice was a distorted by the static, but still understandable.

"What's your status," Irons said, taking the handheld from Jeff.

"I'm on the other side. The tunnel was about sixty feet long. In the middle of the tunnel there was a bulkhead, but it was only partly lowered. Perhaps a defect prevented it from closing completely. Still, it was quite a squeeze to get under it. Green would have completely freaked out!"

"Where are you now? What can you see?"

"There was another panel at the end of the tunnel, but that was easy to move. I can't see anything yet, I've attached the flashlight to my belt. Hang on, it's got caught. Ah, yes, I …" Fields fell silent. "Oh my god!" he whispered.

Jeff started.

"What is it? What can you see?" Irons asked.

"I'm in a room very similar to the one at the other end of the tunnel. But it isn't empty."

"What do you mean?" Irons asked urgently. "Talk, Corporal!"

"There's furniture here. Tables, chairs … some of them knocked over. There's a shelf that's been half tipped over in the corner. In front of it on the floor are silver containers and metallic objects. It looks like a workshop that's been hit by a hurricane."

Jeff's eyes met Irons'. "We've actually found something," Jeff murmured.

"There are papers on the table," Fields continued. "With those alien characters on them. Judging by the furniture and things in here, these extraterrestrials must be very similar to humans. There's an overturned table in front of me. The drawers have handles, just like our desks. In the corner there's a metal plate with a two-pronged silver fork."

"The computer did say the aliens were very similar to us," Irons said.

Jeff felt uneasy. "But the computer also said there was nothing for us to find on the ship."

"Maybe some areas were forgotten when they converted the ship," Joanne suggested. "After all, it is huge."

Irons grunted. "I don't like any of this," he said quietly.

"The room has a door. I'll see what's behind it. I reckon it must lead to the corridor on the other side of the gate. Maybe there's a control panel around here."

Irons leaned over his handheld. "OK, but contact us immediately."

"Understood, Sir."

They waited with baited breath.

If the aliens had left something behind, Jeff wanted to check it out as soon as possible. But why had the computer lied to them? Or did it simply not know about these rooms? Perhaps it was just a small area that had been over-looked during the conversion of the ship, as Joanne suspected. Or was it the other way round? Had the computer purposefully taken them to the only part of the ship that was empty? And how would the computer react if it found out they had gotten to the other side of the gate?

"I'm now on the other side of the gate." It was Fields. "Can you hear me?"

"Loud and clear," Irons said. "What do you see?"

"There's another huge corridor, which seems to lead further into the interior of the ship. Even if I turn my flashlight on full power, I can't see the end. There's stuff lying around everywhere. Boxes, fallen shelves, machines. Something with four tires is tipped over. It must have been some means of transport. There are some burn marks on the walls. I get the feeling a fight took place here."

Jeff gulped. *A fight?*

"And what makes you think that?" Irons asked. "Do you see any bodies?"

"No, no bodies. But everything's a mess. There are bits of broken furniture all over the ground. Even the furniture is made out of metal. And it's not just the walls, lots of things on the ground are charred, too. It's possible that some other catastrophe took place here, but it definitely does not look like the area was simply abandoned."

"Keep searching," Irons commanded. "We'll send Owens and Herrmannsson to you as soon as we reach them." He released the talk button and turned to Jeff. "Where have they got to?"

Jeff looked at his watch. Almost half an hour had passed since they'd last called in. "No idea."

"There's a corridor leading from the room with the ventilation shaft," Fields said. "About a hundred and fifty feet away, a light is shining from a door into the corridor. I'll go and check it out."

Irons hit the talk button. "No! You stay right where you are, Corporal. Do you understand?"

There was no reply.

"He's already switched off," Jeff said.

Where could the light be coming from?

"I told him not to go too far," Irons cursed, his voice unusually sharp. "The corporal is all alone there."

"Typical Fields," Joanne said.

"It was a mistake," Irons was clearly angry with himself. "We should have waited for reinforcement before sending someone through that shaft."

"Owens here. Come in, HQ."

Finally!

Jeff was about to grab the handheld, but the major was quicker. "Where have you been, damn it?"

"Er, we found a room at the end of the corridor and checked it out. But it was empty. And then we took a break and had something to eat."

"Go to the gate. Right away!" Irons handed the device to Jeff.

"What happened?" Owl wanted to know. He sounded scared. Clearly he knew he'd made a mistake and was scared of a dressing down by the major.

"Fields found a way to the other side of the gate. Green is there alone. Get yourselves over there as quickly as possible."

"A way through?" Owl asked, incredulously.

But this was no time for chatting. "Get a move on!"

"Understood."

"How long will it take them?" Joanne asked.

Jeff shrugged. "Twenty minutes. Maybe thirty."

"As soon as Fields calls in, order him to come straight back," Irons said. "We need to plan our next move."

"What do we tell the computer?" Jeff asked.

"I'll think about that when—"

"Come in" Fields' voice was barely more than a whisper. There was something strange about it. Fear? Panic?

"Yes?" Jeff asked quietly.

"There's someone in the room," Jeff hissed, barely audibly.

Jeff hoped he had misheard. "What?"

"I said—there's someone in the room." The mechanic's voice was trembling. Irons and Jeff exchanged glances. The major's eyes were wide.

"Who's in the room?" Jeff asked, after he'd got over his initial shock.

"A … creature …. It's about fifty feet away from me. It's glowing! It seems to be made completely of light. The whole room is lit up with a pale white light. I've never seen anything this weird. It's standing with its back to me and hasn't noticed me. It's doing something at a table. I can't see exactly what."

Jeff didn't respond. He was too stunned by what Fields had told him.

"Get him back!" Irons commanded. His voice had never sounded so urgent.

Jeff's thumb approached the talk button when a loud scream at the other end of the speaker made him jump.

"It heard me. Shit! It's coming toward me."

The blood froze in Jeff's veins.

"No!" Fields screamed in an almost inhuman shrill voice. Then the connection broke off.

Jeff remained rooted to his chair, just staring at the handheld. He felt dizzy and only then did he realize that he had been holding his breath the whole time. He gasped for air.

Irons also had to collect himself. Finally he spoke. "How long do we need to get to the gate?"

Jeff was still staring at his handheld, as if he could use telepathy to get Fields to contact him again. It only gradually dawned on him that his shipmate might never contact him again.

"Captain Austin!" Irons said loudly.

Jeff turned to look at his superior. The major had asked something, but he couldn't remember what. He swallowed, but couldn't get the lump out of his throat. "Sorry, Sir?"

"I want to know how long it would take us to walk to the gate."

It was four miles away. "About three-quarters of an hour."

"Lieutenant Rutherford," Irons said.

"Sir?"

"Wake up Short and McGuinness. I need them on standby. Then I need you to take over communication with the handheld. When Owens and Herrmannsson get to the gate, they shouldn't do anything. They need to wait till we arrive."

"Understood, Sir." Joanne answered and disappeared into the private quarters at the back.

"Lieutenant Castle," the major turned to the WSO, who was standing next to the improvised command table.

"Sir?"

"I need you to come to the gate with me and Captain Austin."

Jeff put the handheld down on the table and stood up. He checked his pistol twice, then went to the alcove beside the kitchen unit to get the rest of his gear from the sled. Lieutenant Castle stooped silently beside him and picked up his own equipment. The major grabbed a portable spotlight.

Less than a minute later, they were out of the door. They had a long way to run through the dark corridors of the ship, on which they now knew without a doubt that they were not alone. Jeff was glad Major Irons was with him this time, but still he kept imagining that he saw one of the light aliens far in the distance.

The whole way to the gate, Jeff asked himself two questions over and again: Was Fields still alive? And what kind of creature had he encountered?

After what felt like an eternity, they finally turned the last corner and entered the cathedral-like corridor, with the gate at the end. A beam from a flashlight fell through the open door that led to the little room next to the gate. Jeff wanted to run straight in, but Irons held him back.

"Green! Are you there?" the major called.

Did he suspect that one of these light aliens was in there instead of Green?

"Yes, I'm in here," Green replied.

Jeff followed Irons into the room along with Castle. Green was standing beside the hole in the wall—the opening to the tunnel, which led to the other side. His hair was soaked in sweat, his eyes were wide.

"Have you heard anything from Fields?" Irons asked.

Green pointed at the hole. "I heard a scream. I think it was Fields." He wiped the sweat from his forehead. "I'm shit scared. Did he report to you?"

Irons ignored his question. "Where are Owens and Herrmannsson? They were supposed to join you."

Green shook his head. "There's nobody else here."

Jeff pulled the handheld out of his belt pouch. "I'll ask Joanne if she's heard anything from them," he said, and pressed the device up against the wall. "Joanne, we're at the gate. Can you hear me?"

"Yes. Are Owl and Finni with you?"

"No, I was just about to ask if you'd heard from them."

"Ten minutes ago. They got lost, I had to get them back on track."

"OK. Any word from Fields?"

Jeff was about to repeat the question when Joanne finally answered. "No, nothing. Is Green with you?"

"Yes, he waited here. Said he heard a scream."

"Shall I send Mac and Shorty down as reinforcement?" she asked.

"No," Irons had come up beside Jeff and was leaning over the device. "They should just stay on standby for now. We'll wait for Owens and Herrmannsson."

"We're here." Jeff looked up. Owens was stumbling toward them, panting. A few seconds later, Mac followed.

"Where were you?" Irons asked.

Owens saluted the major. He obviously had a guilty conscience about the unreported break. "Sir, I apologize for the delay. There was a mistake on the map, and Joanne—"

"It's OK, Private. We've got bigger problems." Irons outlined the situation to Owens, Mac, and Green. The engineer turned pale when Irons described the light alien.

"I didn't see anything."

"But you heard a scream?" Irons asked.

Green nodded. "About half an hour ago or so. It sounded as if Fields was scared to death or in terrible pain. Then suddenly there was silence. I didn't know what to do. I was about to make a run for it."

"What do we do now?" Jeff asked. But he already knew the answer.

"We're all going to go through the tunnel and look for

him," Irons said, without hesitation. He leaned down in front of the entrance to the tunnel, next to which the panel had been carelessly tossed aside. "Let's go. Captain Austin, follow me. Lieutenant Castle will bring up the rear. Be sure to stay as close together as possible. And activate your combat suits." He pressed a switch on the small arm console. Jeff did the same, although it would take several minutes for the reactor to start up.

"It's too tight in here for me. I can't go in there," Green said, pointing at the hole.

"You are coming with us. It is not up for discussion. Get your ass in gear!"

"Shouldn't someone keep watch?" Finni asked. Like Green, it was clear he would do anything rather than crawl through that narrow tunnel.

"No," Irons said. "I don't see any point, and if there really are hostile creatures on the other side, I want as many men as possible. Corporal Owens, please send a short message to HQ." He didn't wait for an answer. He kneeled down and crawled through the hole in the wall.

Jeff wiped the sweat from his forehead. The major was already some way down the tunnel.

"Austin, you still with me?"

Jeff crawled into the passage. "I'm coming."

The floor and walls were made of the same dark metal as everything else on this ship. But while the floor was smooth, there were regular outcroppings on the wall, and Jeff had to be careful not to bump his shoulders. The tunnel was narrow, and they made headway only slowly. After a few minutes, they arrived at a bulkhead that protruded almost halfway down from the ceiling.

Major Irons turned on his back and pulled himself under and past it in one swift, elegant movement.

Jeff continued crawling on all fours, but didn't stoop

low enough, with the result that he banged his head on the bulkhead. If the thing suddenly came down, he would be chopped in half. The mere thought of it made him break out in a sweat, and he crawled to the other side as fast as he could.

He heard groaning behind him. Green was trying to crawl underneath the bulkhead, but his hands were so sweaty he kept slipping. Jeff held a hand out to him, which he took gratefully. Green's eyes were very wide, he looked as if he might flip out at any moment. Jeff pulled his gasping shipmate through and then tried to catch up with Irons.

He had already reached the end of the tunnel. And pulled his gun. "What's keeping you, Austin?"

"I had to help—"

The major cut him off with a movement of his hand. "I don't want to hear about it. Are we all here? Rearguard?"

Meanwhile, Castle had also made it to the end of the tunnel. "Yes, Sir. I'm here."

"Then let's get out of here!" Irons said, and crawled out of the tunnel. A few seconds later, Jeff was standing beside him, shining his flashlight around the room. Fields had been right. It really did look as if a fight had taken place. There was furniture lying around everywhere—some of it destroyed—as well as papers, containers, and equipment. In one corner lay a charred heap of a gum-like black substance. Jeff thought he could smell burned plastic, but maybe he was just imagining it. It was impossible to say whether this devastation had occurred yesterday or a million years ago. Jeff almost expected to see charred, alien corpses.

Groaning, Green crawled out of the hole, pulled his pistol from his holster with a trembling hand, and came and stood next to Jeff. Finally, Castle crept out of the tunnel, cursing.

"Draw your weapon, Lieutenant!" Irons ordered.

Castle wiped his hand on his suit and then pulled his pistol from his holster. "Who knows if bullets are any use against this creature. If it's a ghost, the bullets will go straight through it."

Irons snorted. "There are no such thing as ghosts."

"But Fields said—" Castle began.

"I don't know what he saw," Irons interrupted him. "But I'm sure it wasn't a ghost. Pull yourself together. We're going into the corridor to try and find our shipmate."

"And if this light alien comes along?" Green wanted to know.

"Don't even think about shooting before I do!" Irons said in a threatening tone of voice.

Slowly, the major made his way to the door. Jeff covered him to the left. His eyes wandered over the objects on the floor. Some of them could have been from a human ship. There were cups, pens, containers, even a tool resembling a screwdriver. On the papers he recognized the wedge-like characters that had been on the walls of the ship. It looked like they had been in the middle of working when suddenly disaster struck. Jeff shook his head. What on earth had happened here?

Irons had reached the door. He looked tentatively left and right before stepping out into the corridor. Jeff followed him and took up the left flank. The lamp on his suit illuminated the open corridor.

The passageway was just as wide as the one on the other side of the gate, but so long you couldn't see the other end. At regular intervals along both sides of the walls, there were giant black pillars that met in the middle to form arches high above their heads. Maybe the corridor would take them directly to the center of the ship. Along the right wall, a single rail led from the gate into the distance. Probably, there had been some kind of transportation system here once upon a time.

"The corridor Fields went down must be over there," Castle said, pointing to an intersection nearby. "That's where he saw the light."

"Keep going," Irons said. "But nice and slow."

Step by quiet step, they made their way to the turning. Weapon drawn, Irons peered around the corner before stepping out into the corridor. Jeff followed at a distance of a few feet. There was nothing to see. The only light was from the lamps on their suits. Scraps of paper, some of which looked scorched, lay strewn on the ground.

"There," Irons whispered, pointing to an open door. That had to be the room where Fields saw the alien. The Major pressed himself against the wall beside the door and waited until the others had caught up. Then he glanced around the corner, pointed his gun, and stormed into the room.

Jeff ran into the room behind Irons and took up the left flank again. Something punched him in the back. He spun round in a panic, but it was just Owl, who had caught him by accident on the shoulder.

"Sorry," the radio operator hissed.

Jeff inched his way forward.

There were metal tables lined up against the wall and another long row of tables in the middle of the room. On some of them were pieces of equipment, but Jeff couldn't begin to guess what they were for. Scattered on the floor were containers and more scraps of paper. These were covered in writing.

Jeff picked up one of them and looked at the strange symbols in fascination. What did it say?

An alien language! Jeff swallowed and dropped the piece of paper. But there was no sign of a light alien here—or of Fields.

Irons was now on the other side of the row of tables, scanning the floor. He held his gun lightly in his hand and bit his lips. The major seemed undecided as to how to proceed.

"Where's Fields?" Finni wondered aloud.

"Not here, clearly," Irons replied and slipped past Finni into the corridor.

"And what do we do now?" Green asked. "The light alien must have taken him and dragged him away. Fields could be anywhere on the ship. We may never find him."

"We'll search the immediate area," the major said.

"Shall we split up?" Jeff asked. That way they could cover a bigger area faster.

Irons mulled it over for a moment. "No. We don't know what happened to Fields, or if there's another one of these creatures lurking around. I'd prefer if we stuck together. Captain Austin?"

"Sir?"

"Report back to HQ and check the status."

Jeff nodded. He put his pistol back in his holster and pulled out the handheld. Even from here he had pretty good reception thanks to Green's invention. He outlined the situation to Joanne and how they were planning to proceed. She had nothing new to report. Shorty and Mac were desperate to join the search, but Irons decided against it.

"We're going down the corridor," Irons said, moving on, gun at the ready. Jeff made sure to keep a distance of at least three feet. At one point, he thought he saw a glimmer of light in the distance, but it could have been a reflection from one of their headlamps.

After a few minutes, they reached a door that Irons opened by pressing the small square next to it. Jeff could only just see over Irons' shoulder. They were greeted by the same scene as everywhere else in this part of the ship: broken, charred, and melted-down furniture scattered around the room, and the floor covered in rubbish. There was no sign of Fields. They walked about half a mile down the corridor and searched more rooms, but after half an hour, Irons decided it was time to return to the gate.

Nobody said a word. Irons was tight-lipped the whole time. Jeff had never seen the major so tense before.

Finally they reached the wide corridor with the gate, and Jeff presumed they would return to the other side.

But instead, Irons announced: "Let's look around the corridor a bit more," and headed off. Jeff would have preferred to go back. Everything was so creepy here. He let the light of his headlamp glide over the vaulted ceiling high above his head. The corridor really did look like an endlessly long nave—as if the builders had modeled it on a Gothic cathedral. But a very dark cathedral, with nothing sacred about it.

"There's another door over there," Finni said, indicating a spot on the wall with his headlamp. Jeff turned around. They weren't far from the gate.

Irons opened the door, his gun still raised. He shone his flashlight around the room and then stepped inside. Jeff followed him. It wasn't a big space. Large, cabinet-like furniture lined the walls, while long benches took up most of the middle of the room. On the floor were more scraps of paper and other debris.

Jeff turned his head slowly, so that his headlamp lit up the wall. The place reminded him of a locker room. Irons pushed another door, which swung open. "Nothing in here."

Jeff edged his way along the wall. One of the doors looked a little bent and didn't seem to be properly closed. He pushed against it like Irons had done, but it was jammed. He hooked a finger around the frame and pulled, but it wouldn't budge. He pulled harder and suddenly it opened with a creaking sound. A black shadow that had obviously been leaning against the back of the door fell toward him. *Fuck!* The shadow pushed him to the ground and he felt something cold touch his face. Finni screamed. Jeff tried to push aside whatever it was that was now pinning him to the ground. Finally, he managed to free himself, but as he tried to stand up, he slipped on something wet. Finally he managed to find his balance and pointed his pistol at the thing. But the beam of Irons' headlight had turned the shadow into a human body lying prone on the ground.

The dark-gray combat suit had assumed a strange brownish-red color. The right foot protruded from the leg at an unnatural angle. The boots were missing completely. And where there should have been hair there was a strange, pulpy mass.

"Holy shit!" hissed Owl. "Is that Fields?"

"Who else would it be," Green croaked.

Irons rushed forward, grabbed the lifeless body by the shoulder and quickly flipped it on its back.

Finni turned pale and threw up on the floor.

Castle gasped.

Jeff choked and took a step back.

"What the hell …?" Irons whispered.

The body no longer bore any resemblance to Fields. It looked more like a slaughtered pig. The suit and body had been cut from the sternum to the crotch and gaped wide, as if the ribs had been stretched apart with a mechanical spreader. Jeff was no doctor, but he saw at a glance that much of what should be in a body was missing. Some organ—was it the liver?—was dangling out of the cavity. Part of the intestine had coiled itself around the right hand, on which three fingers were missing.

But worst of all was Fields' face. The eyes were gone. There were two red holes where they should have been. His mouth was open in a silent scream, revealing a toothless cavity. His hair, complete with scalp, had been ripped from his head and lay next to the body.

Jeff retched and held his hand over his nose to block out the horrific smell of flesh and blood, but it hardly helped.

He wasn't sure how long they stood around their shipmate's mutilated body, but it seemed like an eternity.

"Green," Irons barked. As usual, the major was the first one to recover his senses. "Guard the corridor," he commanded. The engineer hastily made his way outside.

Finally, Finni stepped up and covered Fields' face with a large piece of tarpaulin-like material he had found lying on the floor.

"What *happened* to him?" Owl asked. His voice had never sounded so shrill. "That light alien?"

The question was directed at Irons, but he didn't reply. Instead he dropped to his knees and reached under the tarp. "His handheld is missing," he said quietly.

"What do we do now?" Jeff asked, and immediately felt stupid for asking.

Finally, Irons turned around. He fixed his emotionless gaze on Jeff. "We go back to headquarters."

Chapter 12

"Unbelievable," Joanne whispered. She was holding Jeff's handheld and swiping through the photos of Fields' remains that Jeff had taken before returning to HQ. Now they were sitting at the table for supper, but nobody had any appetite. Jeff felt nauseous. The sight of Fields' ravaged body had been too much to take.

"I would like you to go to the gate tomorrow and see his body for yourself," Irons said. "Maybe you can find out what kind of creature did that to him."

Joanne shook her head and handed the handheld back to Jeff. "I don't really see the point. I trained as a paramedic, but I'm not a doctor. I've never performed an autopsy."

Irons looked at her in silence for a moment, then nodded. "You may be right. But what springs to mind when you see the photos?"

Joanne exhaled with a whistle. "During my training, we were shown photos of attacks by wild animals. This looks kind of similar. Maybe a sakkar from New Australia or a bear from Earth. If it was an animal, it must have been very strong, otherwise it wouldn't have been able to open up the rib cage so easily. The wounds are smooth, so I'm guessing they were sharp claws.

"Could this light alien have done it?" Castle asked.

"What kind of creature is it, anyway? What did he mean by 'light alien'?" Mac asked.

Owl grunted. "A ghost, maybe."

Irons raised his hand. "Fields said it consisted entirely of light, but of course he could have been mistaken. The creature may have had some source of radiance that just made it look like it was made of light. Maybe it was some kind of shield or cloaking device."

Jeff shook his head. "It wasn't a cloaking device, that's for sure. It was *because* of the light that Fields became aware of the creature in the first place."

Irons nodded. "You're right. But it could have been a protective shield. "What do you think, Green?"

The engineer was sitting at the far end of the corner, pale and apathetic. His eyes were glazed. He appeared not to have heard the major's question. Castle slapped him on the shoulder.

Green's eyes focused again. "What?" he asked.

"Could the creature's light have been some kind of shield to protect it against our weapons?" Castle repeated the major's question.

Green's gaze wandered unsteadily back and forth between Castle and Irons, then suddenly he nodded. "That sounds logical. But we have to stay as far away as possible from these creatures."

Irons sighed. "What is it, Green? You don't look well. Are you still fighting that infection?"

The engineer really did look ill, Jeff thought, although in the morning he'd seemed to be recovering. Probably the shock of the day's events had caused a relapse.

"I don't feel well."

"Then go to bed," Irons said. "Get plenty of rest."

Green nodded and disappeared to his room without another word.

"What do we do now?" Joanne asked.

Jeff had heard this question being asked more than a few times over the last few hours. But so far, Irons hadn't been able to provide an answer.

Now he sighed. "I have to confess I don't really know what to make of this situation. First, I'd like to speak to the computer."

"Hmm, I'm not sure it's going to like hearing that we bypassed the closed gate and got to the other side," Castle said.

Irons gave him a stern look. "It said we could move around the ship freely. And that's what we did."

"Should we keep exploring the other side?" Joanne asked. Her tone suggested she wasn't keen on the idea.

"We'll decide that after we've talked to the computer," Irons said. "There are certainly plenty of clues about the builders of this ship over on that side. It's probably the only place we'll find anything out."

"You're not serious," Finni raised his eyebrows. "The critter that *killed Fields* live there. We have no idea what kind of monster we're dealing with."

"One more reason to kick ass," Mac retorted. "We'll root out that creature and kill it!"

"I'd like to point something out," Castle began. "We don't actually have many weapons. We have some pistols, a heap of spare magazines, and a few plastic explosives. That's not exactly an arsenal to take on a pack of wild animals."

"A pack of wild animals?" Joanne looked skeptical. "If

they have a protective shield, we're hardly dealing with any kind of animal."

"Or whatever …" Mac said gruffly.

A lengthy discussion ensued. It wasn't the first one that afternoon. Jeff was surprised Irons didn't put a stop to them before they became too heated.

But maybe it was good for the crew members to get the shock out of their systems. Maybe Irons wanted to hear their thoughts. Jeff's mind was whirring. "There's one thing I don't understand: if this creature has some kind of advanced technology at its disposal—some kind of light system or even a light shield—why did it rip Field's body apart with its claws?"

"Maybe it wasn't carrying a weapon," Owl speculated.

"Maybe some of the ship's builders are still on board," Joanne suggested.

"Yeah, right" Castle's voice was dripping with sarcasm. "You reckon they've been hanging around for millions of years?"

"Maybe they're descendants of some of the builders who didn't leave the ship for whatever reason. They could have degenerated over thousands of generations."

A crackling sound announced the presence of the computer. The conversation came to an abrupt end and Jeff found himself, illogically, looking up at the ceiling.

"Hello," said the voice. "I hope you are well?"

Jeff and the others looked at the major.

He took a deep breath. "Today we found a way to the other side of the gate."

"Indeed?" Jeff blinked. Had he detected a hint of sarcasm in the computer's voice? No, he must have been mistaken.

"Through an air vent that we discovered by accident,"

the major continued. "And on the other side, one of our men was killed."

The computer did not answer.

"By a creature that seems to emit light. Does that sound familiar?"

"No," the voice answered immediately. "As I said, I have no access to that part of the ship. It is completely cut off from my systems."

"You are not aware of any living beings on board your ship?"

"No, my sensors have not observed anything of that kind. At least not in the areas over which I have control."

"How many areas *are* under your control?" Irons asked. The major couldn't suppress the cross undertone in his voice.

"About thirty percent of the volume of the ship."

Jeff caught his breath.

Thirty percent?

Irons raised his eyebrows. "That's not very much," he said dryly. "And are these areas evenly distributed throughout the ship?"

"No, I still control the core area and a few sectors in the outer shell, including the one in which you now reside."

"When did you lose the area that is on the other side of the gate?"

"About twenty million years ago."

"And was there a reason?"

What was the major getting at?

"A malfunction in the redundant node."

"And it couldn't be repaired?"

"No. Automatic repair of the area already failed on a previous occasion."

"Couldn't you use a repair mechanism from one of the other areas?"

"No. The different areas are designed for maximum autonomy."

"Why?"

"That is the way the ship's designers built it."

Irons sighed. If he had been hoping for a particular answer, he obviously hadn't got it.

"Where are your systems?"

"What do you mean?"

"Well, yours. The onboard computer."

"Oh." The computer sounded almost amused. "The neural network is decentralized, but the nodal point is in the core area."

"What … and where … is the core area?"

"It is an area with a diameter of sixty miles in the center of the ship. It is where the control systems are located."

"I presume it used to be the crew's headquarters?"

"That is correct."

"And we are located in … in …"

"The outer shell," Jeff helped out.

"Yes, the outer shell," Irons repeated.

"That is correct."

"What is the outer shell?"

"The outer shell is a twelve-mile-thick area containing technical and mechanical systems, and storerooms."

"Are there other subsections of the ship?"

"Between the outer shell and the core is a middle layer."

"And what does that contain?"

"That area was the habitat of the former builders during their journey. There are many large cavitys with artificial atmospheres that simulate the conditions of their home planet."

cavitys? So far they had assumed the ship looked the

same everywhere—in other words, corridors and empty rooms. Or was it referring to the empty rooms?

The major must have had the same thought. "You did not tell us anything about this before."

"I did not think it was important. Besides, those areas are not accessible."

"As I said, we found a way to the next layer."

"Yes, you said that."

"Would it bother you if we had another look around there?"

The computer paused for an unusually long time. Jeff lifted his head again.

"No, but I would not recommend it."

"Why not?"

"I do not control that area and therefore I could not protect you."

"Protect us?" the major asked. "What do you need to protect us from?"

Another long pause. "From possible dangers."

"What kind of dangers?" the major probed.

"Unfortunately, I cannot say because I do not control the area," the computer voice sounded a little offended but the major did not let up.

"But if you mention danger, you must have something in mind."

There was another long pause.

"I would like to inform you that today we made another hyperjump and are therefore a little nearer to your destination."

That was good news, of course, but Jeff was sure the computer was deliberately avoiding the issue they wanted to discuss.

The major must have been thinking the same. "I'm

glad. But I would like to ask again about the danger you mentioned. You said that—"

"I'm sorry, I have to interrupt you. I have noticed a malfunction that I need to attend to immediately."

Once again, the crackling sound that seemed to emanate from invisible speakers filled the room.

"What a pile of crap …" Mac whispered.

"I have to admit, I'm worried," Irons said quietly.

Chapter 13

"We've made it to the other side. Any other instructions?" It was hard to hear Joanne's voice through all the static. Jeff wasn't sure why the reception was worse today than yesterday.

He reached for the handheld, but Irons was quicker. "Please take another look at Fields. Maybe you'll notice something else that wasn't visible on the photos."

"Shouldn't we recover the body and bring it back to HQ?" Joanne asked.

The major shook his head. "That would be pointless. We don't have anywhere to bury him. Lay him straight and cover his body, and feel free to read out the 'Prayer for the Fallen Soldier' which you'll find in the manual on the handheld." He sighed. "Then explore the surrounding area as we discussed. Don't take any unnecessary risks. If you encounter one of the creatures, take cover and call for reinforcements, is that clear?"

"Understood, Sir!"

"Don't go too far from the gate. Maximum two thousand feet, got that?"

"Yes, Sir!"

"And report back regularly. Good luck, over and out."

Irons leaned back in his chair. He and Jeff were alone. They had spent the whole day going over and over the options, but Irons felt they had to keep exploring. If they wanted to find out anything about the builders of this ship, they had to go to the other side of the gate. They'd increased every reconnaissance squad to four crew members, who were not to separate on any account. Jeff hoped it was a big enough group. What if they really did encounter one of those aliens again?

"Let's hope for the best," the major murmured.

Jeff gave his superior a sidelong glance. Irons had been in a strange mood all morning. He seemed distracted and absent-minded. There was nothing of the usual determination in his voice. He had even toyed out loud with the idea of cancelling today's recon. Fields' death must have hit him hard. And yet over the years, Irons must have lost many men and women in combat.

"Everything OK, Sir?" Jeff asked hesitantly. It was the first time he had asked his superior how he felt.

Irons turned to look at him and smiled weakly. "I'm fine, Captain." He was clearly lying through his teeth, and it sounded more like a polite request to stop asking dumb questions.

Jeff nodded and fixed his gaze on the handheld on the table in front of him.

Castle entered the room. His black hair stuck out in all directions. He had taken over the last night watch; Jeff hadn't expected to see him up and about yet. Shorty, who had taken the first night shift, was still asleep.

"Any news?" the WSO asked, as he shuffled over to the kitchen counter. He opened one of the cupboards and took out the can of instant coffee powder.

"They made it to the other side and have started looking around," Jeff said.

"I don't like this," Castle said.

Jeff focused on the handheld again, as if it would enable him to communicate by telepathy with his ship-mates deeper down in the ship. The waiting was unbearable. What if they suddenly lost contact? Their four shipmates might already be dead, and they would never know what happened.

"Do you think there's a chance one of those light aliens might turn up here?" Castle asked. He had joined them at the table with a cup of coffee.

"That's precisely why you took over the watch tonight, Lieutenant Castle," Irons replied dryly.

"I get that we need to be careful. But do you *really* think one of those creatures would turn up here?"

"We don't even know if they're animals," Jeff said, picturing the glowing creature to himself.

"Maybe they're just animals without any kind of advanced technology. There were animals that glowed in the dark back on Earth, too. Maybe they're six-feet-tall hybrids—half vampire, half firefly."

"We have no idea what we're dealing with," Irons said. "At the end of the day, it's all just speculation."

"Hopefully they don't bump into any of those things down there," Castle murmured.

"I hope they do!" Irons reported. "We need to find out what we're dealing with here."

"There are four of them. They should be able to take care of themselves," Jeff added. But he didn't feel too confident.

"Not if they meet a whole herd."

"Enough of your conjecturing," Irons interrupted him sharply.

"But if—" Castle began, but fell silent as a noise came from the handheld.

Jeff hit the talk button. "We didn't understand you, Joanne. Please repeat."

It took a moment before they heard her voice again, this time more clearly. "We're about nine hundred feet from the gate, in a side passage going off from the big tunnel. We're in a room that looks like it used to be some kind of technical facility. There's lots of equipment on one side of the room. Looks a bit like a small cinema or a lecture room. We've decided to take a closer look."

Jeff glanced at Irons. He nodded.

"OK, do that. Have you noticed anything else?"

"No. Owl thought he heard a scream somewhere down the big corridor, but the rest of us didn't hear or see anything."

"All right, but be careful."

"Of course. Over."

And so the unbearable waiting continued. Tomorrow it was Jeff's turn to go to the other side of the gate. His hope of finding some evidence of the alien culture had given way to fear and panic. Fear of the area beyond the gate. And to think that a few days ago, he'd been scared just exploring the empty corridors near their base!

"How many days have we been on this ship?" Castle asked. He could have easily checked on his handheld, but he probably wanted to make conversation.

Jeff was also desperate for any distraction. "Twenty-one days."

"That means another twenty-six weeks to Sigma-7," Castle said. He groaned. "I don't know how I'm going to last."

"You don't have much choice, Lieutenant," Irons joined the conversation.

"In the beginning I found it kind of oppressive—all these dark corridors and everything. But now I'm actually frightened."

Jeff nodded. He felt the same.

"We're all going to die here," Castle whispered suddenly.

Jeff and Irons swung round at the same time to look at him. The usually intrepid WSO was sitting at the table, coffee cup in hand, staring straight through them. His head was swaying slightly, as if he were in a trance.

"What makes you say that?" Irons asked sharply.

Castle's gaze came back into focus and he looked at Irons and then Jeff. His face was completely devoid of emotion. Finally he shrugged. "Just a feeling," he answered.

The major took a deep breath. "Lieutenant Castle. I don't want to hear you say anything like that again, do you understand?"

A few seconds passed, then Castle nodded slowly.

"Pull yourself together," Irons said. "You're an officer in the Imperial space fleet. Behave accordingly."

"Yes, sir," Castle said quietly, then took a sip of his coffee as if nothing had happened.

Irons shook his head and turned away from Castle. He sighed deeply. Jeff and his superior sat side by side in silence, staring at the handheld.

It took quite a while before Joanne checked in again.

"Rutherford here." Jeff started out of his gloomy reverie and almost knocked the device off the table in his eagerness to grab it.

"Speak," he ordered curtly, and wiped his sweaty hands on his trousers before leaning forward again.

"We've found something," she said. Her excitement was clearly audible even through the rustling noise.

Irons was suddenly fully alert. Castle pushed back his chair with a loud scraping sound and rushed over to the command table.

"What have you found?" Jeff asked.

"It really is a projection room. We played around with the switches, and suddenly there was a three-dimensional hologram in the middle of the room!"

Irons grabbed the handheld from Jeff. "Irons here. Nice and slowly, Lieutenant Rutherford. We're having trouble hearing you. What kind of hologram was it?"

"A map, Sir."

"What kind of map? Of the ship?"

"No, stars. It's a star chart. A blue dot in the center probably shows the position of the ship and the surrounding stars. You can change the scale and zoom in and out."

Jeff and Irons exchanged brief glances. Now maybe they *would* find out if they were safely en route back home.

"And where are we? Are we where we're supposed to be?" Irons asked.

"That's hard to say. I need to take pictures and compare them with the data on my handheld. I can do that once I'm back at HQ."

Irons nodded. "All right, Lieutenant. Take all the time you need in the map room."

"Shall we continue exploring after that?"

Irons hesitated a moment. "No. Knowing our position is more important. Once you have everything you need, come straight back to HQ. And don't play around with the switches too much. I don't want something to be set in motion that we might regret later. Tomorrow I'll go look at the room myself."

"Understood, Sir. Over."

Irons leaned back in his chair and whistled.

"A map room," Castle said. "Crazy that the projection still works after such a long time."

"What do you think, Sir?" Jeff asked.

"I don't know. I would have thought a room like that would be in the center of the ship near the command center," he replied, scratching his head.

"Maybe the aliens constructed the ship with decentralized controls. I mean, so that you can control the ship from any area. Or it isn't a map room in the traditional sense, but some kind of scientific facility. An astronomy center. Or some kind of planetarium for the crew."

Irons nodded. "All just wild guesses. The important thing is, we have a chance to find out where we actually are."

"Why didn't the computer tell us any of this?" Jeff wondered out loud. "It said the whole ship was the same and consisted of nothing but corridors. It could have at least mentioned that there were other beings on board, even if it didn't know exactly what was in the other areas."

"Maybe it didn't expect us to go so far from our base and find the gate," Castle said.

"Shall we ask it about the map room?" Jeff asked.

"It depends on what Rutherford finds out about our position," Irons answered and stood up. "I'm going to lie down for a while. I'm exhausted. Make sure they head back soon."

Chapter 14

Jeff swung round when he heard a knock at the door. But Mac was quicker and raced to the door, tore it open, and stormed out into the corridor. He looked in every direction, then shrugged and pushed the kitchen cart with their dinner into the room. "I'd love to know how that computer does it," Mac said, parking the cart next to the big dining table.

Jeff guessed it was robots. Why do they disappear so quickly, as if they had something to hide? Jeff stole a glance at his superior, who was sitting at the table next to him. Irons looked awful. His cheeks were sunken, his eyes glazed. Something must have happened to him in the last few hours.

"I don't get it," Shorty said, grabbing his plate and lifting the lid off the pot. "Even if they have robots that bring us the food, we ought to be able to see them."

"Maybe they beam the food to our door," Green suggested.

"Tomorrow evening I'm going to hang around the corridor and see what happens," Shorty said.

"Watch out, you might end up in the pot!" Mac laughed.

There was a bang. It was Joanne thumping her fist on the command table. In front of her were two handhelds, a piece a paper and a pen, which now rolled across the table. "Can't you jack-asses keep your mouths shut for just one minute? I need to concentrate if I'm going to convert the coordinates accurately."

"Can't you automate it?" Irons asked. He was sitting in front of his empty plate and showed no sign of wanting to eat anything.

"No," Joanne said. "All I have is the pictures of the projection of the star map. I need to make an estimate, as best I can, there's no other way. And then I need to do a coordinate transformation, because the axes don't match up with the ones we use. So zip it, boys."

"I thought women were supposed to be good at multi-tasking," Shorty grinned.

"Pah! Most of the women I know can't even manage a decent sixty-nine," Mac gave a dirty laugh, and Shorty joined in.

Jeff could feel Irons' gaze on him. He had to react, otherwise he'd get an earful later on. Jeff stood up. "Private Short, Private Mac! That's enough. All right?" He shuddered at the way he sounded as if he were begging.

Mac grinned and opened his mouth to say something. Then he remembered that Irons was in the room. He glanced quickly to his left and shut his mouth again. "Of course, Sir." He practically spat out the word "Sir."

Shorty turned to his colleague and whispered something in his ear. Both of them looked first at Joanne, then at Jeff, and started laughing.

"Private Short, Private Mac," Irons said. "Final warning." Irons' voice sounded weak and feeble, it seemed to come from a completely different person than the usually energetic and charismatic major.

"Aren't you hungry, Major?" Finni asked.

As if in slow motion, Irons raised his head and stared at Finni. Finally he nodded, got up, and helped himself from the pot.

Jeff looked over at Joanne. Her brow was furrowed as she concentrated in turn on the two handhelds and wrote down numbers on the piece of paper. "Joanne, come and eat," he said firmly.

She waved her hand without raising her eyes. "I want to get this finished. I'm nearly done. A few more minutes."

"And tomorrow we're going back to the map room?" Owl asked.

"Yes," the major said. "I want to take a closer look at that projector. Maybe it can show us other things apart from the star map."

"Like what?" Jeff asked.

The major briefly raised his eyes, then turned listlessly back to his stew. "I don't want to speculate. Let's wait and see."

If there were chairs in the room, maybe it used to be a lecture room. Or a library for accessing the ship's databases. Maybe they would find information about the alien builders of the ship …. It would be incredible if they could somehow connect the database to their handhelds and make copies to analyze when they got home. "I want to join the expedition tomorrow," Jeff said, though he already knew he'd be terrified the moment he got to the other side of the gate.

"All right," Irons answered, without looking up.

"Major?" Joanne's voice was barely more than a whisper. Jeff looked over at his colleague, his spoon suspended midway between his plate and his mouth. Her face was ashen. Jeff knew immediately what had happened.

The coordinates! We're not on the way back home!

"What is it?" Everyone was staring at Joanne.

"We're not headed toward Sigma-7," she said. "We've moved four light years from our original position, but not in the direction the computer told us."

"Holy shit …" Owl said.

"That bastard of a computer lied to us," Castle spat out his words.

"What do we do now?" Shorty asked.

Jeff closed his eyes. It was what he had feared most— and it was really happening. They were at the mercy of an alien spaceship and its onboard computer, which in the beginning had been so hospitable and accommodating. They had trusted it. No! They'd had no choice but to trust it, there had been no alternative. It had lied to them. But why?

Or was it a misunderstanding? Had the artificial intelligence misinterpreted the coordinates given to it by Joanne and flown in a different direction? But the computer had confirmed they were heading for the Sigma system.

"How far is the ship's trajectory from what we originally specified?" Irons asked.

"Thirty degrees," Joanne replied.

"That's too far off to explain as a necessary course correction. Where is our present course taking us?"

Joanne picked up the handheld from the table and swiped and tapped on the screen. "Deeper into the core area of the Empire. Hang on …" She picked up the other handheld and typed something into it. "Oh …." She opened her eyes wide. "If I extend the course, then we're heading straight for Earth!"

What the hell …?

That couldn't be a coincidence. What did the ship want on Earth? Jeff couldn't see the sense in it. Did the ship's computer want to deliver them to the central planet of the Empire to enter into diplomatic relations? But that didn't tally with what the AI had told them.

"This is crazy," Owl murmured.

Irons stood up. "Computer," he said loudly. His tone of voice was unusually aggressive.

No answer.

"Computer! Answer me!"

"Obviously busy again," Green said dryly.

"I can't wait to hear what it has to say," Owl said.

"That son-of-a-bitch computer has been lying to us the whole time!" Castle screamed hysterically. "That's why it didn't want us to go outside!"

"The billion-dollar question is: where *does* it want to take us?" Owl drummed his fingers on the table.

"Are you dumb or stupid?" Castle snapped. "You just heard! We're heading toward Earth."

"But why?" Joanne asked. She was rooted to the spot in the middle of the room, still clutching the handheld.

"Maybe it wants to blackmail the Emperor and take us hostage," said Shorty.

"Stop these ridiculous guessing games!" Irons ordered.

"Why ridiculous …?" Shorty asked before falling silent.

"And what do we do now?" Joanne wanted to know.

Irons stood up. "I have to think. I'm going to my room and will make a decision by tomorrow morning. If the computer contacts us, please get me immediately. I don't want anyone to talk to it except me. Nobody! Understood?" He fixed everyone in turn with an icy stare. After nobody responded, he turned to Jeff. "Captain Austin, please follow me to my room."

Jeff nodded and stood up. His plate was still almost full,

but he knew he wouldn't manage any more food today. He walked around the table and followed Irons out of the room. His thoughts were racing. What was happening on this ship? Did Irons have a theory?

When they got to his room, the major closed the door behind him and pointed at one of the two chairs by the table against the far wall. Jeff took a seat. The major sat down opposite him.

Jeff cleared his throat. "Major, why do you think—"

"Stop!" Irons' voice was stern. "I have not asked you here to make more conjectures. I need to think about the situation alone first. Tomorrow we can talk about it."

Jeff nodded. "But why did you want to talk to me?"

Irons reached down to his belt and pulled out his hand-held. "You remember the red button on the back of this device?"

"The self-destruct button. Yes."

"On this device are the transponder codes that enable us to fly into the systems of the core worlds without being attacked. But if we're captured, it's my duty too destroy the memory chip."

Why was Irons talking about being captured? He'd never talked like this before. He seemed to be fundamentally reassessing the situation they were in. Jeff swallowed. Captured … yes, they really were prisoners on this ship, and nobody knew what the computer was up to. "Then destroy the chip," Jeff said.

Irons cradled the handheld in his right hand. "Something tells me we're still going to need these codes. In fact, our lives might depend on them."

Jeff got goose bumps. "What makes you say that, Sir?"

The major shrugged. "To be honest, I don't know. It's just a hunch. Call it intuition."

Jeff raised his eyebrows. It was unusual for Irons to be guided by a hunch. "Why are you telling me this?"

"Because I have another hunch. A premonition, if you like."

Hunches? And now premonitions? "What do you mean, Sir?" Jeff asked in confusion.

Instead of answering, the major grabbed Jeff's hand and pressed his forefinger on the display of the handheld.

"Major, I …"

It beeped once, and Irons released Jeff's hand. "Now the device knows your fingerprint. You are authorized to use it, if necessary. If somebody else tries to activate it, it will self-destruct."

"I don't understand …" Jeff fell silent and sagged in on himself.

"I'm convinced Fields won't be the only one to die on this ship," the major said.

Earlier, Irons had reprimanded Castle for having the exact same thought. What was up with the major? "Is everything OK, Major Irons?"

Irons sighed and raised his hand. "Everything's fine, Austin. Don't worry. My only concern is that you have access to my handheld in case anything happens to me. If you find a way of escaping, you'll need the codes as soon as you enter the central system. Otherwise you'll be shot down without warning. But if you don't escape, you *must* destroy the chip before this ship enters Earth's solar system, so that the space fleet can fend it off in time. Is that clear?"

Jeff shook his head in a daze. Was it really that bad? Was it possible this ship wanted to attack Earth? Yesterday, they had been the guests of a helpful extraterrestrial onboard computer, and suddenly they were prisoners of a possibly malevolent artificial intelligence? Hopefully it was all a big misunderstanding.

"Have I made myself clear, Captain Austin?" the major repeated.

Jeff nodded.

"The security of Earth comes first. Destroy the chip if you feel threatened!"

Jeff nodded again.

"Good," Irons said. "And now please leave me alone. I need to think."

Jeff got up and staggered outside. Like in a bad dream, he had the feeling that the ground was moving beneath his feet. The walls of the corridor seemed to be closing in on him.

Jeff staggered back to his own room and collapsed on his bed. He doubted he would have a very restful night.

Chapter 15

"Man, you look like shit," Mac said as Jeff walked into the rec room the next day. Castle was sitting next to Mac and grinned. Joanne frowned. Jeff didn't consider reprimanding the mechanic. He was too tired, and in any case, Mac was probably right. He went straight to the kitchen, where he made himself a coffee with hot water and instant granules, before sitting down at the table with the others. Apart from the major, everyone was up and about.

Jeff grabbed a slice of bread and slapped some peanut butter on it. He took a bite and chewed slowly.

"Who had the last shift?" Joanne asked.

Finni raised his hand, without looking up.

"Did the computer contact us?"

"Nope," Finni replied.

"Boy, we're gonna give him an earful," Shorty said.

"Pfft," said Mac. "It won't give a rat's ass what we have to say."

"I want to know why it lied to us like that," Shorty said.

"And what makes you think it's going to tell you the truth? All it does is lie."

"It's time we took things into our own hands," Castle said.

Joanne rolled her eyes. "And how do you suggest we do that?"

"We confront it with the facts, and order it to take us to Sigma-7."

Joanne laughed. "*Order* it? How do we do that?" Castle stuttered, searching for words, but Joanne continued. "We're in no position to give orders."

"We could go to the airlock and use the plastic explosives to create a hole to the outside," Owl suggested.

"Great," Mac said sarcastically. "And then?"

"Then at least we're out of this prison."

"We should wait and see what Major Irons has to say. I reckon he's made a decision," Jeff said, but nobody took any notice of him.

Finni laughed in Owl's face. "Sure—let's break our way out and we can have fun floating around in the interstellar void. *Jesus.* We might as well shoot ourselves now."

"I just want to get out of here," Owl said in a whiny tone of voice.

"What do *you* think we should do?" Joanne asked Green, who was sitting opposite her at the table. The engineer was no longer as pale as the day before, but he hadn't joined in the conversation at all so far. He was sitting and staring at the ceiling, as if all of this had nothing to do with him.

"Dave!" Joanne repeated.

Finally, Green lowered his gaze and fixed his eyes on Joanne. He shrugged. "No idea. Maybe we should go to the center of the ship. Maybe we'll find some answers to our questions there. After all, it's where the control center is supposed to be."

"Are you mad?" Owl cried. "I want to get out of this

thing, and not go deeper inside it. Who knows what might be waiting for us there."

"Calm down!" Joanne ordered in a loud voice.

But Owl wouldn't calm down. "This ghost ship is cursed! We need to get out of here, or it'll steal our souls!"

Joanne guffawed. "Woah, did you have a bad dream or something? Jeff, what do you think?"

Now all eyes were on him. He sighed. "Major Irons will decide what to do. I'm sure he'll let us know what he decided as soon as he gets up."

Castle looked at his watch. "It's not like the major to sleep this long. Was he on guard duty?"

Jeff shook his head and looked at his own watch. It was already nine o'clock. True; Irons had never slept this late.

"Maybe he's thinking things through," Joanne said.

Jeff was suddenly overcome by a strange feeling as he remembered the almost surreal conversation he'd had with the major the night before. Irons had been so despondent, depressed almost. Surely he hadn't done anything stupid?

Jeff got up. "I'll go and see if he's up already."

"Majors need to sleep late sometimes, too!" Mac said. He wanted it to sound like a joke, but nobody laughed.

Jeff went into the back corridor and put an ear to the major's door. There was no sound. Maybe he really was still asleep. "Major? Are you awake?"

Jeff listened again. No answer. He knocked again. "Major?" He must have heard him this time. Still no answer.

Jeff felt his stomach clench. His hands were trembling. He tapped on the square on the wall next to the door.

From the corner of his eye, he saw the major lying in bed. He sighed with relief. So he was still sleeping. Everything was OK. He was about to close the door again, when the foul smell of blood and dead flesh leapt into his nostrils. He opened the door wider and took a step into the room.

Blood! Blood everywhere!

Jeff let out a twisted scream.

Within seconds, the others had arrived and jostled him further into the room as they tried to get a look for themselves.

The major—or what was left of him—was lying in a red pool on the bed. Blood was dripping onto the floor—there was too much for all of it to be absorbed by the sheets. As Jeff approached the bed, his shoes made a squelching noise in the sticky liquid. He looked at the major and retched.

It was even worse than Fields. A huge wound stretched from his chest, across his stomach, and down to his crotch. Because of all the blood, Jeff couldn't see the organs. He looked into the major's face. His eye patch was missing, revealing the deep cavity of the socket. The other eye was dangling onto his cheek from a twisted thread. His mouth was ripped wide open, as if he were screaming in pain even in death. Jeff tried to look away, but then he noticed that Irons' head was no longer connected to his neck, but lying severed on the pillow.

Shorty pushed his way out of the room, vomiting.

"Oh my God," Joanne whispered. She shoved Finni aside so she could examine the major's body.

"Was it …" Owl began and choked. "Was it an animal?"

Joanne ran her fingers very gently over the bottom of the severed head. "If it was an animal, it must have had damned sharp claws."

Jeff had to force himself not to look away. In any case, it must have all happened very fast, because the major's pistol was untouched in his holster. "He didn't even defend himself." They'd been so nearby in their rooms, and hadn't heard a thing.

Joanne nodded, lifting the major's hands one at a time. "The fingernails are clean. He must have been taken by surprise while he was sleeping. Here, this was lying next to his hand."

Jeff took the piece of paper and turned it over. It was a photo of a little boy lying in the grass and laughing at the camera. It must be Jack—Irons' son. Jeff put the picture back on the bed and shook his head. "I can't imagine he was sleeping when it happened." But something must have taken him by surprise, otherwise he would have tried to defend himself. And suddenly Jeff realized that his own room was right next door. It could have been *him* lying on his bed like this. Jeff remembered his bizarre conversation with the major the night before. Had the major really had some kind of premonition of what was going to happen to him? But how was that possible? And how had the … animal? … got into the room?

"Who was on guard duty last night?" Jeff asked.

"I had the first shift, then Green and Finni," Joanne answered.

"You didn't fall asleep?"

"No—at least, I didn't," Green said. Joanne and Finni shook their heads, too.

"Did you notice anything? Anything at all? Strange noises, maybe?"

All three shook their heads.

"What a fucking nightmare," Owl whispered. "Either we're dealing with some invisible being, or an animal that can walk through walls."

"The light alien!" Castle said. "It must have followed us from the other side of the gate."

Jeff walked around the bed, careful not to step into the

puddle of blood again. He glanced into the bathroom, but didn't notice anything out of the ordinary. Although … part of the wall was slightly dented. He went in and kicked gently at the spot. With a clatter, the piece of wall fell to the ground. Not a wall, a cover. Horrified, Jeff saw a hole that was big enough for a man to crawl through.

"You're kidding me," said Finni, who had come up behind him. "That's like the shaft down by the gate."

"Get a flashlight," Jeff ordered the radar technician.

"At least now we know how the … thing … got in here," said Owl. "There's probably a ventilation shaft like that in every cabin. Fuck! This is a fucking nightmare!" His voice became shrill.

"We're not safe here," Green said, echoing what Jeff was thinking.

"Here …" Finni handed Jeff a flashlight. Jeff dropped to his knees and shone it into the shaft. There was a right turn just beyond the opening. Jeff hesitated a moment. What if one of those things was hiding behind the corner? It was no use. Sending someone else in there would make him look like a coward. He drew his pistol, crawled inside, and shone the flashlight down the tunnel. A few feet further on it forked to the left and right. Jeff had seen enough and backed out of the shaft. "The whole ship is probably riddled with these ventilation shafts," he said after straightening up. He put the gun back in his holster. "Whatever it was must have sneaked in unnoticed and taken the major by surprise."

"At least now we know that these light aliens aren't ghosts," Joanne said.

"How do you know that?" Owl asked.

"If they could walk through walls, they wouldn't have needed the ventilation shaft," Joanne replied impatiently.

Jeff took another sheet from the pile of spare

bedclothes neatly folded on a shelf, shook it open and spread it over the major's corpse.

"What do we do now?" Castle asked after they had left the major's room and returned to the rec room.

Jeff went to the kitchen, took a glass off the shelf, and filled it with water. He felt sick and wasn't sure if he could stop himself from throwing up. He knew the answer to Castle's question, but was afraid to say it out loud.

"Captain Austin will decide," Joanne replied on his behalf. "He has the highest rank now."

Jeff sipped his water, but felt barely any better. He turned around and gazed around the faces of his ship-mates, who were all staring at him expectantly.

"We're dead meat!" Mac said.

"Wouldn't it be better if someone else took command?" Castle asked Joanne. "You or me?"

Joanne gave him a withering look.

Owl whispered something to Finni, who shook his head and looked at Jeff in disgust.

"I'm not taking orders from *him*," Mac said to Shorty, not even bothering to lower his voice.

Jeff swallowed. Perhaps it would be best to hand over command to Castle. Or to Joanne, who was a good at thinking logically, and usually came up with better ideas than he did. But then he remembered his conversation with Irons. The major had trusted him. He would have had Jeff transferred, if he was dissatisfied with his work. What had Irons said?

Your problem, Captain Austin, is your unwillingness to lead.

No, it was his job. It was what Irons had wanted. There was no way he would hand over command to Castle, with his big mouth, or to Green, with his awkward manner. But what about Joanne? She was clever, logical, and decisive—but she'd never shown any interest in taking on a leadership role. And Jeff wasn't sure if she would be able to stand up to Shorty and Mac. No, he couldn't put the burden of responsibility on her. *He* was in charge.

Jeff pulled himself up straight. "I hereby take over command."

Mac groaned. "It'll never work. He doesn't have what it takes."

Jeff knew he couldn't let him get away with talking about him like that. Not anymore. The situation had changed. Irons was gone. Someone on this ship was trying to kill them. They had to pull together as a group. If he didn't enforce his authority now, they didn't stand a chance.

Jeff took a deep breath. "Private McGuinness, I will no longer tolerate your continued insubordination," he said with all the authority he could muster. "You will obey my orders, unconditionally."

Mac stared at him open-mouthed. Joanne blinked in surprise. Jeff wasn't sure if he'd hit the right tone.

Now Mac narrowed his eyes, approached Jeff, and looked down at him condescendingly. "You are not a commander. I only obeyed your orders because Irons was there, and he is no longer around. I'm not listening to your orders."

How should Jeff react? Should he put him under arrest as a deterrent? Would the others support him? What would Irons have done in this situation?

Jeff didn't budge an inch. He had to show Mac, once and for all that he was in charge, and he needed to be sure he had the support of the other officers. There only was one way to find out.

"Private McGuinness, you're under arrest. Lieutenant Castle, Corporal Herrmannsson, please disarm the Private and take him to his sleeping quarters." It was a game. And Jeff didn't have the slightest idea how it would end.

Mac's eyes widened as if he could not believe what he had just heard.

Finally, Castle stepped forward and pulled the pistol out of Mac's belt holster. Finni grabbed the burly man's arm. "All right. Come on."

"You can't do this," Mac stammered.

Joanne opened the door to the corridor. Not even Shorty made a move to support his buddy. Jeff sighed with relief. He had won the game. Or at least this move.

"You can't lock me up. That monster! What if the creature comes and gets me?" Panic had crept into his voice.

"Stop!" Jeff said.

Finni and Castle stopped, and Mac twisted in their grip to look round.

"Private McGuinness. Are you ready to follow my orders?"

Mac stared at him in silence and pressed his lips together. Finally, he nodded. "Yes," he said, barely audibly.

"Excuse me?" Jeff asked.

"Yes, Sir." Mac almost choked on his own words.

"I don't want to hear any more dumb jokes from you. Or I really will put you under arrest. Have I made myself clear?"

A long pause. "Yes, Sir."

Jeff nodded. "Good. Let Private McGuinness go."

Finni and Castle took a step back almost simultaneously.

"My weapon?" Mac asked, almost timidly.

Jeff didn't want to give it back to him. He didn't believe Mac would shoot him from behind, but he needed to teach him a lesson.

"You need to earn it back, Private."

Gradually, Jeff felt himself relax. Since he had been in the space fleet, this was his first real confrontation with a subordinate. It was a test he should have passed much earlier.

"What now?" Owl asked. Then he looked at Jeff. "Sir?" he added.

That was a question Jeff couldn't answer. "I have to think about if first." Then he remembered something. Something very important. He turned around and went back into the corridor to the sleeping quarters.

"Where are you going?" Joanne asked.

"I need to go back to the major. All of you: collect your belongings and bring them to the rec room. From now on, nobody sleeps alone. Later we'll talk about what we're going to do."

He didn't wait for an answer, but opened the door to the major's room, stepped inside, and closed the door behind him. He retched violently as the repulsive smell of flesh and blood rose into his nostrils. He stepped to the end of the bed and pulled up the sheet to the major's waist. He removed the major's pistol from his holster. The butt was smeared with blood. Then he reached into the belt pouch to take out the major's handheld. It was empty.

Had the intruder taken it? Or had the major hidden it somewhere else? There weren't many places to hide something in these rooms. Jeff bent down and shone his flashlight under the bed. Nothing there. Jeff moved tables and chairs aside, but there was nothing behind them, either. That left only the bathroom. Jeff opened the cupboards. Empty. The toilet didn't have a cistern where you could have hidden anything. Jeff couldn't avoid looking at his reflection in the mirror above the basin. He got a shock when he saw the deep rings under his eyes.

He turned on the tap and waited for the water to get

hot. He scooped a few handfuls of water and splashed his face until his cheeks became flushed. He still looked like shit. And now what?

Hot steam rose up, as more and more water gathered in the basin and condensed on the mirror, until Jeff could no longer see his face. But now he saw fingerprints on the edge of the glass. They must be the major's.

But what had the major been doing with the mirror? A glimmer of hope rose up in Jeff and he tugged at the glass. It was attached to a rail that Jeff could push to the side. Behind it was a small niche ... and in the niche was the major's handheld.

Jeff took it out, turned off the water, and put the mirror back in position. As he weighed the device in his hand, he went back into the bedroom and sat down on the chair, being sure not to turn his back to the hole in the wall.

Jeff looked at the back of the device with the red flap beneath which was the handheld's self-destruct mechanism. Gingerly, he lifted the flap with his thumb. The button was tiny, but protruded clearly from a small hollow. The manufacturer had obviously wanted to ensure that even the slightest pressure of a possibly seriously injured commander could trigger the destruction process. Jeff was a little surprised that Irons hadn't destroyed the chip long ago. That he had even taken the risk of letting the codes fall into enemy hands. Especially after the revelation that this huge, sinister ship was set on a course for Earth.

For a moment, Jeff toyed with the idea of destroying the device himself. But what about the major's strange premonition? Had he really foreseen his own death? He had also said that the codes might save the lives of the crew. What if the major had been right about that, too?

Jeff closed the cap. But if worst came to worst, he

wouldn't hesitate to destroy it. And that brought Jeff's mind round to the next problem. He was now in command. What should their next move be? It was up to him to make a decision.

He pushed the chair to the top end of the bed and leaned forward. He could see the outline of Irons' head under the sheet. Jeff laid his hand on the sheet on top of the major's forehead. He had spent over a year with the major. He had always admired Irons; he'd been his role model. Albeit one he would never live up to, no matter how hard he tried.

Jeff sat next to the body for a long time and pondered. Ideas popped into his mind, which he rejected again a moment later. Create an opening to the outside with the explosives, as Owl had suggested? That would be suicide. At least here in the interstellar void. Talk to the computer and hope that it was all a misunderstanding? No. It had lied to them and stalled too often. If they waited here in their quarters to reach Sigma-7, which would never happen anyway, then they would die—one by one. Killed by the sinister something which was responsible for the deaths of Field and Irons. What had Green said? That they would probably only find answers in the center of the ship. The engineer might be right. Jeff was also convinced there was more in the vast interior of the giant ship than the computer was telling them. The longer Jeff thought about it, the more convinced he became that that is what they needed to do. They needed to penetrate further into the ship. The idea terrified him, he was afraid of what they would find—but it was the only option. To escape the abyss, they would first have to descend deeper inside it.

Jeff slipped Irons' handheld into his belt pouch next to his own and returned to the rec room.

The others were sitting at the big table, engrossed in conversation.

"What were you doing?" Joanne interrupted the discussion.

Jeff decided not to tell the others about the major's handheld. "I wanted to say goodbye to Irons," he said simply.

"And what are your orders, Sir?" The last word contained all the hatred that Mac clearly felt toward Jeff.

Jeff tried to ignore his tone. He could make Mac obey his orders, but he couldn't make him like him.

"Has the computer made contact again?" he asked.

Joanne shook her head.

"Computer," Jeff spoke loudly into the room.

Silence.

"Computer!" he repeated.

Nothing. Perhaps the ship's computer knew they'd discovered the truth about their position, and now considered it pointless to continue lying to them. It might never contact them again. But what was it trying to achieve?

"We need to find out what's going on here," Jeff said. "I mean, what's *really* going on."

"And how?" Castle asked.

All eyes were on Jeff. Mac's eyes were full of animosity, Castle's full of doubt. Green's face looked disapproving, Joanne's curious, Owl's fearful, and Finni's confused. Only Shorty was poker-faced and didn't show a trace of emotion.

"We will go to the center of the ship. There must be more to find than the computer is telling us."

Green nodded.

Owl shook his head. "I'm not going deeper into the ship," he said firmly.

"That's three hundred miles," Mac laughed scornfully.

"I'm not traipsing three hundred miles to the core of this thing."

"We have no idea if we'll find anything useful down there," Finni said.

"If we stay here, we won't find anything at all," Jeff said. With a start, he noticed his voice had taken on a whining tone again.

"What if there are more light aliens down there?" Owl asked.

"Well, they can obviously get us here, too," Jeff said. "Besides, now they know where we are."

"Did you hear what I said?" Finni asked. "Maybe there's nothing down there."

"That's exactly what we'll find out. If we sit around here, we can be one hundred percent sure of not finding a way out of our situation," Jeff said.

"Then give me the explosives and we can get out through the airlock," Owl demanded.

"I think it makes more sense …" Jeff began. He imagined he could see Irons sitting opposite him. The illusion shook its head gently and then dissolved into thin air.

Jeff swallowed. Discussing this wouldn't get them anywhere.

"Can I have the explosives?" Owl asked.

Jeff took a deep breath. "No. We are all going together."

"But I just said—" Finni began.

Jeff interrupted him, with some effort. It wasn't right to interrupt others in the middle of a sentence, but he had to make it clear that he was in charge. "I heard what you said. But I've decided. We are going to the core of the ship —together."

"*You* decided?" Mac asked sarcastically. Jeff could almost see that Mac had another insult on the tip of his tongue. He needed to make sure it remained unspoken. His heart was beating like crazy. He hated it, but he had to go through with it. "Private McGuinness, if you have something you want to tell me, then call me Sir or Captain Austin."

Mac's jaw dropped. Joanne grinned.

"Have I made myself clear?"

"Sure …" Mac said, before adding a stifled "Sir."

If the mechanic saw an opportunity to sabotage Jeff's authority, he would take it. That much was clear.

"When …" Green stammered. "When do you want to start?"

"We'll set off shortly," Jeff kept a level tone. "We'll go to the gate and from there to the other side. Major Irons wanted to investigate the projection more closely and that's what we'll do first. We'll take all our equipment with us and work our way, as far as possible, to the center of the ship."

"Should we try and make contact with the computer first?" Joanne asked.

Jeff shook his head. He didn't see the point. "If it contacts us now—fine. But we mustn't believe anything it tells us anymore. It's got its own agenda, that's clear to me now. It won't tell us anything we need to know."

"What if it tries to stop us?"

"It's done that already by feeding us lies."

"Could be that the light aliens and the computer are working together," Owl said.

Jeff leaned back in his chair. He hadn't thought about that possibility. He had assumed the light aliens were degenerated or mutated descendants of the original crew. Or maybe intruders who had come onto the ship sometime over the preceding millions of years, though that seemed unlikely. Either way, the computer might be pursuing its own agenda, but if it wanted to kill them, it could have done so when they were in the airlock. Or it could have simply not let them on board. Ultimately, Jeff had to admit to himself that he didn't have a clue what was going on on this ship.

"No, I don't think so. But I can't say for sure."

"He's not sure …" Mac mocked him in a soft voice.

Since nobody reacted to his comment, Jeff decided to ignore it.

"When are we leaving?" Finni asked.

Jeff would have liked to wait a day or two; have some more time to think things through, but he knew he wouldn't change his mind. And since they obviously weren't safe in their accommodation, perhaps it was best if they kept moving.

"Today," Jeff said. "As soon as we've checked through the equipment."

"And you want us to take everything with us?" Joanne asked.

"Yes, we'll decamp. There's no reason to come back here."

Jeff got up from the table. There was no point discussing this further. The sooner they got going, the better.

Chapter 16

"Here it is," Joanne said.

Jeff followed her into the projection room. A few pieces of furniture, which looked like some kind of exotic, curved metal chairs, stood in three rows along the back wall. At the other end of the room, a broad cylinder stuck out of the ground. Next to it was a table-like structure with controls, which must be the console for the projector.

Joanne slid her medical kit bag off her back and walked briskly over to the console. The buttons, levers, and knobs were not dissimilar to those in the cockpit of the Charon. She pressed a large square at the edge of the console and immediately a hologram appeared above the cylinder. It was a little fuzzy at first, but quickly came into focus.

Jeff could see stars rotating around a green symbol that presumably represented the ship. The whole crew —or what was left of it—gathered around the projection cylinder.

"That's the map. I can zoom in and out," said Joanne.

As if to prove her point, new stars appeared on the edge of the hologram and moved inward.

Jeff already knew about this from the photos Joanne had shown him the night before. Now they needed to find out what else this projector was capable of. "Is it possible to switch to other operating modes?"

Joanne shrugged. "Irons didn't want me to experiment with it too much. That's why I stopped pressing other buttons."

Jeff shook his head. The device appeared to be a projector, pure and simple. He couldn't imagine they would trigger anything dangerous.

"Now I'm in charge. See if you can get any other information out of it."

Joanne nodded and started jabbing around on the console.

Jeff turned and saw Finni pulling something out of the equipment sled. "No," Jeff said, pushing past Shorty to reach the sled. "We have to ration the food." Finni nodded and stowed the package of concentrate bars back in the equipment sled. They could survive for a while with the help of their suits' micro recycling system, but unlike the mushy stuff produced by their suits, the concentrate bars at least tasted halfway decent. He needed their supplies to last as long as possible, there could be no snacking between meals.

"Jeff, come here a sec."

Jeff turned around and walked back over to Joanne.

"What do you make of this?" she asked.

There were now blue characters projected in the air above the cylinder. Sentences that appeared to run from top to bottom. When Joanne rotated a knob, the columns of letters changed color one by one.

"Some kind of menu?" He scratched his head. "But god knows how we're supposed to encrypt the characters."

"I'll just select one of them. I think this is the confirmation button." She touched the button and the projection vanished for a moment. Then new characters appeared. Joanne tried out the different columns, but all that was projected every time was writing.

"Unfortunately we don't have a Rosetta Stone," Castle said sarcastically.

"What's a Rosetta Stone?" Shorty asked.

"He's just trying to say we can't translate what it says here," Joanne answered, without taking her eyes off the console.

"This isn't getting us anywhere," Jeff said. "Go back to the star map and try something else."

"Easier said than done," Joanne grumbled, and pushed various buttons without anything happening.

"It's no use," Owl said in frustration. "Let's go back to the airlock and get out of here. With a bit of luck we'll be picked up by a rescue cruiser or a freighter."

"We will not discuss this again," Jeff said firmly. "And you know as well as I do, the chances of being picked up are about a million to one."

"Hey," Joanne blurted out, and Jeff looked back at the projection. The writing had disappeared. Instead of a star map, he was now looking at a blue, roughly spherical but irregularly shaped structure with many differently sized projections.

"That's the ship!" Castle cried.

"Looks like an outside view," Joanne said.

"What did you press?" Jeff asked.

Joanne pointed to a large square button on the top of the console. "Maybe those are pre-selector switches for different display modes."

"Press the one next to it," Jeff ordered.

When Joanne touched the button, the image of the ship disappeared and the projection was filled with writing, like before.

"No—go back."

The image of ship reappeared in front of them.

"I'll try the little buttons underneath," Joanne said.

The blue sphere gradually became transparent and orange structures came into focus.

"You're kidding me!" Castle said, stepping closer to the projection. "That's a map of the interior of the ship!" He reached out a hand and moved it slowly through the hologram. Wherever he touched the fine lines, the projection became slightly blurry.

"Look," Joanne said. "You can zoom in and out and move it round."

"Now we need to find out where we are," Finni said.

Joanne pressed another button and suddenly the whole upper half of the ship projection was cut off. It looked like a huge cross-section of an apple riddled with holes made by thousands of worms.

"With this you can create and control cross-sections." Joanne turned the knob, and out of nowhere more levels of the "apple" appeared at the top of the projection.

"I'll try this knob here."

Now it was as if a camera had penetrated the interior of the ship. Lines and dots raced through the projection, and then the image came to a standstill again. Jeff could make out individual corridors and rooms. In the middle of the hologram was an orange rhombus.

"Is that where we are?" Finni asked.

Jeff recognized parts of the map. That was the gate with the long corridor. And all the narrow, zigzagging corridors that led toward the hull of the ship. Now Jeff tried operating the console and zoomed out again. There was the airlock through which they'd entered the ship. And those were their quarters—he could even count the ten bedrooms. "Yes, the rhombus marks our location," Jeff confirmed.

He turned the knob farther until the entire circumference of the ship was visible again. From this perspective, the symbol showing their position was at the very edge of the ship. If they really wanted to make it to the center, they had a long way to go.

Jeff turned to Joanne. "How far are we from the outer shell?"

She shrugged. "My guess would be about six miles. As the crow flies."

Owl burst out laughing. It was a desperate laugh. "Then it's only three hundred miles to the heart of the ship. Just a stroll in the park."

Mac laughed hollowly.

Jeff pursed his lips. Owl was right, of course. It was a very long way. Even if they didn't have to take any detours and made good headway, he reckoned they would need at least a week and a half.

"Maybe there's some means of transport that still works," Joanne said hopefully. "An elevator or something."

Jeff imagined an elevator that ran hundreds of miles into the depths of the ship. But he was determined—they had to give it a try. It was their only chance.

"OK, let's use the map and try and work out a route to the core." He looked at Joanne. "Plot it all on your computer. Then we'll transfer the map to the other handhelds."

Joanne nodded.

Jeff zoomed in further and moved the center of the

hologram so that their position was now on the left edge of the projection. "First we can go down this long corridor. It leads directly toward the center.

"Pretty long …" Owl remarked.

Jeff nodded. "Yup, probably over sixty miles."

"It ends at this weird, shaded area," Joanne said.

"What *is* that?" Green wondered. "Looks like a giant ellipse that has been halved along the long axis."

"Maybe we can rotate the view to get a different perspective," said Jeff, trying out various knobs. Finally he was able to turn the image slightly and the cross-section changed. The outline of the large area remained, but the shading disappeared.

"Oh my God," Owl whispered.

Jeff whistled through his teeth. It appeared to be a hollow chamber. And it was humongous.

"Is that what I think it is?" Joanne asked, hardly able to hide her disbelief.

Jeff nodded. "It seems to be a huge cavity. Deep inside the ship."

"If it's a cavity, then it's the biggest one I've ever seen," Shorty said.

"At least one hundred and twenty-five miles long. And almost as wide," Finni said.

"The highest point of the roof is over forty-five miles high," Jeff added.

"Holy shit!" Even Mac dropped his surly tone for a moment.

"Well, I wouldn't mind taking a look at that," Green said dryly.

"I'm happy to give it a miss," Owl said. "Who knows what we'll find there."

"We'll have to walk through part of it," Joanne said. "It

takes us to this corridor, which leads directly to the center." She turned to Jeff. "Can you zoom out again?"

Jeff turned the knob.

"This corridor," Joanne said, pointing.

"Maybe it isn't a corridor, but an elevator," Green speculated. "That's possible, isn't it?"

"I guess we'll find out," Joanne said. "The main thing is, it takes us straight to the core."

"Not quite," Jeff said and turned the view slightly counterclockwise. "There's another cavity. It's about the same size as the first one. We need to pass through that one too, to get to the core."

Finni frowned and peered more closely at the hologram. "What are those things? Huge warehouses, maybe?"

"I dunno, but they're situated along the main corridors," Joanne said. "That makes them easy to reach from anywhere on the ship."

Jeff nodded. "Yes, the corridors only seem to have that fractal structure in the outer areas. Down there, it looks more like one of our ships or stations, with main axes leading from one section to all the others."

"At least we've found a good way to reach the core of the ship," Joanne said. "I've loaded the approximate coordinates onto my handheld. I'll transfer the data to your computers later."

Jeff continued to study the hologram. The corridor they'd been talking about ended in a circle, which was filled with white on the map. "The map doesn't show the core of the ship," he said.

"Luckily it's not that big," Green said.

"Thirty miles in diameter, I'd say," Joanne said.

Owl shrugged. "Then we'll have to find the way ourselves."

"I wonder why that area isn't on the map? As if there's

something hidden there, which we're not supposed to find," Joanne said.

Nobody answered her.

Jeff ended the uneasy silence after a few seconds. "Let's get going."

Chapter 17

"How much further do you want us to go today?" Owl asked. He sounded tired. "Surely we've gone far enough."

Owl's weary voice jolted Jeff out of his reverie, and he realized that for some time he'd just been trudging along mechanically staring down at his boots. They'd been walking down the same gloomy corridor for hours; it seemed to be endless. Of course, they knew approximately how long it was from the hologram, but in reality, the march through that sixty-mile-long nave-like corridor, with its lateral columns at regular intervals that joined into black arches high above their heads, was like walking through a surreal horror-movie set. Only occasionally did corridors turning off to the left or right. Even less often were there doors leading into rooms, none of which was more than a few square feet in size.

More than once they heard sinister noises: a mournful moan, a grinding sound, and one time Jeff thought he heard the cry of a madman echoing from far away. But because of the echo, they could never tell if the noise was coming from in front or behind. The mere thought of some weird creature following them in the darkness made Jeff's stomach turn.

He threw a glance at Joanne, who was stoically marching alongside him. She returned his glance and nodded. She knew what he wanted to know. She held up her handheld. "Twenty-two miles from the gate."

Jeff wiped the sweat from his brow. He thought they'd covered a greater distance in the last eight hours. At least that's what his aching feet were telling him. With every step he took, he felt a stab of pain shoot through his big toe. He was sure he'd find a big blister when he took off his boot. And no doubt the others were suffering, too. But he wanted to carry on just a bit longer. The faster they got to the core of the ship, the sooner they would find out what was what —and hopefully also find a way of steering this ship in the direction they wanted to go. Also, he didn't want the men to think he was a quitter, the first one to need a rest. And something in the pit of his stomach told him they didn't have all the time in the world.

But finally Jeff decided there was no point in carrying on for the day. If they exhausted themselves too much today, they'd just cover less distance tomorrow. "All right. Let's look for somewhere to camp for the night."

"Night …?" Castle laughed. "It's always night here. It's always as dark as a shit-house. It's starting to drive me crazy."

Jeff didn't respond. "We'll carry on until we find a room we can camp in for the night." He didn't want them to spread out their sleeping bags in the middle of the corridor. Beneath this cathedral-like ceiling, and with those awful noises, he wouldn't sleep a wink. No, they needed a larger-than-average room that they could barricade from the inside, and set up a guard post outside.

"Over there. I see a door." Finni pointed to the left.

The radar technician was right. As they came closer, Jeff saw there was a narrow window in the wall beside the door. Good—that way they could keep an eye on the corridor from the inside, making it harder for potential intruders to take them by surprise.

"There's a turnoff into a corridor," Joanne noticed.

She was right. About forty feet away, there was a turning into a narrow passage. But that made no difference to Jeff's decision to use the room in front of them as their quarters for the night.

The door into the room was closed, and Jeff shone his flashlight through the window. He pushed against the door. It swung open noiselessly and with little resistance.

Apart from a few tables, the room was empty. It wasn't very big, but just big enough that they would all be able to lie down relatively comfortably. The gray table legs were far enough apart for them to spread out their sleeping bags underneath the tables.

"Put the equipment sled next to the door. When we sleep, we'll use it to block the exit."

"What should we eat?" Castle asked, carelessly dropping his backpack on the floor and sliding down the wall to a sitting position.

It was a stupid question, and in any case, the WSO knew the answer. "We'll get the concentrate food out of the sled shortly," Jeff replied tersely.

Mac crouched down, took the small, wrapped gray bars out of a container, and distributed them. Everyone got one bar, and Mac made a point of handing one to Jeff last of all. If that was going to be Mac's only act of rebellion, Jeff wouldn't complain. He put his backpack on one of the gray tables and sat down next to it. He ran his fingers through his hair and was surprised to find that it was damp with sweat. He checked his multifunction watch and clicked his tongue.

"What?" asked Joanne, who was in the middle of unwrapping her concentrate bar.

"It's gotten warmer."

Owl and Shorty looked down at their watches.

"You're right," Castle said. "Seventy-five degrees Fahrenheit. I hadn't noticed. I guess the temperature rises the further down into the ship we go."

"If it carries on at this rate, it will be over a hundred and twenty degrees at the core," Finni calculated.

"Let's wait and see," Joanne said.

"This stuff tastes like shit," Mac said, spitting the last bit of his concentrate on the floor.

"You're welcome to slurp the food made from your excrement out of your combat suit," Castle said sarcastically. "I'll happily take your share of the concentrate."

Shorty yawned loudly. "I'm so tired. I just want to sleep."

Jeff looked at his watch and nodded. "Let's get some rest. We're going to take a ten-hour break and then continue."

"Ten hours?" Joanne asked. "Then it will be four in the morning."

Jeff sighed. Perhaps it would be better not to mess up their sleeping patterns completely. It was not for nothing that a uniform time had been introduced for all ships of the Empire, which the crews had to stick to. But he couldn't shake the vague and disturbing feeling that they didn't have much left to save themselves from the situation they were in. It was as if an invisible stopwatch were counting down to their doom. Jeff tried to snap out of it; he didn't know where the feeling came from. Then he remembered the major's premonition, which had cruelly come to pass, and decided to listen to his gut feeling. But the others didn't need to know about it. "As Castle said, it's impossible to tell night from day here, and ten hours' rest should be enough."

"Shall we set up a watch?" Joanne asked.

"Yes."

"Then I'd like to take the first shift," she said.

"Are you sure?"

Joanne nodded. "I'm not that tired."

"OK. I'll take over in two and a half hours. Then Green, and then Finni."

Jeff spread out his sleeping bag so that he was lying half under one of the tables, and then pressed the button that inflated the integrated mattress. He sat down wearily and pulled off his heavy boots with a groan. Despite the breathable material, the odor that emanated from his feet was anything but pleasant. He pulled off his socks and examined his right foot. He winced. On one of his toes there was a big, pus-filled blister. He resisted the urge to pop it and instead applied a wound-healing strip, which he took out of Joanne's medical kit.

Then he sighed and slipped inside his sleeping bag. For a moment he watched Joanne, who had pushed a table in front of the window, and was now settling herself down on it to keep watch. She checked her weapon and laid it on the table beside her. Then she dimmed the lamp so far that Jeff could only vaguely make out his surroundings. Somewhere next to him he could hear Finni snoring.

Jeff closed his eyes. Although he was utterly exhausted from the long day that had begun so horrendously, it took him a long time to relax. Again and again in his mind's eye, he saw the major's ravaged body lying on the bed, and couldn't help wondering which of them would be next.

After what felt like an eternity, Jeff drifted off into a restless sleep.

Chapter 18

"Psst … wake up!"

Jeff was ripped out of a deep sleep when Joanne shook his shoulder. It was pitch black, and Jeff could hear but not see his companion.

"Turn on the light," he husked, trying to shake himself awake.

"No," Joanne hissed. "There's something outside!"

Now Jeff was wide awake.

What the hell?

He sat up straight as a rod and hastily undid the zipper of his sleeping bag. "What do you mean?"

"Come with me," Joanne whispered and grabbed his hand.

Rubbing his eyes, Jeff stood up and stumbled after her. He could just about see the window. On the other side, the corridor was illuminated by a pale light. Weak, but unmistakable. "What is it?"

"I don't know. It started a few minutes ago and it's been gradually getting brighter. But I can't see anything out there."

The light seemed to be coming from the left, from the center of the ship. Jeff pressed his cheek against the window but could only see a little way down the endless corridor. They should have set up a mirror on the other side of the pane. "I can't see anything, either."

"It's as if someone had switched on a lamp at the end of the corridor," Joanne murmured. "What the hell could it be?"

"We'll have to go out," Jeff said, and reached down for his gun. There was nothing he wanted to do less, but they had to find out what was going on outside.

Jeff fumbled his way to the door, weapon in hand, and moved the equipment sled aside with his boot. As he pushed against the door, he noticed that his hands were shaking. He opened the door a crack and peered around the corner. Nothing. He had no choice but to go out. With a deft movement, he opened the door all the way before stepping out into the corridor. He thought he could hear his heartbeat echoing in the corridor. He peered into the darkness—and then he saw the creature.

"Oh my god," Joanne whispered from behind him. "What is that?"

It was at least three hundred feet away from Jeff and Joanne and was standing motionless in the middle of the corridor. It had the rough outline of a human being and appeared to consist entirely of light—a ghostly light. Like an angel of death that had returned from the hereafter to get them. Jeff's hand was clenched on the handle of his pistol. He knew instinctively that the weapon would be useless if the creature decided to attack. That must be the alien being that had killed Fields—and maybe Irons. Or it was one of them, because of course there might be more.

Joanne clung to Jeff's left arm. "It's scary."

Jeff nodded. He had never seen anything like it. It

reminded him of the ghosts that had haunted his imagination as a child—and which he'd dismissed as a figment of the imagination long ago. He had been sorely mistaken.

He hardly dared to breathe. But the creature must have noticed them by now. He couldn't recognize any details of the face, as the light was so dazzling, but the sinister being seemed to be looking directly at them. Jeff felt as if it was staring straight into his soul, plumbing the depths of his mind for the essence of his very being. He shook himself.

"It's just standing there," Joanne whispered. "Is it looking at us?"

"I … I think so," Jeff stammered. His mouth was completely dry.

The light radiated by the creature was cool, almost chemical. In fact it was probably less bright than it seemed, because it didn't light up the corridor very far. Although the creature appeared to lack any clear contours, it cast wave-like white shadows across the wall. The pretty patterns had an almost hypnotic effect, and Jeff suddenly had trouble focusing.

"I'm scared," Joanne said, and Jeff flinched as she tightened her grip on his arm. They had to wake the others and prepare for an attack.

Then, suddenly, the creature began to glide toward them.

"Jeff!"

Open-mouthed, Jeff noticed that the ghostly figure wasn't moving its legs. It hovered just above the ground and floated toward them noiselessly.

"Jeff!"

"Yes," he croaked. He was unable to move, as if the light alien had cast a spell that rooted him to the spot.

Jeff began to tremble. The ghost had already moved around eighty feet in their direction and Jeff still couldn't move. He wanted to run away, scream, pull his gun and shoot at the approaching danger, but he couldn't. He had lost control of his body. Helplessly, he watched the creature approach, waited for it to reach him, to tear out his soul and ravage his body until it was left like the corpses of Fields and Major Irons.

"Jeff!" Joanne's voice was no more than a whimper.

Jeff wanted to shut his eyes. He didn't want to see this apparition coming toward him, but he was transfixed.

Then, all of a sudden, the creature changed direction, floated to the side of the corridor, and disappeared down a narrow passageway. For a brief moment, a shaft of pale light gleamed from the opening, then it was pitch black again, as if nothing had happened.

Gradually, the adrenalin leaked from his body, but Jeff was shivering as if he had a fever.

"I thought it was coming to get us," Joanne whispered. She was still clutching Jeff's arm.

"I thought so, too," Jeff said. "I couldn't move. It was like it had hypnotized me." Tentatively, he took one step forward and one step back, to reassure himself that he had control over his limbs again.

"When Fields called in the last time, he sounded as if he were scared to death," Joanne said. "Now I understand why."

Jeff nodded. As his ability to think returned, his anxiety grew. He sensed they had no power over the aliens. Even if they could use their weapons against these creatures—which he doubted—that was of little use if they had the power to root them to the spot.

"I don't get it," Joanne said.

"What don't you get?"

"We've got deflective shields in our combat gear that

are meant to protect us from psychic influences. How was it able to put us under a spell like that?"

Jeff shook his head. "The deflectors protect us from telepathic or magneto-psychotic interventions, but they don't work against visually produced hypnotic effects. And let's be honest, maybe we were just paralyzed by fear."

"So how can we protect ourselves against them?"

"No idea. And we still don't know if our weapons would have any effect."

"And if they don't?"

"Then all we can do is run."

Joanne gave a desperate laugh. "And that worked really well just now."

Jeff took a deep breath. He was as despondent as Joanne, but wasn't it his job as commander to spread a little optimism? But where was he supposed to get that from? Just one thing reassured him a little. "It didn't come closer, and in the end it disappeared."

"It didn't have the same scruples with Fields and Irons."

"Maybe it didn't dare to come closer because there were two of us. If we always stick together as a group, maybe we stand a chance.

"Hm," Joanne was skeptical. "And what do we do now? Shall we wake the others?"

Jeff thought feverishly. Maybe we should change location in case that … thing … returns with reinforcement. On the other hand, in this enormous and endlessly long corridor, they could be spotted from miles away. If the aliens wanted to find them, they would, no matter which room they hid in.

Jeff looked at his watch and shook his head. He had to take the risk. "No," he replied firmly. "We need to rest if we want to make progress tomorrow. We'll go back in and block the door."

"And if that ghost simply floats through the closed door?"

Jeff wouldn't have been surprised to find the creature was capable of it, but he didn't want to discuss it.

"Your shift is almost over. Get some sleep. I'll take over."

"I doubt I'll be able to sleep."

"Then try, at least," Jeff said, blocking the door again with the equipment sled.

Joanne slipped into her sleeping bag and Jeff sat down on the table near the window. He tried to relax, but his heart was pounding louder than ten orbital canons. He was sure Joanne must be as wired as he was, but she didn't make a sound. He couldn't stop thinking about the light alien, what it was, what its intentions were … but ultimately all he could do was speculate. Every few minutes he pressed his face up against the window and squinted down the corridor, but the luminous apparition didn't reappear.

Chapter 19

"Over there!" Owl yelled so loudly it made Jeff jump. He saw immediately what the radio operator was talking about. Well, they'd been expecting it for a while now.

For three long days they had continued their monotonous journey along the corridor. On the first day, they had talked with each other about their mission, the ship, and above all about the light alien, but by the second day they had lapsed into almost complete silence. Since setting off from their second camp that morning, they had hardly exchanged a word, even during breaks. The mood in the group became gloomier the further their journey took them into the interior. Since the sinister encounter the night before last, they hadn't seen another light alien. But Jeff couldn't shake the feeling that they were all doomed.

Now the first part of their journey to the center of the ship had come to an end. In front of them the long corridor ended in a huge wall.

"Finally!" Finni groaned in relief. "I couldn't manage another yard of that damned corridor."

Joanne was the first of the group to reach the end of

the corridor. The smooth wall was made of the same black material as all the other walls on the ship. She turned around. Her face expressed relief and Jeff guessed she was feeling the same way as he was.

"I thought the corridor ended in one of those huge cavitys we saw on the hologram," Castle said, letting his pack slide to the ground. He pulled his water bottle out of the side pocket of his pack and took a big gulp. Beads of sweat trickled from his temples and down to his chin before dripping to the ground. No wonder, the temperature had risen again and now hovered at just under ninety degrees Fahrenheit.

"There are only two narrower corridors leading off from this one," Green said.

Joanne pulled out her handheld and jabbed at the screen. "This corridor didn't end directly at the cavity, but it must be close. Four to five hundred feet at most."

"Which way do we go?" Green asked, shining his flashlight down the corridor to the right.

Joanne turned the handheld slightly and looked irritated. "I'm not quite sure. I can't tell from the scale. I think the one on the left, but I could be wrong. The direction is roughly correct, in any case."

"What now, boss?" Mac asked.

Jeff pursed his lips. McGuinness had been doing this for the last three days. With every comment and every question he addressed to Jeff, he added a sarcastic "boss," which he stretched out like chewing gum.

Jeff ignored him. He looked at his watch, but his heavy legs and waves of fatigue told him it was time to start looking for a place to set up camp. Still, it would be good if they could find the entrance to the cavity first, to get an idea what they would be up against the next day. They might also come across an empty room in the process, which they could use for shelter.

"We'll start searching for the cavity," he decided.

Joanne nodded. "Together, or shall we split up?"

"I think we should split up," Castle said in a tired voice. "It'll be quicker that way."

Jeff looked down each of the dark corridors leading from the intersection. He wiped his hand over his dry mouth. On the one hand, they would be stronger together if they faced a threat. On the other, the cavity couldn't be far away, and if they split up into groups and searched for half an hour, they were very likely to find it.

"We'll split up," he decided. "Green, Finni, and I will take the left-hand corridor. Joanne, Castle, and Mac, you take the right-hand corridor. Owl and Shorty will keep watch here, and stay in contact with us.

Shorty sighed with relief, leant against the wall and slid down to the floor. The long march had been tough on him. Jeff had noticed him repeatedly clutching at his lower back and wincing with pain. Because of his height, Shorty was prone to backaches. Green had survived the march surprisingly well, considering how ill he'd been a few days before.

Owl took his handheld out of his pocket, placed it against the wall so that the rod antenna touched the metal, and sat down with his shipmate.

Joanne switched on her flashlight and set off down the right-hand corridor with Castle and Mac. Castle didn't look happy. He would have preferred to stay with Owl and Shorty, but he appeared to have some energy left, and Jeff saw no reason to leave him behind. He turned to Joanne's group. "Listen up. Explore the corridor, but don't go too far. We'll meet back here in one hour, max."

Joanne nodded. "The cavity can't be more than about five hundred feet from here."

"Yeah, we got that," Castle said testily.

"And see if you can find a room where we could camp for the night."

"Yes, Sir," Joanne replied, and immediately set off down the corridor. As a lieutenant, she had the same rank as Castle, but there was no question that she would lead the group, even without Jeff placing her in charge. Castle shrugged and followed Joanne with a sigh. Mac snorted loudly, spat on the ground, then grudgingly followed the others.

Jeff looked at Green and Finni. "Come on, we should get going too." He led the way and shone his flashlight down the left-hand corridor. It was considerably narrower than the main, giant corridor they had left behind. It was only just wide enough for two people to walk side by side. The ceiling was no more than eight feet high. Jeff was surprised there wasn't a larger corridor leading off from the main one. It would be impossible to carry any bulky items down here. Was that intentional? Or had modifications been made after the aliens had left the ship?

Jeff wiped the sweat from his brow. So many questions which they would probably never be able to answer. He set off with as much determination as he could muster. Green and Finni followed him at a distance of a few feet. So far there were no further turnoffs.

"I wonder what we're going to find," Finni said quietly.

"What do you think?" Green asked.

"If that hologram was correct, the cavity will be nearly a hundred and thirty miles long. And forty-five miles high. The whole of Lake Almazan could fit inside it."

"Lake what?"

"One of the biggest lakes on Astana. I went on vacation there once."

"What are you trying to tell us?" Green asked.

Finni sighed. "I mean this cavity will be fucking huge."

"If we ever find it," Jeff responded, pointing to where the corridor forked about forty feet in front of them. One corridor went off at a ninety-degree angle to the left. The other at an acute angle to the right. "What direction is the cavity?" he asked.

Green tapped around on his handheld. "I'd say right."

"This way, then," Jeff said, and turned right. After just a few feet, the corridor ended in a big room. Jeff stepped through the open door and looked around.

"Well, that's something new," Finni said.

The room was about the size of a small gymnasium. On the opposite wall was a long, metal table. Behind it, shelves made out of some glassy material were attached to the wall. Above them was a brown symbol, vaguely reminiscent of a sun with stylized rays. The symbol was marbled, as if it had been made out of the finest mahogany.

Along the other walls were seats, big enough for a human to sit in comfortably. Vase-like structures as tall as a person and made out of a transparent material were distributed at regular intervals around the room like bizarre works of art.

"Shit, looks like the Hilton on Ceres," Finni said.

Jeff nodded. He had never been to the asteroid, but the room really did look like a modern hotel lobby decorated by an abstract artist. Big open doorways led out of the hall on all four sides.

"What now?" Green asked.

Jeff looked around uncertainly. He had no idea which opening they needed to go through to reach the cavity. And they ran the risk of getting hopelessly lost. On the other hand, this was the first time they had come across a room of this kind—they might find something interesting. He walked over to the nearest wall and touched it with the antenna of his handheld.

"Owl? Shorty? Can you hear me?"

A few seconds passed, then Jeff heard Shorty's basso voice. "We're holding the fort. Everything OK?"

"Yup, we're fine. Have you heard anything from the others?"

"Yeah, Joanne contacted us a few minutes ago. They were going down a long corridor that led directly toward the cavity. At least that's what they thought."

"But?"

"But after several hundred feet they came to a dead end. Now they're in a parallel corridor."

"OK. Thanks. We've found an interesting room. A kind of lobby. I'll get back to you."

"Maybe it's some kind of transit area," Finni murmured so quietly that Jeff could barely hear him.

"What do you mean?" Green asked.

Finni gazed around the unusual hall. "We know the cavity we're looking for is huge; it's no ordinary cavity. Maybe this is a kind of transit lounge leading to it."

Jeff was silent for a moment, then nodded in agreement. Finni could be right. Access to the cavity may have been controlled by bulkheads. A bit like the gateway from the outer part of the ship to the central corridor. Maybe one of the passages led directly to the cavity. But which one?

Jeff made his way to the first doorway on his right.

"What are you going to do?" Green asked.

"We'll see where they all lead. At least the first few feet."

The first opening led into a narrow corridor, which turned off to the right after a few feet—in the direction from which they had come. Jeff doubted it would lead them to their goal. The next opening was right next to the long table. This one was wider and higher than the others. It led into a smaller room, at the other end of which was another door and a glass pane in the wall.

"Wait here," Jeff ordered and stepped into the room. "I want to see what—" He stopped short when he heard a loud hissing noise behind him and whirled round—just in time to see a hatch come thundering down to the ground from the ceiling.

"Green!" Jeff screamed and raced to the door. His flashlight fell out of his hand and skittered across the floor. The beam of the flashlight on the ground immersed the room in a ghostly light. Jeff banged his fists against the metal and screamed the names of his shipmates. "Finni! Green!"

No answer. He took a step back and looked to see if there was some kind of opening mechanism. To the left of the door, a dark-gray rectangle was embedded in the wall. He touched it, but nothing happened. Jeff groaned. It *must* be a control panel for the door, considering it was right next to it. Some automatic mechanism must have caused it to close. But why didn't the manual control work?

Frantically, Jeff took his handheld out of his pocket. He had to get Finni and Green to look for a control mechanism on their side. Maybe the one on this side was just broken. With trembling hands he held the antenna against the wall. "Green! Finni! Can you hear me? You have to—" There was a clinking sound as the antenna snapped off and fell to the ground.

Shit!

He had pressed the device too hard against the wall. Now he was completely cut off from the others.

After trying in vain to reattach the antenna, he banged his fist against the door, cursing loudly. But it was no use, it didn't budge. He had to get a grip. Finni and Green would of course do everything in their power to open the door from their side.

Jeff tried to suppress the panic welling up inside him. What if they didn't manage to get it open, and there was no other exit out of this and the surrounding rooms? Then he would starve to death in here.

Jeff tried to gather his wits and push those dark thoughts aside. He turned around, picked up his flashlight, and shone it around the room. It was completely bare, and not very big. Just a few feet lay between Jeff and the opposite wall, where there was another open door and a window. Maybe there was another way out that would lead him back to the lobby.

He walked toward the window, but all he could see was the bright reflection of his flashlight. Then he shone his flashlight through the open door. The room on the other side was bigger and higher than this one, as big as the gym at his old school on Luna. Behind the door were a few steps leading downward. Slowly, he let the beam of his flashlight wander round the room.

He gasped in surprise. At the end of three long rows of tables were machines of some kind. They were twice as high as a tall man and looked a bit like the old phone booths they used to have on Terra. They also reminded Jeff of the security controls at a civilian spaceport.

He stepped up to the first row of tables. They were covered with twisted and distorted metallic objects. He picked up one of them: a long tube that was bent in the middle, with a small black box at one end of it. Whatever it might have been, it had definitely been destroyed. He placed it back on the table and continued to look around. The hall was oblong in shape. On each of the two short sides there were two doors. The ones to his right were open, but led in a completely different direction from the way he had come into the room. The ones at the other end, behind the "phone booths," were closed off by heavy bulkheads. He wondered if he should wait here, hoping that Finni and Green would be able to open the door, or if he should venture into one of the open passageways. Maybe it would lead him back toward the "lobby" … And anyway: if his shipmates hadn't managed to open the hatch by now, they probably never would. Jeff picked up his handheld and checked that the inertial navigation was still working so that he wouldn't get completely lost.

He turned to look at the openings. They were both narrow and high and had arch-shaped recesses at the top, like the portal of a church—or like a cross-section of the long corridor they had been walking down for the last few days. They appeared to lead into two parallel corridors. If he went down one of them, he had to make sure he took a right turn as soon as possible so he didn't move too far away from the group.

He got to the opening and stopped. He felt a warm gust of wind on his face and started. It was the first time that he had felt anything like a breeze on this ship. He could barely bring himself to put even a single foot forward. He wavered as he peered into the corridor. There must be something up ahead that was reflecting the beam of his flashlight. He swung the beam to the right, but the light did not change. So it wasn't a reflection!

Jeff quickly switched off his flashlight. He was enveloped in darkness. Only the pale white glow further down the corridor remained.

It must be one of those light aliens. He began to tremble. He tightened his grip on his flashlight so it wouldn't slip out of his hand. He wanted to take a step back, but couldn't. As if something had blocked the neural paths from his brain to his muscles.

The glow in the corridor got brighter.

Jeff had to get out of here. Somehow. He bit his lower lip so hard he tasted blood. He bit even harder. The pain triggered something in him, and with a huge effort he managed to take a step back. And then another. As if in slow motion, he turned around and somehow heaved himself to the other end of the room. He had to hide so that the sinister creature didn't find him.

Finally, he reached one of the phone booths and crouched down behind it. He peered around the edge just as the creature reached the hall.

Jeff thought he could hear the hammering of his heart echoing through the room. The creature must have seen the light of his flashlight. But it didn't seem to know where he was now. It stood there very calmly. A pale ghost that resembled a slender, almost human figure, a little smaller than Jeff. It wasn't wearing any clothes, had no visible sexual features, no hair on its head, and no face. Jeff wasn't sure which way it was looking. But it must have some kind of sensory organs. Light surrounded the being like an aura, white, with a pale-blue shimmer.

The creature entered the room very slowly. It didn't make a sound. It simply floated over the ground. Jeff was sure it could move much faster than he could run.

It stopped abruptly at the first row of tables. Could it be the same creature he and Joanne had seen in the corridor the night before last? Was it the same creature that had brutally murdered Irons and Fields?

Now his life depended on whether the creature noticed him or not. It must know that something was hiding in here. Maybe he could somehow sneak past the alien and flee down one of the two back corridors. Or had he maybe overlooked an exit? If he turned on his flashlight now, the creature would know immediately where he was. In front of Jeff were the two big closed-off doors. But over there, several feet away, was another little door that he hadn't noticed before. It, too, was closed. But next to it was another one of those small squares embedded in the wall. It must be a manual control for the door. If he was quick enough, he might be able to run to the door, slip through, and close it from the other side before the creature reached him. But the question was: would the manual control work? If it didn't, he was a dead man.

The creature was still standing calmly next to the table at the other end of the hall. It appeared to be waiting for him to make a mistake and give away his location. If only he could see which way the creature was looking!

Minutes passed, during which time Jeff remained crouching rigidly in his hiding place. His heart was beating so hard he was sure the creature must be able to hear it. But the alien did not move an inch and gradually it dawned on Jeff that he would never get past his enemy. His only chance of escape was through the little door in the wall. Jeff tried to estimate how long it would take him to run there, open the door, and close it behind him, but he couldn't think clearly.

He had to make a decision. And he knew it was a life-or-death decision.

Suddenly, the image of the gutted major appeared in his mind's eye. Jeff shook his head. He didn't want to end up like that!

He sprung up, stumbled, and almost fell flat on his face. He only just managed to regain his balance. Then he ran.

Don't turn around! Don't fall!

He assumed the creature was now coming after him. The question was, at what speed? He expected a cold, pale hand to grab him from behind at any moment. Mechanically, he counted his steps.

Twelve, thirteen …

Too many, but finally he reached the door. Still running, he hit the small square on the wall before crashing headlong into the door. Nothing happened. He pressed on the square again. Still nothing! The door didn't budge.

This was it. He was about to die. For a moment he considered closing his eyes. He didn't want to see the ghost rush toward him and start to slice him up. He just hoped it would be quick. But in the end he couldn't resist the urge to turn around.

The creature hadn't moved! It was still standing by the table, waiting.

Of course! It knew the door was closed and so it could take its time. Jeff's heart was racing. Frantically, he looked around for another escape route, but there was nothing. He would never get past the creature. He needed to confront it, although he knew it was pointless.

Finally, he remembered he had a weapon with him, and with shaking hands, pulled out his pistol. He pointed it at the creature. *This damn trembling! It was impossible to aim accurately!*

Then the creature began to move. Jeff remained glued to the spot. It was coming toward him. But very slowly, as if in slow motion.

"What do you want from me?" Jeff cried out.

He pulled the trigger. The noise reverberated around his ears. The bullet exploded in a shower of sparks against the back wall.

Shitshitshit!

The second shot also missed the target by several feet.

The creature was now barely more than a few feet away from him.

"No!" Jeff shrieked.

Bullseye!

But the shot simply whipped through the middle of the creature. The bullet left a fine white line in the creature's body that immediately dissolved again. Jeff cried out in horror. The weapon clattered to the ground.

He was done for. Any moment now, this creature would grab him.

Suddenly he heard a hissing sound behind him and a gust of wind in his hair. The ghost stopped abruptly.

Jeff turned around and saw Green stepping out of the now open door with his pistol drawn. He grabbed Jeff by the shoulder. "Shit!" the engineer screamed and pointed his gun at the creature.

"No use," Jeff cried and stumbled backward. "The bullets go straight through it. Let's …"

Suddenly, the ghost swung round and glided away at great speed.

"Jesus, it's fast," Jeff whispered. The creature had already disappeared down the corridor down which it had come. For a moment, the eerie glow continued to illuminate the tunnel entrance, then it was pitch black again and only the flashlight in Green's hand provided a little light.

Gradually, the tension in Jeff eased. He stooped to pick up his pistol and his hands grasped the weapon. It had been close. Too close.

He turned round to his shipmate, who was still staring slack-mouthed at the doorway through which the alien had vanished. "Thanks," Jeff croaked. "If you hadn't turned up, I'd probably be dead by now."

Green gave a nod, then turned to look at him. "Yup, looks like it," he replied.

"How did you find me?" Jeff asked. He wiped his clammy hands on his suit. His pulse was still racing.

"We looked for another corridor that led to the other side of the closed gate. One of the doorways in the lobby branches off into a total labyrinth of corridors and rooms. I looked around a bit and heard shots close by." He shrugged. "It was luck, mostly."

Jeff nodded. There was no doubt he'd been extremely lucky. "Where's Finni?"

"He stayed behind in the lobby. He wanted to keep the others updated and keep trying to make radio contact with you. Why didn't you contact us with your handheld?"

Jeff shrugged. "I was clumsy, and broke off the antenna by mistake."

Green nodded and checked out the room with the beam of his flashlight. "Interesting."

"Yes," Jeff agreed. "Looks a bit like a transport hub in a space station or asteroid."

Green looked at his handheld, then pointed at the big, closed doors. "The cavity ought to be exactly in that direction."

"Maybe this is where passengers had to check in," Jeff mused.

"If the others haven't found anything …" Green began.

"… then we have to go this way," Jeff ended his sentence.

"We can try and open the doors," Green said, walking toward them.

"No," Jeff said, and grabbed him by the arm.

Green turned around in surprise. "You're still trembling."

"Whatever," Jeff said. "I want to get everyone together again first. Let's go back to Finni and get the others to come to the lobby."

Green shrugged. "If you say so." Then he turned on

his heel and went back through the door. Jeff followed him down a short corridor that led to another from which further forks led left and right at regular intervals. Green was right. It really was a labyrinth. By now, Jeff had completely lost his sense of direction and Green kept looking down at his handheld.

Jeff took his own computer out of his pocket. Although the antenna was broken, the inertial navigation still worked fine. "But that's not the way to the lobby," he said out loud.

Green nodded, without turning around. "No. But a little further on there's a turnoff that leads back to the lobby."

"It's a miracle you found me at all."

"I told you, I was lucky."

"Without our handhelds we'd never find our way out of this maze," Jeff said. "We really need to be careful not to split up again. If someone's handheld really breaks, then they won't stand a chance."

"I don't know why that damned hatch suddenly closed," Green said and turned left down another corridor.

"Maybe it was triggered by a sensor. But I don't understand why it didn't open again."

"Maybe the manual controls are broken."

"Possible," Jeff replied. "After all, there seems to be more than one way of getting to every destination. How much farther is it?"

"Not far, we're nearly there. Down there, round that curve, and then the first door on the left."

Jeff followed Green and a few minutes later they were walking into the lobby. It was pitch black.

"Finni?" Jeff called. Why hadn't he put on his flashlight?

"Where are you, man?" Green shouted.

Jeff shone his flashlight on the closed door that had

separated him from his shipmates earlier on. He walked toward it and pressed on the small square next to it on the wall. As he expected, the door didn't budge. Jeff turned around and followed the beam of Green's flashlight as it panned around the room.

"Maybe he went back to the others," Green sounded uncertain.

The cone of light fell on an object on the floor.

"Stop! Hold on, there was ..." Jeff switched on his own flashlight and walked toward the spot.

It was Finni's handheld. It was completely destroyed. The rear panel was shattered and small electronic components lay scattered all over the floor.

"Looks as if he flung it full force against the wall," Green said.

"Finni?" Jeff called, shining his flashlight around the lobby again.

Had one of the light aliens been here? Had it abducted Finni? Or had Finni run away and was now in one of the other corridors?

"Green! Try and contact Owl and Shorty, and ..." Jeff trailed off as he saw Green, standing stock still at one of the doorways leading out of the lobby, his flashlight directed at something Jeff couldn't see from where he was standing. But he guessed what it was. Or who.

The body of their shipmate was lying face down. He could only tell from the mussed up hair that it was Finni. He was lying in a huge pool of blood, his arms stretched out on either side of his body as if he were trying to fly.

"Fuck," Green finally whispered.

Yet another one of them had been murdered. This couldn't be happening.

"How long was he alone?" Jeff asked hoarsely.

"Since just after you got separated from us."

Jeff felt anger welling up inside him. "You shouldn't have left him alone," he said.

Green turned around and looked at him coolly. "Sure. Then *you* would now be ..." He didn't finish his sentence.

Jeff took a deep breath and turned away. Was the engineer right? If Green hadn't found him, Jeff would probably now be lying slashed up on the floor of that strange check-in hall. Instead, Finni was dead.

It's my fault! Mine alone!

Jeff shook himself. He mustn't think like that. Neither he nor Green was to blame for the actions of these savage creatures. Hopefully the rest of the group was OK.

"Try and contact the others. Give them the coordinates for the lobby and precise directions. They should come as quickly as possible."

Chapter 20

"He was slit open," Joanne said, after she'd finished examining Finni's body. She was very pale. "From the lower lip down to his anus."

Jeff shuddered. "To his anus? But …"

"His penis and testicles were cut off and inserted into his abdominal cavity." Joanne swallowed. "Together with his eyes."

"Jesus fucking Christ," Owl put his head in his hands.

"No!" Castle moaned. "No! Who would do something like that?"

Nobody answered.

"You shouldn't have left him alone," Mac snapped at Green.

"I was trying to find Jeff." Green appeared nonplussed.

Mac snorted. It was obvious whose death he would have preferred.

"You should have gone in search of Jeff together," Joanne said calmly but reproachfully. Green shrugged and turned away to pick up the remains of Finni's handheld.

"All three of you might have died," she continued.

"And we would have had to come searching for you in this labyrinth and possibly never found you."

Jeff pursed his lips and nodded. Joanne was right, of course. It had been a dumb decision to split up the group. He had wanted to save time, and now Finni was dead. If he had made a different decision two hours ago, his shipmate would still be alive now. Never mind the fact that the damn hatch had crashed down behind him wasn't his fault, and the same thing might have happened if they'd all come to the lobby as a group.

Green shouldn't have gone looking for him alone, but Jeff hadn't really established any rules for that kind of scenario. He would lay down some ground rules now, but that didn't change the fact that Finni was dead.

Jeff pulled a thin, striped blanket from the equipment sled. He stepped gingerly into the pool of blood, which was unpleasant, but it was so big, he had no choice if he wanted to reach the body. Then he spread the blanket gently over the body of his shipmate and placed his backpack with his personal belongings beside him. He touched the blanket where Finni's shoulder must be, and muttered a short prayer. Although most of his family had been churchgoers, he had never really been a believer, and the prayer gave him little relief.

He retreated slowly to the lobby. "Does anyone else want to say something?" he asked quietly.

When he got no answer, he hit the square on the wall and the door slid down.

"I don't get it." Joanne was standing just behind Jeff.

He turned around. "What don't you get?"

"The light alien that you saw."

"What about it?" Jeff asked.

"Why it ran away when Green turned up?"

"Maybe they only dare to attack us when we're alone.

Remember—the one we saw when we were together also didn't attack."

"You said you shot at the creature and the bullet went straight through it," Castle said.

"Yes," Jeff nodded.

"If our weapons have no effect, why should they be afraid?"

"I don't know," Jeff admitted.

"And if they're immaterial like ghosts, how can they cut people up like that?" Owl asked.

Joanne frowned. "Maybe it's some kind of protective light shield, which they can turn on and off at will."

"Or only their weapons are material," Castle suggested.

"God help us …" Joanne whispered.

"I don't believe they're intelligent, technically advanced beings. If they were, things on this ship would look different," Mac said.

Jeff shook his head. They'd been over this a thousand times. They just went round and round in circles. "Let's face it, we have no idea, and that's one of the reasons we're going to the center of the ship. To try and find some answers."

"If we haven't all been killed by the time we get there," Mac said phlegmatically.

"I think it's a bad idea," Owl whined. "We should have gone to the shell and blown our way out. It's not too late—we could still go back."

Shorty nodded grimly.

Now the arguments were going to start all over again—which is exactly what Jeff wanted to avoid. Not that it was surprising, in light of Finni's horrific death. "Come on! We've got this far. We've nearly reached the center of the ship. We can't give up now."

Mac gave a shrill laugh. "*This far?* We've only gone about sixty miles. We've still got another two hundred and fifty ahead of us."

"I say we turn around before we're all dead," Owl said.

Jeff's gaze roved over the faces of his team. Owl, Mac, and Shorty were in favor of returning to the outer shell. Jeff was sure Owl and Mac would have no qualms about disobeying him, but would they be prepared to commit mutiny without the backing of at least one officer?

"I'm also not sure if we should go further into this hellish ship," Castle said.

Shit!

As if Mac and Owl had been waiting for this, they immediately swung round to the WSO.

"Then we'll go back!" Mac announced. "Let Boy Wonder here go and explore the ship alone, if he's so crazy to see what's there."

"What do you think?" Castle asked Joanne.

"You're a damned idiot," Joanne hissed and came and stood next to Jeff.

"Private Short! Private McGuinness," Green suddenly spoke in an icy tone that would tolerate no contradiction. Even Jeff started. "Captain Austin is our commander, and he has decided we will continue to the center of the ship. We will all obey his order, is that clear?"

Mac stared at him open-mouthed. Jeff had never seen this side of the usually phlegmatic Green. Maybe Finni's death had hit him harder than he thought. Or maybe he had a bad conscience because he'd deserted Finni.

"Is that clear?" Green repeated.

"Yes, Sir," Owl answered flatly.

Mac said nothing but lowered his head and nodded.

Jeff let out a sigh of relief. If Green hadn't reacted so quickly, he might have had a mutiny on his hands. Now it was important for him to take control again. "We will spend the night here in the lobby, and tomorrow we'll go in search of the cavity," he said. He made an effort to sound firm, but all that came out of him was a feeble croak. "To prevent another attack, we will stay together from now on and not split up on any account. From tonight, we will always have two people on watch. Any questions?"

"Who'll be next?" Owl muttered, so quietly that Jeff pretended he hadn't heard him. But if he was honest with himself, he was wondering the same thing.

Chapter 21

"These are supposed to lead to the cavity?" Castle asked, gazing up at one the huge gates in front of him. He rapped his fist on the metal, but all that came back was a hollow clanging sound. The doors must be very thick.

Jeff yawned. He was having trouble concentrating. Another—sleepless—night had come and gone. But what did "night" even mean in this strange place, where the only source of light came from their headlamps and flashlights. When they were switched off, they were surrounded by utter darkness. While Jeff had been slipping in and out of sleep during the night, he'd had the surreal feeling that time in this ship was literally frozen. He flinched when Joanne tapped him lightly.

"Don't fall asleep," she whispered, before walking over to Castle with her handheld. "At least this is the right direction—if we can trust the hologram in the map room. We can't be more than forty feet away from the cavity."

"Now all we need to know is how to get these things open," Shorty said.

Jeff looked over at Mac and Owl, who were standing

by the metal stairs talking to one another in subdued voices. They kept glancing in his direction. He had won yesterday's dispute, but clearly they were scheming. He would have liked to separate them, but in the circumstances that wasn't possible.

"How will we get them open?" Shorty repeated his question.

"I have no idea," Jeff admitted. "If this is really some kind of transit hub, there must be a control system—a switchboard or something."

"We've searched the whole place already—there's nothing" Castle said.

"Apart from these small squares," Joanne said, pointing to the one next to the gate in front of her.

"Which we all know work flawlessly …" Castle said sarcastically. To prove his point, he punched one of the squares on the wall. Nothing happened.

"Maybe they changed everything to remote control after renovating the ship," Shorty suggested.

Jeff shrugged. Another wild guess.

"If this was some kind of security control area, then it was for living beings to pass through. After they all left the ship, it would have become obsolete. So why would they have needed to change anything?" Joanne asked.

"If this *was* a security control," Castle said quietly and went over to one of the long tables. He ran his hand over the metallic surface and looked around again. "It looks like something else to me."

"Oh?" Joanne said. "Like what?"

The weapons expert scratched his head. "I could be wrong, but I think it's a kind of airlock."

"An airlock?" Joanne asked, unimpressed. "Why would they need an airlock inside the ship?"

"Perhaps as a security measure," Castle answered. "In

case the ship was damaged and the air escaped, you could safely enter the evacuated area here wearing a space suit. Look at the thick doors. Everything about this place is designed for a big change in pressure."

Jeff gazed around the room and nodded. Even the little door through which they'd entered was extremely thick and had membrane seals.

Joanne looked skeptical. "Even if you're right, how's that going to help us open the gates?"

Castle frowned and rubbed his chin. Suddenly his eyes widened. He grinned and pointed upward with his right forefinger. "Watch!" He sprinted toward the open gates on the other side of the hall.

Jeff watched him in confusion. What was he doing?

Once the WSO had arrived at the gates at the far end of the room, he punched one of the squares on the wall. With a loud grinding sound, a thick metal door emerged from the ceiling and began to slide down, eventually hitting the ground with a crash. Castle did the same with the other gate. Then he came back to them. "Close the other doors as well. We need to close them all."

Mac shrugged and climbed a short metal staircase to close an open door at the top.

Now Jeff understood what his shipmate was doing. He went back to the door through which they'd entered the room and closed it, trying to ignore the queasy feeling in his stomach. He hadn't forgotten his encounter with the light alien, when he had been unable to open the door from the inside. But in any case, for now they didn't want to go back, but forward, to the center of the ship.

"Will it work?" Joanne wondered.

"If it's an airlock, it might be a safety mechanism," Castle said, after they'd reconvened at the gate they wanted to pass through. "Maybe both sides can't be opened at the same time."

"You reckon the big gates will open now?" Owl looked doubtful.

"We'll find out in a few seconds," Castle said and headed for the closest of the big gates. His smile suggested that he was pretty sure it would work.

But nothing happened.

Castle turned around abruptly and scratched his chin. "I thought the gates …"

"You were wrong," Mac snapped caustically.

"Psst," Joanne hissed. "Do you hear that?"

Jeff and the others fell silent and listened. Yes, there was a noise. A low whistle, although Jeff wasn't sure which direction it was coming from.

"What is that?" Shorty asked.

Suddenly Jeff's ears popped.

Oh shit!

He realized immediately that they had made a dreadful mistake.

The color drained from Castle's face. "Oh God, the pressure is falling. The air's escaping."

"There must be a vacuum on the other side," Joanne screamed. "We're going to suffocate."

Owl ran to the nearest door and whacked the square on the wall in desperation. But nothing happened. They could no longer stop the process they'd started.

"Our suits!" Castle screamed. "We have to activate our suits!" Frantically, he fiddled around with the controls on the arm of his combat suit.

Jeff didn't even try. The micro-reactors of their deactivated suits would take several minutes to power up. The life-support systems would take even longer before they started to supply any air. He cursed inwardly. They should have left their suits on standby the whole time, however uncomfortable that may have been. Now it was too late.

Jeff was already having trouble breathing. His pulse was racing and his chest felt tight.

Mac grabbed Castle by the collar. "You fucking asshole! You've killed us all!"

"Wait," Joanne said. "It's stopping. Do you feel it? It's stopping."

Jeff was struggling to keep calm. But then he also noticed the whistling had stopped.

"The air pressure has stopped falling," Green announced. He had remained surprisingly calm throughout the ordeal and was now swiping around on his handheld. "The pressure is 600 hectopascals."

"Shit," Castle groaned. "I thought we were all going to bite the dust."

"We nearly did," Mac roared. "It's an *airlock*, for Christ's sake!"

"I'm sorry," Castle said. "I wasn't expecting a change of air pressure. I thought it was just an emergency safety measure integrated by the builders."

"Next time we talk things through first," Jeff said, addressing the whole crew and not just Castle. "No rash decisions, is that clear?"

"Why is the pressure different on the other side?" Joanne asked. "It doesn't make sense."

A loud metallic grinding noise reverberated around the room—as if a huge, rusty bolt were being drawn. Then the left-hand gate slowly rose up in fits and starts and with an almost unbearable screeching noise. Jeff covered his ears.

A reddish light flooded the room. A gust of wind ruffled Jeff's hair and the stench of rotten eggs filled his nose.

Joanne choked loudly.

The gate disappeared into the ceiling with a resounding boom. On the other side, Jeff saw a short corridor, no more than a dozen feet long, but with a very high ceiling. An open doorway at the end of the corridor led into a room that was bathed in a dark, ruby-red light.

Jeff moved forward hesitantly. The air was even warmer here than where they'd come from and far more humid, and immediately the sweat began to pour down his face. It was worse than the tropics. But worst of all was the revolting stench of rotten eggs.

Sulfur!

"Jesus, this is gross," Shorty groaned.

Castle pointed into the room. "What's that over there?"

They made their way forward tentatively, until they reached a platform. It was about the size of a small glider landing pad and was bounded by a railing along the front and sides. To the left was a kind of scaffolding that ended several feet above the platform. When Jeff looked up, he saw a reddish-gray sky … and a ruby-red sun.

A sun? Here?

It emitted a faint light that was mostly swallowed up by a hazy mist.

Jeff looked over the railing, and immediately got vertigo as he gazed into the endless depths.

"Where the hell are we?" asked Joanne, who had appeared at his side.

Jeff looked down at a hostile, craggy landscape that appeared to consist of nothing but black volcanic rock. Here and there were little pools and lakes, from which gray vapors rose into the air. The landscape lay far below them. In the distance, the horizon was shrouded in mist.

"Have we come out on a planet's surface?" Shorty looked perplexed.

"Of course not," Castle shot back. "This is the cavity

we saw on the hologram map. It's so big that the other end is shrouded in mist."

"And why can't we see the ceiling? How did they even get that sun up there?" Mac asked, wiping the sweat from his face.

"God, we've been so dumb," Joanne blurted out.

"What do you mean?" Jeff asked.

"We underestimated the dimensions of the cavity. It's so big, the illusion of being on the surface of planet is perfect."

"A very grim planet …" Owl quipped.

Joanne ignored him. "The room is so high, it practically goes beyond the atmosphere. That's why we can't see the ceiling. The sun is probably an oversized floodlight, fed directly from a reactor. It also explains why the air pressure is different here."

"Why?" Castle asked.

Joanne spread her arms wide. "We came out quite a few miles above the ground. No wonder the air is thinner here."

Jeff nodded. It made sense. But only to an extent. "Why doesn't the airlock lead directly to the bottom of the cavity?"

Joanne shrugged. "Maybe there are other airlocks. We may even have been lucky. Imagine if we'd come out six miles further up."

"Then we'd be dead," Owl said dryly.

Jeff turned around and looked up. The gates were embedded in a smooth, dark-gray metal wall, the top of which was lost from view somewhere in the haze.

"Maybe they lived here," Castle speculated.

"Who?" Mac asked.

"The builders of the ship. Maybe they modeled these

cavitys on their home planet so they would feel at home during their generations-long flight."

"You reckon their planet looked like this?" Owl was dubious.

"It's possible."

"Looks worse than where I come from," Mac muttered.

"It's creepy. Really creepy." Castle shuddered.

"And now?" Owl asked.

"We need to go down and walk about halfway across this cavity," Joanne said.

"Down?" Castle asked. "But how?"

"This might be some kind of elevator," Green said, examining the scaffolding-like structure. Jeff followed him.

The engineer was right. In the middle of the scaffolding there was a smaller, square platform, at the end of which a control panel jutted out of the floor.

"Come on," Jeff called, waving his shipmates over to the platform. When everyone was standing on the elevator, Green pressed the only button on the panel.

A small railing rose up from the floor, separating the elevator from the platform. Then a horn sounded and the platform began its descent with a loud rattling noise.

"Well, it seems to work," Mac commented dryly.

"Or our journey would have ended here," Owl said, with a hint of regret in his voice.

"No it wouldn't," Joanne said. "We just would have had to look for another airlock further down."

Owl grunted.

Castle looked up. "That sun is very weak."

"It's probably designed to provide light but not heat," Jeff guessed.

"Just as well, it already feels like a sauna in here," Joanne said.

They stood huddled together in silence as the elevator slowly descended. Jeff had to constantly wipe the sweat out of his eyes in order to see anything at all. His head was pounding and he wondered if it was from all the pent-up tension or the horrendous heat.

The descent seemed to go on forever. The platform they had come out on must have been very high up. But finally they reached the ground, and Jeff was the first to step out onto the rocky terrain. Up close, the landscape didn't look one jot friendlier than it did from above.

"Strange," Joanne said, looking around. "We've come out in the middle of a wilderness. No paths, no streets, no buildings. It doesn't look as if anyone ever lived here."

"Maybe they dismantled the buildings when they got to their destination planet," Castle suggested as he bent down to touch the ground. He ran the palm of his hand over the sharp rocks.

"But then there would still be roads, and foundations," Owl retorted.

"Or they never lived here," Jeff said. "Maybe it was a kind of nature reserve and they came here to recuperate."

"Recuperate?" Shorty guffawed. "Here?"

Jeff shrugged. "Let's keep going," he ordered. "Which way do we go?"

Eyes fixed on her handheld, Joanne turned around in a circle several times. She appeared to be having difficulty orientating herself. "I think we need to go this way," she said finally, waving an arm.

"Are you sure?" Castle asked.

"Pretty sure," she replied, and marched off. "If not, we'll notice soon enough and change our course."

Castle shrugged and trotted after her.

"How far still?" Jeff asked.

"About eighty miles," Joanne answered. "Then we

should hit the outer wall of this cavity and get to the corridor that leads to the center."

"And how deep inside this ship of horrors are we now?" Owl asked.

"About seventy-five miles."

The radio operator groaned. "Not even a third of the way. Unbelievable. Feels like we've walked thousands of miles already."

"And now we have to walk hundreds more without getting any closer to the center," Mac said.

Joanne shook her head. "You're wrong. Every step takes us closer to the center of the ship."

"Bullshit," Mac scoffed. "We're not even going downhill."

Joanne sighed. "Actually we are. The ground of this cavity doesn't run parallel to the outer surface of the ship, it slants down at an angle of more than sixty degrees."

"Yeah, but—" Owl began.

"Dumbass," Shorty interrupted. "Think of the corridors up near the surface. They changed the vector of gravity again here. In this ship, down is not simply down."

Owl and Mac didn't respond.

Even Jeff had trouble imagining that this huge cavity was slanting downward toward the center of the ship.

They trudged on in the direction Joanne had indicated. They wouldn't manage eighty miles in a day. Even if they kept up a good pace and didn't encounter too many obstacles, they would need three full days. Or probably four, because despite his sturdy boots, Jeff's feet were already aching from clambering across the rugged terrain.

Chapter 22

Jeff's neck was aching when he woke up. He looked at his watch. He'd slept four hours since his watch. It felt more like four minutes. He yawned.

"Here you go!"

Joanne was standing over him with a cup of coffee.

"Great service!" he struggled to smile.

"You've been tossing and turning for the last half hour. I thought you'd wake up sooner."

Jeff sat up, and took the cup gratefully. He looked around. Apart from Owl, everyone was up already. Mac and Shorty were sitting a little to the side, talking in low voices. Green was fixing something on his suit. Castle was heating up his cup of coffee with the immersion heater.

Jeff took a big gulp of the lukewarm brew. It would take a while before he felt the invigorating effect of the caffeine. "Anything to report?"

Joanne shook her head. "Nothing," she said. "Absolutely nothing."

"No sign of the light aliens?"

Joanne shook her head. "Maybe they only exist in the area of the ship we left behind."

Jeff blinked in the light of the reddish sun. "Day and night don't seem to exist here, either."

"No, apparently not," Joanne said. "Eternal darkness in the other parts of the ship, and perpetual depressing reddish-gray daylight here."

"I'm surprised the aliens didn't shut down these areas when they left the ship."

"Don't expect me to give you an explanation."

Jeff shrugged. "Of course not, I've given up trying to understand anything about this ship." He finished his coffee and placed the cup on the ground beside him.

"I'll go and wake Owl," Joanne said.

Jeff waved a hand. "No need, I'll do it."

"OK," she said and returned to the equipment sled, which formed the heart of the camp.

Jeff groaned as he stood up. Every bone in his body ached. As he walked over to Owl's sleeping bag, he looked around at the depressing landscape. The light was extremely weak. The scene resembled a dreary November day on Terra at twilight—making it all the more odd to look up and see the sun in its zenith. It was uncanny, and he had to admit that he almost preferred the depressing darkness of the wide corridors of the alien ship.

Jeff bent down and shook Owl's shoulder. "Wake up!" he said. "We have to get moving."

There was no reaction from Owl and Jeff felt a shiver run down his spine. He moved his hand to his shipmate's neck to feel his pulse and sighed with relief when he felt a heartbeat. But Owl's skin was very cool.

"Owl! Wake up!" Jeff said loudly.

Finally, Owl scrunched his eyes before slowly opening them. He looked up in silence and Jeff felt another shiver run through his body. His shipmate's eyes were glazed, as if he had a fever or taken drugs.

"Owl?" Jeff asked quietly. "Can you hear me?"

Several long seconds passed. "What is it?" Owl finally asked in a toneless voice.

"Are you OK? Do you feel all right?" Jeff wanted to know.

What had happened to the man?

He motioned to Joanne to come over to him, and she immediately sprang up.

"I don't know," Owl whispered.

"What do you mean?" Jeff asked.

"I don't know if I feel all right," Owl asked in a strange, throaty voice. "Should I feel OK?"

"What is it?" Joanne asked.

Jeff stood up and whispered softly in her ear. "He seems so apathetic."

Joanne nodded and dropped to her knees. Jeff took a step back. She felt Owl's carotid artery, his forehead, and shone a little flashlight into his eyes. His pupils didn't contract.

"Can you hear me?"

"Yes, I can."

"How do you feel?"

"I don't know."

"What don't you know?"

"How I feel."

"Are you in any pain?"

"No."

"What's your name?"

"Edward Owens, Corporal."

"Where are we?"

"On the alien ship."

"Who am I?"

"What kind of a dumb question is that? Can I get up now?"

Joanne nodded, stood up and went back to Jeff.

"And?" Jeff asked quietly, while Owl got up and searched for his belt.

"No idea. He doesn't have a fever and doesn't seem to be confused, either. Maybe we woke him up from a dream and he's just a bit off kilter. Let's wait and see."

Jeff shrugged, went back to his camping spot, picked up his sleeping back and rolled it up. He used the belt to tie it into a small bundle that he stowed on the equipment sled. He glanced around. "Where's Castle?" he asked, when he noticed the WSO was nowhere in sight.

"No idea," said Shorty, who was also stuffing his sleeping bag onto the sled.

"Joanne!" Jeff called.

"Yes?" Joanne turned away from Mac, with whom she was immersed in a conversation.

"Where's Castle?"

She hesitated. "Call of nature."

Jeff groaned. "Didn't I say we should use the recycling systems in our suits? What way did he go?"

Joanne shrugged.

"Castle," Jeff called. Despite the haze, there was visibility of about a mile. Castle couldn't have gone far.

"Castle!" he called again.

The others stopped talking.

"Did anyone see what direction he went?" Jeff asked but nobody answered.

Jeff shook his head. He was upset rather than angry. Everything was falling apart. How was he supposed to lead the group if nobody listened to him?

"Castle!" he called again as loud as he could.

It was pointless. Joanne returned his concerned glance. "Shall we split up to search for him?"

"No. We stick together," Jeff replied firmly. "We'll look for him together. We'll circle outward from the camp."

"What about the equipment?" Green said, pointing at the sled. "Should we leave it here?"

"No. We'll take everything with us. Pack anything that's still lying around and then we'll leave."

"I'm here!"

Jeff looked up to see Castle running down a small hill. He could feel his blood pressure rise. "Damn it, I told you we need to stick together. What should we do, if—"

"I found something," Castle said, gasping for breath. "Over there. You've got to come and see!" He pointed in the direction he had come from.

"What did you find?" Joanne asked.

"Come and have a look for yourselves," he said excitedly, and started running back up the hill.

"Mac! Shorty!" Jeff called and pointed at the equipment sled. Then he scrambled after Castle.

When he reached the top of the hill, he saw what looked like a big trench a few feet below them. It was filled with something.

"What is that?" Joanne asked, as she came panting up behind him.

Castle clambered down the hill until he reached the edge of the trench. It was about three hundred feet long and sixty feet wide. Jeff joined him and peered into the hole.

"Oh my god," Shorty said, letting go of the handle of the sled. Mac cursed as it tipped over and some unsecured objects fell to the ground.

Jeff squeezed his eyes shut in the hope that his imagination was playing tricks on him. But when he opened them again, he was greeted by the same sight. Bones. Whole skeletons. Hundreds of them. Thousands. It was a grave. A mass grave. The skeletons had two legs, two arms, ribs, a skull. Were these the extraterrestrial builders? There was nothing that distinguished them from human skeletons. Jeff could have sworn he was looking at a human grave.

"The aliens?" Shorty asked quietly.

"Who else?" Mac retorted.

Joanne crouched down on the edge of the pit and then jumped in among the bones. The edge of the grave reached up to her chest. She bent down and lifted up one of the arms of the corpses. "Four fingers and a thumb. Exactly like a human."

"Any idea how old the grave is?" Jeff asked.

Joanne stroked one of the naked skulls and finally shook her head. "No idea. I trained as a paramedic, not a coroner. It would depend on the environmental conditions, too. It's very warm and humid here. Depending on the microfauna, it can go very quickly. I would say anything between a month and a million years."

"Maybe this is where the aliens buried their dead during their journey," Shorty suggested.

"And why did they never cover them with anything?" Castle said. "No, I think this happened after the aliens left the ship."

"What makes you say that?" Joanne asked.

Castle shrugged. "Nothing. Just a feeling."

Joanne snorted.

"Can you tell how they died?" Jeff asked, feeling increasingly queasy gazing into this mass grave.

Joanne took her time examining some of the skeletons.

"It varies," she answered finally. "Some of them have terrible injuries. This one had his skull smashed in, that one had his chest crushed, as if he was put in a vice. But some of them don't appear to have any injuries."

"So how did they die?" Jeff asked.

Joanne shrugged. "How should I know? They might have been poisoned or gassed."

Jeff helped his shipmate out of the pit. "Weird that they're just like humans …"

"Maybe we have common ancestors," Castle speculated.

"Not likely," Joanne said. "How could we have common ancestors if they come from another galaxy?"

"Maybe the computer lied to us, like it did about almost everything else," Mac said.

Jeff frowned. "Come on, let's get going," He hoped against hope they would find answers deeper down in the ship. He swung his backpack over his shoulder and marched off. The others followed him.

"What's up, Owl?" Mac cajoled his shipmate. "Come on, get a move on!"

Jeff turned around. Owl was still standing at the edge of the pit. As Jeff approached him, he turned his head and looked at Jeff with glassy eyes.

"What is it?" Jeff asked.

"They died," Owl said in a completely monotone voice. "The ship killed them."

Jeff swallowed.

"And we're next," Owl added indifferently. Then he turned around and followed the others.

Chapter 23

"I can't stand another day in this depressing place," Joanne said quietly to Jeff, taking an unenthusiastic bite from her concentrate bar.

Jeff shrugged. What could he say?

"I'm almost looking forward to leaving the cavity and getting back into the dark corridors." Joanne's eyes were red—possibly because of the terrible air in the cavity, or from lack of sleep.

"I kind of wish we'd gone with the other option and tried our luck in space," Joanne concluded her monologue.

Jeff sighed. Was even Joanne losing heart? Was he the only one who wanted to carry on? No, *wanted* wasn't the right word. He didn't *want* to go deeper. He'd seen enough of this damn ship. But they *had* to go deeper. It was the only logical way out. Their last chance. They *had* to find something down there. Quite apart from the fact that he wouldn't have the strength to go all the way back the way they had come. Back across this bleak and desolate terrain. Back through the same corridors of the ship, only to vege-tate in their quarters with the fear of being killed at any moment. No, it wasn't an option. And he hoped that the second cavity, which they still had to cross, would be more hospitable.

The gloomy atmosphere was dragging them all down. Even Mac and Shorty's open defiance had given way to resigned silence. As if this cavity were slowly but surely robbing them of their energy and free will, turning them into soulless robots. Owl was the most afflicted. He had stumbled along behind them all day without a word, without a gesture, his eyes glassy and unfocused like a zombie. And now he was just sitting there, the concentrate bar Castle had given him dangling limply and uneaten from his hand.

"Owl? Don't you want to eat?" Jeff asked him gently.

His shipmate appeared not to have heard him. He looked past Jeff toward the hazy horizon, beyond which the outer wall of this cavity must lie, and which they would hopefully reach tomorrow.

"Owl!" Jeff repeated, this time a decibel louder.

"Yes?" Owl replied quietly, without looking at him.

"Aren't you hungry?" Jeff asked.

As if he'd been given an order, Owl bit off a little corner of his bar and chewed slowly and mechanically.

Jeff shook his head. He threw a glance at Joanne, but she seemed to be immersed in her own thoughts and uninterested in Owl's state of mind.

Jeff sighed and got up. "I'm going to sleep. Castle, Joanne, you're on first watch."

Castle nodded, then rummaged around in his backpack.

Jeff crawled into his sleeping bag, which he had already prepared before dinner, and pulled up the zipper. He closed his eyes and within a few seconds had fallen asleep.

· · ·

"PSST!" Joanne was shaking his shoulder. Jeff was wide awake within a second.

"What is it?" he hissed.

"Owl!"

"What's the problem?"

"I don't know exactly." She pointed toward a small hill. Jeff sat up and saw Owl standing with his back to them. Both his arms were stretched out slightly from his body. In his left hand he was holding a long knife. It looked like it was covered in blood.

Jeff scrambled out of his sleeping bag and together with Joanne crept over to where Mac and Shorty were already standing a few feet away from Owl.

"For God's sake, what are you doing?" Jeff asked.

Mac turned around and looked at him wide-eyed. He was white as a sheet.

"What …?" Jeff asked. He saw that something was dripping out of the front of Owl onto the ground. What was he doing? Was he vomiting?

"Owl!" Jeff yelled. He wanted to run to his shipmate, but something stopped him. "Owl!" he yelled again.

Owl turned round as if in slow motion.

Jeff cried out in horror.

"Oh my God!" Joanne whimpered.

Mac retched.

Shorty threw up all over his boots.

There was a huge wound from left to right across Owl's entire abdomen. Blood was running in thick rivulets from the wound and dripping to the ground. With every breath he took, Owl's intestines bulged out of his abdominal cavity. One loop was already dangling in front of his crotch.

"What are you doing?" Shorty asked hoarsely. "What have you done?"

Jeff wanted to run over and hold his shipmate upright, but he was rooted to the spot.

Owl's face was completely impassive. He seemed to feel no pain, or even to notice what he was doing.

To Jeff's horror, he now jerked the knife up into his chest.

"Don't do it!" Joanne screamed.

To Jeff's utter amazement, Owl began to laugh. He turned to look at them. "I am now part of this ship," he said, with a wild joy in his voice, as if he were announcing his upcoming wedding. "And you will be soon, too!" Then he thrust the knife deep into his chest.

Within a split second, his eyes became completely clear and his face was distorted with pain.

"What …?" he gasped. He looked down at the loops of his intestines, which had slopped down to his feet and at the knife in his hand that was still halfway inside his chest. Owl stared at his shipmates, mouth agape, eyes wide. Then he dropped to his knees, pulling the knife out of his body. The blood gushed out in a thick stream. The weapon clattered to the ground. Owl had time to scream before he fell forward and his face fit the bare rock.

Chapter 24

"The outer wall of the cavity is over there," Joanne said huskily. "About one more mile."

Jeff nodded. The haze had cleared a little and he could see the dark-gray, vertical wall that seemed to rise never-endingly into the sky. He couldn't yet make out any details or see an opening.

They had been walking nearly all day. In silence. Nobody seemed able or willing to talk about Owl's gruesome death. Jeff needed to process it himself. They had left their shipmate lying on the rocks covered in just his sleeping bag. What else could they do?

Jeff simply couldn't get his head around what Owl had done. Had this strange place driven him mad? Jeff remembered his dilated pupils. Had Owl secretly taken some drugs that he'd smuggled on board? Unfortunately they couldn't do an autopsy, so they would never know.

Jeff glanced over at Joanne, who was marching alongside him but at a slight distance. Her lips were pursed and her eyes were fixed on the wall in front of them. "What do you think happened?" he asked her tentatively.

She shrugged.

"Drugs?" Jeff asked.

"Possibly," she replied. "If we were anywhere else, I'd bet on it. A hallucinogen with a dissociative effect. Maybe phencyclidine or an overdose of ketamine. But I'm not an expert."

"And if it wasn't drugs? Could he have lost his mind?"

Joanne shook her head. "Not from one day to the next."

"Not even under the influence of the ship?" Jeff pointed in front of them, where the wall of the cavity reached seemingly endlessly up into the sky.

She shook her head again. "We haven't gone mad. No, I can't imagine it. Yesterday he was fine."

"Could it happen to the rest of us?"

Joanne didn't answer.

Jeff flinched. It was a nightmarish thought. To wake up in the morning completely out your mind and slit open your own stomach with a knife. He shook himself.

This goddamn ship. What was going on? Maybe Owl had been right. Maybe they never should have come on board. But now it was too late. From now on they were closer to the core than to the outer shell.

"There's a ramp going along the wall," Mac said.

Jeff could see it, too. It was wide enough that even the Charon would have fit on it comfortably. It led to a huge gate, set into the wall, through which you could have pushed an entire building. But it was closed.

After a few minutes the group had reached the ramp. The angle was flat enough that it required no effort to climb up. When Jeff reached the gigantic gate, he was overwhelmed by its sheer size. He had visited cathedrals on Terra that were smaller than this. The question was whether they would be able to open it.

"There's one of those squares on the side," Castle said, moving past Jeff to the edge of the gate, which was clearly marked with a swath of yellow paint. He pressed it, and Jeff took a step back. But the gate didn't budge.

"And now?" Mac asked wearily. His voice had all its former hostility and cynicism.

Joanne pointed to the left edge of the ramp. "I think there's another smaller door." She set off and Jeff followed her. She was right. There was another doorway, just big enough for a person to pass through without having to bend down. Joanne pushed the square and the door swung inward.

"We've found a way in!" She waved to Castle, Green, and Shorty, who were still standing in front of the big gate.

Jeff let the others pass, and then took a last look at the vast cavity they were about to leave behind. They would be passing through one more on their way to the center of the ship, and Jeff wondered if the same kind of scenery awaited them. They would find out soon enough. Tomorrow, hopefully. They had another thirty miles to cover.

"Are you coming, or do you want to carry on staring into space?" Castle asked, holding the door open for Jeff.

Jeff gave a start and turned around. Somehow it was easy to get lost in thought down here. He put it down to the weak light and gloomy atmosphere. He tried to refocus and pulled the door shut behind him.

Joanne had already switched on her flashlight. Jeff wasn't surprised to find they were in another airlock. It was small and only just big enough for the six remaining members of the team and their equipment sled. Suddenly there was a hissing noise, which quickly died away. No need for a big pressure equalization here, then. But unlike the airlock through which they had entered the cavity, this one was at ground level.

Joanne easily swung open the hatch at the far end of the airlock and stepped through the opening. Jeff was the last to enter the corridor that lay on the other side. It was no more than forty feet long. At the end of the corridor was a door, and on the side wall next to it, another door. Without waiting for an order from Jeff, Joanne headed toward them. There was nowhere else to go, in any case.

When Joanne reached the end of the corridor, she pushed on the square next to the door, but it didn't open.

Castle came up beside her and rapped his fist against it. There was a loud clanking noise, but it still didn't budge. "I think the big airlock is behind this door—the one on the other side of the big gate that we couldn't open out in the cavity."

Jeff hoped the other door in the corridor would open. Castle must have had the same thought, and pressed on the square. The door slid upward with a loud hissing noise.

Warily, Castle stepped through the opening and shone his flashlight around the room. Jeff followed him.

"This is interesting," Shorty said, coming up behind him.

Jeff looked up and nodded. Gray-brown rock face stretched up in every direction. Although the whole space was probably as big as a sports stadium, Jeff felt like he was in a chimney. Castle pointed his flashlight upward, but the beam of light petered out some way above them. The room must be several miles high. Most bizarre of all were the warm drops falling on his face.

"Is this some kind of tropical shower?" Mac asked.

Jeff stepped up to the rock face and ran his hand over the rough surface, which was completely wet. He looked up again, but closed his eyes instinctively against the drops of water.

"I think the room is so high, the humidity in the thinner air higher up is condensing," Castle mused.

"Rain?" Joanne asked incredulously.

Castle nodded.

"Why did they even go to the effort of building cliffs in the cavity and parts of the interior of the ship? Just so they would feel at home?" Shorty wondered.

"I reckon this ship used to be an asteroid," said Green, who had been very quiet over the last few days.

"What makes you say that?" Jeff asked.

"I think the aliens took an asteroid or minor planet with a high level of iron from their system, and used that iron to help build the ship. Maybe some original parts of the asteroid were left over and simply incorporated into the structure."

Castle shook his head. "Why would they do that? This much rock is heavy and would have slowed them down."

"Maybe they wanted to take along a little bit of home," Green shrugged.

"Can we get out of this damn rain already?" Mac asked and started marching over to one of the doors on the other side of the chamber.

"No," Joanne said. "That way." She pointed to another door. Mac grunted and changed direction. He reached the door, but waited for the others to join him before pressing the square. It slid upward.

On the other side was a huge hall, but instead of rock, the walls here were made of a gray-blue metal. And again, the ceiling was so high it was barely visible. Jeff turned on his headlamp and let the cone of light glide along the wall. The beam didn't reach far enough to light up the other end of the room. He shook himself. The dimensions inside this ship were beyond comprehension. Somewhere far in the distance shone a faint, red light.

"Is that another one of those cavitys?" Mac asked.

Joanne looked at her handheld and shook her head. "It wasn't on the hologram, that's for sure. It can't have a diameter of more than a few miles, or else I'd be able to see it on the map."

"Which way now?" Jeff asked.

Joanne turned in a slow circle as she looked down at her handheld, then stopped abruptly and pointed forward. "This way. After about half a mile the corridor should branch off and go down."

"Down?" Castle asked.

"I presume the vector of gravity will change again," she said.

The red light was coming from exactly the direction they were about to take. Jeff took a deep breath and set off. "Come on, let's go."

Joanne, Green, and Castle trudged after him. Shorty and Mac brought up the rear with the equipment sled. They made their way through the spooky hall in silence.

Gradually, the red light grew stronger and they could see it shining a few feet above the ground. Beneath it was a platform covered in yellow and grey stripes and surrounded by a low railing. It was big enough that they could all fit on it. Attached to the middle of the railing was a narrow box with a square. It was similar to the elevator that had taken them down to the bottom of the cavity.

"No gravity vector change here," Castle said laconically. "Just an ordinary elevator."

"What are we doing?" Shorty asked.

Mac snorted. "What kind of a dumbass question is that? Our *commander* is sending us down into the abyss."

"Quit complaining. If the hologram is right, this will take us straight to the next cavity," Joanne retorted. "Would you rather have walked?"

Mac waved off her comment and helped Shorty push the equipment sled onto the platform.

Jeff was standing a few feet in front of the elevator and regarding it critically. Could a simple construction like that really take them down sixty miles? He suddenly felt a wave of nausea wash over him, and an inner voice was whispering to him not to get into the elevator and travel into the depths.

"Jeff?" Joanne asked. "Everything OK?"

He rubbed his chin. "I don't like this. The elevator I mean. We shouldn't use it."

"I don't want to get in that thing, either," Castle agreed.

"If it gets stuck in the shaft going down, we're dead meat," Mac added.

"Let's look for another way down," Shorty suggested.

"Is there another way?" Jeff asked, turning to Joanne.

She swayed her head from side to side uncertainly while jabbing at her handheld. "A few miles further on there seems to be a corridor that also leads down. Looks a lot like the wide corridor we came down at the beginning."

Jeff glanced at the screen and nodded. "We'll use the corridor, even if it means more walking."

"What's that?"

Jeff looked up. Castle was standing on the edge of the platform and pointing into the darkness. Jeff looked in the direction he was indicating but couldn't see anything. "What are you talking about? What do you see?"

"Turn off your lights," Castle suddenly hissed.

Jeff and Joanne quickly switched off their headlamps. Now only the faint red light illuminated the platform.

Now Jeff saw it, too. There was a pale shimmer—over in the direction from which they had come.

"Is that …?" Shorty began, but the words dried up in his mouth.

"Yes, it is," Jeff answered quietly. "It's standing at the door we came through. I wonder if it's been following us the whole time."

"Let's go," Joanne said urgently and turned in the direction of the corridor she hoped was there. But after just one step she came to an abrupt halt. "There's another one."

Jeff swung around. She was right, there was one standing in the middle of the path they wanted to take.

"And there," Joanne was screaming now as she pointed in another direction. "We're surrounded!"

"Are they coming … closer?" Castle was trembling.

It was the first time he had seen more than one of the light aliens. Were there so many of them because they were deeper down in the ship? Or had whatever was following them brought in reinforcement? The light they emitted was getting stronger. "Yup, they're coming toward us," Jeff said in a voice so calm he surprised himself. "Everyone on the platform. It's our only escape route."

"I don't want to go down on that thing," Shorty whined.

"You're welcome to stay here …" Mac snarled.

Jeff shoved Joanne onto the platform. Green pulled Shorty on by the arm.

The aliens were nearing them at breakneck speed.

"Press the button!" Jeff yelled at Castle, who was standing right next to the control panel.

The WSO obeyed.

Nothing happened.

Oh God, we've had it!

"Shit!"

Then, finally, Jeff felt a faint vibration beneath his feet.

Another railing rose out of the ground, enclosing the platform, which began to descend, slowly.

Too slowly.

The first light alien was already there. It came to an abrupt stop in front of the sinking platform. Mac and Castle tore their pistols out of their holsters and fired. Two fine lines traced the path of the bullets through the semi-transparent body of the strange being and then dissolved again.

"Shit!" Shorty yelled and threw himself on the ground. Without thinking, Jeff took a step back and wondered if the creature would jump down onto the platform.

But suddenly two door halves slid out of the wall and closed the shaft above them.

Mac helped Shorty get up. "Damn, I thought they were going to get us that time."

"Did you see that?" Castle asked, his pistol still in his hand. "The bullets went straight through it."

"We don't stand a chance against those creatures," Joanne said, catching her breath. "Next time I doubt we'll be so lucky."

"At least we've shaken them off for now." Green was smiling with relief.

"What's to grin about?" Castle yelled, and stuck his weapon back in his holster.

Gradually, Jeff felt the adrenalin drain from his body. Around them the walls slid upward and doors closed at regular intervals as they passed. Castle suspected this was to keep the air pressure in the shaft stable. Nevertheless, they progressed at a snail's pace. If the elevator really did take them to the next cavity, Jeff estimated they would have to spend almost twelve hours on this platform. They would have to set up camp for the night here, strange a location as it was.

After they had been traveling for a few hours, they warmed up some of the remaining cans of food with the immersion heater. Soon all they would have left was the concentrate bars. Then Jeff assigned the watches and lay down in his sleeping bag. Despite the humming and slight vibration, he had no trouble falling straight to sleep.

Chapter 25

"Damn it, how much further down is this thing gonna go?" Mac asked.

Nobody answered him. Jeff had slept, completed his watch, and slept again. The platform had been descending for over twelve hours. According to Joanne's calculations, they'd already covered sixty miles. His shipmate picked up her handheld. "It can't be much further. We're approaching the end of the shaft that we thought from the map was a corridor. We should reach the bottom any minute now."

"And how much further to the cavity?" Castle asked.

"Not far. A few hundred feet."

"And we have to cross the whole thing?"

Joanne nodded. "Almost. About fifty miles."

Suddenly the platform screeched to a stop. Shorty, who was bending over the equipment sled, fell to the ground with a curse.

"And now?" Castle asked.

Jeff looked around. They were stuck. They were surrounded only by the metal walls of the elevator shaft.

"Shit and damn," Mac said. "Didn't I say that—"

"Shhh!" Joanne put a finger to her lip. Mac fell silent.

Jeff heard a soft hissing noise coming from above. "Sounds like the air pressure is being adjusted again. I'm sure …"

Suddenly one of the walls rose up into the ceiling and turned into a door.

"There we go," Green looked pleased. "That was much faster and more comfortable than traipsing through miles of corridors." He stepped out of the elevator and into a long corridor with rock walls.

Jeff followed him. The corridor was just wide enough for two people to walk along side by side. The elevator had been pleasantly cool, but down here the air was hot and humid again. Beads of sweat were already running down Jeff's face.

"This air is unbearable," Mac gasped as he maneuvered the sled into the corridor.

"Ninety-four degrees," Joanne said crisply. "One hundred percent humidity."

Castle was the last to leave the elevator. "Why the hell isn't this ship rusting away under our asses. I don't get it." The hatch closed behind him. Jeff felt a slight lurch in his stomach as he noticed there was no manual control next to the hatch. There was no going back. But that wasn't the plan, in any case.

He shrugged and began to stride along after Green down the long corridor. Some distance in front of them, the corridor was illuminated by a pale red light. But it was still too far away for them to know if it came from a lamp or had some other source.

"Joanne?"

"The corridor leads straight to the cavity."

"And what are we going to find there?" Shorty asked.

"Probably the same as in the last cavity," Mac said. "Lousy air, rocks, mass graves, and an atmosphere that will drive one of us to commit suicide."

"Zip it," Jeff growled. He'd had enough of Mac's griping.

"You know it's true," Mac spat back, but quietly.

They marched on in silence. The light didn't seem to get any closer. Jeff frowned. "I thought it was just a few hundred feet away."

Joanne looked down at her handheld. "By now we should be inside the cavity."

"Maybe that hologram wasn't up to date," Green conjectured.

"But it's been completely accurate up to now," Joanne was confused.

"There's something up ahead," Castle said.

Jeff could see it, too. The corridor seemed to be leading into a room. The structure of the walls was also changing. The craggy rocks gave way to smoother ones, which in turn were replaced by light sandstone. Strange symbols, different from the ones further up in the ship, were carved into the rocks. The writing they had encountered before was cuneiform, these resembled Egyptian hieroglyphs.

Finally, they entered the room. It was light enough that Jeff could turn off his headlamp. The whole chamber was the size of a small hangar, with walls of light sandstone. In the corners, columns adorned with bizarre curlicues rose up to the ceiling. Every square inch was covered with drawings. Opposite them was a large, double-winged gate out of black metal. Reddish light filtered through a crack in the middle of the gate, casting a thin strip of light on the floor. A brownish mist swirled beneath the ceiling.

Castle whistled through his teeth. "Look at these drawings!" He was standing in front of one of the walls and gently running a finger across the grooves of the alien symbols carved in the stone.

Joanne leaned forward and pulled a face. "That's disgusting," she said and turned away quickly.

Jeff swallowed. The drawings were of humanoid creatures that might well be humans. And they were unremittingly violent. Some of the figures were holding huge knives, others were lying on the ground with severed limbs. Some of them were burning at the stake. One of the figures was tied to a cross with its head hanging down and its stomachs ripped open, red coils dangling in front of its face.

Jeff took a step back, turned around and walked to another part of the wall. The whole room was covered with scenes of violence and torture. But why?

"We shouldn't enter the cavity," Joanne whispered.

Jeff swallowed. Again he felt that peculiar feeling in his stomach as he looked at the gate opposite them. Next to it was a small square with which they could probably open it. But *should* they open it? What kind of hell awaited them on the other side? Jeff was afraid to find out.

Green seemed less concerned and reached for the square next to the gate.

"Green, wait!" Jeff cried.

But it was too late. With a horrible scraping noise, the gate slowly swung open. Gloomy, blood-red light filled the room.

Jeff approached the entrance, but stopped short a few feet in front of it. Beyond it was a kind of terrace. It was bounded to the left and right by a parapet of beige sandstone.

"There's no other way to go!" Green said, in response

to Jeff's accusing look. He led the way out, and Jeff and the others followed him.

A rock wall rose up behind them, disappearing into thick gray and red clouds that swirled across the sky. The outline of the pale sun was only just visible through the haze. Jeff walked up to the edge of the platform. A broad, stone staircase led down to bare rock below, which looked as rugged and inhospitable as in the other cavity. And the landscape was just as bleak and monotonous. The ground was at least 300 feet below them. Fires flickered here and there on the naked rock, as if some kind of natural gas was rising from the earth and being kindled. The stench of decay was so pungent that Jeff gagged several times.

Castle pointed into the distance. "Do you see that? What is it?"

A few miles away there appeared to be a group of small buildings. Little black dots were moving around them. Jeff grabbed the binoculars from the equipment sled.

Something was running along the side of a stone hut. Was it an animal? Jeff adjusted the binoculars, and finally the image came into focus. His heart skipped a beat. That was a … no, it couldn't be. He lowered the binoculars, wiped his eyes and raised them back up.

Yes it could! He had seen correctly!

"You won't believe it," he whispered.

"What is it?" Joanne asked agitatedly. "Tell us!"

"Humans!" Jeff spoke in a husky voice.

"What?" Castle blurted out.

He was sure he wasn't mistaken. It was a group of people. No, two groups. But Jeff couldn't see what they were doing exactly. They were wearing only pathetic scraps of cloth. Their skin glistened with dirt.

"It can't be," Joanne whispered.

"Incredible," Green added.

Shorty was more pragmatic. "And what should we do? Shall we go and talk to them?"

Jeff lowered the binoculars. He chewed his lower lip as he tried to organize his thoughts. Were those really humans? Or were they aliens that just looked like humans? Holograms? He couldn't get his head around what he was seeing. They had to go and find out. "Yes, we'll go and talk to them."

Mac was dubious. "Might be a trap set by the aliens."

"What aliens?" Joanne snapped. "The light aliens?"

"No," Mac shot back. "I meant those … over there …" He trailed off.

"We'll go and find out if we can communicate with them," Jeff said. He found it hard to believe it was a trap. What would be the point? He also couldn't imagine they were extraterrestrials that just happened to look like humans. Well, they would find out soon enough. He began to descend the stairs, the others close on his heels.

It would take at least a quarter of an hour to reach the bottom. Through the mist, Jeff thought he could see other buildings and groups of people. But was it possible? How could humans possibly have found their way here? Had other spaceships landed on this ship and tried to save themselves by going into the interior?

Jeff and the others gathered at the foot of the steps and set off.

Tentatively, they approached the nearest group, which consisted of a good dozen people. Jeff could hear them yelling and shouting. They were running round and round the building, which looked more like a derelict stable than a dwelling. They were running in pairs, each pair was pulling a bundle on two ropes.

What is that? What are they dragging over the rocks?

Jeff's stomach clenched as the bundle in front of him raise an arm.

That's a human!

Yes, they were human bodies, and they were alive.

Jeff found himself rooted to the spot a few feet away from this grisly scene. His shipmates huddled around to look. Joanne's eyes were wide. The group appeared to take no notice of them. One of the bodies was dragged right past them by two angry, screaming men. It was a woman. She was naked and moaning softly as she was dragged on her back across the jagged, rocky ground. She was covered in open wounds, and a big one on her left thigh was leaving a trail of blood on the ground. Shorty retched.

Jeff shook his head. *What was going on here?* He gripped the butt of his pistol, but left it in the holster. Then he stepped in the path of two more men who were pulling another naked woman behind them. She was whimpering. In horror, Jeff realized the skin on her left leg was completely rubbed off, exposing the muscles underneath.

"Wait! Stop!" he said loudly.

The men stopped and stared at him angrily. Joanne grabbed Jeff's arm. He checked to see that his shipmates were all close by.

Jeff took a deep breath.

"Can you understand me?" he asked as casually as he could manage.

"Move! You're in our way," said the man on the left. He looked around fifty years old, was of medium height and had a gray beard. He squinted a little, which made it difficult for Jeff to decide which eye to focus on.

He felt a chill running down his spine. The man had spoken Cosmocration, the standard language in the Inner Sector. He wasn't an alien, but a human. Was it possible?

"What are you doing here?" Jeff asked.

"What does it look like? Punishing the whores," the other man answered. He had a huge birthmark under his right ear, and also spoke flawless Cosmocration. He addressed Jeff in a tone that suggested he'd asked the stupidest question of the century.

Maybe it was smarter not to pursue this line of questioning. "May I ask where you've come from and how you ended up here?"

The two men exchanged glances. The one with the birthmark shook his head as if he couldn't grasp Jeff's stupidity. The other one fixed his gaze on Jeff as if were about to tie *him* to a rope.

"Are there more people here?" Jeff asked.

The man on the left burst out laughing. The other man shook his head again, and they continued to drag the moaning woman behind them.

"Hell is full of people," the one on the left shouted.

Jeff watched them for another moment before returning to his shipmates. "What do you make of that?"

Joanne stared after the men, wide-eyed.

Green rubbed his forehead and shook his head.

Castle ran a hand through his sweat-soaked hair. "If we were anywhere else, I'd say they'd lost their minds."

"But they're humans," Jeff said. "So where are they from? What are they doing on this ship?"

"What did the guy mean by 'punishing the whores'?" Mac wondered aloud.

"Should we talk to them again?" Shorty asked. "Shouldn't we stop them from dragging those women to death?"

"Better not," Jeff said, remembering the murderous gaze of the bearded man. "We don't know what's going on here. They could attack us and do the same to us."

Joanne sighed. "So what *do* we do?" she asked finally.

Jeff rubbed his temples. "I say we keep going. There seem to be more people here. Maybe there are some we can actually talk to."

They picked up their belongings and continued walking.

Joanne was marching alongside Jeff. "I don't get it. How did those people get here? Did they crash land like we did? Were they taken in like us and then lost their minds? Where do they live? What do they eat?"

Jeff didn't have any answers. But he hoped to find some soon.

They were nearing another group of people. Jeff could hear the screams from afar and swallowed. It was no better than what they'd just left behind. Ten wooden crosses stood on a small hill. On each of them hung naked men, bleeding from multiple wounds. Some were unconscious or dead. Around the crosses stood a crowd of twenty or thirty men and women covered only in tattered loincloths. The women hadn't bothered to cover their breasts. Some of the men at the front were holding long, lance-like weapons in their hands, and were repeatedly prodding the flesh of the men hanging on the crosses. The rocks below were colored dark red.

Mouth agape, Jeff stopped about thirty feet away from the scene and watched the angry mob.

Joanne came up beside him. "What the fuck is going on here?" Her voice was barely more than a whisper. "What *is* this place?"

A large woman was in the process of attacking one of the men on the crosses with a lance. The sharp tip plunged deep into his thigh, and blood gushed over the blade and down the man's leg. His screams turned into whimpers and then stopped altogether as he slumped down on the cross, held up only by the ropes around his arms.

"I don't know," Jeff replied quietly. He wanted to speak to someone, but was scared. Scared of ending up on a cross himself.

A small, blond woman was standing a little to the side. She looked calmer than the rest of the pack. Jeff beckoned to Castle to follow him and approached her, keeping a tight grip on the butt of his gun. Given the number of potential opponents, it wouldn't help him much, but the touch of the bare metal gave him some reassurance.

"Excuse me," Jeff addressed the woman tentatively.

She took no notice of him, her gaze was fixed on the nearest cross, on which a bearded man with gaping chest wound hung apathetically. The woman was mumbling something to herself. Jeff thought he heard the words "Bleed, you sinners!"

"Excuse me?" Jeff spoke a little louder this time, and tapped the woman's bare shoulder. She briefly turned in his direction. Jeff got goose bumps. The woman was a good head shorter than him. She had a pretty, striking face with narrow, expressive lips and a button nose. But the pupils of her eyes were completely dilated. She looked mad. Jeff was reminded of the look on Owl's face before he had slashed open his stomach. Then she turned around again and continued with her mumbled litany.

It was pointless.

Jeff took a step back. The people here had evidently all lost their minds. They needed to think of something if they were going to get anything out of anyone.

He looked around. The rest of his shipmates were gathered at the bottom of a small hill, huddled around the equipment sled. Then Jeff had an idea. Maybe they could learn something if they separated one of the people from the rest. The blond woman, perhaps? Yes, it was possible, because the others were so busy watching the men being tortured on the crosses, they weren't paying attention to anything else.

Jeff waved Mac and Castle over. They listened to him with strained expressions, while he explained the plan to them.

"And you reckon that'll work?" Mac sounded doubtful.

"They could kill us," Castle added.

Jeff sighed. "We have to take a risk if we want to find out what's going on here. Let's go."

Mac shrugged, crept up behind the blond woman, flung one arm around her chest and covered her mouth with his other hand. Castle grabbed her by the ankles. The woman writhed, but Castle tightened his grip. She didn't stand a chance. Hurriedly they dragged her behind the little outcrop. Jeff and the others followed, glancing around nervously to check that they hadn't been seen. It looked like nobody had noticed them.

"Put her down over there," Jeff ordered.

Castle loosened his grip and the woman immediately started kicking. Mac struggled to keep her under control.

"Looks like she's gone mad. Like Owl. Is there anything you can do?" Jeff asked Joanne. She was pale but composed and immediately started rummaging in her medical bag. She took out a small pre-filled syringe and injected the clear solution into the woman's stomach. Immediately the woman began to calm down.

"What did you give her?" Castle asked.

"An antihypertensive. But the stuff is also used as an antagonist for various psychoactive substances. Might work."

"How long till it has an effect?" Jeff asked.

Joanne shrugged. "I don't know if it will work at all."

But finally the woman stopped kicking. After a few

minutes, Jeff nodded to Mac to take his hand off her mouth.

"You should be hanging from a cross," the woman's voice was slurred. Her pupils were still very dilated.

"Don't worry," Jeff spoke in a reassuring tone. "We just want to talk to you. We have a few questions."

"*What* have you got?" The woman looked at him uncomprehendingly.

"A few questions. Please don't worry."

"What kind of questions?" the woman asked, as if Jeff had made a stupid joke.

"What are you doing with the men on the crosses?"

"Punishing them, obviously. What did you think?" The woman stared at him as if she were dealing with an imbecile.

"What did they do?"

"They're sinners," the woman said.

"Sure, but what are they being punished for?"

"They sinned," she said firmly.

"Are you saying you don't even know?" Joanne asked.

"It doesn't matter. Who cares. They're sinners and must be punished."

"Yes, but who says they're sinners?" Jeff asked.

"Everyone knows it."

Jeff shook his head. They weren't getting anywhere.

"How did you get here?" he wanted to know.

The woman stared at him like a ghost. "What do you mean?"

Jeff could feel anger welling up inside him. He took a deep, slow breath. "It's a simple question: How did you get here?"

The woman regarded him in silence for a moment, then finally opened her mouth. "I died. How else would I have gotten here?"

294

Jeff's draw dropped. The woman must really be mad. There was no other explanation. "Where are you from? I mean, what planet did you live on?"

"On Deneb-6," she replied.

No, that can't be. Jeff bit his lip until he tasted blood in his mouth.

"I died when the planet exploded."

Dad died when Deneb-6 exploded. Jeff was unable to continue.

"Where are you now?" Joanne asked quietly.

"Pfft, where do you think?" The woman replied. "In hell!"

Chapter 26

"This is all too crazy," Joanne said. "In hell?"

It's beyond me, too, Jeff thought.

They had been unable to get any more information out of the woman and had finally let her go. She had immediately rejoined the group and cheered on the torturers beneath the crosses. What choice did they have but to continue on their way?

They had encountered more people. One group had been occupied in chopping off the limbs of "sinners" with long machetes, so that they bled to death. Another group had been lowering people into giant cauldrons of boiling water. With bared teeth, and pure hatred in their eyes. Jeff hadn't dared to intervene or to speak to any of them. The blond woman had been right: this was hell!

But one thing bothered Jeff above all: if the woman had really been on Deneb-6 when the planet was blown up by the rebels, was it possible that his father was down here in this madhouse? Jeff had told the woman his father's name, but she had shaken her head.

Now they were passing another group. Four men were

lying on the ground screaming in pain, while a dozen others impaled them on iron bars. An older gray-haired man was still alive when the bar emerged out of his body through his mouth. Jeff turned away.

"I can't take any more of this!" Joanne whimpered and covered her ears.

"This is a fucking madhouse …" Mac looked down at the ground as he continued to pull the equipment sled behind him.

They encountered more people as they progressed to the middle of the cavity. Jeff didn't see any real houses. Where did these people live? The whole thing was surreal. Were they just holograms? A huge show to frighten Jeff and his crew? No. He had touched the blond woman. She had been warm and obviously consisted of flesh and blood. Jeff had even smelled her sweat.

They were coming up to another group that was pushing heavy rocks up a steep hill. Once at the top, the big chunks of stone immediately began to roll down the other side of the hill, followed by the people who ran after them screaming. At the bottom, the whole exercise was repeated, as if Sisyphus himself had organized a competition for his most devoted followers.

Jeff and his shipmates stopped and watched the bizarre show. There were about a hundred people taking part in this crazy spectacle.

"I don't get it," Castle said. "What makes them do this bullshit?"

Shorty was wide-eyed. "They must have lost their minds!"

Green ran his fingers through his hair and shook his head. Since they'd entered the cavity, he'd hardly spoken a word. There was a strange sheen to his eyes, and Jeff hoped he wouldn't be the next one of them to fall victim to madness.

"Some of them are completely exhausted," Shorty frowned. "Why don't they just stop?"

"They can't," Joanne countered. "Look!"

Jeff followed her gaze. One of the unfortunate men was so exhausted he was stumbling around aimlessly. Again and again he paused for a moment, only to keep on running, his face distorted with pain.

But what—?

Then Jeff's eyes fell on the man's feet. As soon as he stopped for just a moment, the rock beneath him began to glow. With horror, Jeff saw that the man's soles were already burned black.

Jeff couldn't stop himself. He stepped forward and shouted: "Frank? Frank Austin?"

He didn't get a reply. Not that he had expected one.

Chapter 27

Finally they started to near the other side of the cavity. They had taken two breaks. The first time behind a small outcrop, the second time in a hollow in the ground. During the first break, Jeff had been unable to sleep. As soon as he'd closed his eyes, his mind had been filled with the horrific images he had seen—and with so many questions. The more he thought about it, the harder it was to come up with a single explanation that made any sense. Joanne knew about his father, but he'd had to explain to the others why he had shouted out his father's name. During the second break, however, he managed to nod off. His body was so overwhelmed with tiredness, that not even his restless mind could stop him falling asleep. But when he woke up, he felt anything but rested. Like zombies, they dragged themselves past more groups of people carrying out the most unimaginable atrocities on one another. And each time, Jeff forced himself to check that it wasn't his father who was being hacked to pieces, whipped, stretched, or disemboweled. And every time he called his father's name, he hoped he wasn't among the tormentors. But he neither saw his father nor received a reply from anyone.

Finally, they reached a flat summit and Jeff saw a broad staircase, similar to the one they had walked down to enter the cavity. It extended upward around eighty feet. At the top, there was a black gate, which hopefully offered a way out of this chamber of horrors.

They passed the last group. Several men were standing around some stone structures that looked like ancient altars. Naked women lay on them, motionless, and Jeff didn't want to know what the men were doing with their chained bodies. Almost out of habit, he called out the name of his father.

"Austin. Frank Austin."

He didn't even make the effort to lift his head.

"You'll find the sinner back there."

Jeff stopped in his tracks, as if struck by lighting, and looked up. A man with long brown hair was pointing vaguely toward an area to the left of the exit, then turned back to what he was doing.

"Excuse me?" Jeff asked. He had spoken so softly, he had to repeat himself immediately, but he didn't receive an answer.

He turned to his shipmates. They, too, had stopped in their tracks and were staring at him.

Jeff's horror was reflected in Joanne's shocked face. This simply couldn't be!

Joanne stepped closer to him. "Jeff," she said quietly and laid a hand on his shoulder. "Don't do it! Don't let yourself be manipulated!"

Was that what this was about? Was someone trying to manipulate him? To force him to do something? Had he heard correctly or was he starting to lose his mind? No, he was thinking clearly. And he knew what he was going to do.

"I have to know," he answered quietly.

Joanne looked at him beseechingly for a moment, then relented. "Of course. We'll go with you."

Mac cursed, but Castle and Green nodded understandingly. Jeff marched ahead. He could feel his heartbeat in his throat. They walked around the group at the altars, and a several hundred feet ahead of them, Jeff saw another cluster of people. About a dozen men and women were piling up logs and erecting poles. It was a pyre, there was no doubt about it.

A little to the side, four people lay on the ground, again wearing only loincloths. Their hands and feet were bound. There were three women and …

"Dad!" Jeff cried with a sharp intake of breath. He began to run.

"Jeff, wait!" Joanne screamed after him.

Jeff ran to his father as fast as he could. He had almost reached him when a tall man with curly black hair blocked his way.

"Where do you think you're going, kid?" the man asked.

"I want to go to my …" Jeff swallowed. "I have to talk to that man over there."

The curly-haired man shrugged and made way for him. "Be my guest. You don't have much time, in any case. He's gonna burn in a minute."

Jeff ran the last few feet. He stumbled and fell to the ground in front of his father. He scraped his knee on the sharp rock, but barely noticed the pain.

"Dad!"

"*Jeff?* Is that you?"

It was unbelievable! Jeff had never expected to hear his voice again. He took his father's face in his hands and looked him in the eyes. His cheeks were sunken. He looked thinner than Jeff remembered. His pupils weren't dilated. He looked at him without a trace of madness. But his lips quivered. "Is that really you, Jeff?"

"Yes," Jeff sobbed and pressed his father's head against his chest. He breathed in his father's familiar smell. He couldn't believe he was hearing this voice, which he knew so well. This couldn't be a hologram. This wasn't a deception. This was Frank Austin. Flesh and blood.

"I'm so sorry," his father said.

Jeff wiped the tears from his eyes. "There's nothing for you to be sorry about, Dad. Nothing at all."

"Oh yes there is. I didn't know, I didn't want it."

"What do you mean?"

A stray tear ran down his father's cheek. "I'm so sorry you're dead, too. I'm so sorry you're also in hell."

Jeff's felt his stomach cramp. "I'm not … you're not …" He swallowed. "We're not in hell."

"It's hard to come to terms with," his father said, his voice thick with tears. "The sooner you realize you're dead and in hell, the sooner you'll accept it."

"No, Dad. I'm not dead. And nor are you."

Frank Austin shook his head. "I saw it, Jeff. I felt it. The Quagma bomb on Deneb-6. I felt the heat consuming my body. I could feel my soul leaving my body. I was hovering over the inferno together with all the other souls that died. Together we flew into the red tunnel and together we were born again here. To suffer eternal damnation in hell."

Jeff shook his head. His mind was racing. How the hell had his dad come from Deneb-6 to this ship? How could he explain this to him? That he wasn't in hell but inside an alien spaceship that had somehow captured him.

"Dad, do you trust me?"

"Of course, son," Frank said without the slightest hesitation.

"I'm not in hell. You're not in hell. We are inside a huge spaceship." His father looked at him incredulously. Jeff pointed to his shipmates who were lined up behind him. "These are the crew members of the bomber Charon. Our ship was damaged. We had to abandon it and were picked up by a huge alien ship. And we ended up in this hell, which …"

Frank began to sob again. "Oh, Jeff. It's different for everyone. Everyone arrives in hell in a different way. It seems so unreal. When it's fast, you barely even notice you've died. Probably your ship was destroyed and you all came here together."

Jeff shook his head. "Our ship was destroyed," he said softly but firmly. "But we weren't killed."

"No, Jeff. I know how it is. The spirit looks for a way out. It takes time until you accept the inevitable. You're dead and your soul is in hell. And here we will be punished together for all eternity for our sins."

Jeff closed his eyes. He felt a painful throbbing behind his temples. None of this could be true! How the hell had his father ended up on this alien ship? He began to wonder if *he* was losing his mind. Or had he lost it already? Could his father be speaking the truth? Had their ship been shot down in the attack on Acheron-4? Had everything that had happened been an illusion, a hallucination, which his mind had used to alleviate his descent into hell?

He opened his eyes again and looked at Frank. The kind, blue eyes. The smile lines around his eyes.

No! His father wasn't a sinner. If there was one man in the universe who deserved salvation and paradise, it was his father. He had always put others before himself: his family, his friends, his work colleagues. And he had been one of the few people who still attended church regularly.

No, Jeff didn't know what game was being played here.

But he was not dead, and this place certainly was a kind of hell, but not hell itself.

"Do you trust me?" Jeff asked again.

"Yes, I trust you."

"Then come with me and let me prove to you that this is not hell!" Jeff was sobbing now himself.

"Oh, Jeff. That won't be possible."

"Why not?"

His father turned his gaze to the right, where the pyres were standing. "They won't allow it," he said quietly. "And they're right. I deserve to suffer."

"No!" Jeff began to cry in earnest now. "I will not accept it. I—"

A hand grabbed his arm and jerked him aside. Jeff landed face-first on the rock and hit his head hard. He put a hand up to his forehead and felt blood running through his fingers. Castle helped him get up.

He saw the man who had dragged him away pulling his father to the nearest stake. The three women had already been tied to the other wooden stakes. They were all staring blankly into the distance as if they had surrendered to their fate. Several men holding burning torches stood ready and waiting in front of the pyres.

Rage welled up in Jeff. Without conscious thought, he ran after his father's torturer, pulled his pistol from his holster, aimed, and fired. He hit the burly man in the back. A woman standing on the other side was suddenly covered in blood and bits of brown tissue. Jeff rushed forward and grabbed Frank's arm before the falling man pushed him down with him. The other men cried out in anger. One of them grabbed Jeff by the arm and he struggled to free himself from his grasp. A woman tried to grab his father. Jeff shot her down. He felt as if someone had switched him onto autopilot. All that mattered now was saving his father's life.

Another man stood in his way. He was holding a heavy club and swinging it over his head, ready to strike. There was a shot, and the man's skull exploded above the nose. Green had hit him in the back of the head.

"Jeff, you can't do that!" Frank gasped, but ran with him.

"Trust me!" Jeff screamed. "I'm going to get us out of here."

More shots were fired, and several men and women fell to the ground. Others weren't deterred, and stormed toward them. There were too many of them.

"Run!" Shorty screamed, as he fired another shot.

"Fuck this," Green cursed, running toward the exit, which was just a few hundred feet away.

The attackers were close on their heels, but with their bare feet, they couldn't run as fast across the rocky terrain as Jeff and his shipmates in their boots. Only Frank screamed in pain. Jeff pulled him on, regardless. Better for him to have injured feet than to die.

They reached the stairs. Green and Castle ran ahead. Mac cursed the whole time.

"No, Jeff!" his father screamed. "Don't go any further. We're not allowed there."

"Trust me," Jeff said, pulling Frank along behind him despite his father's increased resistance. They almost both fell. The first attackers had reached the steps but stopped in front of them. They, too, seemed afraid of doing something forbidden—whoever it might be that had forbidden them.

The others had reached the door and were waiting.

"We're not allowed in," his father screamed again. "It's

not allowed." He put his arms around Jeff's chest so tightly, he could hardly breathe.

"Help me!" Jeff hissed.

Mac grabbed Frank Austin by the arms and pulled him away. Jeff was able to free himself and grabbed his legs.

"It's going to be OK. You'll see!"

"No!" His father howled as if in fear of his own life. "He'll punish us."

Finally, they reached the plateau. Mac dragged Jeff's father through the door and into a lobby, which—like the one through they had entered the cavity—was covered in hieroglyphs and drawings.

"*Who* will punish us, damn it?" Jeff gasped.

"HE will!" his father screamed. "HE will punish us."

Suddenly Jeff's hands, which were still clutching at his father's ankles, were burning. The pain made him cry out. He let go and staggered back.

Mac had fallen backward and hit the wall. His hands were smoking.

Frank Austin screamed. His burning legs kicked like crazy.

"Dad!"

Jeff stumbled forward. He tried to put out the flames with his bare hands; they were blazing as if his father consisted of gelled gasoline.

Joanne and Green pulled him back.

Those screams!

He knew he would never be able to forget them.

Joanne placed a hand on his shoulder and together they watched as his father was reduced to a pile of ashes.

Chapter 28

Jeff opened his eyes, and stared at the black ceiling.

Joanne was immediately by his side. She knelt down and laid a hand on his shoulder. "How are you feeling?" she asked gently.

How was he supposed to feel? He had found his father, who he had believed to be dead, in this crazy and most unlikely of places—only to lose him again.

Jeff's shipmates had carried him deeper into the ship's interior after he collapsed. They had set up a camp for the night in the first suitable room they came across. He had been aware of Joanne treating the burns on his hand with an ointment, before drifting off into a fitful sleep.

"Jeff?"

"S'OK. I'm OK," he said weakly.

"Do you want to talk?"

"Later maybe."

Joanne nodded and handed him a concentrate bar and his water bottle.

It took a long time before he was able to get up and join the others, who were sitting in a semicircle around a spotlight on the floor of the dark room. Here again, the walls were made of the gray-black alloy of the ship. He sat down next to Joanne, who was sucking listlessly on her food.

"What next?" Shorty asked. His question was directed at Jeff.

Jeff looked around the faces of the others and tried to marshal his thoughts. He had no more energy. All he wanted to do was crawl back into the corner and close his eyes. Someone else could lead the group. What was the point of it all?

He shrugged. "No idea," he said weakly.

Nobody spoke.

It was Mac who broke the silence. "No idea," he repeated. "I don't want to hear that from you, Captain!"

Jeff looked up.

"You dragged us down here into this hell," Mac spoke quietly, but his voice was tight with anger. "Fields died as a result, and so did Owl. And now you're kicking the can?"

"Mac!" Joanne raised a hand.

"No. I won't accept it. We followed this bastard all the way to *hell*. He has no right to wallow in self pity just because he came across his dead daddy."

Anger welled up in Jeff and brought him back to his senses a little. "Watch what you say about my father."

Mac stuck his arms up in the air. They were wrapped in thick bandages. "See this, big shot? I burned my hands for you and your pop. I've earned the right to shoot you dead. And you know what?"

Jeff didn't say anything.

"I told you I thought you were a mamma's boy and an aristocratic asshole. But over the last few days I changed my mind about you. You brought us down here, which I never would have had the guts to do. You were convinced that our only chance of survival was to get to the center of this Satanic ship." He squatted in front of Jeff so their faces were level. "And now move your ass, get us to the goddamn center, and prove to me you were right!"

Jeff closed his eyes. He knew that what Mac was saying was true. What would have been the point of all the deaths, the suffering, the fear, if he gave up now?

Jeff opened his eyes again and wiped Mac's spit from his face. He pressed his lips together and stood up.

"All right," he said hoarsely.

"Finally," Mac said, and backed off.

"We'll keep going," Jeff commanded. "Get the equipment sled ready."

"I'm afraid that won't work," Green said.

"And why not?"

"Because it's still with the crazies down in the cavity," Castle said. "We had to leave it behind when we fled."

Jeff bit his tongue. All that was left was the medical kit that Joanne had on her back. Their supplies, water, and lots of useful equipment were all on the sled. On the other hand, Jeff had no desire to go back. The mob would probably attack them immediately.

"We'll continue without it," Jeff said. "We'll activate our suits and rely on their supplies."

Shorty suppressed a groan.

Jeff turned to Joanne. "How far still to the center, and what route do we need to take?"

Joanne took out her handheld. She swiped across the screen, then pointed to one of the exits. "If we go out that way, we'll soon reach a corridor that's about ten miles long and leads directly to the center of the ship."

"Ten miles," Jeff repeated. "That's doable. And then we're at our destination?"

Joanne hesitated. "That takes us to a large room

directly bordering the central area. I can't say what lies beyond it, because the hologram doesn't show anything."

"How big is the central area?" Castle asked.

"It's got a diameter of sixty miles," Joanne answered. "When we reach the border and find a way in, it's thirty miles to the actual epicenter of the ship."

God only knew what awaited them there.

They would find out soon enough. "Let's go."

As he led the way, Jeff activated his suit's remaining systems. A hologram appeared in front of his face that only he could see. It consisted of a few displays and a series of status lights that alternately switched from red to yellow and finally to green. He shuddered as the catheters for urine and feces were activated.

The next room was round, and the door on the far side was much bigger than the other ones. Joanne led the way into the long, high, corridor.

"We need to go this way."

They continued along the dark corridor in silence. Joanne marched alongside Jeff, but they didn't speak. Jeff was lost in his own thoughts. The encounter with his father already seemed like a surreal dream. He and his mother had mourned deeply for his father. Then as the months passed, he had slowly come to terms with the fact that his father was dead and that he would never see him again. And now this unbelievable encounter—only to be immediately parted from him again. What power in the universe could be so cruel?

He tried hard to suppress his dark thoughts and to concentrate on what lay ahead. Today they would reach the center of the ship. What awaited them there? Would they finally learn something useful? Find some answers … some way of steering this ship back to where they wanted to go … or would they be confronted by a new catalog of horrors?

Jeff expected one of those pale light aliens to appear in front of them at any moment. Then it would all be over, in any case. There didn't seem to be any turnoffs from this corridor down which they could escape.

But thankfully, none of the sinister creatures appeared.

As if in a trance, Jeff trudged on and barely noticed the time passing. Finally they were standing in front of a big, gray, metal gate. They waited for Joanne, who had fallen behind a little. She was pale and her eyes were bloodshot.

"Everything OK?" Jeff asked her.

She looked at him with glazed eyes, and Jeff was about to repeat his question when she answered. "I'm fine. Got a bit of a headache, that's all. We can go on."

Jeff hoped it was just a headache, and touched the square next to the door. The door slid up and retracted into the ceiling with a loud hissing noise. It opened into a large room.

Jeff wanted to go through the opening, but Green grabbed him by the arm and held him back. "What is it?" Jeff asked.

"Careful. Something's not right here."

"What do you mean?"

Green pointed at a yellow line on the floor, then at a ladder, which appeared to be mounted horizontally along the wall. The engineer took a concentrate bar from his pocket and threw it into the room. As the bar flew over the yellow line it didn't fall down, but accelerated upward towards the opposite wall, as if magnetically attracted by it.

"I see. Thanks," Jeff said. Clearly the gravitational vector had changed yet again.

He crossed the threshold tentatively, then grabbed the nearest rung of the wall-mounted ladder with both hands.

Then he took another step forward. His legs were suddenly flung upward. He was only able to hold onto the rung with great difficulty, and his feet slammed into the ladder.

His coordinate system had changed from one moment to the next. The floor had turned into the wall, and the opposite wall into the floor, at least fifty feet below him. If Green hadn't warned him, he would have fallen to his death.

"Watch out! You have to be really careful here," he warned the others.

A cylindrical-shaped corridor led out of the small room and was so narrow that Jeff had to crawl down it. As he squeezed his way along it, he was repeatedly pushed to the side. It took him a moment to realize the direction of gravity was changing again. After a few feet, he looked back and saw Shorty bringing up the rear, crawling along the ceiling of the corridor. He immediately felt dizzy, and focused on looking ahead before he was actually sick. The ceiling had now turned into the floor.

He forced himself to continue. Again and again, in his mind's eye, he saw his father burning alive. And every second his mind wasn't overwhelmed by this image, the same questions kept popping up: How had his father gotten here? Had it really been his father, or just a deceptively similar illusion created by this nightmarish ship?

He reached a closed hatch and waited a moment for the others to catch up before opening it. Like an iris diaphragm, the individual sections of the hatch disappeared radially into the wall. He blinked as he was dazzled by a bright blue light.

Shit! A light alien!

He rolled to the side and pulled his pistol from his holster.

But then he realized the light was simply emanating

from the new room. He clambered out of the tunnel and stood up. Except for the cavitys, it was the first illuminated room since leaving their quarters; the first sign that here, in the center of the ship, something was different. The room was spacious, like a warehouse. But Jeff couldn't see the source of the light, it seemed to be coming from every direction at once. The walls were white and smooth, with narrow, rectangular hatches embedded on the left- and right-hand sides.

He helped to pull the others out of the tunnel, and noticed that Joanne looked worse than ever. He wondered if they should set up a camp for the night here, but he wanted to find an entrance to the central part of the ship. Then they could have a rest before going any further.

"Joanne, how are you feeling?"

She coughed slightly, shaking her head as if it might dispel her drowsiness. "I feel dizzy. Like I drank a couple of glasses of champagne. But I'm OK."

"Sure?"

Instead of answering, Joanne studied her handheld. "We can go through either of the hatches. They both lead directly to the center of the ship—which is only few feet away from here."

Jeff nodded. "OK." He chose the hatch on the right and headed straight for it. The others followed and took up position behind him.

He reached out a finger, but didn't speak. Turning around, he studied the faces of his shipmates. Joanne looked dazed; Mac and Shorty were clearly exhausted; Green's eyes were fixed on the ground; and Castle appeared tense. Somehow, he felt he ought to say something and took a deep breath.

"We've reached our destination. We've nearly made it to the center of the ship. I don't know what's behind this door, but I'm sure of one thing. If we're going to find a way to get back home, the answers to our questions will be behind this door." He hesitated. "In any case, I want to thank you for following me here."

Joanne nodded tiredly. Mac looked him in the eyes, hesitated a moment, then nodded too. The others didn't react, and just waited.

Jeff took another deep breath and pushed the button next to the hatch. He heard the inner hatch closing behind them.

Then a loud alarm tone sounded from the loudspeaker of his helmet. Several indicator lights on his neck console flipped to red and he heard a cracking sound in his ears.

"Shit!" Castle screamed.

The emergency release on Jeff's helmet activated. The molded plastic cover shot out of his neck, wrapped itself around his head and locked with the ring round his neck.

Within seconds, the air had been sucked out of the room, creating a vacuum. The lights flickered briefly. If they hadn't activated their suits in advance, they would have all been dead by now. In front of Jeff, the hatch went up, revealing a narrow staircase illuminated by strips on the walls that emitted a pale white light.

Jeff took a deep breath and looked around. His ship-mates all had the plastic visors of their helmets pulled down in front of their faces.

"Lucky again," Green said laconically.

"Let's go," Joanne said.

Jeff began to climb the stairs. They led up just a few feet. One step at a time, Jeff climbed the stairs until he was standing on a wide platform.

What a view!

"Oh my God!" Castle said.

The platform was curved and made of pale-gray metal.

Jeff felt like he was inside a huge bowl or a giant balloon. The strangest thing, however, was the enormous dark-gray sphere hovering above them, which took up almost the entire sky. It was covered in a regular pattern of fine black lines. Here and there on its surface were faint dots of lights and black areas. Some of them looked like they might be doorways.

"What the hell …?" Mac whispered.

"What is that? I don't get it! What are we looking at?" Shorty ogled the hovering orb.

"That," Joanne began, "is the spherical center of the ship."

"What?" Mac was confused. "Above us? But …" He trailed off.

Jeff understood, although it was completely unintuitive. "They work with artificial gravity. We've seen that already. There is no direct access to the central area. They've separated it from the surrounding central area of the ship with a vacuum."

"Let me get this straight," Shorty said. "That huge sphere above us is the epicenter?"

"Yup."

It really was breathtaking. The whole orb was bathed in a soft light. The horizon of the rising floor merged with the outer shell of the epicenter, which was perhaps twenty or thirty miles away.

"How can it just float there like that?" Mac pondered.

"It's probably gravimetrically coupled," Castle replied.

"What?" Jeff asked.

"Imagine a steel ball suspended from metal springs," the weapons expert explained.

"And?" Mac asked impatiently.

"Replace the metal springs with gravitational fields."

Jeff could picture it.

"How far away is it?" Shorty asked.

"Almost exactly six miles," Green said.

"How do you know that?"

"You can calculate it from the angles," he replied. "If you take the tangent from the big—"

"OK, OK," Shorty gave a dismissive wave. "Forget it."

"I'm wondering something completely different," Castle said.

"Yup," Jeff nodded. "How do we get across?"

"The gravity is too strong for the jets on our space-suits," Joanne said.

Jeff thought feverishly, but couldn't come up with a solution. Was their long journey going to end here? Had it all been for nothing?

No, there had to be a way!

"Maybe there's a bridge or some kind of crossing over there," Shorty suggested brightly.

"Take a look around," Mac grunted. "All as smooth as a baby's ass. There are no bridges here."

"You can't be sure," Shorty grumbled. "Maybe beyond the horizon."

"I don't think so," Green said thoughtfully. "I think they isolated the central orb from the rest of the ship for a good reason."

"And what reason is that?" Castle asked.

But Green just shrugged.

If the engineer was right, they had failed.

"Shit!" Mac cursed.

They stood there for some time, staring silently up at the silver sphere, so near and yet so far away.

"There is one possibility," Shorty said finally. "But nobody will like it."

Jeff swung around.

"Out with it," Castle said.

Shorty sighed. "On the equipment sled, there are four levitation belts. We could use them to take turns pulling ourselves over.

Jeff closed his eyes.

"No!" Mac cried. "I'm not going back to those lunatics."

It was also the last thing Jeff wanted. But it was probably their only chance of reaching their goal. "Come on," he ordered the others and started back down the stairs.

"Where are you going?" Castle asked.

"Back to the antechamber. We'll close the hatch, let the air back in, and rest for a few hours."

"And then?"

"Then we'll go back to the cavity and get the levitation belts."

Mac put his head in his hands. "Holy shit!"

Chapter 29

Jeff awoke to find Castle shaking his arm.

"What is it?" Jeff looked at his watch blearily. He had only slept four hours and didn't feel in the least refreshed.

"It's Joanne" Castle said. "I'm really worried about her."

"What's wrong?" Jeff asked, but he had already sprung up.

Joanne was lying in the corner with her arms wrapped around her chest. Her lips were trembling.

When Jeff looked into her dilated pupils, he got a shock. "Joanne!" He leaned over her.

"We're all going to die," she whispered. Saliva was dribbling from the side of her mouth.

Jeff stood up again and pulled Castle over to a corner. "It's just like Owl. That's how it started."

"What can we do?" the WSO asked.

"We need to make sure she doesn't harm herself, we need to watch her vigilantly."

"What about that drug?" Castle asked.

"What do you mean?"

"The stuff she gave the woman in the cavity. Maybe it'll work on her."

"I'm just wondering—" He heard a noise beside him and whirled round.

Damn it, what the—?

He was looking into Joanne's contorted face. She was holding a knife in her hand. Jeff jumped backward, stumbled, and fell to the ground. Castle screamed and threw up his arms.

Jeff tried to get up, but his boots kept slipping on the floor. Then the blade pierced Castle's neck. His scream turned into a gurgle. Blood gushed from a huge wound in his throat. He fell to his knees and then collapsed in a heap.

Joanne took a few steps back. Her eyes were wide open. Her face was splattered with drops of blood. As if in slow motion, she raised her hand with the knife.

"No!" Jeff screamed, finally getting to his feet as she guided the blade to her own neck. "Don't do it!"

But Mac was already by her side. He grabbed her and pulled the knife out of her hand. Then he pulled her hands behind her back. The blade clattered to the ground.

"Give me something to tie her up with," Mac shouted.

With trembling hands, Shorty handed him a strap from Joanne's backpack. Mac tied her hands together behind her back.

"Give me another one," he ordered Shorty, and tied her feet together.

Joanne was completely spaced out. Saliva dribbled down her chin.

Jeff turned to Castle. Green was already kneeling beside him. "He's dead."

"No! No!" Mac wailed.

Jeff covered his face in his hands. This couldn't be happening. *Not another one! And not Joanne!* He stumbled forward a couple of steps and thumped the walls with both fists. "Jesus fucking Christ!" he screamed. "You fucking ship from hell. Leave us alone!" His knees gave way. Leaning back against the wall, he slid to the floor and began to sob. "I can't take any more. I've had it." He tipped his head back and whimpered.

He wasn't sure how long he sat there like that, but finally he got to his feet. He had to support himself against the wall as he got up. He looked around the group. Mac and Shorty were sitting next to Joanne. Shorty's eyes were red, he must have been crying, too. Mac was staring at the ground rubbing his wrists. A bit further away, Green was leaning against the wall staring at them all blankly.

Jeff's anger turned into cold hatred. Hatred for this damn ship, these damned aliens.

The reason for all this misery, all this pain, all this horror, dwelled in the center of this ship and was waiting patiently for them. He wanted to go there and kill it. Whatever it was.

"Mac! Shorty! Green!" he spoke in a rasping voice.

"Yes, Sir?" Shorty asked weakly.

"Get up. We're going back to the cavity to get the levitation belts."

"What about Joanne?" Mac asked.

Jeff ran his fingers through his hair. They couldn't possibly drag her all the way back, bound up like that. But they also couldn't leave her here.

What to do?

"I'll wait here with her until you get back," Green said.

Jeff looked up. He didn't want to separate the group.

Every time they had done it before, something dreadful had happened. But what choice did they have?

"Are you sure?"

The engineer nodded. "I don't think we're in any danger here. It's been a while since we've seen one of those light aliens. I'll look after Joanne till you get back."

Jeff nodded gratefully and beckoned to Shorty and Mac. "Let's go."

Together they crawled through the narrow tunnel and climbed down the ladder into the wide corridor, which would take them back to the cavity. They had around ten miles to cover; Jeff hoped they could make it in about two hours.

"This ship is really starting to piss me off," Mac said.

"Me too," Jeff agreed.

"Do you think there might actually be extraterrestrials in that central sphere who are controlling all this?" Shorty asked.

Jeff didn't want to speculate. He knew they wouldn't get to the truth by guessing.

"Maybe the onboard computer is part of all this?" his shipmate persisted.

"Listen, Shorty," Jeff replied crossly. "I don't know. I really don't. All I know is that we'll find the answers we want in the center of the ship. And we're going to get them."

"Ooh, the boss is mad," Mac quipped. Jeff ignored him.

Finally, they reached the anteroom to the cavity, where everything was as they had left it. The pile of ash that had been his father was still lying on the ground. Jeff swallowed and hurried past it.

They stepped into the dim light of the huge cavity and

looked down at the barren landscape. In the distance, Jeff could see the group his father had been a part of. And he could see the equipment sled—no more than a black dot—beside on of the little hills. They made their way to the group of people, keeping themselves hidden from view as best they could. It looked like the group had found new victims, who were lying on the ground and watching stoically as the torturers built up the funeral pyres. Did they never sleep? Or eat? Jeff simply didn't get it.

"Shall we just take the belts? Or shall we try and take the whole sled?" Shorty asked quietly.

Jeff considered. If they slunk up from behind and took out the bag with the belts, they stood a better chance of going unnoticed than if they tried to take the whole sled.

"We won't take any risks," he decided. "We'll grab the belts and get out of here."

"OK," Mac nodded.

They had almost reached the sled. The men and women in front of them were still busy building the pyres and took no notice of them.

Jeff dropped to his knees and crawled the last few feet. The bag with the belts was now right in front of him. He stretched out a hand, easily pulled it out from under the straps and hung it around his neck. They'd done it. Now all they had to do was get out of here.

Jeff lifted his head to take a last look at the men and women.

His eyes fell on a thin man who was helping pile up the pyre. The man turned and looked in his direction.

"Dad!" Jeff screamed.

The men and women turned round to look at him.

Shit, what had he done?

But it was too late. They'd seen him.

"Seize them!" his father said sternly.

Jeff jumped up and wanted to run away. But a powerful hand had grabbed him by the shoulder. Mac cursed and fired his pistol. A slender woman fell whimpering to the ground. Then a man with a broad back knocked the pistol out of Mac's hand.

Another woman pulled Jeff's weapon out of his holster and tossed it away in a high arc. Two muscular men in loincloths grabbed Jeff by the arms and dragged him toward the pyre—directly in front of his father, who stood, straight-backed, in front of him.

"You were dead! I saw you burn!"

"I told you. We're already dead. We can't die anymore," his father said tonelessly.

Jeff looked him in the eyes. Yesterday they had been clear and focused. Today his pupils were dilated and his eyes glazed.

"What happened to you?" Jeff asked quietly.

"I've been born again," his father replied icily. "Just as everyone here is born again and again to contribute to the eternal cycle of punishing and being punished. And this time I've been born again to punish." He leaned his face forward until his nose touched Jeff's. "And today you will be punished. Because you have done something forbidden, and are therefore a sinner in the eyes of *Him*."

"Him?" Jeff asked in desperation.

"The Prince of Darkness, who watches over us from the center of hell, commanding us to punish and suffer, as is his right and his task."

Jeff felt a shiver run down his spine. "Dad! Please!"

His father took a step back and pointed at Mac and Shorty. "Bind them to the free stakes," he ordered the surrounding men and women. "So that they are exposed to the purifying fire."

Shorty screamed as they dragged him to the nearest stake and tied him to it.

"Fucking bastards!" Mac cursed, as he was tied to the stake next to it. "I'll kill you all!"

Jeff's father picked up a burning torch from the ground. The throng of people cheered as he set light to the pile of logs.

Jeff tried to break free, to help his shipmates, but there were too many hands holding him back. "You can't do this, you pigs!"

As if someone had dumped accelerant on the piles of wood, they immediately caught fire and Jeff's shipmates were quickly engulfed by flames. Shorty's hair burned like tinder. Jeff closed his eyes, but he couldn't block out their shrill screams of pain. And it got worse. In the end, the sounds they made sounded almost inhuman. Finally they fell silent and the only thing Jeff felt was the burning heat of the fire on his skin.

When Jeff opened his eyes again, Shorty's body had collapsed onto the pyre. Mac, however, was still tied to the post with his feet on the pyre; a human torch. Jeff would be next.

As Mac collapsed, too, the guards around him hollered and raised their fists in the air.

At that moment, Jeff broke free. He almost stumbled, but he was free, and he ran.

"You will not escape your punishment," his father shouted from behind him. "You will be back, and together we will punish ourselves for all our sins."

Jeff bit his tongue and ran. He ran like he had never run before in his life. He looked around and saw that some men had taken up the chase, but they soon gave up and turned back. The last thing he heard was the maniacal laughter of his father.

He stormed up the steps, through the antechamber and into the corridor, where he closed the hatch that led back into the cavity. Then he slumped on the ground and closed his eyes, overwhelmed by fits of sobbing. He tore the bag with the levitators from his shoulders and threw it on the ground.

Chapter 30

Jeff stumbled back down the corridor. He had to stop several times to wipe the tears from his face. He knew he was close to collapsing. He had no more energy left.

He had no idea how long he had sat in the corridor, howling.

Now Shorty and Mac!

Their death screams echoed through his head, and every echo pierced his very being like a hot, glowing knife.

Now only Green and Joanne were left. And who knew if she would ever recover from her fit. Would any of them reach the center of the ship? Jeff had his doubts.

He dragged himself, one foot at a time, down the dark corridor, when he saw a faint light. Hastily he switched off his headlamp.

He wasn't mistaken. In front of him, not far away, was one of the light aliens. And it was coming closer. It was hard to tell how fast. Jeff wanted to turn around and run back, but he didn't stand a chance of reaching the cavity before it reached him. And what would be the point?

The creature was now close enough that Jeff could see

without his headlamp. A little way back down the corridor there had been a turnoff. Maybe he could hide himself there somehow. It was his last chance. He ran.

He raced down the corridor that branched off from the main one and which, a little further on, turned a corner. He looked back. The corridor was illuminated by the pale light of the alien being. It must be just past the fork.

Jeff slipped through an open door into a room. He briefly flicked on his headlamp to get his bearings. The place looked like it had once been a lab or a workshop. There were several tables and various large implements attached to the walls. In the back wall was another door. As quietly as he could, Jeff slipped over to it. Once through, he briefly switched on his headlamp. He was frightened almost to death when he realized it wasn't a way out, but a small chamber without any further doors. He had fled into a dead end.

He swiveled round in a panic. A shaft of white light fell from the hallway into the lab. Any moment now, the light alien would float through the door. He looked around frantically but there was no other way out. Nowhere to hide. It was over. Once and for all. Now he was going to die.

He resigned himself to his fate. Maybe it was for the best. Then this nightmare would finally come to an end.

The light alien had already entered the room. It stopped in the doorway and turned around slowly, as if it were searching for him. It must have seen him, because it remained motionless just a few feet away from him.

As with the light alien he had encountered before, this one had no discernable eyes. And yet it seemed to be looking straight into his soul.

Jeff's hands automatically reached down to his holster, but of course it was empty. He didn't have a weapon anymore. And in any case, a gun would have been point-less. Trembling all over, he surrendered himself to his fate.

The light alien was moving closer. It came toward him slowly but inexorably. Finally it was right opposite him. If he stretched out his arm, he could have touched it.

"You won," Jeff croaked. "Now do what you have to do."

But the being didn't move. It stood motionless before him.

What felt like an eternity passed. Jeff's heart was pounding like a drum. Why didn't it just kill him, like those other beings had killed Major Irons and Fields? What was stopping it?

Fascinated, Jeff looked at this creature that was slightly smaller than him. The head seemed to shine from the inside and the light flickered slightly. It was like looking at a light just beneath the surface of rippled water.

"What are you?" Jeff whispered.

Very slowly, the creature raised both arms. It stretched them out, palms first, and Jeff was reminded of old paint-ings of a benevolent Christ giving his blessing. Then the creature floated back a little way and turned around. It lowered its left hand, lifted its right one a little, showing him the back of the hand.

Jeff stood completely rigid. This wasn't the behavior of a creature that wanted to kill him. Gradually, his fear began to subside, although his heart was still pounding like a jackhammer.

But what does it want?

The creature had now retreated as far as the door. It stopped there and continued to hold out its hand in Jeff's direction.

Does it want me to follow?

Robotically, Jeff took a step forward, but then hesitated.

Should he really follow this creature? What if it was a trap? On the other hand, it hadn't attacked him like it had Fields, Irons, and Finni. Jeff was suddenly overcome by a dreadful feeling that he may have completely misjudged the situation. What if the light aliens hadn't been responsible for the deaths of his shipmates? But then what was? Or were there good and bad versions of these creatures?

Jeff took a deep breath and clenched his fists until his nails dug into his palms. The pain triggered him into action. There was only one way of finding out.

Jeff walked toward the alien being. It waited until he had almost reached the door, then drifted down the corridor. Jeff followed it back down to the long corridor that connected the cavity and the central area. There, it swished round to the right. Jeff looked over his shoulder nervously, fully expecting to see a whole group of light aliens, but there were none to see.

For a few minutes, Jeff followed the ghostly creature and wondered if it wanted to take him to Green and Joanne. But at the intersection, it turned left and took him on a zigzag course through the bowels of the black ship.

Finally, it stopped in front of a door. Jeff waited a few feet behind the creature; the door opened as if by magic. The creature floated in and Jeff followed.

The room resembled the projection room where they had found the map of the ship. Several armchair-like objects were dotted around the room. It reminded Jeff of the small movie theater on board the Orpheus space base. Did the creature want to show him a film?

The alien floated to the front of the room to the projection screen and came to a stop in front of one of the armchairs. Then it raised an arm and touched it with the palm of its hand.

Was the thing telling him to sit down?

Nervously, Jeff stepped closer. Could he trust this creature?

Finally he sat down, not taking his eyes off the alien.

He sat there tensely while the figure hovered in front of him. It lifted both arms and moved its hands backward slightly.

It wants me to lean back. But why?

Jeff tried to relax, and rested his head on the back of the chair.

Suddenly there was a hissing noise. Something cool wrapped around his head and he couldn't move anymore. His hands shot up in panic. With his fingers he could feel a piece of tight-fitting metal covering his head. Only his face was left uncovered.

And now what? Was he going to be tortured? Had it been a mistake to follow the alien? He broke out in a cold sweat.

The creature made a soothing gesture.

Jeff tried to calm himself.

It drifted to another chair and lowered itself into it. Jeff could only watch it from the corner of his eye.

Suddenly the projection screen at the front of the room lit up. Unlike the other map he had seen, this wasn't a hologram. Individual characters were projected onto the wall one after another.

"I'm afraid I can't read that," Jeff whispered more to himself than the alien.

"But I'm sure you can understand me," replied a sonorous, robotic voice from an invisible speaker somewhere in front of him.

"Yes," Jeff whispered.

"Good. Finally we can communicate."

Now Jeff understood why they had come here. The device seemed to be some kind of translation machine.

Finally, he would get some answers! But would this creature tell him the truth? He had to think of Irons. He couldn't rule out the possibility that one of these creatures was responsible for the deaths of his companions. And not to forget all the lies the onboard computer had told them.

"Who are you?" Jeff asked finally.

"My name is Jerry, I am an—"

Jeff pulled a face. "You're kidding me, right? *Jerry?*"

There was a short silence. Then the voice could be heard over the crackly speaker again. "It is unlikely that my actual name exists in your language. I imagine the translation system selected a name at random."

That made sense.

"Sorry for interrupting. Please continue."

"I am one of the last survivors of the original crew of this spaceship."

"How is it that you're so … so …?" How should he phrase this?

"Don't be deceived. This is not my actual body. This is a hologram with limited manipulative abilities. An avatar, so to speak."

"An avatar," Jeff repeated in confusion.

"I will explain later. My real body is in stasis in another part of this ship."

"So some of you *did* stay on board after you reached your destination," Jeff said.

"I don't understand. We never reached our destination."

Jeff pricked up his ears. "You didn't?"

"No."

"But the onboard computer told us you left the ship before it embarked on a discovery expedition."

"What onboard computer?"

Jeff was utterly confused.

"The computer that controls the ship."

There was a pause, which seemed to last an eternity.

"This ship is not controlled by a computer."

"It isn't?" Jeff was baffled.

"No."

"Then who controls it?"

"*He* does."

"He?"

A long silence.

"The demon."

Chapter 31

"Our galaxy was doomed. Several supermassive stars at its center burned out and died in a massive hypernova. The expanding gamma-ray flash gradually erased all life in our galaxy. With our drive technology, we could not travel more than a hundred light years per year, so we built this ship as a way of escape. A ship constructed from an asteroid that would be able to accommodate all the inhabitants of our world. Ten billion of us, approximately. And we began a journey that would take us to the next galaxy in twenty-five thousand years, where we hoped to find a new home," the voice explained.

"And all those billions of people lived in cavitys, like the ones we saw?" Jeff asked.

"Only their avatars."

"I don't understand what you mean by avatars," Jeff admitted.

"We are freedom-loving beings and our home world had a beautiful, dark-blue sky. We couldn't bear the thought of living for hundreds of generations in the cavitys of the asteroid ship without ever seeing our new world with our own eyes. We also wanted to spare our children and future generations this fate. That's why we used a cryo-genics system.

"You went into hypersleep?"

"We thought that when we awoke from our frozen state, we would be able see our new world with our own eyes and spend the end of our days under an open sky instead of an artificial one."

"So why the avatars?"

"Our lifeless bodies could survive over millennia. But our souls could not. The soul wastes away during the inac-tivity of cryostasis and cannot be revived after thawing. As a result, the body dies with it. The only solution was to create avatars that could occupy themselves in the cavitys during the flight."

"But what could you do in the cavitys as disembodied spirits?" Jeff asked.

"Do not be deceived. This is just an emergency avatar."

"Emergency avatar?"

"I will come back to that. Our original avatars were exact replicas of us. We could use them like our actual bodies. They could feel love, joy … but also pain, anger, and hatred."

The screen on the wall in front of Jeff lit up again. The characters disappeared and the body of an alien being appeared against a blue background. It had a leathery brown skin, two thin legs, two skinny arms with thin fingers, and a plump body with a big, lumpy brown head resting on a long neck with large, human-like eyes. Jeff was reminded of an old movie he'd seen as a kid, about an alien who kept trying to "phone home."

"That's you," Jeff said.

"Yes, that is correct. That was my body."

Something about the choice of words bothered Jeff. It took him a moment to realize what: "You said *was*. I thought your body is still somewhere on the ship in a cryogenic pod."

"It is, but millions of years have passed. There are limits to our cryotechnology. My body is mostly decomposed and will no longer be viable outside the pod. I can feel it, I am dying. And it is the same for my companions."

"But I still don't understand why you didn't reach your target world."

"I'm coming to that. The spaceship was flown and operated by a crew of about a thousand individuals. I myself was part of the unit that took care of the reactors. Many of us are still doing so today."

Jeff said nothing but his mind was racing. He was talking to a being that had been spooking around this ship for millions of years. The extraterrestrials were immortal because of their cryotechnology combined with their avatars. Or if not immortal, they at least led impossibly long lives. Jeff was sure there were many people—especially those getting on in years—who would happily be put in a cryopod and spend their days as an avatar, if it meant they could carry on their lives with a substitute body and never get old. But he didn't understand where the alien was heading with its story. Only one thing was clear: something about the aliens' plan had gone terribly wrong. "Please continue."

"We set off. At the central core of the spaceship was the command center. This is where the commander—you would say *captain*—lay in a cryopod next to eleven of his closest staff."

"And their avatars?" Jeff asked. "Were they also in this command center controlling the ship?"

"No," the alien replied. "The ship itself was their avatar."

Jeff tried to process what he was hearing. "The ship?"

"Correct. They merged their consciousnesses together and controlled the ship with their minds. The ship is their substitute body."

It was beyond belief. After hearing about their slow hyperdrive, Jeff had assumed these aliens weren't as advanced as humans, but in some aspects, they were clearly far ahead. "What happened then?"

"The twelve controllers were the best, brightest, most dedicated, and cleverest of our species."

The alien paused a moment. Jeff was about to ask something when the creature continued. "But one of them was evil. Evil through and through—a *psychopath*, you would say in your language—and clever enough to hide it until after our departure. He was also telepathic; able to read and manipulate other people's minds. We call him the demon."

Jeff felt a chill go down his spine.

"After traveling through space for several years, it happened. Without warning, from one moment to the next. The demon took over control of the ship. He drove the other commanders, including the captain, mad. He managed to make them turn off their own cryopods, and they suffocated to death. Now he had sole control of the ship. Of all of its systems. The engines and the computers, but also the cryopods, the avatar generators, and the environmental simulation systems in the cavitys. With his telepathic powers, he was even able to override the security mechanisms and steer the avatars himself, while the spirits of the passengers were trapped in their substitute bodies."

Jeff swallowed.

"The crew members, including myself, were robbed of

their avatars and instead provided with emergency avatars with limited freedom of movement. He forced them to continue their work on the ship."

"But not you?"

"No. My superior was one of the commanders in the center of the ship. While he was dying, he disconnected some of the cryogenic pods from the main system and isolated them with a protective shield. Including mine. I and around fifty other maintenance workers are the only free beings aboard this ship. We are condemned to walk through the bowels of the ship as ghosts, waiting for our bodies in the cryopods to decompose enough that we can die.

Jesus Christ! This creature had been transformed into a ghost by the demon ship when men on Earth still resembled monkeys.

"It's a miracle you haven't lost your mind," Jeff whispered.

"Those of us who are left support each other and help one another stay sane. But little by little, my companions are dying off."

"Has the … demon never tried to hunt you?"

"He cannot control us and he has no access to our cryopods. Which makes him powerless against us."

"Have you never tried to kill him?"

"It would be pointless. He blocked all access to the center of the ship and closed himself off. We have no way of reaching him."

Jeff remembered the gigantic hovering sphere. So there really was no way of reaching it.

"And what happened to the rest of you? To the passengers in the cavitys."

"We cannot enter the cavitys with our emergency avatars, so we have never been able to see it with our own eyes. But traces in the ship's surveillance computers indicate that the demon forced the avatars to hurt and kill each other. He is a sadist who takes pleasure from inflicting the greatest possible suffering on others. Because the avatars cannot die—or at least are recreated as soon as they are destroyed—he has a god-like power over all the beings in the cavitys. He forced our people to torture, mutilate, injure, and kill each other. And every day afresh, until their spirits could no longer bear it and their souls were extinguished.

Jeff could feel the tears running down his cheeks. The horror, the suffering, the pain. It was simply inconceivable to think about what so many living beings had endured in those cavitys. And these tortured souls now also included humans. Among them his father.

Could he trust this alien being? Was it telling the truth? At least what it was saying made sense. It seemed logical. That's why his father had burned when he left the cavity only to be resurrected. It wasn't really the body of Frank Austin, but an artificially created substitute body, a copy of the original. His father's real body must be in a cryogenic pod somewhere on the ship. Practically immortal—exposed to new, unspeakable torments every day. No wonder the people believed they were in hell. But how had they gotten onto the ship in the first place?

"We came across humans in the cavity," Jeff said. "From worlds destroyed by rebel bombers. How can that be?"

"My people, the original passengers, all died long ago. My companions and I believe that the demon, as he travels through the universe, seeks out intelligent life to bring to the ship so that he has new victims. It is possible he discovered inhabited worlds in this galaxy of humans."

"Is there a way of finding out how the ship got here?" Jeff asked.

"Yes, I have limited access to some computer systems. One moment, please. It will take a little time. I need to redirect the data so that the demon does not suspect anything."

Minutes passed that seemed like hours to Jeff. "How did you learn our language?" Even if the computer did the work of translating, it must have its knowledge of the language from somewhere.

"The sensors of the ship pick up radio signals by default. Subsystems with artificial intelligence extract translation routines out of these. That had already been planned before the ship was built."

Jeff wanted to nod, but couldn't because of the metal cap around his head.

"May I ask you a question?" the alien asked.

"Of course."

"How did you come on board the ship?" It is the first time that strangers have entered the ship without being transferred immediately to cryopods."

Jeff took a deep breath. Then he told the creature about their war, the attack on Acheron-4, how the antimatter chambers had failed, and how at the last moment they'd spotted this ship, which had taken them on board. He also told the alien about their journey through the interior to here, the edge of the core area. As he recalled their adventure, it seemed to him as if they had been on this spooky ship for years. If it was really controlled by this demon, why had it taken them on board in the first place? He presented this question to the alien.

"I do not understand it, either. But he seems to be allowing you to penetrate to the core of the ship unscathed.

Either he is playing an extremely perfidious game for his own amusement, or you have something he wants."

Jeff snorted. "I wouldn't say he let us through unscathed! My crew are being killed off one by one. At first we thought you light aliens—I mean avatars—were responsible."

"We are not responsible. No emergency avatar can harm a living being."

"But I am being followed by emergency avatars." Jeff thought of the incident a few days ago, when he'd believed he had only just escaped with his life.

"Yes, that was me," the alien said. "I tried to contact you in the transit hub before your companion arrived. Then the situation became too confusing for me. Later, we wanted to stop you from going into the cavity and exposing yourselves to the dangers there. But we did not reach you in time. In fact, we have been watching you since your arrival."

Jeff was about to interject with a question, but the alien continued. "I have the data you wanted."

White dots, distributed in a bluish grid, appeared on the black screen. Then a red line zigzagged across the map.

"This is the course the ship has taken in this region of your galaxy."

Jeff pulled his handheld out of his pocket and held it in front of his face, as he couldn't bend his head to look at it. He called up the navigation screen and rotated his own star chart until it matched the projection. He traced the course of the alien ship with his forefinger. Then he pressed a button and a list of the star systems that the ship had passed through popped up.

Holy shit!

"Grimaldi-2, Alderon-8, and Deneb-6. Those are all systems that were attacked by the rebels." The alien ship must have followed the rebels and then taken the humans who were doomed to perish.

But immediately Jeff realized that something was wrong with this theory. He had misunderstood the situation completely. And even worse: all of humanity had made a terrible mistake. The rebels weren't responsible for the downfall of those worlds. Those who had doggedly claimed that humans would never be so malevolent as to destroy inhabited worlds had been right all along. The rebels hadn't been responsible. It had been this ship, controlled by the demon! He must have somehow gotten hold of Quagma bombs and destroyed those worlds after bringing parts of the population onto his ship and putting them into cryopods.

"What have we done?" Jeff whispered under his breath. They had taken revenge on behalf of the Empire. He himself had wanted to avenge the murder of his father by destroying rebel bases on which civilians also worked. If they now also attacked an inhabited planet, as some hardliners had been demanding for months, then this orchestrated mass murder would be carried off to perfection.

And the demon at the heart of this ship probably followed the radio communications and reveled in the misery he had inflicted, while at the same time abducting people to his hellish cavitys where they were forced to torture one another.

He had to stop this. Somehow. He had to do something. Or at least inform the fleet, so that no more fatal errors were committed.

"What can we do?" Jeff asked quietly.

"There may be a way out," the creature's voice replied. "If the demon really wants you in the center of the ship, then you must try to get into the control room."

"And then? Should we try and destroy his cryopod?"

"You would not succeed. The cryogenic pods in the control center are hermetically sealed and cannot be reached without detailed knowledge of the systems. But there is an emergency mechanism that can override the system. A console with a switch with this symbol."

An image appeared on the screen. It resembled a company logo: a yellow circle surrounding a smaller black circle with eight rays. Like a black sun in front of a yellow background.

"If you find this, press it."

Jeff wasn't very hopeful about making it to the control room, and yet he was curious about this switch. "What happens if we do?"

"It is an emergency device that only the captain knew about. It was a safeguard, in case a foreign power invaded the ship. Not even the demon knows how important it is."

"How do *you* know about it?"

"I installed parts of the system while building the ship, including the switch, and was sworn to secrecy."

"And what happens when it's activated?"

"Several things," the alien replied evasively, which bothered Jeff. "But it will give us back some control. And it will give you a chance of escaping this ship."

"How?"

"That is more than I can explain right now."

"All right." Jeff imprinted the logo in his memory before the screen darkened again.

"You should return to your fellow crew members now," the alien said. "Otherwise the demon will become suspicious."

"If he's surveying the ship, he's probably aware of our conversation," Jeff said.

"I hope not. There are several areas of this ship that cannot be monitored due to technical defects. Don't forget, he is controlling the ship as an avatar, by controlling most of its computers."

"And the part we are in now …"

"… is not under his surveillance. Incidentally, it would be better if you didn't mention our meeting to your ship-mates for the time being."

"Why not?"

"Because I can't rule out that the demon is controlling one of you."

Joanne! So that was it. The demon had taken control of her and that's why she had killed Castle. And Owl? Had he also been controlled by the demon when he slashed his stomach? Had one of them perhaps also killed Fields and Irons? And all this time they had assumed the light aliens were responsible.

"OK, I won't say anything. And you're right. I know who has been taken over."

"Then be careful. I wish you well."

"Thank you, I have no idea if …"

With a loud hissing noise, the metal hood retracted back into the chair.

Rubbing his head, Jeff leaned forward and got up just in time to see the light alien darting out the door.

Jeff felt dizzy and slumped back down in the chair again. What he had just learned was almost too much to process.

After a few minutes, he was finally able to get back on his feet. Did they really stand a chance of getting to the center of the ship? There were only three of them left—or two, really, assuming Joanne was under the control of the demon. And if they did, was there really a way out of this ship? Perhaps even a way of saving his father? He was annoyed with himself that he hadn't asked the alien about this. More and more questions flooded his mind which would now remain unanswered.

Jeff felt sick just thinking of the burden of responsibility if he failed, and what would happen to the prisoners, whose avatars were still torturing each other in the cavitys.

Slowly, he made his way back to the main corridor, and back to Green and Joanne.

WHEN JEFF ENTERED THE ROOM, Green looked up. He was sitting next to Joanne, who was still tied to the floor, asleep. Green looked tired, but that was hardly surprising.

"Where are Mac and Shorty?" Green asked.

"Dead," Jeff answered, picking up Castle's weapon.

He sat down next to Green and stared down at the ground.

"Oh god … what happened?" the engineer wanted to know.

"Don't ask," Jeff mumbled.

"But …"

"Not now," Jeff said. "Please."

"All right." There was resignation in Green's voice. "So the mission failed."

In response, Jeff threw down the bag with the levitation belts.

"You got them?" Green was amazed. He took one of them out of the bag, turned it around slowly in his hand, and put it back. Then he pointed at Joanne. "What do we do with her?"

"Has she said anything?"

"No," Green answered. "I gave her a sedative. I reckon she'll sleep for a while. Shall we leave her here or take her with us?"

Jeff didn't need to consider long. "We'll take her with

us. I don't want to leave her here alone." Even if she was under the control of the demon, he couldn't desert her. Maybe there was a way of freeing her from the devil's influence.

"OK," Green said. "So are we leaving?"

We ought to get going right away, Jeff thought. But he was so exhausted, he knew he wouldn't manage it. He had to sleep—just a few hours. And Green looked pretty exhausted, too.

"We'll rest for four hours, then we'll go."

"Who'll keep watch first?"

Jeff wanted to laugh out loud, but stopped himself. What was the use of keeping guard? Joanne was tied up. And if he or Green were taken over by the demon in their sleep, they were doomed in any case. Their only chance was to get into the ship's control room as quickly as possible and find that switch. But he didn't tell Green this. Nor did he say anything about his encounter with the light alien. Perhaps Joanne was only pretending to be asleep in order to follow their conversation. Which meant the demon would be listening, too.

"Forget it," Jeff said shortly. "We'll risk it without keeping watch."

"OK," Green said. He yawned and curled up on the bare floor. After just a few seconds, he started to snore.

It took Jeff longer to fall asleep. He couldn't stop going over and over his encounter with the alien. Too many questions were still unanswered. And he was terrified of failing.

Chapter 32

"How far to the sphere again?" Jeff asked.

He looked up at the dark-gray orb—the ship's epicenter.

"Six miles," the engineer answered. "Who'll take Joanne?"

Jeff sighed. "I'll do it." He leaned over his still unconscious companion and activated the levitation belt. He adjusted the inertia negation. Joanne no longer weighed anything and Jeff lifted her up effortlessly until she was hovering level with his waist. He attached her belt to his own with a hook and placed his left arm under her hip.

"Let's go!" Jeff said. "You fly ahead."

Green didn't answer but drifted upward like a helium balloon whose string had broken.

With his right hand, Jeff activated his own levitator and followed the engineer up into the alien sky.

The inner wall of the outer part of the ship was so smooth and featureless, it was very difficult to judge how high above the ground they were—and how far it was to the surface of the sphere. Only the radar on his suit provided numbers, which the computer projected onto the HUD of his helmet.

The view was truly breathtaking. Surreal. As if he had taken off from the bottom of an enormous bowl and was now steering toward the huge orb that hovered over it. It was the stuff of a feverish dream.

Jeff was almost level with Green when his legs suddenly jerked upward. Frantically, he manipulated his flight belt, trying to stabilize himself. It took a while until he stopped spinning around his own axis.

Green was having an easier time of it. But he wasn't carrying Joanne, who did add extra bulk although she weighed nothing.

"The vector of gravity has changed again," Green stated. As if Jeff hadn't noticed. The ground was now no longer the inner shell of the outer ship area, but the surface of the central sphere.

He felt like he was about to vomit.

These damn gravity changes!

Finally they reached the new ground. Green pointed at a light-gray square a few miles away. "That could be the door to the lock," he said.

Jeff shrugged. "Let's give it a try. Lead the way."

Green flew ahead, and a few minutes later they landed next to a square door that really did seem to be an airlock hatch. Several feet in diameter, it was more than big enough for them to get through. Jeff carefully laid Joanne down on the ground, but made sure her belt was still activated. Somehow they had to get into the airlock. He looked around. There were no control mechanisms. If the interior really was hermetically sealed, they would never be able to get in, and this whole journey would have been in vain.

"Hey," Green nodded at the hatch. "It's opening on its own."

He was right. The hatch retracted slightly and then slid sideways into the wall. The chamber behind it came into view.

Green stood on the threshold, jumped up, and floated inside with the help of his belt.

Jeff hesitated. It made no sense to hermetically seal off the interior, if the hatch simply opened every time someone came along. He was pretty sure it was an invitation. Did the demon really want them to enter the epicenter of his kingdom? And if so, why? What made them so damned valuable? Or was this all just some kind of perfidious game?

"Are you coming?" Green asked. "I don't want the hatch to close again and end up in here by myself."

Jeff nodded. Their aim had always been to get to the center. But they had to stay on their guard more than ever. Gently, he picked up Joanne, stepped onto the threshold, and sank to the ground on the other side. He had barely reached the bottom when the hatch closed behind them. This was followed almost immediately by the whistle of incoming air.

Finally, a hatch opened on the opposite wall. Jeff checked the air pressure and opened the helmet of his suit. Cool, fresh air stroked his face.

"Ahhh," Green closed his eyes in appreciation after also taking off his helmet.

"Wow, for the first time since we've been on board this ship, the air is good." Jeff stepped through the hatch and found himself in a sterile white room about the size of a small auditorium. It was a typical airlock antechamber; it could have been on board a terrestrial ship. Cabinets, shelves, and equipment were dotted around the room. Double doors led to the other side. Green was already heading for the doors. Jeff followed with Joanne.

Green punched a button on the wall and the hatch slid open easily. Behind it was a room only a few square feet in size. Controls were mounted in the wall, and when Jeff entered, he realized he was standing in an elevator.

He laid Joanne down on the ground and stood next to Green to inspect the panel. There were two rows of vertically arranged buttons, with golden lettering next to each one.

Jeff took a deep breath. "Hmm, now what?"

"I'd say we want to go right down to the bottom," Green said, and pressed the lowest button on the panel without waiting for a reply. Immediately, the door closed behind them, and the whole cabin shuddered slightly. Was it supposed to be this easy?

There was no indicator panel to show their current position. Only the constant vibration suggested they were actually heading toward the core of the ship. They were still twenty-five miles from the center, so the ride might take a while. On the other hand, they had no idea how fast the elevator was traveling.

After less than a minute, the elevator came to an abrupt stop. The doors opened with a hiss. Jeff lifted Joanne out of the elevator, and as he looked around, his eyes widened. By now, nothing ought to surprise him, but *this* …?

They were in a huge hall. It was dark, and Jeff could only make out vague outlines. The elevator they had just stepped out of was embedded in a huge, gray pillar, hundreds of feet high, which is what they must have traveled down. And there were more pillars all over this chamber, but at odd angles that led upward and sideways to a hemispherical ceiling that was so high above them, you could have fit several cathedrals on top of one another. The entire room was in fact a vast hemisphere with a diameter of at least a third of a mile. There were hatches at irregular intervals along the walls, some of which were open and emitting a shimmering reddish light. In the center of the room was another hemisphere, the shell of which was so black, it was like an enormous blind spot in Jeff's field of vision.

"Well, I guess that's the center of the ship," Green said, marching resolutely toward a dark-gray hatch around eighty feet away from them.

Could it be? Was this hemisphere the control center of the ship? Had they really found it? And would the demon —or rather its hermetically sealed cryopod—be waiting for them inside?

Green seemed pretty convinced that they had reached their goal. Having almost reached the hatch, he beckoned to Jeff. "Come on. We're there." He grinned.

Jeff stood rooted to the spot. Something about Green bothered him. It had been bothering him the whole time. Subconsciously. The engineer had changed since coming on board this ship. True, they had all changed, but Green more than the others. Jeff remembered how sick the engineer had felt after they had moved into their accommodation. What had been the matter with him? A headache … dizziness. He'd had the same symptoms before. But where? That was it! On the Charon—during the attack on Acheron-4. When they had been hit by psychorays and Green had discovered his deflective shield was defective.

His deflective shield was defective.

Jeff felt a shiver go down his spine and stars dance in front of his eyes. How could they have been so blind? How could *he* have been so blind?

Jeff let Joanne slide to the floor and straightened himself. Green stared at him, his face still frozen in a grin. He must have guessed what was going on in Jeff's mind, because he began to walk toward him. "Everything OK?"

Jeff took a step back and shook his head. "It's *you*!" he husked. "You're the demon."

Green came closer. His grin widened. "Now, now," he said, as if admonishing a child. "Who would want to be so rude as to insult his host?"

There was something in Green's face—something strange that Jeff hadn't noticed before. An evil grimace just below the surface that was now revealing itself. Jeff felt his pulse quicken and his hands turn clammy. He was standing right in front of the demon that had caused so much suffering, simply for his own perverse pleasure. All he had to do was reach out his hand to touch him. Instinctively, he knew he was no match for this sinister creature. He had to get away.

As if Green had read his mind, he began to laugh. It was a tinny, cackling laugh.

Jeff turned around and made a dash for the open hatch. He couldn't face his opponent here. Green's laughter echoed after him.

Chapter 33

Jeff stumbled through the dark corridor, gasping. Every few feet he passed blood-red lights embedded in the wall. Finally, his panic subsided. He turned around. The demon hadn't followed him. He gasped for breath and grabbed onto a yellow and black wall strut.

What should he do? He didn't stand a chance against this creature.

How could he have been so wrong? He'd been convinced Joanne was the one who was possessed, like Owl before her. Was it possible that the demon was able to possess several people at once? Was Green also responsible for the deaths of Fields and Irons? What if Jeff simply went back and shot Green? Would the demon allow it to happen? And if he succeeded, what then? Maybe he'd already replaced Green with an avatar. Would he be able to stop this devil from turning *him* into an avatar in this pseudo-hell, too?

It was all too much. Jeff lowered his gaze and glanced furtively at the pistol in his holster. Wouldn't it be simpler just to shoot himself? Then at least he could rest in peace and not end up the plaything of an insane, godlike creature.

No, he knew he couldn't do it. He had to find a way out of here. But how?

He trembled as he tried to breathe normally. Slowly, he continued to make his way down the corridor. A few feet further on, he came across a dark-gray metal door in the wall. The edges were marked with black and yellow paint. Maybe Jeff could find something that would help him or at least give him an idea.

He touched the square on the wall next to the door. On the other side was what looked like a big hall. Jeff stepped through the hatch and his heart skipped a beat.

The hall was gigantic, with a diameter of at least several miles. It was filled with shelves and Jeff's first thought was that he'd stumbled into a warehouse. But then his eyes fell on the neat rows of rectangular boxes that filled the shelves. He touched one of them gingerly. It was made of black metal and on the right-hand side were a series of depressions and switches.

Jeff ran a finger over the strange material. It was cold as ice. These must be the cryogenic pods of the passengers and crew. He walked back to a railing a few feet away. The shelves with the sarcophagus-like containers continued not only upward but also downward. He couldn't begin to guess how many levels this gigantic hall had, because the rows of shelves disappeared into a reddish mist far below. There must be thousands, no, millions, of cryogenic pods in this hall alone. And God alone knew how many of these halls were on the ship.

Was his father lying in one of these containers somewhere in this hall? It would be impossible to find him.

"Jeff!" Green's voice echoed through the hall.

He looked around but couldn't see anybody. He must be hearing the voice over a loudspeaker.

"Jeff," the voice repeated. "I know where you are."

Jeff closed his eyes and sighed in resignation. Of course, the demon had him under constant surveillance. He was trapped. It would never let him out again.

"What do you want from me?" Jeff cried out in despair.

Laughter echoed around the room. "What do you think?" That laugh again. "I want *you*!"

"What do you want from me?" Jeff repeated. His hands were balling into fists.

"I want you by my side. Come back to me."

"And if I don't want to?" Jeff asked angrily.

Another chuckle—this time quieter.

"There's someone here who wants to see you again," the voice said. "Describe the situation, my dear."

Jeff's stomach contracted. He knew whom the demon was referring to. He had forgotten about Joanne. He'd run off in such a panic, he'd left her behind in the clutches of the demon.

"Jeff!" She sounded desperate. "I'm lying on the ground, I'm tied up. Green is leaning over me and holding a knife to my stomach."

"Come back to us, Jeff," Green said in a sickly sweet voice. "Or I'll cut open your little friend's stomach and describe what I'm taking out of it." He cackled. "That is, if you can hear me through all the screaming."

Jeff felt the blood draining from his face. He couldn't bear that. He looked down at his pistol again and considered turning it on himself. But what would become of Joanne? She, along with his father, would still be at the mercy of the demon.

"Shit! Damn it!" Jeff punched the wall.

"Now, now," Green's too soothing voice came through the loudspeaker.

Jeff clenched his teeth. There must be something he could do!

The pistol …

He breathed deeply in and out. He wasn't sure whether it would work. Above all, it would probably mean killing the real Green—if his spirit was still somewhere inside his body. But it was probably too late to save him, in any case. "OK. I'm coming."

He retreated from the warehouse and stepped back into the corridor. It took him only a few minutes to get back to the antechamber."

He could see Green some distance away, standing next to the entrance to the central hemisphere.

"Where's Joanne?" Jeff asked.

Green tilted his head to one side and smiled. "She's already gone ahead." He pointed at the door next to him. "After you."

"You're really letting me into the innermost … sanctum?"

Green nodded. "Why not? There's nothing you can do to me there. You can't harm me. And anyhow, it's necessary."

Jeff didn't even bother asking why. He didn't want to go in, but he had to convince himself that Joanne was really there.

"After you," Jeff said.

Green shrugged and turned around. "If you insist." The door opened with a hiss and Green stepped through. Jeff followed him, although every cell in his body was urging him to go the other way.

Once inside, Jeff was reminded of holograms he'd seen of the Pantheon in Rome on Earth. A huge dome with a small hole at the very top. Along the walls were console-like instruments, but they were all unlit and did not seem to be in operation. There were no other doors. The only way in or out was through the door they had come. In the middle of the room was a round pillar. It had a diameter of several feet and was almost twice as tall as Jeff. A reddish ray of light slanted from the hole in the ceiling, illuminating the pillar like a surreal altar.

Joanne was lying on the floor a few feet away from him. Jeff hurried over and knelt beside her. He could see her chest rising and falling. She was alive, but unconscious.

"There's your girlfriend. She's doing well," Green said with a sneer. He was standing right behind Jeff.

Now or never!

With a fluid motion, Jeff rose to his feet and at the same time pulled the pistol out of his holster, spun round, and squeezed the trigger.

The bullet entered Green's forehead and exited out of the back of his head. In an explosion of red, it tore out bits of skull, brain, and blood with it.

Green's expression froze in disbelief and surprise. He staggered, but somehow remained on his feet. Then his face twisted into a nasty grin again. A thick trail of blood ran down his cheek from the wound on his forehead. He began to laugh again—and fell forward. He landed on the floor with a thud and fell silent.

"*Bastard!*"

Loud, inhuman laughter sounded from hidden loud-speakers that echoed around the room. Jeff knew he hadn't killed the demon, but maybe it would buy him some time. He ran along the edge of the room. That button the alien had told him about—it must be here somewhere.

But Jeff hadn't gone far when he heard the door hissing

behind him. He spun round, clenching his hands. Who would enter the room now?

Or what?

It was Green. He stood in front of the door until it closed behind him, then made a histrionic gesture with his arms like an over-enthusiastic entertainer. "I told you—you can't do me any harm here."

"Green was just an avatar," Jeff said dryly. "Since when?"

The demon grinned. "Oh, not long. If you hadn't run off in a panic, your plan might have worked." He cocked his head. "Or perhaps not. But then there would have been other ways and means. In any case, you won't be leaving here."

That was no surprise. "Why?"

"Why what?"

"Why are you doing this?"

Green grimaced and rolled his eyes. "Because it's fun. Especially with you humans. You make such funny noises when you're in pain."

"You're sick!" Jeff shouted.

Green shook his head slowly. "No I'm not. I'm God." He paused a moment. "Or rather the other one. You know who." He chuckled. "A very interesting concept, by the way, your hell. A place of eternal torment and punishment —I was delighted to hear of it when you humans came on board. I redecorated the cavitys especially!"

"You destroyed inhabited planets!"

Green nodded. "I found some bombs aboard a damaged ship and wanted to give them a try. You certainly like playing at war. In fact, there isn't such a big difference between you homo sapiens and me. And I certainly had a lot of fun destroying your worlds after I'd taken several thousands of their inhabitants on board."

"How did you even get them onto your ship?" Jeff asked, his throat completely dry.

"Teleportation, of course."

Jeff swallowed. Humanity had been trying to master that technology for centuries—but in vain. "Teleportation?"

Green laughed. "What did you think? That billions of passengers were bought on board with ferries? That would have taken decades. No, the individuals were captured on their respective planets, teleported, and immediately rematerialized in the cryopods."

Jeff shuddered.

One moment you might be walking down the street, the next moment you would be in this simulation of hell on the black ship. No wonder the people thought they had been killed in a surprise attack.

"Why didn't you beam *us* straight into the cryopods when we turned up?"

Green shrugged. "I happened to be busy with a—shall we say, interesting—game in hell, and only noticed your presence rather late. What's more, the teleportation process is rather time-consuming; the field projectors have to be prepared first."

"You could have teleported us straight from our cabin to those pods."

Green laughed. "You're right, that would have been very convenient. But no. Because of the large projector surfaces, matter can only be brought aboard from a certain distance. There's no other way, unfortunately."

Jeff took a deep breath. "And what do you want from me now?"

"I want to show you something. Come with me."

The demon turned around and strutted across the

room toward a console. Jeff followed him at a distance of several feet.

When Green reached the console, he flipped a switch and a small door slid opened. Behind it was a compartment the size of a microwave oven, illuminated by a yellow light. "This is a universal analyzer. It scans everything you present it with, atom by atom, and transfers it as a model to the computer."

Jeff was confused. "And?"

The demon grinned again. He seemed to be enjoying giving Jeff the runaround. Then he stretched out his right hand.

"What?" Jeff asked.

"Major Irons' handheld, please."

Jeff was frozen to the spot. Suddenly he understood what the demon was planning.

"No."

The demon nodded. "Yes. I have already tried approaching your central worlds. But they are too well protected. But with the access code, I'll have free rein, and once the people realize what's happening, it will be too late." He chuckled. "My first stop: Earth. How many inhabitants does it have again?"

"Ten billion," Jeff croaked automatically.

Green clapped his hands. "And I have just about that many empty cryopods on board. What a wonderful coincidence. My, we're going to have a lot of fun together!"

Jeff closed his eyes. He should have deleted the data long ago. Why hadn't he? At the latest after they had encountered the light aliens—that would have been the time to do it. But perhaps it wasn't too late. Very slowly, he reached down to his belt pouch, where Irons' handheld was tucked in next to his own.

But before he could take it out, Green punched him in

the stomach. Jeff dropped to his knees with a groan. He had to support himself with both hands and was only half aware of Green taking Irons' handheld out of his pouch.

"I'd rather take no chances. I wouldn't want you to do something stupid."

The pain gradually subsided. At least he could lift his head again. He looked up just in time to see the demon close the door of the compartment and press a button.

"It should be quick," Green said, rubbing his hands as he watched the hologram that had appeared in front of him, and which displayed symbols in the aliens' language. "Yes, the analysis is starting. Ah, I see!"

He turned around and grinned. "It was a good idea to bring you here."

Then the demon lunged at Jeff.

What the …?

Jeff tried to push Green away from him. He didn't succeed. Then Green's knee rammed into his stomach and he collapsed to the ground. Jeff felt his hand being tugged at. He tried desperately to pull it away, but it was useless.

Green's head jerked forward. His bit into Jeff's index finger, and Jeff felt his hand explode with pain. He screamed, and tears filled his eyes. He almost lost consciousness.

Then the searing pain suddenly stopped. Jeff groaned. Green let him go and fell to the ground. He blinked, and struggled to regain his vision. He propped himself up on his left elbow and looked at his right hand.

My finger!

His finger was missing. A small piece of white bone protruded from the wound. Blood was pulsing down his hand and dripping onto the floor in a steady stream.

Jeff looked up. Green's chin was bloody. He reached into his mouth and pulled out Jeff's finger.

He had bitten it off!

"Thank you for your fingerprint," the demon said, licking his bloody lips. Then he placed the finger next to the handheld in the analyzer. "I really appreciate your sacrifice."

It beeped, and then he reached into the device and pulled the handheld back out.

Jeff looked at his hand, which was still bleeding heavily. *My finger!*

Gradually a dull ache spread through the remainder of his finger and hand, and grew stronger.

He had to get to Joanne, who was still carrying the medical kit on her back, and treat his wound.

"Yes, that's better," Green said. He had pushed the handheld back into the machine.

"Aha. Interesting. Well, most of the data on here is unimportant. But there it is: general and specific access codes. Oh … password protected. I thought so." He turned to Jeff. "The password please!"

Jeff was trying to stem the flow of blood with his left hand and stood up with difficulty. He wanted to look the demon in the eye when he said what he had to say. "I'm afraid I have to disappoint you. I don't know it. Irons didn't tell me." He laughed bitterly. "Even if you torture me for a thousand years. I really don't know it."

Green cocked his head. "Well that *is* a shame."

Jeff wondered why Irons had given him the code to the handheld but not the password. Had he forgotten it? But that wasn't like him. Or had he assumed Jeff knew it? And suddenly Jeff *did* know. It could only be the name of his dead son. Jack!

"Thank you," Green cried suddenly. "That's all I wanted to know. Excellent. It accepted the password."

Oh Jesus, no! He had made a dreadful mistake.

"Correct, Jeff. I am telepathic. Unfortunately, I have not been able to sabotage your deflective shield and therefore cannot possess you completely, but if I concentrate very hard, I can read your mind." He laughed a dirty laugh. "And with that you have fulfilled your purpose. But I *would* like to thank you. In fact, I have made special plans for you."

Jeff backed away along the row of consoles. He didn't want to know.

"I will make you my chief assistant. You will become my inquisitor and foreman. We will let the people of Earth torture each other over millennia in the cavitys." The demon chuckled gleefully. "And when the time is ripe to destroy them for good, you will take over the job and deliver the final death blow. Bit by bit, you will destroy the soul of every single human being. Is that not an honor? A privilege?"

The room had started to spin, and Jeff was afraid he would pass out at any moment. Irons had entrusted him with the codes and warned him to destroy it sooner rather than later. He had failed. He had delivered humanity into the hands of this demon.

"You can begin by practicing on your father," the demon said. "We have plenty of time before we reach Earth."

Jeff backed away slowly from Green along the wall of consoles. But Green followed him so that they remained the same distance apart.

Suddenly, Green stopped and took a long, thick cylinder from a bracket on one of the consoles.

Jeff swallowed as he continued sidling backward.

The demon pressed a button on the underside of the cylinder and the tip lit up blue. It emitted an electric crackling noise.

"I'm afraid I am going to have to stun you," Green explained, moving closer. "So that I can put you in a cryo-pod. I have had a special avatar made for you that will do justice to your new role. It is almost ten feet tall, has hooves, a whip-like tail, very sharp teeth, and two long horns. How do you like the sound of that?" He chuckled again. "We'll meet again in the cavitys. You'll get to see Joanne and your father again. You can celebrate with a nice threesome—I've already thought up some nice games for you to play!"

This couldn't be happening. He must be dreaming. He should have shot himself while he still had the chance. He had failed spectacularly. It was all over. Now all that remained was never-ending horror.

The demon aimed the cylinder at Jeff.

A wave of dizziness washed over him, and he had to support himself on a console to stop himself from falling.

"Don't worry. It won't hurt," Green grinned. "At least not when I stun you. The pain comes later."

Right next to his hand Jeff saw something yellow. A logo. *The* logo! *A yellow circle with a black sun!*

It was his last chance!

He took his hand off the console and immediately lost his balance. At the same moment the demon fired his weapon. Jeff collapsed onto the console and a blue ray of light flashed past his shoulder. Before he crashed to the ground, Jeff managed to jab his elbow into the switch. It made a loud clicking noise and flashed brightly.

Green's smiled faded. "What was that? What did you do?" Then he closed his eyes, as if to listen to an inner voice.

Jeff struggled to his feet. His legs were like jelly and he had to support himself on the console. Nothing appeared to have changed. Only the glow of the switch indicated that something was in progress.

Complete silence reigned. Trembling, Jeff looked at the demon in Green's body. He understood that a battle had commenced deep in the bowels of the ship. A battle between the commands given by the demon and the computer routines programmed millennia ago. And it was not clear which would win.

Minutes passed. To Jeff they felt like years.

Then suddenly a metallic sound echoed through the room. So loud that Jeff thought his eardrums would burst —as if gigantic hammers were striking planetary-sized anvils. The acoustic inferno lasted only a few seconds, then all was quiet again except for a reverberating echo.

The demon ripped his eyes open. All color had drained from his face. He didn't even seem to notice as the stun gun fell from his hands and clattered to the ground.

"What did you do?" Green croaked. "What did you *do*!" He stood there motionless, staring at Jeff with undisguised hatred. Any moment, and he would lunge at Jeff and kill him with his bare hands.

Jeff stumbled backward and braced himself for the moment when the demon would pounce.

But it didn't happen. Green turned toward the door. "No!" he screamed in desperation.

The door opened.

Light aliens floated into the room. One after another and incredibly fast. Faster than Jeff could run, they moved toward the demon in Green.

The light aliens had changed. They were considerably smaller and came up only as far as Jeff's chest. They were no longer fully transparent and had discernible shapes. For the first time he could see eyes and a mouth. And their luminosity had diminished, too.

Two of the beings had already reached Green. They grabbed him by the arms and dragged him to the middle of the room, while the others began to busy themselves at the man-high pillar.

"No, don't do it!" Green screamed. Then suddenly he began to rave in an alien language.

Jeff walked around the pillar so he could see what the creatures were doing. About two dozen of them were gathered around the column, blocking Jeff's view.

Suddenly, a gray box slid noiselessly out of the post. Now Jeff understood what was happening. It must be the demon's cryopod. Two of the light aliens began tapping on one of the consoles.

Green screamed in terror. Then all of a sudden he fell silent and his eyes glazed over. As the light aliens released him, he collapsed on the floor like a rag doll.

One of the light aliens took a small box from a console on the wall and approached Jeff. He stopped right in front of him. Now he looked like the picture Jeff had seen on the projection.

"Jerry?" Jeff asked.

The creature nodded like a human.

"Yes," came a synthetic voice from the little box.

"Is it over?" Jeff wanted to know.

The creature nodded again.

"The demon is dead."

Chapter 34

"Can you hear me?" Jeff asked. Joanne did not react. Her lids were half open, her eyes glazed. But she was still feeling the effect of the strong tranquilizers. Jeff hoped she would recover quickly once the medication wore off. She had only been under the demon's influence a short time, and he was sure she would be able to make a full recovery. Or would she?

Jeff tugged at the bandage he had wrapped around his finger, got up and turned to the aliens. Jerry had remained by his side. "What happens now?"

"I will take you to a rescue pod that was intended for the ship's controllers. It will take you to the next inhabited star system."

Jeff sighed deeply. He and Joanne were the only ones left. Two out of the original ten. And he couldn't stop thinking about his father, and all the other people still trapped in cryopods. "Do you have access to the cavitys again? And the avatar controls?"

Jeff looked around. The aliens had spread out around

the room. They were standing at the consoles, which were flashing back to life one by one.

"Yes," Jerry said. "The avatars have been deactivated and the cavitys are no longer in use."

Finally there was an end to all the suffering.

"Good," Jeff said shortly. He wondered what the safest way would be of transporting all the people to the next world?

"I suggest I take you and your shipmate to the escape pod now."

Jeff shook his head. "No, thank you. We won't leave our fellow humans alone here. We will stay until we've reached the next star system and disembark together."

The alien shook his head. "I'm terribly sorry. But we can't help the other members of your species."

Can't help them?

"Why not?"

"Because the ship will self-destruct in … forty minutes."

Jeff couldn't believe what he was hearing. It was impossible. It couldn't be. "What did you say?"

"I'm sorry. The ship will be destroyed in forty minutes."

"But why?"

"It was the only way of stopping the demon. The button you pressed ejected the refrigerant used for the reactors. It was the only way to activate emergency access to the central area. Without sending the coolant into space, we couldn't have come in here."

"And what will happen to all those people?"

"I'm sorry."

"Can't we distribute them among the emergency escape pods?"

"I'm sorry."

"Or rescue them some other way?"

"I'm very sorry."

Jeff cupped his head in his hands. He had thought they could save those poor people. Now they had been freed from their nightmare but he had sentenced them to death.

His father! He had to at least save his father!

"I met my father in the cavitys. I won't leave the ship without him," he said firmly.

"I'm not sure there is enough time."

"I won't go without him."

"Follow me," Jerry ordered.

Jeff followed him to one of the consoles. Jerry fiddled around at the controls and several screens lit up.

"You met him? In the cavity? Did you talk to him?"

Jeff nodded.

Most of the screens were covered in symbols. It took several long seconds, and Jeff hopped nervously from one foot to the other. Finally a fuzzy image of his father appeared on the screen. His eyes were closed and he appeared to be asleep. The background was black. "That's him!" Jeff cried.

Suddenly the screen went blank and Jerry turned around. "Follow me."

Jeff followed Jerry to the exit and through the big antechamber. They turned into one of the dark corridors and after a few minutes' walk reached an elevator. Jeff wasn't sure if Jerry was taking him up or down. When the doors reopened, they stepped into the big warehouse with the countless cryogenic pods.

Hurriedly, Jerry led him past the endless rows of shelves, through which a reddish mist wafted. Finally, they stopped in front of one. Jerry punched something into a control panel and a few seconds later a small platform descended from above. On it was a cryopod. The platform with the coffin-like container made of black metal stopped directly at his feet.

Jerry punched several buttons on the console on the side of the container. First came the faint humming of a pump, then a metallic sound of latches snapping back. At last, the lid hissed open. Jeff's heart was pounding.

He leaned forward. The container was filled with a greenish liquid, but it quickly receded. Floating in the liquid was an emaciated body, which bore little resemblance to his father's formerly muscular physique.

"Oh my God!" Jeff whispered.

The person in the container turned his head slightly in Jeff's direction and moaned softly. Then he opened his eyes and Jeff recognized their deep blue color.

"Jeff," his father said in a weak voice and stretched out a hand.

"Dad!" Jeff sobbed, lifting out the bizarrely light body. Carefully he laid him on the metal floor and held him tight.

His father no longer had any hair. His skin was pale, almost transparent. His bones stuck out of parchment-like skin, beneath which there was no sign of fat or muscle.

"What happened to him?" Jeff asked, stroking his father's cheek.

Jerry was still fiddling around with the console, on which a small screen displayed changing symbols.

"The demon," Jerry said. "He changed the nutrient supply in the chambers. He must have wanted to ensure the bodies would no longer be viable outside of the cryopods."

"You mean, my father is dying?" Jeff asked.

"His muscles have completely atrophied. His body can no longer function on its own. I fear the answer to your question is: yes. The man is dying."

Jeff sobbed. His father opened his eyes again for a moment and his gaze was very clear. "Where are we?" he asked in a trembling voice.

"On the black ship," Jeff whispered.

"Hell was really just an illusion? I'm alive?"

Jeff nodded. He wiped the tears from his cheeks. "Yes."

How could he explain it to his father? How could he tell him he had woken him from the dead, only to let him die again?

"But I'm so tired," his father whispered. "I think I need to sleep now."

Jeff nodded. He couldn't speak because of the lump in his throat.

"Will you stay with me until I've fallen asleep?"

Jeff squeezed his father's hand. "Yes."

His father looked him straight in the eyes, as if he wanted to hold onto Jeff and to life with his eyes. But then they glazed over and his head fell limply back into Jeff's arms.

The console made three long beeping sounds.

"I'm sorry," Jerry said after a short silence.

Jeff sobbed and hugged his father's body.

"I think you should make your way to the escape pod now. It is only another fifteen minutes until the reactors overheat."

Jeff was unable to move. He couldn't go on. All he wanted to do was curl up beside his father and close his eyes. But he had to think of Joanne. He was responsible for her, too. Jeff bit his lips, until the salty taste of blood filled his mouth. He had to get up. There would be time to mourn later.

Gently, he laid his father's body on the ground and loosened the last cords and cables that connected him to the cryogenic pod. He stroked his cheek one last time and then got up.

"Let's go."

Jerry led the way. Jeff followed him into the elevator.

"What'll become of you?" Jeff asked as they waited.

"We are tired after eons of roaming this ship, and now that the demon has been destroyed, we are looking forward to being finally released."

"You don't mind?"

"Not in the least."

The doors of the elevator opened and Jeff followed Jerry into a narrow corridor at the end of which was an oval hatch.

Jeff frowned. "That doesn't lead to the control center."

"No, but to the escape pod."

Jeff turned around. "I still have to get Joanne!"

"My friends have already taken her on board, everything is ready."

Jerry opened the hatch, and then another one right behind it. Jeff found himself in an elongated, oval cabin with a few seats and two large windows at the front. Joanne was sitting unconscious in one of the seats, already strapped in. At the back of the capsule were five open cryogenic pods.

"How am I supposed to fly this thing?" Jeff asked, looking down at the controls on the two front seats.

"As I said, everything has been prepared. As soon as the hatch closes, go to the front and strap yourself in. Then press the illuminated button. The escape pod will take off and leave the mother ship."

"And how do I get to the next star system?"

"The pod will continue its course as programmed by the mother ship."

"You mean, the ship is flying toward Earth?" Jeff asked.

"I don't know. The target is a G-class system, the third planet from the sun. According to the database, it has a satellite and large amounts of liquid water. And it—"

Jeff gave a wave of his hand. "OK. That sounds like Earth. How long will the flight take?"

"Since the escape pod has a lower mass, it can make longer hyperjumps than the mother ship. The computer calculates a flight time equivalent to one hundred and twenty of your days. Upon arrival at your destination, the spacecraft will automatically search for a landing site and initiate the appropriate maneuver."

Jerry pointed to the back of the cabin.

"The cryogenic pods are very easy to use. You lie down in it and press the oval button in front of you. The device will do everything else. It will wake you when you have reached your destination."

Jeff nodded and stretched out a hand. "Thank you, Jerry."

The alien took his hand. It felt cold. "We thank you for freeing us from our suffering. I wish you and your species all the best. I hope you enjoy a better fate than ours."

Jeff swallowed. "Thank you. I would like—"

"There's no more time." Jerry withdrew his hand and hurried back out of the hatch. "Another sixty seconds. Close the hatch and prepare for departure. You must hurry if you want to live." Then he closed the hatch of the mother ship. Jeff pulled the lever on the inner door of the flight capsule and it closed with a dull thud. A pneumatic hiss told him the hatch was sealed.

He hurried along the narrow cylinder of the ship's hull. Joanne was groaning and holding her head. She seemed to be slowly regaining consciousness. "Everything's going to be OK," he said as he walked past.

He sat down in the chair. It was too small for him and he had to squeeze himself into it. He reached for the harness, which was very similar to one on a human ship, pulled it over his waist, and snapped it shut.

A yellow button shone directly in front of him.

He took a deep breath and pressed it.

Immediately he was pushed forward against his belt. The capsule was going to be ejected backward. He looked out of the window in front of him into a dark tunnel, whose dimly lit walls slid past at breakneck speed. The capsule vibrated violently and he was thrown back and forth in his seat.

For what seemed like an eternity, they raced backward through the long tunnel, reminding him once again how gigantic this ship was. Surely the sixty seconds must be up. Jeff fully expected a giant explosion to tear apart the ship, the tunnel, and the escape pod, sending him into the afterlife.

Then, suddenly, they were outside!

He could see a few stars; more and more appeared as the demon ship retreated from view, until it was barely more than an outline.

Just a few seconds later it had disappeared completely. Any moment now … Jeff was wondering what would happen when the ship's reactors exploded, when he was almost blinded by an incredibly bright flash of light. Jeff closed his eyes, but the light penetrated his closed eyelids.

He forced himself to open his eyes again and saw a giant yellowish orb in front of him, growing larger.

It will devour us!

But the brightness of the explosion subsided and

collapsed in on itself until only a faint, red afterglow in space indicated the former existence of the alien ship.

Jeff sighed with relief. They'd done it!

He unbuckled himself and stood up. At least there was artificial gravity in this escape pod. He went over to Joanne, who was slumped in a seat two rows behind. She had opened her eyes. Her gaze was clear as she looked out of the window. Jeff leaned over her.

"We're in space," she said.

"Yes, we got away. We made it, and we're on our way to Earth."

"That bright explosion just now. Was that the black ship?"

Jeff nodded. "Yes, it's been destroyed." He forced himself to smile. "Everything's going to be OK. How do you feel?"

"Not too bad. I'd like to get up. Can you undo my belt?"

"I think you should rest a bit more."

"Please," she implored.

Jeff sighed and leaned forward to undo her belt.

From the corner of his eye he saw Joanne raise her arm but thought nothing of it.

Pain exploded through his temple and he blacked out.

Chapter 35

Jeff regained consciousness, groaning. His head hurt so badly, he thought it would break into a thousand pieces at any moment. He had to force himself to open his eyes.

"You've woken up," he heard Joanne's voice somewhere behind him. He wanted to turn around but couldn't. He was shackled to the seat in front of the window, where Joanne had just been sitting. His arms were tied to the armrest with thin straps. His feet were hanging freely above the floor, but they were tied together at the ankles.

Joanne came into his field of vision from the right-hand side. She was grinning. But he could see immediately that it wasn't Joanne's grin. The demon had taken off her combat suit, she was wearing only a white top and skimpy white panties.

"You're still alive!" Jeff said. He couldn't believe it.

"Yes. I'm surprised myself that it worked," said the demon. "It seemed that the prospect of death helped my consciousness make the leap to her body."

"But the shield in Joanne's suit—"

The demon gave a dismissive wave. "Green broke that

already. It was the only way to take possession of her. Worked with Owl, too." He chuckled. "And you dimwits didn't notice a thing."

Jeff jerked forward but the restraints were too tight.

"Don't even try." the demon said. "You don't stand a chance." He laughed, and globules of spit landed on Jeff's face. "In the end, I won after all."

"But the ship is destroyed."

Joanne's body shrugged. "But now I have a nice new, young body. That's worth something." The demon ran a hand over Joanne's breasts.

"Do you want to know what I'm going to do?" the demon asked. He didn't wait for Jeff to respond. "I will go to Earth and take over your Emperor. He'll soon develop a few new hobbies. In the cellar of his palace there's plenty of room for a nice dungeon, full of nice toys. It was starting to get a bit boring on the ship anyway."

"You're gross," Jeff hissed.

"You're repeating yourself," the demon said, rubbing between his legs with Joanne's left hand. In the other, he was holding a slender knife with a black handle. "That's a nice feeling. I never did understand human sexuality. My former body didn't have anything like this. We still have a little time till we get to Earth. Maybe we can use it to experiment a little." He came nearer and sat down on Jeff's lap. "I could ride you. That way it's enjoyable for both of us. Oh yes, let's do that." Then he raised his other arm and examined the knife. "And while we do it, I'll slowly slit you open and keep on riding you till you're dead. What do you think of that?"

Jeff's eyes narrowed to slits. He didn't answer.

"It was almost too easy."

"What do you mean?" Jeff couldn't stop himself from asking.

"After I took over Green, it was no problem killing the others. I didn't actually want to bring you to the center of the ship, I just wanted to have a little fun. Green was supposed to kill you all, one by one, like he did Fields and Irons."

"You were lucky that Green's deflective shield was broken."

Joanne shrugged. "I only found out about your protection fairly late. I'd been wondering why I couldn't take over any of you. I tried it with you, too."

The headaches he'd had—that they'd all had! It had been the demon's unsuccessful attempts to possess them.

"And then you pretended to be the computer. A clever idea."

"Yes—that was a lot of fun. Improv theatre, so to speak. But some of Irons' questions got me into a bit of a sweat."

"And who put the food outside the door?"

Joanne laughed loudly. "That was particularly amusing. I sent one of the ship's avatars and dissolved it as soon as it had knocked on the door. You should have seen your faces!"

Jeff shivered as Joanne's hand caressed his face almost tenderly.

"Actually I wanted to kill you and not Irons that night. But when the Major told you about the codes on the device, I changed my plans."

"You were listening in?"

"Of course! I heard every word you spoke."

Jeff shook his head. "Then why didn't you kill me and have the Major bring the handheld to the center of the ship?"

"Irons was too stubborn for me. He might have destroyed the thing too soon."

"So why didn't you just kill me later and have Green bring you the device with my finger? You didn't know about the password any more than I did."

Joanne nodded eagerly. "That's true. I didn't know. But I thought I could turn it into a nice little game and kill you all, one by one, until only you were left. The fact that you guessed the password was a stroke of luck. I never would have thought of it myself. But it was fun, wasn't it?" The demon moved his face even closer, so that Jeff could smell Joanne's breath. He needed all the willpower he could muster not to turn his head to the side.

"Then you sabotaged Owl's and Joanne's suits," he said.

"Yes, that was easy. All I had to do was break the connections to the shields and then I was able break their spirits."

There were no bounds to this creature's evil!

But he had to keep him talking until he came up with an idea. His mind was racing. "One more thing—in the first cavity we found the bones in the mass grave. Were they from the avatars?"

The demon shook his head. "Those were real humans. I didn't put all of them in cryogenic pods. I took some of them straight to the cavitys to experiment with them. But it wasn't much fun because they broke too quickly. It's more fun to slowly destroy the soul than to quickly break the body."

Joanne stroked his cheeks again. "But now we've chatted enough. Let's finally have some fun." The demon leaned over him and before Jeff could react, kissed him on the mouth. He could feel Joanne's tongue on his lips, which he pressed together as tightly as he could.

Finally the demon laughed, pulled back his head, and stood up. He went to the back of the capsule and rummaged around in a compartment. "Of course, we need protection. You always need to protect yourself during sex, that's what I've learned." He chuckled and returned to Jeff. In his hand he was holding a thin, silver metal cylinder that looked like a pen.

"What's that?" Jeff asked as his heart started to beat faster.

"Just something to help you relax. So that I can take off your suit more easily. Don't worry, you won't be completely unconscious. You'll still be able to enjoy the sex. I promise you: it will be the best sex you've ever had!" He cackled as he approached Jeff's face with the syringe.

Jeff looked down at his bound feet and then at the window, which was literally right in front of him. He had an idea. His suit was deactivated, so he couldn't save himself, but if it worked, at least the demon would be destroyed once and for all. And he wouldn't have to be the demon's sexual plaything. He had only one chance. He was running out of time.

Jeff stretched out and lifted his feet as far as he could. Then he writhed around until he was lying half on his side. The shackles cut into his skin and he cried out in pain. Then he tilted his feet and kicked.

"What are you doing?" the demon asked reprovingly. "You'll only hurt yourself and you won't achieve anything."

Jeff kicked as hard as his bound legs would allow. The diamond tips of his boots struck the window full force.

A loud crunching noise penetrated his ear, as if a hundred demons were dragging their fingers across slates. Then there was an almighty crash as the window shattered into thousands of pieces. A storm raged through the cabin and began to suck them out.

Joanne's body was ripped into the air. For a moment

the demon tried to cling to Jeff's seat, but the vacuum was too strong. With a silent scream, the demon was sucked out of the window into the eternity of space. It was the last thing Jeff saw before he fell unconscious.

THE FIRST THING he felt was amazement that he had awoken.

Shouldn't he be dead? Suffocated and frozen by the vacuum of space?

When he opened his eyes, he realized he was still sitting in the escape pod, tied to his chair.

The window?

There was no more window. A big, metal plate covered the hole where it had been.

An emergency cover!

Like on the ships of the Imperial fleet—the aliens had also provided their windows with emergency covers that were activated automatically when the windows were damaged. Unlucky for the demon that it hadn't closed faster.

Jeff managed to wriggle his hands out of the shackles, which seemed to have been loosened slightly by the storm in the cabin. Once he had freed his hands, it was easy for him to remove the other restraints.

Jeff stood up with a groan. His head was throbbing. He looked at the undamaged window to his right. Countless stars studded the sky.

The demon was dead—and this time for good. For all eternity, he would drift through space in Joanne's body as a dried, frozen corpse.

Jeff stood up and searched the cabin for anything that might be useful. He found a packet of some green substance that might be alien food, but he didn't feel like trying it. His suit would have to keep him alive; he reached down to the switch on his chest that activated the life-support system. A beep confirmed that it was on.

Jeff went to the back of the cabin and stood in front of one of the open cryogenic pods. The bottom of the container was filled with a greenish liquid. If he got into it, he would sleep the whole way back to Earth. But he only toyed with the idea for a second. He couldn't bring himself to lie down in one of those alien pods that had already caused so much misery and misfortune. He would manage to while away the hundred days back to Earth.

Instead, he simply lay down on the floor next to the hatch. And suddenly he had a thought. What would happen when he left hyperspace in a few months and entered Earth's Solar System? He no longer had Irons' handheld with the authorization codes. In the worst-case scenario, the Orbital Space Guard would shoot him down as he approached Earth.

Or had Jerry transferred the correct code to the onboard computer of the escape pod? He had no idea.

Overwhelmed by tiredness, Jeff closed his eyes.

He would find out soon enough.

Also by Phillip P. Peterson:

TRANSPORT

"Transport? Transport to where, Sir?" - "Possibly straight to hell!"

An extraterrestrial object is discovered off the coast of California; a sphere that transports humans to other solar systems. Death-row inmate Russell Harris and nine other convicts are given the chance to save their lives by agreeing to travel as test subjects on the transporter. But when the first volunteer dies a gruesome death, it becomes clear to Russell and his comrades that the venture is little more than a merciless death mission on which they will all perish. Their only chance of survival is to uncover the secret of the mysterious object, but that too seems hopeless – because no trace of the transporter's constructors can be found

Stargate meets The Fly meets The Dirty Dozen - a suspense-packed science-fiction thriller from Storyteller Award winning author Phillip P. Peterson

"Highly Recommended. Five HAZARDOUS Stars" - RBSProds

Book at amazon

Also by Phillip P. Peterson

FLIGHT 39

For a top-secret research project, airline pilot Christoph Wilder is recruited to fly an A380 equipped with a time machine. But on the maiden voyage, activists hijack the plane and force Christoph to take them back to 1939. Their goal: to kill Adolf Hitler! But the price to pay for averting the Second World War exceeds Christoph's worst nightmares. He has to decide whether to save the dictator's life in order to prevent the downfall of humanity in the present day.

+++A fast-paced high-tech thriller from Phillip P. Peterson, the author of Transport and Paradox.+++

"The book is more thoughtful than its simple premise suggests, and while the plot follows the typical time-travel narrative arc, Peterson does a good enough job hiding the ball that the twists feel satisfying. A well-executed time-travel tale." – Kirkus Review

Book at Amazon

Also by Phillip P. Peterson

PARADOX - On The Brink Of Eternity

Travel to the Stars . . . A Dream Fulfilled or Humankind's Worst Nightmare?

Ed Walker's last mission almost ended in catastrophe. Although he had been able to save the lives of his crewmates, he's still in danger of going down in history as the commander of the mission that wrecked the International Space Station. So he can hardly believe his luck when he's chosen to head the first manned exploration of the outer solar system.

One of his new crew members is the young physicist David Holmes, who is studying the mysterious disappearance of three space probes. But as their spaceship approaches interstellar space, humanity's most pressing question is no longer: **Are we alone in the universe? It is rather: Are we ready for the truth?**

"Peterson manages to satisfy ... sci-fi fans of both the Arthur C. Clarke cosmic-wow variety and the more techno-minded aerospace yarn-spinners of yesteryear such as Frank G. Slaughter and Martin Caidin with their launchpad melodramas. But when the plot finally reaches the unknown void beyond Pluto, the payoff goes into macro-cosmic territory, the stuff of Carl Sagan's finale to Contact--but far more bitter than that scientist/speculator's ultimate optimism. A sometimes-stirring space trek tale, with intriguing science and dark matter along the way." - **Kirkus Review**

Book at Amazon

The dark ship
June 2019
First published in German as
Das dunkle Schiff
October 2018

Author:
Phillip P. Peterson

Publisher:
Peter Bourauel
Auelswiese 2
53783 Eitorf
raumvektor@gmx.de

German editors:
Anke Höhl-Kayser
Andrea Weil

Translator:
Jenny Piening

English editor:
Laura Radosh

Cover:
Rafido/99designs

83427432R00231